WHO'S AFRAID OF THE BIG BAD WOLF?

JANIE MARIE

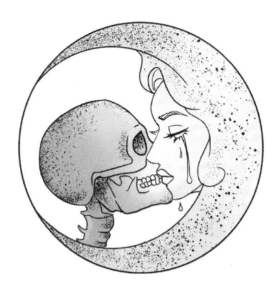

First published in March 2019 by Janie Marie
This edition published in October 2020 by Janie Marie

Copyright © 2020 by Janie Marie

This book is a work of fiction. Names, characters, places, and incidents are either a product of the author's imagination or are used fictitiously, and any resemblance to actual persons, living or dead, events, or locales is entirely coincidental.

All rights reserved.
No part of this book may be reproduced, distributed or transmitted in any form or by any means, including photocopying, recording, or other electronic or mechanical methods, including information storage and retrieval systems, without written permission from the author, except for the use of brief quotations in a book review.

ISBN: 979 8690683351
Cover design & Illustration by Thander Lin
©2020 Thander Lin
Editing by Emily Vaughan
First edition edit by Emily A. Lawrence, www.lawrenceediting.com

For Keira Natalie

*It has always been for you.
Never give up on your dreams and remember it's possible to glow, even when it's dark.*

*Love,
Mama*

HOW TO READ THIS BOOK

Who's Afraid of the Big Bad Wolf? is the first book of The Big Bad Wolf Trilogy, a spinoff series of Janie Marie's Gods & Monsters trilogy.

Without reading the trilogy, you might feel left out of the loop when *Gods & Monster*s readers are screaming with excitement. Still, you'll enjoy a full story and the connections it shares with the G&M trilogy, without it giving too much of the trilogy away.

If spoilers bother you and you're considering reading the related titles, read the trilogy first. They won't seem related until read together.

"What are you doing, Jane?"

She felt tears falling down her cheeks. "Saving you from her fire." She turned his arm and kissed his markings. They were weak, sloppy kisses, but she pressed the longest to the star next to the moon. "I will find a way to save you and stop the fire."

He breathed out, closing his eyes for a moment. "Sleep, Jane. Build our kingdom. I must insist—no vampire princes."

"Yes, my king." She chuckled, her eyes fluttering shut as blood oozed down the sides of her body and her throat. "Perhaps only sexy bad boys, wolves, and fairy tales. You did kill my dearest wolf."

"How did I already know you would say that?" He pressed his hand to her neck as the other touched her temple. "Rest now. I will find you, and we will complete our kingdom together."

"My wish?"

"I haven't forgotten. Sleep, my queen."

A pair of cold lips touched hers.

Then light . . . Just light.

-*The Light Bringer, Gods & Monsters Book 3*

CONTENTS

1. GRIMM EXPECTATIONS — 1
2. CATEGORIES — 16
3. FUCK THE BIG BAD WOLF — 26
4. PAIN VS PAYNE — 42
5. LIKE A MOVIE — 53
6. GYM TALK — 69
7. INTO THE WOODS — 76
8. DATING — 82
9. ADDICTED ON THE FIRST TRY — 106
10. EXPOSED — 132
11. I'M SORRY, IDIOT — 160
12. THE BAD KIDS — 168
13. HIS PAST — 188
14. PLAYING — 207
15. LIAR — 227
16. CREEP TO FREAK — 232
17. SUPER FREAKY — 257
18. ALWAYS THE ONE — 277
19. MY GIRL — 293
20. REMEMBER THIS — 308
21. I AM TRUTH — 318
22. DOUBT — 336
23. THE PADAWAN — 356
24. BROMANCE — 375
25. RED RIDING HOOD — 384
26. KISS IT BETTER — 408

1
GRIMM EXPECTATIONS

White . . .

Just white.

Kylie preferred it when Trevor wore baby blue because the color brought out his stunning slate-blue eyes, but today he had chosen a plain white T-shirt. It really didn't matter what color he wore—Trevor Grimm would look attractive in anything. No matter the hue, no matter if he picked designer or pulled on a ratty gym shirt, she would still be taunted by the lucky piece of fabric touching his skin. She always felt like the designers had a bet on whether she would dare to reach out and touch him that day.

Sons of bitches.

"I really appreciate you coming over to help me, Kylie." Trevor's deep voice saying her name almost had her choking on her own spit.

This was the second time he had spoken it. The first was when he walked up to her in the cafeteria with the entire school watching and asked if she would come over today. It was no big deal, really . . . Okay, it was a huge deal. Trevor Grimm, Blackwoods, Oregon's golden boy and Blackwoods

High's star athlete—all drop-dead-sexy six feet of him—had asked her, Kylie Hood, to come over to his place. It had already flooded social media.

It might have felt like this was the beginning of a fairy tale—the loner girl who hid under her hood was asked out by the Prince of Blackwoods—if people hadn't been making fun of her. Definitely not the best debut after hiding her face every day. Still, Trevor asking her to go to his apartment was something she would make sure she never forgot.

"Kylie?" Trevor had been talking over his strong shoulder as he led her to the kitchen, but now he stood waiting in the entrance, staring at her with an uneasy expression. He pushed his hand through his blond hair, waiting for her to respond.

"I'm sorry," she sputtered, her face heating up. "I, uh. Yeah . . ." She shook her head at her sudden lack of intelligence, breathing frantically. "I mean, it's no trouble." *Lie.* "I'm happy to help."

His blue eyes twinkled and he smiled, stealing her heart as if he didn't already own it.

"Still," he said, turning to enter the kitchen. He must have already known she'd follow him anywhere. "It's a huge help to me."

Kylie was happy to hear this. He needed—no, wanted—her help. Out of all the girls in school, he'd asked her.

"So," she said as he plopped down on one of the chairs, returning to the half-eaten sandwich on his plate. She rubbed the sweat from her forehead, not sure if it was from the twenty-minute walk to his apartment or just nerves. "Um, where are we going to work then?"

Trevor gestured to the chair beside him. "I have to go get everything."

Kylie nodded, hiding herself under her hood as she sat by him. He didn't pay too much attention to her as he ate. She figured he was starved since he'd just finished practice. He was a growing boy, after all.

"I'm lucky your mom ran into me," he added, not looking up.

Kylie stiffened, unsure why he would bring up her stepmother. "Lorelei?"

Trevor took a drink of water. "Yeah. She was the one who suggested I get your help."

Kylie's heart squeezed with fear as she wondered what Lorelei had told him. When had he even met her? How? She waited for him to explain, but he stood up instead.

"I'll be right back with everything."

Not having the guts to ask him more, or to correct him about Lorelei not being her mom, she nodded and turned her attention to the table in front of her. Trevor left the kitchen.

What is Lorelei up to? Kylie wondered. Her stepmother didn't want people to see her face, didn't want them to remember the girl she was before. The girl with golden hair and lovely green eyes she'd inherited from her dead father. No, both her stepmother and her stepsister, Maura, wanted the world to forget Kylie Hood, and they had done a perfect job over the past four years. Now she was the weird girl who wore a red hoodie all the time. Whether it was hot or cold, her wavy, golden hair was always kept covered, never complimented. Even if her hood slipped, the unflattering bun she twisted it up into each day kept any potential admirers away.

That was okay. The lack of attention was something she embraced now. Hiding meant staying alive.

For the briefest moment, she thought about life before the hood became her shield. Before she could even get a glimpse of the girl she used to be, she shoved her memories into the dark. It sent a twinge of pain through her head, but she breathed out and shook off the headache. She'd need to remember to keep her medicine with her.

"I'll be there," came a male voice that wasn't Trevor's. "Put five on me. Yeah, I have it."

Kylie snapped her head up and forgot the growing pain behind her eyes, because what she was seeing could only be a gift from God.

It was a boy. No, he was a man. A man-boy. He was more mature than the boys she went to school with, but not that much older than her—maybe early twenties. A hot twenty-something, at that. With the perfect body, glistening with a light sheen of sweat, he was glorious. Solid and lean—not an inch of fat. Just pure muscle and sun-kissed skin painted with beautiful tattoos along his arms, chest and—dear God—the attractive V dipping below his low-sitting shorts.

Breathe, girl.

She sucked in a breath. Thank goodness he hadn't noticed her sitting there. He rummaged through the fridge, his phone still pressed to his ear. It looked as though he'd found what he wanted because he stood, shutting the door as he lifted an apple to his lips.

The man was a god. And he was about to see her sitting there. Staring at him.

"Nah, I think I already fucked her, didn't I?" He took a bite of the apple, finally making eye contact with her. He froze, staring at her with the same shocked expression she had stamped across her face.

Kylie gulped, unsure of how to explain who she was and what she was doing there, eavesdropping, all while admiring the apple juice dripping down his chin.

"What?" he said, shaking out of his daze but not looking away from her. "No, I'll pick one later." He wiped his chin, and with a jerk of his head, his black hair shifted away from his dark-brown eyes. "I said, I'll pick. Yeah. See ya."

Kylie started sweating under his intense stare as he ended the call. At first, he just kept staring at her. His gaze drifted over what he could see of her face and body, which couldn't have been much, but even with her hood up, she felt as if he could see right into her soul.

Too afraid to speak, Kylie looked back down at the table, hoping he would just leave her alone. He was too intense for her, and she didn't need to know him to understand that.

"What's your name?" He spoke roughly and to the point.

She knew he wouldn't care that she was the freak of their school. It was easy to see he was the kind of person who demanded and received.

She started to say, "Ky–" but Trevor's return prevented her from answering him.

"Hey," Trevor greeted the man who had yet to stop his inspection of her. "I didn't think you'd be here today. Don't you have a fight tonight?"

Trevor dumped his work on the table, causing her to flinch.

The man-boy narrowed his eyes on her. "I do," he told Trevor, still watching her. "Are you going to ignore your friend, or introduce me?"

Trevor looked over at her and said, "Oh, this is Kylie. Kylie, this is my cousin Logan. I live with him while my dad is overseas."

Logan took another bite of his apple as Trevor took a seat. She nodded in acknowledgment and looked away. She wasn't used to meeting new people anymore, especially sexy guys like Logan.

"What's your last name?" Logan asked.

Kylie couldn't stop herself from jerking her head up. He had moved closer, standing opposite her now. His eyes never left her face. He no doubt figured she was a freak like everyone else did.

"Hood," she said, wringing her hands together on her lap. "Kylie Hood."

The small twitch at the corner of his mouth threatened to turn into a smirk, but he took another bite of his apple, finishing it and tossing it into the trash.

"Well, Kylie Hood," he said, sounding amused, "it's a pleasure to meet you." He stuck out his hand as he cut Trevor a dark look, but he focused on her as he grinned. "Logan Grimm."

She stared at his hand and the detailed tattoos running up his forearm all the way to his bicep—horrifying depictions of demons engaged in battle with all sorts of monsters. Witches and scary candy cottages with children smiling happily as they wandered into the trap. A girl with a red hood on his other arm caught her eye. Little Red Riding Hood. Just like the fairy tale, she was traveling through the woods as the twisted limbs of the forest welcomed her to darkness. And the wolves. He had so many wolves mixed throughout the different scenes. Every image was beautifully drawn.

Grimm popped into her head. Fairy tales. He must have been playing on his name. That didn't surprise her in this town. After all, Blackwoods, Oregon, was the most famous of the American Fairy Tale towns. Texas, Colorado, and Canada also had towns with rich history concerning the various fairytale discoveries, but Blackwoods was the most famous. It was the place where the first tales were uncovered. She felt stupid for never thinking of Trevor's last name as having anything to do with fairy tales.

Kylie couldn't look away from Logan's tattoos. They were beautifully menacing, and she had an unshakable urge to run her fingers all over the detailed designs. But her hesitation came from the fact that contact with boys was forbidden—another stupid rule she had followed since her freshman year.

He chuckled, leaving his hand out. "Are you afraid?"

"No," she said, though *yes* was the real answer.

"Then shake my hand. I won't bite."

"Right," she said, sticking her hand out, surprised to see a faint smile on his full lips. "It's a pleasure meeting you as well." Their hands made contact and she almost peed herself. It wasn't that his touch felt strange or magical—only that she was touching such a perfect specimen of a man. A man-boy. A still shirtless man-boy.

"See?" he said, caressing the back of her hand with his thumb before he let go. "That wasn't so bad, was it?"

He moved back, still staring at her like a predator stalking its prey.

"No." Kylie swallowed, unable to look away from his stare. "I'm sorry. Just a little distracted, I guess."

Trevor cleared his throat, making her jump back. Logan smirked as Trevor glared in his direction.

"Do you need something?" The bite in Trevor's tone revealed agitation Kylie hadn't expected.

Logan shrugged, walking back to the fridge. "I was just getting a snack. What are you two up to?"

Kylie bit her lip, casting a small glance at Trevor before returning her gaze to Logan. He had pulled a bottle of water out and was guzzling the entire drink in one go.

"Kylie is here to help with a project of mine," Trevor answered.

Logan narrowed his eyes at Trevor but didn't say anything else. Kylie felt like she was in the middle of a fight about to break out as they glared at one another. Whatever problems they had going on, she didn't want to find herself caught in the middle. As fit as Trevor was, Logan looked like he could kill him with one arm tied behind his back.

"How much have you done so far?" She kept her gaze away from Logan, even as she felt his stare burning a hole through her forehead.

Trevor rubbed the back of his neck, cringing as he avoided making eye contact with her. "Well, with football practice and our recent away games, I haven't started."

Kylie's mouth fell open as she looked down at his syllabus. "But this is due tomorrow, Trevor."

Logan snorted, but she didn't look at him. She ran her finger over the list of bugs he needed for the assignment. Twenty. He needed twenty different bugs, and he had none.

"Like I said, I haven't had time." Trevor gave her a sweet smile that made it seem like he'd found a perfect solution and tapped on the syllabus. "But it says they can be sketched."

She nodded. At least they didn't have to catch bugs.

"I've heard you're a great artist, so I thought you could get those done for me in no time."

She stared at him in shock. He expected her to draw detailed sketches of twenty bugs, and have it all prepared for turn-in tomorrow? She was the solution to his problem because she could draw. That was all she was to him. It wasn't that he noticed her or that she was anything special; he just needed someone who could draw.

This was Trevor though. Trevor Grimm—the boy she was in love with. The boy who'd asked her for help. She'd do anything for him. He was counting on her. This was her chance to let him see how great she could be for him. Maybe then she would be special.

Casting a quick glance at Logan, who looked irritated, she returned her attention to Trevor. His blue eyes sparkled at her unsure smile.

"Okay," she murmured. "They might not be as good as I normally do, but if you start writing up the fact sheets, I think we can get it done." Her smile grew bigger as she grew more confident in her decision. But then she noticed his frustrated expression and her confidence wavered.

Is he upset my sketches won't be their best?

"Well," Trevor said in a semi-apologetic tone, "you see, I kind of have somewhere to be tonight. It's a prior commitment I can't get out of. You understand, don't you?"

Kylie's smile vanished and her stomach clenched. He expected her to do it by herself. There would be no *them*. She couldn't even find her voice.

Logan could find his though. "Is this the project you told me about?" His tone was almost violent. "The class you're making up?"

Kylie slowly let her eyes move to the fierce glare he had trained on Trevor.

"It's none of your business." Trevor's icy tone sent a shiver down her spine. She had never heard him speak with so much hostility before.

Logan pushed himself away from the counter and stood across from them. "While your dad is gone, you are my business." His voice held just as much venom. "You've had this assignment since the first day of school. Are you really going to bring some girl here and dump it on her to finish in one night?"

"Fuck off." Trevor stood up. "Go find one of your little bitches and mind your own shit."

Kylie almost wanted to cry. They were so filled with hatred. And it was over her.

"Do you really want to test me, little cousin?" Logan's muscles flexed, either for effect or in anger. "You know how that would end."

He scared her shitless, and the threat lining his statement made her nervous about Trevor's well-being. She knew he was right without even knowing Trevor's fighting abilities. Logan could probably kill anyone he wanted. Her fear for Trevor had her blurting out words before she could think. "No, it's fine. I work better alone anyway."

That earned her a fierce glare from Logan.

"See?" Trevor smiled at her. It helped soothe the sting across her heart. *Maybe he really does have a commitment.* Of course, football cut into his studies. It was the reason teachers were so lax with athletes, at least at their school. "Thanks, Kylie."

Logan grunted and walked out of the kitchen. She cast a glance at his back before returning her smile to Trevor.

"I really am sorry—and grateful, Kylie." Trevor gave her another heartbreakingly beautiful smile. "It just slipped my mind, you know?"

She nodded, consumed by his soft tone.

He reached out slowly and caressed her cheek with the backs of his fingers. The action and tender look on his face had her paralyzed. "You should smile more."

She couldn't believe he was touching her. Trevor Grimm was caressing her cheek and telling her she should smile more.

"Okay," she said, making him chuckle. The sound warmed her heart.

"You're the best." He gave her a trademark wink. "I gotta go now."

The warmth became a chill, yet she couldn't even shiver.

"Oh, and you can work in my room if Logan gives you trouble. He probably won't stay long. He has a fight tonight. But he could come back with a girl, so unless you want to see and hear that, try to finish before midnight."

Her heart sank. Not because of the details of Logan's activities, but because Trevor was practically giving her a deadline to get done and get out.

But she loved him. She wouldn't have the chance to do something for him again.

"Okay. I'll try to finish before then."

He smiled and stood up. "Great. Just shut the door on your way out. No need to worry about locking up. No one messes with Logan's stuff."

She didn't respond as she stared at the humongous load of work she was about to start. This was her moment with Trevor, and it was ruined by some prior commitment. He would forget all about her, but she refused to fail. There was always the chance he'd be so grateful for her help that he'd see her as someone truly special.

"See ya, Kylie. Thanks again."

She looked up in time to see his back retreating out of the kitchen. Then she heard the front door slam shut. She let her eyes water as heartache consumed her.

"Are you really going to do his project?"

Kylie gasped, lifting her gaze to find Logan standing at the kitchen entrance. He had a shirt on now, thank God, but his dark eyes still gleamed with hate.

"Yes," she stuttered. "Of course, I will."

He shook his head, making some of his hair land in his eyes. It looked good that way, but even better when he jerked his head to move it. "You shouldn't let people take advantage of you just because you have feelings for them."

"He's not taking advantage of me. He asked for help and I agreed." She didn't want Trevor to come off as a bad guy. It wasn't his fault that practice took up so much of his time, or that he had another commitment.

"Does he know you're in love with him?" There was so much disgust in the question.

"What?" She cringed as her voice screeched.

"It's a simple question." He looked her dead in the eyes. "Does he know you love him?"

She felt her chest tighten and shook her head.

His expression was blank, his tone empty. "Has he ever talked to you before this?"

Again, she shook her head, and that burning feeling you get before crying stung her eyes and nose.

"Did he offer you any sort of payment or favor in return?"

"No," she whispered, hating the point he was making. She didn't want to give up hope that Trevor was interested in more than just having her do his project.

Logan stayed quiet as her eyes watered and her breath hitched. She didn't even know him, but the degradation she felt under his judging eyes was far greater than she ever remembered feeling.

He studied her for a few more seconds before turning and walking away. She sighed and looked down at her workload. Logan's opinion shouldn't have bothered her, but it did. No matter how long she sat there, just knowing he was disappointed in her made her feel so much more pathetic.

◆◆◆

"Crap." The pencil fell from Kylie's cramped fingers as she flexed them. Three hours had passed, and she'd only completed five sketches and six descriptions. She rubbed her eyes and looked at the clock. It was nearly nine. "They're going to kill me tomorrow," she said, groaning at the fact she'd feel Lorelei's wrath whenever she made it home. Better hers than Maura's though.

"Who will kill you?"

Kylie yelped, jumping from her spot on the floor in Trevor's room. She had moved in there after Logan kept making noise in his room. She had no idea what he was doing, but it had sounded like he was throwing furniture around for hours.

Now he was standing in the doorway, watching her the same intense way he had been earlier.

"Do you have to keep doing that?" She was surprised by how snappy she sounded, and by the amused glint it caused in his brown eyes.

"I thought you weren't scared of me?" He shoved off the doorframe and walked into the room.

Her face heated up as she remembered their meeting a few hours ago. "I'm not. I just find people sneaking up on me annoying."

He chuckled and threw something down on her sketches.

"Hey," she yelled, grabbing up the binder he'd thrown, ready to throw it back at him.

"Get up," he told her.

"What?" She glared up at him as he stood over her.

"That's his project," he said, nodding to the binder in her hands. "He asked me for it weeks ago when he told me he didn't feel like doing his."

Kylie looked at the binder and opened it. Sure enough, it was the same project, done with sketches instead of actual bugs. Her fingers trailed over the intricate drawings. They were amazing.

"This is yours?"

A sort of sadness flitted across his eyes too quickly for her to understand. "They're my sketches."

"Why are you giving it to me? Your drawings are beautiful by the way."

He shrugged, briefly glancing at her sketches. "He asked for this because he knew I had it. I told him to fuck off and do his own damn work. I didn't know he would go get some girl and force her to do his shit."

She looked at the binder and smiled. "So why give it to him now?" Slowly, she peered back up at him.

His expression gave nothing away, but his words sure as hell warmed every cell in her body. "I'm not giving it to him. I'm giving it to you."

2
CATEGORIES

"It's going to be hectic in there."

Kylie looked at Logan as they walked side by side. He grinned down at her. The sight of his smile almost had her tripping over her own feet.

"Are you sure it's okay for me to be here?" She glanced at the lines at the entrance.

"What do you mean?"

They reached the side door he was leading them to, and she walked through as he held it open.

"I mean"—she grimaced at the corridor full of scantily dressed women—women who all had their hungry eyes on Logan—"I'm not eighteen yet. Isn't that illegal or something?"

He laughed. It was a deep sound that sent tingles between her legs. "Am I taking you on a drug run or to watch me fight? Do you have a curfew?"

"I don't do drugs, so I hope this is just a boxing match. And I don't have a curfew. At least I don't think so." She noted that his smile hadn't faded since they left his apartment. He didn't tell her any more about Trevor, or his drawings. When she had asked him if he was certain he was okay giving it to Trevor, he closed off and told her to get up because she wasn't getting it for free. The payment was her company tonight.

"I told you, it's mixed martial arts, not boxing." He glanced at her like she was stupid before asking, "When are you eighteen, by the way?"

She remembered he'd explained the type of fight he would be in, but she didn't realize confusing it with boxing was offensive. "I was just saying I feel a little out of place."

He followed her line of sight to see she was making it clear that she did not look like the other females here. His arm suddenly fell over her shoulders, and he pulled her to his side.

Yelping from both pain and surprise, she tried to push him off. Logan loosened his grip but kept her close as his eyes ran over her body. She didn't want him to figure out she was hurt and looked away. Only, she ended up subconsciously leaning into him for safety anyway. The malicious glares being sent her way spelled trouble.

"When?" His stern tone had her focusing on him rather than the jealous stares.

She didn't know if he was asking about her birthday or what injury she might be hiding, but she hoped he only meant her age. No one could find out about her. "September twenty-eighth," she whispered, noticing the satisfied spark in his eye.

He looked thoughtful before he nodded and squeezed her tighter. She started to cringe but stopped when he softened his grip.

"Good, then you're my date tonight, Hood." He lowered his mouth to speak softly in her ear. "I'm the champ. My girl doesn't need to fit in."

Before her shock could settle in, a guy approached them.

"The Big Bad Wolf has arrived." The man greeted Logan with a grin.

"You know not to call me that," Logan told him, all the playfulness now absent from his tone.

"Fine." The guy rolled his eyes. "Have it your way. The fans like the bad wolf thing—it's catchy. But whatever you want. Are you ready? I've got the girls waiting," he said before looking at her with a frown. "Who's the kid?"

She dropped her gaze to the floor. He was right, after all. She was a kid in a place only the elite, older crowd should be.

"Get rid of the girls," Logan told him instead of explaining why he had brought a seventeen year old to his fight.

"Come on, man. I spent thirty minutes standing out there, picking the hottest in attendance."

Logan shrugged, still holding her close. "Kylie's my date tonight." He grinned down at her and heat spread over her cheeks. "Isn't that right, Hood?"

Unable to do anything else, she smiled and nodded at him. She didn't know why he was being so nice to her, but she was loving his attention.

"Are you high?"

Logan exhaled sharply and pinned his friend with a fierce look. "Chris, I have company. Take them with you for all I care."

The man, Chris, just looked at him like he'd lost his mind, then dropped his gaze to her, trying to see the appeal, before Logan gave a throaty grunt.

"See that Kylie is taken care of while I'm in the ring," Logan added. "I'm holding you responsible for her. Put her in the front row and stay with her. Got it?"

Chris sighed. "Got it."

"I have to go get ready." Logan gave Chris a dark glare. "Just send Mark and Gloria."

"All right," Chris said, nodding as he took her in once more before leaving.

"Don't worry about him," Logan told her. He began walking her down the hall again. "He's my manager. And a dick. He's always had a problem with my—" He shook his head. "Never mind."

She didn't have any idea what he was going to say, but she was more focused on the fact that she wasn't good enough to be at his side. "But he's right," she whispered. Even though she had felt insignificant for so long, she could not deny that she wanted to make him proud. It didn't make sense to her why she wanted to please him—she just did.

"Hood," he said, not looking at her, "you have to quit thinking so lowly of yourself. I brought you with me because I wanted you here. I can have any woman I want."

She couldn't believe he was so conceited.

He shrugged at her look, adding, "It's true. My point is, I brought you."

"I don't know why you did."

"I'll tell you why soon."

She didn't look up at him until they arrived at a door with his name taped on it. The words separating his first and last name had her raising her eyebrow at him. "The Reaper?"

"Yeah." He frowned as he studied his name. "You don't like it?"

Smiling at his somewhat worried expression, because it was adorable as hell, she shook her head. "No, I like it. It makes you scarier than you already are."

He grinned, happy with her compliment.

"But why don't you like The Big Bad Wolf? It fits your name and your tattoos."

His smile fell. "Let's get inside."

Letting him push her inside the room, she decided to investigate this whole dislike of the wolf thing later. What was so wrong with the big bad wolf anyway?

"My masseuse and coach will be here soon," he said, putting his bag on the table. "We have a few minutes alone." He gave her a sexy smirk as he raised an eyebrow.

Her body was aflame, but she glanced around the locker room and pretended to be interested in the case of water sitting on a table as she said, "If you brought me here for some freaky warm-up sex, I'm sorry to disappoint."

"You sure?" He grinned, his gaze slowly falling over her. "Not even non-freaky sex? I hear I'm a great lover."

She squeezed her legs together. "Well, I'll just have to take your word for it."

He sighed and shrugged his shirt off. "And here I thought I was impressing you with my gentlemanly behavior."

She shook her head, trying her hardest to not look at his body.

"Not even a little hug for giving you my project?" He stuck his arms out toward her, smiling adorably.

"I thought me keeping you company was payback?" God, she really wanted to hug him. But she knew he'd find her weird when she refused to let go.

Without any sort of warning, Logan smirked and dropped his jeans.

"Logan," she screamed, covering her eyes.

He laughed loudly. "I'm not naked."

She peeked through her fingers before moving her hand. He already had his fighting shorts on.

"You don't just undress in front of people!"

"I've never had an upset audience," he said, still smirking. "Do you want a closer look, Kylie?"

She blushed, making him laugh and turn back to his bag.

"So tell me," he said while he dug through it.

Kylie walked to the only available chair, a leather couch, to get comfortable. She tried her damnedest to not stare at his back. How was it that a man's back could be considered sexy? She really didn't know but decided, yes, Logan had the sexiest back she'd ever seen.

She shook her head and went to sit so she wouldn't keep staring at him. Not anticipating the couch's firmness, she bounced up rather high.

Logan chuckled, catching her surprised expression. "You all right?"

She wanted to hide her face for plopping down like a little kid but ended up smiling and nodding at him anyway.

"Good," he said. "Now, I was wondering how long you've been in love with Trevor."

Her eyes nearly popped out, and she dipped her head down to hide her humiliation.

"Love at first sight, huh?"

She nodded slowly and peeked up to see him staring at the wall with a far-away look.

"Yeah." He nodded. "I know the feeling."

"You think I'm stupid, don't you?"

He shook his head before walking to sit beside her. A shaky breath slipped out of her mouth as his large hand closed around her thigh. Her jeans covered her skin, but the heat from his touch almost had her shaking with a need she'd never felt before.

"You're not stupid," he said. "Innocent and inexperienced, yes. But you're not stupid."

Kylie was still focused on his hand and the way his thumb was drawing little circles on her thigh.

"I'm going to be honest with you," he added.

"What?" She finally tore her eyes away from his hand and found him staring down at her.

"I brought you here because I want to help you," he said.

She frowned and went to open her mouth, but he squeezed her leg and spoke before she could.

"You'll never get noticed if you keep hiding under your hood. You need to see that the only way to get what you want is to come out confident and go after what you want. I can help you gain that confidence. Because if you keep letting people push you around, one day, you won't get back up." He paused, his eyes drifting down her body before adding, "I saw the way you flinch."

He narrowed his eyes at her, daring her to argue.

She didn't.

"I don't like people taking advantage of the weak. And honey, right now, you're as weak as they come."

Her eyes watered.

"I can help you get stronger," he murmured, sliding his hand along her thigh. "I'll teach you how to defend yourself. And I'll give you the experience you need to be confident."

"I don't need your help." She wasn't what he thought she was.

Logan exhaled, letting go of her leg, and rested his forearms on his knees. "Hood, don't take my bluntness as an attack. I'm just being straight with you."

She looked away, almost in tears.

"Do you want Trevor to see you as more than an easy tool to get out of homework?"

She didn't answer him, but that didn't stop Logan from telling her what he thought on the subject.

"Because that's all he sees with you right now. Hell, he probably hasn't even noticed you up until this project."

"I know that," she whispered.

"He's stupid for not noticing you," he muttered.

She didn't look at him because she didn't want to read into his comment.

"Did you know that guys put girls in categories?"

She turned to look at him, wondering what he was going to enlighten her with now.

He looked happy to have her attention and began his explanation. "Well, for starters, we don't have the whole

'She's just a friend' thing. Girls are never just friends. You all might do that to us, but for guys, it works like this. There are the girls we make our girlfriends and eventually wives, then there are girls we'd like to fuck, and last—the girls we'd consider fucking if we're in a zombie apocalypse and all the hot babes are already dead. 'Cause then you could end up having to choose between the chick that smells like farts or your hand."

Her mouth was hanging open from the moment he listed *girls they'd like to fuck*, but he was still speaking as if he were telling her about the weather.

"Me, personally, I'd go with my hand before I stick my dick in Smells Like Ass Nancy—but that's me. I have standards."

"That's awful, Logan."

He laughed loudly. "I'm just fucking with you."

She shook her head, not sure whether to throttle him or feel giddy because of his amazing laugh.

Logan's laugh quieted to a chuckle, and he continued, "What I really mean is that those are the girls we hardly know exist, and if we do, we use them for whatever we need at the moment. For example, someone to dump our large project on to complete in one night." He gave her a pointed look before adding, "While most of those girls fall short in the looks department, some are just unnoticeable."

"Which category do I fit in?" It was a stupid question but too late for her to retract, so she waited.

His tone was soft and his gaze almost tender. "For Trevor—right now—you're just a girl who hides under her hood—a girl to use for the moment." Her heart began to crush. "For me, though"—he grinned, putting his arm over her shoulders and pulling her to his side—"you're most definitely high on my 'Want to Fuck' list."

3
FUCK THE BIG BAD WOLF

It felt like days were passing as Logan made a few phone calls and various men came in and out of the room. Kylie stayed quiet, never looking too far from him but avoiding eye contact whenever he looked at her.

She checked the clock on the wall. Five minutes?!
How the hell—
"I want to help you with Trevor."

Kylie jerked her gaze from the time-fuck of a clock to stare at Logan. "You want to help me with Trevor?"

He hesitated before nodding. "I want you to be able to go for something you want. If that's my douchebag cousin, I want to help you become the type of person you're supposed to be—someone he'd notice, not a girl in the apocalypse-only category."

She gave him an annoyed look.

He shrugged off her irritation. "You know what I mean. He doesn't see you the way you want him to. I can help you with that."

She decided to humor him. "Say I take you up on your offer, what would your service include?"

The corner of his eyes crinkled as he smiled. *God, he's so attractive.*

"My service?"

Kylie rolled her eyes. "Just spit it out already."

"Well, the best way to get a boy to notice you is to have a rival male's interest first." He hitched his thumb toward himself. "Trevor's greatest rival is yours truly. I might be his guardian when his dad's gone, but we really do despise each other."

"Why?"

Rage lit up his eyes like fire. "Don't worry about it. It's not like you'll view him differently just because I say he's a piece of shit."

Her heart pounded. "How could you say that about him? Trevor's perfect."

The inferno in his eyes roared. "I know him better than you do but it's not what I think of him that matters. You like him. So I'll take interest in you and make it known that it's in a sexual way—not that I'm just using you for something—and he'll begin to look at you in a different light. But I don't want him to take interest and fuck you just to spite me either. So we have to get him to want you in the 'girlfriend' category. To do that, you have to come out of hiding." He flicked her hood. "No more hiding under this. You need to show off what you've got."

Not really paying attention to the fact he was offering the most ridiculous form of help, she blurted out her insecurities. "I have nothing, Logan. I'm not going to be one of those girls standing in the hall for you. I know I'll never have a guy like Trevor. It's pathetic to like him, but what can I do?"

"You're right," he said. "You're not one of those girls—you're better than them."

She turned stare at the wall instead of his face. He was too gorgeous to look at for an extended period of time. Looking at him while he implied such a thing would only hurt her later when she was foolish enough to believe it.

"This is the stupidest idea I've ever heard." She bit her lip, worried about sounding nasty, but there was no annoyance in his eyes, only humor. "Why are you looking at me like that?"

"You're hot when you're angry," he said, chuckling softly.

"Is that all you ever think about?" she snapped.

"Oh, come on, Kylie. Don't be angry with me. I just want to help you."

She huffed and crossed her arms, very aware of his fingertips trailing up and down the side of her arm where his hand rested. Her eyes followed the movement in a trance, and for the first time in a long while, she wished she wasn't wearing her hoodie so those fingers would glide over her skin instead of just her clothing. "But you said girls and guys aren't friends. This proves you're full of it."

He smiled, shaking his head as he squeezed her to him again. "Baby, I told you what list you're in for me. We're not friends." His dark eyes roamed over her face slowly. "There's just a need to protect you that I can't get over. Hooking up is what I want, but I don't want to hurt you. So the fact you don't like me that way and you're in love with my cousin won't hurt. 'Cause, essentially, you're using me."

"I don't want to use you," she said, frowning. "That's wrong."

"Maybe I want you to use me," he said, chuckling.

Kylie sighed, feigning frustration as she fought the smile trying to form on her lips.

Logan saw it and grinned, adding, "What's so bad about getting what I want while making sure you're safe? Besides, when we're done, you'll have Trevor."

Her body relaxed into him, but her heart hurt. It was heartwarming that he wanted to keep her safe, but for him to admit that his eagerness to provide this protection was because he wanted sex made her sad. She shouldn't be sad though. She couldn't let herself think of Logan as anything more than a sex god with a kind heart. He had to remain just that, and she needed to remember it was Trevor she loved—the boy she always dreamed of—and this was Logan's plan for her to have him.

"And if I don't want to give myself to you?" She exhaled, feeling his hot breath around her ear.

"You don't want me?"

She closed her eyes as his lips brushed her ear, sending her body into a new heat she'd never experienced before. Her mouth went a little dry, and she swallowed when his tongue lightly flicked her earlobe.

"I don't want to be used," she whispered, though her body was now begging him to use it however he wished. "I—I don't want to be taken advantage of."

A rumble sounded from him as he whispered in her ear. "Like Trevor used you?"

She snapped her eyes open and shifted away the same time he did.

His look had darkened considerably, and his voice turned cold. "Because he did, honey. And you let him without putting up any sort of fight. If it weren't for me, you'd be at my apartment, tired and hungry, all while Trevor is fucking whoever is on his list tonight. Maybe you'd be there to see it, maybe not. Either way, deep down, you'd know the truth—he used you. No matter how tough you think you are right now, you'd be sobbing, wishing for someone to care when the truth about Trevor hits you." He grabbed her chin, keeping her face up when she tried to hide her brimming tears by looking down. "I'm telling you, for some reason, I care about what happens to you—and I want to make sure Trevor, or any other dicks out there, know they'll have me to answer to if you get hurt."

Kylie watched his angry face through her burning eyes. "But you're still using me."

He dropped her chin and sat back. "Just think about it. I do really want to help. And it's more like we would be using each other."

She scooted farther from him as he leaned back and stared up at the ceiling.

"But I'm not going to lie to you," he continued, "I'm still just a guy who wants to get in your pants, and that won't change."

She turned to wipe her tears away, his words slicing her heart.

He sighed and leaned over, grabbing her chin again, only gentler this time. She squeezed her eyes shut, not wanting to see his beautiful face as he said such hurtful things. It didn't even matter they'd only just met—he was the first person to show real interest in her.

"Open your eyes." His voice slid over her skin and into her bones.

"I don't want to," she said, squeezing her eyes shut tighter, hoping her tears wouldn't fall.

"Why?" His voice was closer, but it was cold once more.

"Because you're hurting me," she whispered, trembling from his touch and her sadness.

"Open them."

The power in his order demanded obedience. So, afraid and sad, she opened her eyes to see his face right in front of hers, maybe an inch away.

"Hood," he said softer, moving his hand from her chin to hold the side of her face, "I promise to never intentionally hurt you, okay?"

She nodded as the warmth of his hand seeped into her skin. She would have tilted her face more toward his palm if she didn't think he'd laugh.

"There's no pressure," he went on. "Just think about it. Besides, it will be good practice for you before entering the adult world."

"What do you mean?" She had calmed a lot now that he wasn't looking or sounding like he was ready to kill someone. It was strange how he could achieve these sudden jumps in mood and make her nearly forget all sadness and frustration.

"I'm just taking a guess," he said, "but you don't strike me as a girl who knows her way around the male sex."

"So?"

He chuckled. "Don't you want to be confident when you decide to start a relationship?"

"I'm fairly certain I won't have the opportunity anyway."

He watched her for a few seconds. "You have no idea what awaits you. I'm just giving you the chance to embrace yourself without some piece of shit taking you without your consent and breaking that sweet little heart of yours." A strange look flitted over his face before he went on. "I wasn't joking about which list you're on with me. I know there's a hottie just waiting for me underneath this hoodie. I'm going to enjoy unwrapping you."

She couldn't help but smile at him. He was so inappropriate, but she liked how blunt he was with her, and she was happy to have him teasing her again.

"I won't hurt you, Kylie." He pulled her to his side. "Do you want some jerk to come and feed you sweet lines, then screw you and leave you used on the floor?"

She shook her head.

"Do you want to have no idea what you're doing so you're either made a complete fool of, or taken in a way you were never ready for—or against your will?"

Again, she shook her head.

"Would you rather have someone who genuinely cares for you be the one you experience your firsts with?"

She nodded. All she wanted was to be someone's whole world.

He continued, his tone tender like a sweet caress across her heart, "Would you want that person to understand that you're innocent and hurt? To understand they need to be gentle and patient with you?"

She sat quiet next to him, listening to his steady breaths and relaxing in his warmth and scent. It was stupid to ponder this. She couldn't do what he was asking. She couldn't be the girl he was sure she'd be if she stopped hiding. But it was nice to savor his company, to imagine what he could teach her and fantasize about him fighting to protect her. But it was wrong to dream. "Thank you for your offer, Logan, but I ca—"

Knock, knock.

Logan looked at the door, then back at her. "Don't decide yet. Sleep on it, okay?" He smiled and leaned forward until his lips faintly brushed her cheek. "And make sure we're both naked when you dream about me."

She smiled as his lips pressed against her cheek, then she watched him jump to his feet to go open the door. He unlocked it and greeted the fierce-looking man outside.

Kylie watched him, noticing all signs of the happiness and softness he had shown her were gone. It intrigued her that he was so different with her. His exclusive affection made her feel special and excited. Her giddiness quickly halted, however, and her heart pounded wildly when a beautiful woman stepped inside.

Logan's normally unreadable expression came to life, killing the happiness he'd built inside her.

"Logan, *mi amor*," the woman said, receiving his quick kiss to her cheek.

"Hello, beautiful," he said, smiling and hugging her to him.

The man squeezed past Logan and the woman, nodding to Kylie when he caught sight of her.

Kylie couldn't even nod back. She was feeling so many emotions as she continued watching the pair by the door.

"You know I love hearing you call me that," she said, her voice thick with her Spanish accent.

Kylie balled her hands as she watched the woman all over Logan. She wouldn't stop touching him. She was running her stupid manicured fingers across his chest as he smiled down at her.

"It's been so long, *mi corazón*. I hate when you make me wait so long to see you." Her arms wrapped around Logan's waist as she pouted her red lips up at him.

Kylie tasted blood as Logan's hand reached up to caress the woman's cheek.

His deep chuckle angered her now instead of melting her like it had all other instances, and she couldn't even understand what he was saying to the woman in a low voice. She could hear her heartbeat in her ears and felt that maybe she was vibrating until Logan's voice became clearer.

" . . . her name is Kylie," he was saying.

Kylie blinked, realizing she must have been in some sort of daze as Logan led the woman toward her. She couldn't tell what he expected from her. Meeting one of his sex buddies wasn't high on her bucket list.

"Kylie!" His snappish tone startled her, and she jumped in her seat before looking up at him. They stood right in front of her now, and he was looking at her with an odd expression as he spoke. "Are you all right? I was talking to you, and you were just sitting there turning red in the face."

"I'm fine," she said, speaking just as sharply as he had with her. Her eyes flickered over to the woman, easily picking up the glare she was receiving.

"Good," he said, gesturing to the woman. "I want you to meet Gloria, my masseuse. Gloria, this is Kylie. I brought her to watch me fight tonight."

Kylie glared at him. "She's just your masseuse?"

His eyes trailed over her angry features as he nodded. "What's your problem?"

Kylie looked over to see a smug look on Gloria's face and saw red before she focused on him again. "That's not one of your categories."

He was staring at her like she was insane, and his condescending tone didn't help. "I'm just introducing you to someone. That's Mark over there."

"You know what, Logan?" She didn't like him talking down to her. He'd just made her feel so special—now he was treating her like a nuisance, so she blurted out the first thing that came to mind. "I wonder if your ass is jealous of all the shit that comes out of your mouth."

"What the hell?" he asked, laughing.

It fueled her anger and heartache. Why her stupid heart was already hurting, she didn't know, but she didn't like it. Still, she meant every bit of her accusation. He was a smooth talker and nothing else. She stood quickly and made her way to the door, glaring at the huge guy who had come in earlier as he laughed. "Nice meeting you, Mark."

Mark laughed harder.

"Where are you going?" Logan called after her.

She could hear him behind her as she fumbled with the doorknob. Her hands were shaking so bad she couldn't even open the door like a normal person. She was practically playing patty-cake with the thing as she continued to slap it. "Away," she said, finally turning the knob. Only, she was yanked backward once she made it out the door.

"Stop, Hood," he whispered, pulling her back against his chest. She thrashed in his hold, hurting her ribs but still fighting him. "Baby, stop. *Shh.*"

"Let me go." She whimpered from the onslaught of physical and emotional pain consuming her. She had no idea what she was feeling, why she was angry, sad, and hurt all at the same time.

"No, Kylie." His tone was so soft.

She opened her eyes, realizing they had been closed as she stood there crying.

"What's wrong?" he murmured, still holding her from behind. "What did I do?"

"You know what you did." She flung her arms out since they were alone in the hall.

"No I don't." He took one of her hands. "Tell me."

"Her!" She cried because she felt so stupid. He'd managed to make her feel special and pathetic in the span of such a short time. Now, just after offering to help her, he was flaunting the top of his fuck-list in front of her. "How can you just put me face-to-face with your all-star fuck buddy?"

He hugged her from behind, chuckling. "I haven't fucked Gloria, and she's not on my 'Want to Fuck' list. Honest."

Her chest heaved up and down as she tried to wipe her eyes. "I don't even know why I care. But I know you're lying. And it makes me . . . I don't even know."

He squeezed her gently. "Hey, don't be jealous of Gloria. You shouldn't even be mad—you and I just met. This is the kind of shit you need to learn, okay? But I promise I haven't fucked her."

She didn't like him telling her what she had to learn, but she was so focused on what he'd said about Gloria that she ignored it. "Really?"

"Yeah. I mean, she gave me head once when I first met her, but I stopped it at that."

"That's not exactly better, Logan." She wanted to gag and cut out her heart. Why did such simple words affect her so deeply? "No way is she not on your 'Want to Fuck' list."

Logan laughed softly and surprised her by kissing her cheek from behind, his earlier kiss still lingering on her other one. "Trust me, she's not a woman I want my dick getting close to again."

Frowning at him, she let him hold her face after he turned her to look at him. "What does that mean? If she's not on your fuck list, then which category do you put her in?"

He grinned and wiped her cheeks. "She's on my apocalypse-only list. She gives horrible head."

"Logan." Her face burned from his words as he laughed.

"What?" He kissed the top of her head. "Trust me, it was awful. I was terrified to imagine what she would be like in the sack."

"What a jerky thing to say." She was laughing as he pulled her back to the door. Already, her anger with him was slipping away.

"Ah, but I'm a jerk who doesn't want to see you hurt. Remember that."

With a smile on her face and her sadness forgotten, she let Logan pull them back inside his room.

◆◆◆

"He's undefeated," Chris said, staring ahead.

Kylie briefly looked up at him before returning her attention to the ring, or rather the octagon, that Logan stood inside. "That's good, right?" she said, trying to be polite. She didn't want to talk to Chris, but with her improved mood after Logan exposed his past with Gloria, she wanted to put aside her anxiety. She used to have no problem talking to people.

Her head throbbed as she forced herself not to think about the past. All that mattered was the present.

Kylie breathed out as her building headache vanished. At last, she could simply recall how she basked in her small glory and even smiled smugly when Logan had tossed her little glances and repeatedly winked in her direction while Gloria massaged a muscle he'd recently pulled.

Gloria, however, had looked ready to claw her eyes out, especially after Logan suggested Kylie take notes so next time she could do Gloria's job. It was an even sweeter victory when he added that maybe he'd buy a better lock to keep Mark, his coach, out of his room because they'd be shagging for hours. At that, she chose to throw a bottle of water at him, and he shut up. For ten minutes, that is. Then he went on to tell Mark—and Gloria—how sexy he thought Kylie was.

She was in heaven with all his attention while Mark kept smacking Logan on the head, eventually telling him that gentlemen didn't speak so crudely about the women they loved. Apparently the 'L' word was all that was needed to succeed in shutting Logan up. After that, he became more focused and allowed Mark to tape his hands before they started some exercises. Then Chris came to take her away.

"Yeah, it's a very good thing," Chris said. "And he's at the top of his division. It's promising for such a young fighter. He has the potential to become a legend."

She faintly processed Chris' words as Logan stared at his opponent. His eyes almost looked black under the harsh lights of the ring, and his beautiful smile was nowhere to be found.

The crowd roared upon hearing his name, and she clapped excitedly when it appeared they were getting ready to start. Violence should bother her, but the fact she was about to watch him do something he was clearly passionate about had her blood pumping with excitement.

"I'm so nervous," she said, thinking that Chris was not really listening to her. Her heart was hammering with anticipation, and when Logan's eyes scanned the crowd and stopped at her, winking, she nearly fainted. It was so quick, and his face didn't show any other emotion, but she felt her heart flutter.

Her mind caught up with her heart at that moment, and she accepted that her heart was attaching to Logan Grimm. And maybe she didn't mind. Maybe it was possible to like someone so quickly.

"You know," Chris spoke softly as the referee went over some stuff, "you're not the only girl he's asked me to sit in the front row."

Her breath hitched, and she turned to look at the man next to her, not really hearing the bell ring as the fight started.

"Just saying," he went on. "Don't think you're special because he turned down a few babes tonight. I've had to entertain one he couldn't get his hands off of. And he ain't looking at you the way he did her."

Her lips trembled, and she looked down, then up to see the fight already in full swing. Logan looked incredible as he dodged and ducked punches and kicks, landing a few hard punches instead.

"You seem like a good kid," Chris said in her ear as her eyes watered. Logan delivered several hard jabs to the other fighter's face. Blood was quick to flow from the force of his punches. "I just don't think you should believe whatever bullshit he's told you to put that smile on your face. Because I know Logan. After he gets done banging you tonight, he'll have Gloria or some other eager chick down on her knees, bent over his bed—or more than likely, both. Trust me, you're not his type. He has a thing for brunettes—one in particular. He's just biding his time with you until he can have who he really wants."

All her happiness vanished and her heart crumbled as she glared at the octagon.

The other fighter landed a punch to Logan's side before trying to put him in a hold of some sort, but Logan wasn't having it. Kylie watched with the crowd as he lifted the guy completely off the ground before slamming him down on his back. The pain was felt by everyone in the stands as they *ooh*'d briefly, then cheered as Logan maneuvered himself to lock the man in a choke hold. They screamed out, excited when the other fighter tapped out and the ref shoved Logan off the beaten man.

"Take care of yourself, kid," Chris told her as she stood and headed for the exit.

Kylie didn't respond. She just kept walking with her head down, and she let the roar celebrating Logan's victory fade behind her.

Logan was a fairy tale. A grim fairy tale she'd not be taken a fool by. He could feed his bullshit to the next slut ready to spread her legs for him.

It was time for her to return to the dark. Her nightmare. She had her own monsters, and Logan Grimm would not be another beast waiting to feast on her bones.

"Fuck the Big Bad Wolf," she whispered, shoving the exit door open, letting darkness once again wrap her in its wicked arms. "Fuck Logan Grimm."

4
PAIN VS. PAYNE

Fire exploded over the right side of Kylie's face, pulling her out of one nightmare and throwing her straight into another.

"Enough! Wake up and tell me where you were last night?"

Finally opening her stinging eyes, Kylie held her cheek and stared into Lorelei's green eyes as she glared at her from the foot of the bed.

"I told you," Kylie whispered, staring fearfully into the hate-filled gaze of her stepmother, "I had to help a boy from school with his project." Kylie pulled her hand away and inspected her fingers, expecting to find blood. There wasn't any.

Lorelei let out a cruel laugh. "Yes, I forgot. Trevor Grimm wanted your help. Did you have a good time?"

Kylie didn't respond as she pulled herself into a sitting position.

Lorelei continued, "Did he end up falling madly in love with you after getting to know your sparkling personality?"

Kylie rubbed her throbbing cheek and looked down as last night's events ran through her head. "Of course not, Stepmother. He left me to finish the project alone. That's why I was so late. I had to walk home—I got lost."

"Of course you did." Lorelei tossed some concealer on her bed. "Cover that bruise. Kevin is downstairs, and you know I don't want him focused on you."

She nodded with watery eyes as Lorelei walked away.

"You really shouldn't walk in the dark, Stepdaughter. It's so easy to trip and fall."

"Yes, Stepmother," she said, knowing this was the excuse she was expected to give Kevin, Lorelei's new husband, regarding the injury.

"Good girl. Now hurry and come down for breakfast. School starts in an hour. Kevin's here, so you'll ride with Maura instead of walking through those woods of yours."

Kylie nodded, listening to the door click shut. She would rather walk in a hailstorm than endure five minutes with Maura, but she had no choice. Lorelei didn't like Kevin to suspect they weren't one big happy family. So she would have to put up with whatever wrath her sister wanted to dish out.

Sighing and praying Maura was in a good mood today, she got out of bed and made her way to the attached bathroom. At least both she and Maura each had their own. Kevin Blackwood was loaded—not surprising since his family founded the town, and he owned most of it. His wealth was a relief to Kylie though. God knows what she would have had to put up with if he hadn't bought them this huge house after marrying Lorelei.

"Shit," Kylie muttered, wincing as she poked the swollen skin on her cheek. "Stupid witch and her bony hands."

Kylie closed her eyes as blinding pain radiated through her head. She cradled her cheek, exhaling as she pushed her anger away. She took a deep breath, panting harshly as the pulsing pain faded. For a few minutes, all she could do was stare at her reflection. Her cheek actually wasn't as bad as she'd first thought.

She whimpered, opening her medicine cabinet to get the pain medicine Lorelei hid in there for her. Thinking of Lorelei sent her anger to dangerous heights. Kylie wanted to fight back so badly, but she knew it would only bring more trouble. Lorelei wanted her alone, hidden, and she would make sure no one ever saw her.

Again, her head throbbed, but she pushed it away, her thoughts drifting unintentionally to Logan and how he'd promised to keep her safe. Maybe she should have talked to him before leaving last night.

"No," she said out loud, trying to stop thinking of him. It was stupid to get close to him anyway. No one could help. No one really wanted to protect her, keep her safe or believe her. She'd known that for years now. And even though Logan was likely being honest about his concern for her, he still had an ulterior motive.

While thoughts of him wanting her in a sexual way excited an unexplored part of herself, she was terrified to allow him such a thing. After all, his chaste kiss to her cheek was the first kiss from a boy she'd ever received.

Her face flushed even redder as she thought of his lips on her skin. He was so attractive—and he'd admitted to wanting her. It was beyond exciting, but she couldn't act on it. Maybe one day she would have the experiences he was willing to give her, but for now, she'd add them to her many fantasies and daydreams. Because Logan was a fantasy. Allowing anything more than her silly dreams would be asking for trouble. Lorelei would see to it. She and Maura would ruin everything.

"Soon," she said, opening her eyes slowly. "Soon I'll be out of here, and I won't have to see any of them ever again." Kylie focused on her reflection and began the task of carefully covering yet another bruise marking her cheek.

This was what mattered. Not Logan.

She'd never see him again anyway.

"Good morning, Kylie," Kevin greeted her as she took a seat. "Did you sleep well? Your mom said you came in late." He took a sip of his coffee, eyeing her over the top of his mug. Kevin was a kind man, completely clueless, but nice nonetheless.

"Yeah, sorry about that," she murmured, briefly taking in his dirty blond hair and light blue eyes. She hated to admit it, but Lorelei had managed to snag a gorgeous man with Kevin Blackwood. He was in his early forties, and he had the whole hot older guy thing going for him. Unfortunately for him, even his looks, money, and kindness couldn't keep his wife loyal to him. He married a monster.

"I ended up having to walk, and it was farther than I thought."

"Why didn't you call your mother to pick you up? Or me?"

Kylie jerked her head up to stare at Kevin. She slowly looked over to see a forced smile on Lorelei's perfect lips.

"Honey," Lorelei said sweetly, "you know she won't carry a phone, and she won't let us purchase one for her."

Kevin shook his head at Lorelei. Kylie knew this was going to end badly. Kevin always unknowingly caused her to receive even more of Lorelei's wrath.

"She should have one for emergencies, at least. And she could've borrowed her friend's phone to call you."

Kylie hated when they talked about her like she wasn't there. Briefly, she darted her eyes across the table at Maura. Maybe her stepsister would grow upset with all the talk about her and cleverly shift the conversation to something about herself instead. Unfortunately, Maura looked too preoccupied with her own thoughts.

"I guess she didn't think about that," said Lorelei. "I'll look into getting her one."

Kylie darted her eyes away from Maura's downcast expression. "I couldn't call," she told them. "Trevor had to leave, and I stayed to finish his project by myself."

Maura dropped her fork and glared at her.

"Your friend left you by yourself?" Kevin asked, not catching the hateful look on Maura's face.

Kylie's mouth opened and closed as she shifted her gaze between all three people. Kevin looked shocked and angry that she had been abandoned, Maura—well, judging by that fierce gleam in her green eyes, she was no doubt planning ways to make Kylie pay on the way to school. Then there was Lorelei, just as Kylie knew she would be, trying to hide her glee over her misfortune.

"He said he had a previous commitment he couldn't get out of. I told him I would stay and finish, then leave."

"Who is this boy?" Kevin demanded.

"Why?"

He roughly set his fork down. "No boy should ask a girl, or anyone for that matter, to take care of his assignments, then leave them all on their own. And without a ride or a phone. Christ, you could have been killed walking all alone in the dark. And you were alone in his house without anyone there?"

She shook her head quickly, stuttering, "I-I wasn't alone."

Kevin sat back, waiting for her to continue. Even Lorelei looked interested in her statement.

"Well?" said Kevin.

She swallowed as her time with Logan played out in her head. She didn't really think it wise to tell the truth here. "He lives with his cousin while his dad is overseas. His cousin knew I was staying behind and didn't mind."

She wrung her hands together as Kevin seemed to cool off a bit, while Lorelei wore a calculating look before she spoke. "Maura, darling, weren't you telling me that a Trevor was supposed to take you out last night? Could he be the same friend of Kylie's?"

Kylie's eyes widened as she returned her attention to a still fuming Maura.

"I had been waiting for Trevor to ask me out forever," Maura said as she glared at Kylie. "He finally did, and then

I'm waiting for him—all dressed up—and he doesn't call or show up. Do you have to have everyone to yourself?"

"Kylie, do you know something about this?" Kevin asked, reaching out to put a comforting hand on Maura's shoulder. Besides the sadness in her stepsister's watery eyes, Maura looked ready to jump over the table and beat her.

"No," Kylie said. "He didn't tell me what his plans were—only that he'd had them for a while. I promise I don't know anything, Maura."

Lorelei's happiness with the turn of events could only be registered by Kylie's terrified eyes. She wanted to say more, but she knew nothing would help. Maura was pissed and hurt. She wasn't going to let her get away without suffering.

"Calm down, Maura," said Kevin softly. "Clearly, this Trevor boy lacks common decency. If his father was around, I'd talk to him myself, but I very well can't go disciplining a boy who is not my son."

"I'm sorry, Maura," Kylie whispered as a tear fell from her stepsister's eye.

"Just hurry up," Maura spat, slamming down her fork and standing. "I'll be in the car."

Everyone watched Maura flee the room with her shoulders shaking. Kylie would have felt bad if she didn't hate Maura's guts. As far as Kylie was concerned, Maura deserved every bit of sadness she was experiencing, and she silently thanked Trevor for showing her she wasn't as important as she thought she was.

"Oh, dear," said Lorelei as Maura disappeared. "I think she must've really liked that boy."

"It's probably a good thing I don't know where to find this Trevor," Kevin muttered, taking another sip of his coffee. "Goodness, Kylie!"

She jumped at his sudden exclamation.

"What happened to your face?" he asked.

Instinctively, her hand went to her cheek. "Nothing. I just fell when I was walking home."

"It looks like someone hit you." He leaned forward, trying to inspect her puffy cheek.

"You know she's just clumsy, Kevin," Lorelei said, standing to clear off the table. "The girl is always banging into walls and tripping over air."

Kylie looked down, trying to avoid his stare as she let her hood fall over more of her face.

Kevin narrowed his eyes at his wife before looking back at her. "Sweetheart, is there anything you need to tell us? Did this Trevor boy hurt you?"

"Of course he didn't," Lorelei yelled, slamming a plate down. It was unlike her to lose her cool. But everything was a little odd this morning.

"Lor, this boy might have hurt her," Kevin said, his voice still raised with concern.

"She fell." Lorelei huffed angrily before she pinched the bridge of her nose. "Kylie, darling, get your things and don't keep Maura waiting."

"Okay," she whispered, putting her fork down as Kevin continued to stare at his wife. Kylie knew Lorelei was going to have to fix her slip in composure. She rarely lost it in front of others, but when she did, she used her looks to cover up any suspicion. "Bye."

"Goodbye, sweetheart," Kevin said, smiling at her before looking back at Lorelei.

Kylie didn't wait to see Lorelei fix this. She bolted from the room as fast as she could, wincing when each step set off a twinge of pain in her chest.

After stumbling back downstairs with her backpack, she darted past the breakfast nook, barely catching a side-eyed glimpse of Lorelei kissing Kevin.

Kylie shook her head and ran out to the car. Lorelei sure worked fast. She just hoped Maura's heartache would be debilitating rather than further fueling her urge to inflict pain.

Pulling open the car door, Kylie carefully took her seat. She didn't dare meet Maura's angry gaze and kept quiet as they began heading to school.

Her body was coiled tightly, clutching her bag to her chest as they sped down the streets to Blackwoods High School. She knew something was coming, and the silence was filling her with dread.

The throbbing in her head returned, but she ignored it as a sudden urge to console Maura rose in her. "Maura?" Her voice shook, and she tried to subtly move farther away. She chanced peeking over to see her stepsister gripping the steering wheel tightly, but the pain in Maura's normally vindictive eyes was what tugged at something inside Kylie. "I'm really sorry, Maura. I don't know where he went."

"Just drop it, Kylie!"

Kylie flinched from the high pitch of her voice and turned her head to look out the window, knowing without a doubt what Maura Payne was going to deliver tonight.

Pain.

✦✦✦

Logan rubbed his tired eyes as he stumbled toward the kitchen. His head was killing him. "Shit," he muttered, shielding his eyes from the refrigerator light.

Growling in frustration, he grabbed eggs, cheese, and bacon before shutting the refrigerator and dropping his ingredients on the counter, cracking a few of the eggs. "Goddammit!" he yelled, picking up the broken eggs and hurling them at the sink. He breathed heavily, bracing himself against the counter as his mind went to a girl he shouldn't have been thinking about.

"Do you need help?"

Logan slowly turned his head and peered over his shoulder, narrowing his dark eyes at the pretty brunette wearing only a large T-shirt.

She toyed with the hem of her shirt. "Maybe I can make you breakfast, or get you some aspirin?"

Logan didn't respond right away. His grip tightened on the edge of the counter when she tried to step closer. "Who the fuck said you could still be here in the morning?" He glared at her as he stood to his full height.

"I-I—" she stuttered and stepped back. "I didn't know I couldn't stay."

"Get out of my fucking apartment," he shouted, slapping the counter. The loud sound echoed and the girl shrieked, running from the kitchen. Logan grabbed his pounding head as he listened to her crying until the front door slammed shut.

"Dumb bitch." He shook his head and put the still usable breakfast items back in the refrigerator, grabbing a water bottle in the process and retrieving a bottle of aspirin. He poured out two pills and took them quickly before returning to his room.

As he picked up his jeans from the floor, he dug out his mobile. Not stopping to read his messages, he searched through his contacts and pressed call when he found the one he wanted.

His muscles flexed as he paced his room, snatching up a towel and fresh clothes. "Chris," he said, stopping in his path.

"Logan, listen, I'm sorry. I–"

He growled, tightening his hold on the phone. "Save it, or I'll break your other arm." He studied his bloody jeans before marching toward his bathroom. "Just tell me what you told Kylie last night."

"I only told her you had a thing for brunettes." Chris stayed quiet for a few seconds. "I was keeping your head straight, brother. You know how you get."

He squeezed his phone to the point he heard it crack. "You're lucky I didn't know this before I put you in the hospital. You're fired."

5
LIKE A MOVIE

The five-minute chaos between classes was probably the most annoying part of Kylie's school day. If she looked to her left, a dumb jock had his tongue down some cheerleader's throat, and to her right, a bad boy wearing a black leather jacket was glaring at the world as a mass of students parted for him.

Kylie rolled her eyes as Ryder Godson, Blackwoods High's notorious bad boy, pushed some unsuspecting jock into a locker, causing an all-out melee between Ryder and his three brothers—who always came out of nowhere—and jock-boy's teammates.

"Idiots," she muttered, stumbling a bit after being shoved by eager teens all rushing to see the fight. She had to admit that Ryder Godson was practically a god—and not the kind of Greek god Trevor was. No, he was the complete opposite of Trevor. Like the god of darkness . . . and sex.

He wasn't her favorite daydream, but it was nice to watch him do just about anything. If only he wasn't a heartless asshole.

She sighed, pushing her way through the crowd to get to class. That's when she realized the jerks Ryder and his brothers were pummeling were the same jerks who often threw wads of paper at her and stuck gum on her chair.

On second thought . . . class can wait.

Kylie turned to enjoy the sight of Ryder in all his hunky glory as he pinned Philip Miller down and punched him over and over. She cringed as she watched Philip's face swelling, and the little spray of blood that shot out of his mouth.

Violence wasn't something she condoned, obviously, but she found herself enjoying the sadistic smirk on Ryder's face after he'd knocked Philip out cold. Her lips twitched with a smile, and she didn't really care that it had to do with someone else being hurt.

Philip had repeatedly embarrassed her in the past, and for a tiny moment, she fantasized that Ryder and his brothers were doing this for her.

Her smile disappeared when Janie Mortaime, Ryder's girlfriend, pushed her way through the crowd. The girl was waving her hands about, shouting nonsense, as Ryder wiped his bloody hands on Philip's shirt.

Kylie sighed when Ryder ignored Janie's glare and kissed his girlfriend senseless as he lifted her up, wrapping her legs around him, and marched down the hall.

There goes today's Ryder fantasy. It would've been more appealing if Ryder really was just a heartless asshole, but he did care about one person. His girlfriend.

It wasn't fair to watch everyone else matter but her.

Kylie's thoughts drifted to Trevor. His face morphed into Logan's, and before she knew what she was doing, she imagined it was Logan carrying her off as she watched Ryder and Janie get farther away.

It was stupid to think about him. Logan didn't want a girlfriend—he'd told her what he wanted from her. She shouldn't even care about him; he was a player. But . . .

"Ow!" Her books spilled to the floor when someone knocked her from behind. She turned to see who pushed her, but they had already continued running down the hall.

Turning back to gather her things, she grimaced from the old pain in her side. "Stupid fuckhole," she muttered, adding extra insults in her head as she tried to arrange her books.

"Did you just say fuckhole?"

Kylie whipped her head around to see none other than Trevor Grimm kneeling beside her.

Opening and closing her mouth a few times, she finally responded to his smiling face. "Yes," she whispered as he handed her one of her folders. "Someone made me drop my books. I was just angry."

He chuckled, handing her the final piece of paper she had dropped. "I wouldn't have guessed you had that kind of mouth."

Kylie frowned as he looked her over. She had a feeling he meant something other than her use of language. Yesterday, she would have turned into a blushing mess because of the smile he was giving her, but today, all she could think about was Logan's words: A girl to use for the moment.

Pushing away her thoughts, she spoke. "Well, my mom always told me that people who didn't cuss were less trustworthy than those who did." That was a lie. She really didn't remember much about her mom. She'd just seen a quote about it.

Trevor laughed as he stood up, offering her his hand. "Well, I was about to say that I don't like to cuss, but I guess that would make me untrustworthy, wouldn't it?"

She hesitated but took his hand. "Thanks," she said, letting go. "I'm sure you're trustworthy, Trevor."

He grinned, making her stomach flip. Even though he had done her wrong, he was still her dream guy. It was pathetic, but that's what dream guys were for.

"Well, thank you. I hope to keep your trust," he said, watching her tug her hood into place.

"Yeah." She took a step back. "I, uh, should get to class. I think I'm late now. Thanks for helping me."

He nodded and stuffed his hands in his pockets. "Sure. I was hoping I'd see you. I wanted to thank you for your help. Mrs. Lewis was impressed with all the drawings. I think I'm going to get an A."

She smiled, but only because she remembered Logan's project was the one he turned in. He'd dug around for hours looking for it. For her. "I'm glad you're going to pass." Again, she prepared to leave; this whole conversation was nothing but awkward. She couldn't even look at Trevor like she used to without thinking of Logan, but she suddenly couldn't stop herself from speaking again. "Can I ask you something, Trevor?"

He was taking a step away. "Yeah."

"What did you have to do last night that was so important you couldn't stay to help me?"

Trevor looked a little surprised, but he answered, "I told you—I had a thing."

"Yeah, I remember what you said. But I'm curious as to why you never showed up to take her out if you abandoned me." She had to stop her eyes from showing shock as she waited for him to respond. It was so unlike her to confront someone. Especially the boy who'd had her heart for so long.

"Her?" He scratched his head. "I don't know who you're talking about. I had to go see a coach from one of the universities I applied to."

A bit of her adrenalin faded. "A coach? But what about Maura?"

His face scrunched up in confusion. "Your sister?"

Kylie stood still as he appeared to remember his date.

"Oh, shit. I completely forgot about her. The coach thing has been scheduled for months." He rubbed his face. "It was your mom who suggested I take her out—I don't even like Maura. She's hot, but, you know—I date nice girls." He gestured to her somewhat, making her heart speed up. "Maura ran into me the next day. I guess your mom let it slip about me taking her out. I was on the spot . . . I asked, and she said she was free. I wasn't even paying attention to the dates."

"Oh," she whispered. It all made sense. Lorelei did often suggest boys take Maura out—not that she needed advertisement. All the boys knew Maura.

"Is she mad? Was she crying or something?" He was so stressed.

He looked more like the Trevor she'd always imagined him to be. A good guy. Her dream guy. Only, he was worried about Maura, not her.

She nodded. "Yeah, she thought I had something to do with you not coming."

"Damn." He grabbed her shoulders and looked her in the eye. "I'm sorry, Kylie. I really didn't mean to forget. And I felt like a total dick for leaving you. That's not like me at all. Honest."

"I believe you," she said, her voice way too breathless, but she couldn't fix that. He was so close.

"I'll talk to her, explain it all, okay? I'll make sure she knows you knew nothing. I'll make it up to both of you."

"Okay," she whispered, staring into his big blue eyes.

Trevor smiled brightly, looking a lot like Logan for a second, then moved her hood back and leaned forward to kiss her forehead. "Thanks, Kylie. I promise to fix this."

The whole time he spoke, he left his lips on her skin. Her body and mind went to mush. Every fantasy she'd ever had of this boy came forward, and she was frozen.

"And, Kylie"—he moved back to look at her, still wearing that big smile—"I meant what I said. I'm not interested in Maura."

With those final words, he winked and dropped his hands, leaving her standing dumbstruck in the middle of the hall.

"What the hell just happened?" She looked around when he turned down the next hall and realized she was ten minutes late for class. "Shit!"

Kylie tugged her hood tighter to her head as her gaze drifted to the side of the room where Ryder Godson sat. He'd been moved to her English class today. Girls were dying to get a class with him or one of the brothers, and somehow, Kylie managed to get all four Godsons in her class.

Yep, all four of them were now in her class. All sitting just feet away. From her understanding, they were quadruplets—not identical—but she'd heard the boys often refer to Ryder as the 'big brother.' Maybe he was the first born. Either way, they were the gods of Blackwoods.

First, there was Archer. He was hot in a unique way. He had hair so blond, it looked white, like really white, and he had the palest blue-gray eyes, almost matching his light skin. He was the funny one of the group, always cracking jokes or pulling pranks to amuse himself.

Next, there was Savaş. No one could miss him. He was huge, bigger than Ryder in height and bulk—and his golden skin and bright red hair made him stand out even more. He got in more fights than Ryder, but he was polite whenever he spoke to people whereas Ryder made you feel like you didn't matter at all.

Then there was Tercero Godson—the calm brother. He looked almost identical to Ryder, except he had more of an emo look about him. Where Ryder was bigger, tanned, and just oozing sex and danger, Tercero was lean with a very pale complexion, and he had a quiet, intelligent aura. He reminded her of the anime characters that girls always had secret crushes on. He even had long, straight black hair. Normally that was a negative thing for her, but he pulled it off, especially with the way he dressed. He always wore all black, and it made his light skin stand out even more against his black eyes.

This was the first time Kylie had ever had a class with any of them. She was certain it was only because Janie Mortaime had this class. Normally, Kylie ignored anything to do with the girl. Every time Janie opened her mouth to argue with the teacher, Kylie blocked out her voice and focused on her work. Today, Janie wasn't in class, and kids were whispering she'd been kicked out of school. With Janie gone, and the Godsons showing up with slips confirming their change in class period, Kylie was fully absorbed in the buzz.

It was especially wonderful because the boys they fought earlier were nursing their wounds on the opposite side of the classroom. Maybe now Kylie wouldn't have to put up with those guys anymore.

Tercero muttered something to Ryder, and she hid her smile when Ryder grinned. *God, he's gorgeous.*

She sighed, trying to focus again. It was becoming more frustrating by the second that she was looking at every bad boy now. She knew why bad boys were on her brain. Logan Grimm.

"Ryder Godson?" called Mrs. Demoness.

Ryder didn't look up or reply.

The teacher sighed. "Your assignment, Mr. Godson—where is it? Just because you switched periods when you have me does not change the fact that your work is still due during class."

Finally, Ryder looked up. "My girlfriend has it, and you already know she's at the principal's office. I'll turn it in later."

So Janie wasn't expelled. Well, at least she wasn't there to ruin Kylie's mini-fantasy that put her in the center of the Godson brothers.

Mrs. Demoness was one of the few teachers who didn't cower from Ryder, and she didn't now as she stood up, bracing her hands on her desk to look intimidating despite her five-foot stature. "Your girlfriend is not the homework bin, Mr. Godson. Your assignment on *The Little Moon* fairy tale was due yesterday. You can thank Miss Mortaime for your drop in grade."

"Watch what you say about her." Ryder shifted in his seat.

Kylie darted her eyes back and forth. Every student was tensing in their seat. It was well-known that Ryder didn't have a problem arguing and getting into fights with teachers. He'd even gotten into a fist fight with the old principal, and the new principal, who'd been the vice principal at the time, had to wrestle him off with the help of the brothers. They said the old principal couldn't walk or talk anymore because Ryder had beaten him so bad. At least, that was the rumor she'd heard since starting at Blackwoods her junior year.

She'd heard about him getting into a huge fight with an older boy who used to rule the school when Ryder was only sixteen. It was the only fight he'd lost, but he'd apparently lost it on purpose to win Janie. That didn't make much sense, but that's what people said. They were probably all lies, but looking at his emotionless stare, Kylie wondered if some of it was true.

Mrs. Demoness glared at him. "Is that a threat?"

Archer chuckled, leaning back in his seat as if he was preparing to watch a showdown.

"A warning," Ryder said, his eyes narrowing on the teacher. "You know damn well I know more about the fairy tales than you do."

Mrs. Demoness' face reddened. "That doesn't change when your assignment is due."

Ryder stared at her and a terrifying smile stretched over his perfect face. "Then let me give you a sample of my assignment, orally. Your interpretation of *The Little Moon* is full of shit because you, like every other lonely hag, loathe the goddess it's about, simply for the fact she has a good heart and more than one man. Now sit your ass down, get on with your lesson, and leave me the fuck alone." Ryder didn't spare her another look and went back to talking with his brothers.

Kylie swallowed as she watched Mrs. Demoness' face scrunch in rage. Ryder had a point about her teachings of the Blackwoods Fairy Tales. Kylie wasn't a fan of them, but clearly Ryder was. There was a collection of related stories that were found in Blackwoods, Colorado, Texas, and Canada a long time ago. Learning them was now a requirement in both History and English Literature. So it was strange for a teacher at one of the famous towns to speak so negatively about them.

All through the lesson for *The Little Moon*, Mrs. Demoness made hateful remarks about how American storytellers were fools obsessed with a weak woman who used her promiscuity to blind men. Why on earth Janie had such a big problem with that, Kylie didn't know, but she'd clearly relayed everything to Ryder after arguing with the teacher yesterday. Kylie realized that must be why Janie wasn't in class—she was in trouble, and Ryder was pissed.

What Kylie wouldn't give to have someone that protective of her.

"Everyone, turn to page 394," Mrs. Demoness snapped, sitting down.

Kylie sighed as she opened her book, not eager to work on the gloomy stories.

Mrs. Demoness started speaking again, "We'll be comparing the classic Grimm's Fairy Tale of *Little Red Riding Hood* and—"

The door opened as Janie Mortaime entered. Mr. Prince, the principal, was right behind her. Janie quickly made her way to Ryder. He sat up, reaching for her when she got close.

"Take a seat, Miss Mortaime," said Mrs. Demoness. "I don't have all day for you to reunite with your boyfriend."

Mr. Prince leaned against the doorway, his vibrant sea-green eyes on the teacher. "She's not staying. Neither is Ryder."

"What about us?" Archer asked, looking ready to bolt.

Mr. Prince smirked. "I don't need you pestering me. Stay put."

Archer flipped Mr. Prince off, who merely laughed with the other Godson brothers.

Ryder stood, snatching Janie's bag and greeting her with a kiss.

Every girl sighed.

Tercero leaned over, handing Janie a folder. "Get me out of here, *tesoro*, and I'll buy you a Dr Pepper and let you drive my car."

"Deal," Janie said, kissing Tercero's cheek before looking at the principal. "Mr. Prince, Tercero has something of mine in his car. Can he get it?"

Mr. Prince rolled his eyes at her. "Come on, Tercero."

Archer glared at Mr. Prince, then grabbed Janie's hand. "Spring me, too, beautiful. I'll give you a massage and a ride in my car. Way better than your Camaro."

Savaş snorted before laughing at Ryder's glare.

"Bye, handsome," Janie said, giggling when Ryder punched Archer in the shoulder.

"Don't call him handsome," Ryder growled, kissing Janie once more before dragging her toward the door.

"There is no kissing on campus, Mr. Godson, especially not in my class," Mrs. Demoness snapped.

"Ryder," Mr. Prince said, his tone a warning as the bad boy began to turn to the teacher. "Let's go."

"I expect them to be punished, Mr. Prince," Mrs. Demoness said as Janie shoved Ryder out the door.

Mr. Prince's retort was instant and harsh. "And I expect you to teach the curriculum outlined by the board without voicing your negative views on our town's beloved history, Nia. Check your email after class."

Ryder and Tercero could be heard laughing in the hall as Mr. Prince shut the door.

A few students snickered as Mrs. Demoness' face grew red with rage. She looked downright psychotic with her wild curly hair, but it had to be stressful dealing with a bunch of rich kids opposing you and having no power to stop it. Because everyone knew Ryder would be let off. The Godson family was loaded—probably richer than Kevin—and they contributed to the school financially.

Ryder probably should've been expelled at least twenty times, but here he was, more than likely getting Mrs. Demoness fired.

"Read the story to yourselves," Mrs. Demoness said, her voice screeching like a bird. "I want absolute silence. Your assignment and homework is on the board. Get to work!"

Kylie swallowed her annoyance as she read the board.

Read: *Little Red Riding Hood* and *The End of Gods & Monsters*.

Assignment: Summarize and provide your interpretation of each tale. Provide examples of similarities in style, structure, and content between the traditional Grimm Fairy Tale and the Blackwoods Tale.

Great, *The End of Gods & Monsters* was long and way too emotional for a fairy tale. She was going to be up all night.

"Archer, wake up and start your assignment," Mrs. Demoness said.

Archer had his head on his desk, and he didn't move.

"He seems to be unwell," Savaş said. "I think I should take him to the nurse."

"You will do no such thing," Mrs. Demoness shouted.

Archer dramatically reached out for Savaş. "Help me, brother. I am certain I have something contagious. I believe I may faint."

Everyone laughed, including Kylie, when Savaş jumped up and lifted Archer's limp body into his massive arms.

"Sit down, Mr. Godson."

Savaş glared at the teacher. It was terrifying enough to make everyone stop laughing. "You are well on your way to starting a war with our family, Demon-ess."

Kylie's jaw dropped. Did they all talk to teachers like this?

"I suggest you learn your place quickly," he added.

Archer snickered but kept his eyes closed.

As Savaş started to leave, he dropped a bag right by her desk.

Archer peeked an eye open. "Mind helping a sick man, Red?"

Kylie felt her cheeks burn as she reached down and picked up the bag to hand it to him.

"Thanks, gorgeous." Archer winked, moaning as he took the bag. "Make haste, brother. I feel the cold hand of Death closing around my heart."

Savaş laughed, rushing out of the room as the class lost it.

Mrs. Demoness let out a little growl before snapping, "Get to work, everyone. Now!"

◆◆◆

"This is gonna suck." Kylie looked down at the puddle of water pooling around her feet, then back inside the dark house. It looked like no one was home, but she knew better.

After being left to find her own way home from school, Kylie began the trek through the woods nearby. It was a normal occurrence for her—one she didn't mind, but today, a terrible storm had decided to blow in. Now, completely drenched, she stood at the foyer of her house, debating her best options before going in.

A door slamming upstairs at the same time lightning lit up the sky made Kylie jump. A lump formed in her throat.

This was like a setup for some scary movie, but for her, the scary movie was real.

What she wouldn't give to have Logan there. He had no problem putting his arm around her and telling everyone to fuck off. She couldn't help but wish she'd at least had his number. She stopped herself from hoping for too much with him. First of all, she had no phone, and second, he would expect her to repay him with sex when he kept her from getting hurt.

And my problem with that is what exactly?

"Seriously, Kylie," she whispered to herself as she shut the door. "I'm not going to be a whore to get a guy to like me."

"Talking to yourself again?"

Kylie screamed, dropping her wet things on the floor as she spun around to face Maura.

"Kevin would worry, you know," Maura said. "If he found out that you still talked to voices in your head. He might worry about a lot of things."

Kylie slowly tried to distance herself from Maura, taking in the bat in her hands. Maura was team captain of the Girls' Softball team. She must have just gotten home before it rained.

"I was just thinking out loud, Maura."

Maura grinned, her lips expressing false happiness. "I saw you in the halls today—when you were drooling over Ryder Godson. Did you fantasize you were Janie fucking Mortaime? Did you imagine he was kissing you instead of her?"

Yes, but she wasn't going to say that. "I was just watching like everyone else, Maura."

A twisted sneer graced Maura's face. "I saw you when the fight was over, too. With Trevor."

Kylie froze. "Maura, it was nothing. He was just helping me pick up my books and thanking me for the project."

Maura screamed, swinging her bat at the vase nearby, smashing it. "Don't lie to me! I saw him kiss you. You knew I liked him!"

Kylie stumbled backward, hating herself for not looking around because she fell over a chair. The old pain in her side stabbed her, and she cried out as Maura moved closer. "Please, Maura," she cried as she held her hands up to protect her face. "It wasn't like that. I even confronted him about standing you up."

Maura yelled, raising her bat.

Kylie screamed, but continued to blubber out her findings. "He said he forgot. He had a thing with a coach." She cried as Maura swung her bat to knock the chair away. "He didn't mean it, Maura. He said he would make it up to you. He felt bad."

The crazy gleam in Maura's eye had Kylie more frightened than she had been in a long while. She knew the beatings had increased lately, but she didn't understand why.

"Then why did he kiss you?" Maura's voice was low and steady, her green eyes fierce with hate. "Why did I hear him tell you he was never interested in me?"

"Maura," she screamed as Maura yelled and swung right for her.

6
GYM TALK

"Logan."

He looked around the punching bag he was currently imagining was Chris to see Mark making his way closer. "Hey," he said, resuming his work on the bag.

"Still pissed at Chris, I see."

Logan didn't respond.

"I saw him today. He came by, asked if I'd seen you."

Logan grunted and continued his workout.

"He said you fired him."

"I did." Logan flicked his head, moving the hair from his eyes.

Mark sighed, putting his hands on his waist. "Over that girl? It's not like she was—"

Logan cut him off, "You work for me, Mark. Not the other way around. I don't run my decisions past you."

Mark held his hands up, smiling. "I was just trying to figure out what happened. I wasn't picking a fight. You know I never had a problem with—"

Logan held his hand up, stopping him. "He just pissed me off."

Mark nodded in understanding. "And ruined your game."

Logan shot him a dirty look.

"What?" Mark laughed. "You telling me you weren't trying to get into her pants?"

"She's seventeen," Logan muttered, picking up his bag to leave.

Mark laughed loudly and followed him.

"Shut up."

"Are you that hard for some virgin pussy?"

"It's not like that." Logan nodded to a few guys, greeting them as they walked by.

"Then what's it like?"

Logan stopped and glared at his coach. "Why are you asking?"

"I'm just curious why you would beat the shit out of Chris over a seventeen-year-old girl who looks like she's never even seen a guy naked before. And why she apparently means enough to you that you would fire him." Mark shook his head. "Seriously, man. You've known Chris for years, and you didn't fire him for the shit he pulled with—"

Logan glared at him.

Mark rolled his eyes. "I'm not picking a fight. How long have you known this girl?"

"Do you have a point to all your questions?"

"I'm just curious about the big reaction."

Logan was tired of this. Mark was a cool guy, probably the closest to a friend he had, but he didn't need any new friends. "I don't answer to you."

"I'm asking you as a friend." Mark watched him. "You don't just fire people—get drunk and try to fight everyone around you—all over a random girl."

Logan sighed, looking around the gym before he focusing on Mark again. "Someone's hurting her."

Mark frowned. "Like her feelings, or like *hurting* her?"

Logan knew Mark had a problem with girls getting abused. His girlfriend had been in an abusive relationship before, so he told him about Kylie, hoping it would be enough to get him to lay off. "She flinches and limps. I know you saw it. I just met her."

"Yesterday?" Mark asked, folding his arms. His muscles were already jumping, probably thinking about his girl.

"Yeah. She was at the apartment when I came home. Trevor was dumping his project on her."

"You let her around your cousin?" Mark gave him a once-over.

He glared at him. "No, dumbfuck. I just told you she was already there. He'd brought her over on his own. I don't think he's noticed she's kinda hot."

"That's good." Mark sighed. "So, you find out who hurt her? Is it a boyfriend?"

"No." Logan was getting uncomfortable. He didn't expect to see Kylie ever again, but he couldn't help thinking about her, worrying if she made it home okay. "I offered to help her out."

Mark made a weird face at him. "With the project?"

"No." Logan felt a tight sensation around his chest. "Well, that too, I guess. I gave her an old project of mine so I could get her to come with me. I didn't want to leave her there alone."

Mark laughed, wiping his eyes. "Logan Grimm bribed a seventeen-year-old chick to get her to come out with him?"

"Do you want to know what happened or not?" Logan's anger was coming back, and by the looks of it, Mark knew to lay off.

"Sorry," Mark said, calming down. "Continue."

"You know I'll fuck you up if you keep laughing at me."

Mark just smiled.

"Dick."

Mark waved his hand. "Just waiting for you to explain."

Logan exhaled a frustrated breath. "First off, I wasn't bribing her. I just can't stand Trevor. I wanted to take her to piss him off, but I changed my mind, I guess. I noticed her flinching, and I wanted to find out what was up. But I knew she'd run if I came on to her like I normally would. She looked like she was going to pass out when I introduced myself—I had to soften her up."

"Yeah, looked like a baby deer when I walked in on you two. That is, until she noticed Gloria." Mark gave him a warning look. "Definitely has some fight hidden inside that little body of hers."

Logan glared at him. "Don't say that."

"What?" Mark grinned. "Little body? Did you already get a peek?"

"No, just don't look at her body."

"Okay," Mark said, still smiling.

"I told her I'd protect her."

"And she refused you?" Mark looked confused.

"She was thinking about it. But Chris fucked up my plans by saying that shit he did. Now she's gone, and I'm just . . . I don't know. I wanted to keep her safe, and now I don't know if I should try to find her. If I ask Trevor, he'll only make shit worse."

"Yeah," Mark said. His joking was gone. "Well, I have good news for you then, Casanova. I know who she is."

"How?"

Mark nodded to the benches nearby, and Logan followed him to sit. "She looked familiar, and when you introduced her, I thought it sounded like I've heard her name before. Do you remember that doctor who died in that bad accident? The one from Wolf Creek?"

Logan frowned, thinking it over. "I think so. The one they couldn't find for a while?"

"Yeah," Mark said. "His name was Dr. Oliver Hood. He used to stop by when I was in high school—sometimes helped when Evander wasn't available. He fixed my dislocated shoulder one time."

"He's her dad," Logan said quietly.

"Yeah. She was with him once. Cute girl, I remember. She didn't have the whole hoodie look going on then. I never would've put together she was the same girl you had here, but it was the name . . . Anyway, she's his kid."

"But he's dead." Logan was trying to figure out what Kylie was hiding. Usually family members were the abusers. "So Kylie just has her mom?"

"No, her mom is dead, too. For a long time, I think. Because I remember her stepmom. Every fucker in the room had a hard-on the moment she walked in."

Logan narrowed his eyes at Mark. "So Kylie doesn't have parents? What the fuck? Is she homeless?"

"Chill, bro." Mark held up a hand, quieting him. "I said she has her stepmom. And hottie stepmom got married recently."

"To?"

Mark grinned. "The lady married Mr. Blackwood."

"You're fucking with me." This wasn't good.

"Nope." Mark chuckled. "Kevin Blackwood, the dude that signs our paychecks—owns this gym, arena, and practically the whole damn town of Blackwoods—is Kylie's new daddy."

"Shit." Logan looked around the gym. Everything here belonged to Kevin Blackwood, including his contract.

"Do you think it's him hurting her?" Mark asked, eyeing some girl who smiled at them as she walked by.

Logan watched lightning dance across the sky. "I don't know. He doesn't seem like the abusive type, but you never know."

"Well, how bad is she?" Mark asked. "Like are you talking Stacy-type abuse?"

"I'm not sure." Logan knew Stacy, Mark's girlfriend, had been beaten badly. The guy she used to date was on his team, and everyone made sure Zack got what was coming to him after they stumbled on Stacy bleeding with a broken nose. It was awful; he'd never seen anyone beaten by a boyfriend before. Kylie didn't have a boyfriend, and she didn't have a busted face, but she was hiding under her hood. His thoughts drifted to that hood, but he shoved his rising feelings down.

"Do you want to go to the cops?" Mark nudged him. "I mean, I know you don't trust cops to do right, but you know it's not the same anymore."

"Just keep quiet about it." Logan's memories of how the cops in their town dealt with that kind of shit made his heart burn. "I'll handle things myself if I ever see her again."

"You got it." Mark started walking away but added over his shoulder, "Let me know if you need anything. I could always ask Stacy to talk to her."

Logan's mind went to a different girl, and he shook his head. "I gotta run."

"Can't beat yourself up forever, brother." Mark's voice trailed off as he got farther away.

"Yeah, I can," he muttered, shoving the exit door open.

7
INTO THE WOODS

"But, Mommy, why did Little Red Riding Hood go into the woods? The woods are scary." Kylie was probably five as she stared at her mom, who lay cuddled beside her.

Her mom closed the book she'd just read and set it on the table. "Because, Kylie, she was going to help her grandmother. But she didn't listen to her mother. Instead of staying on her path, she listened to the wolf."

"I won't ever listen to the wolf," said Kylie, yawning softly and shutting her eyes.

Her mom leaned forward and kissed her forehead, her tone soft like a lullaby now. "I hope not, darling." She stood and arranged Kylie's quilt, adding, "Because you might not have a chance to run. The wolf is not always what he seems."

Kylie pried her eyes open, the action painful due to dried tears. The more she woke, the more distant her dream became. She knew it was likely a memory, but the contents of her dream already began to blur, making it impossible to remember what it was in the first place.

"Oh, good, you're up."

Kylie looked over to see Lorelei setting out her breakfast.

"Kevin will be back tomorrow," Lorelei said as she walked around the room, gathering items, almost like a kind mother would. "Your face is almost healed, but you need to keep applying the cream I gave you. And ice that swelling around your cheek and ribs like I told you. It would have been healed by now if you had done as I instructed."

"Yes, Stepmother," Kylie whispered, trying to sit up. She bit her lip to not cry like she wanted to. Three days had passed since her incident with Maura. It was Friday, and while Maura got to carry on like nothing was the matter all week, Kylie had been confined to her room with Lorelei doctoring her wounds, feeding her and helping her to the bath.

The night Maura had attacked her, Kevin and Lorelei had been in town having dinner together. Kevin was then dropped off at the airport. Apparently, his mother was ill, and he was going home for a few days to make sure all was taken care of.

So, while Lorelei was being pampered by Kevin, Kylie was fighting for her life. After Maura had bashed her across the ribs repeatedly, she slapped her on the same cheek Lorelei had bruised that morning. When Kylie fell unconscious, Maura must have decided that was enough and left to go to the movies with a few friends.

It was much later when Lorelei had come home and found her. And while a normal human being would immediately call 911, Lorelei simply dragged her upstairs and dumped her on the bed with a bottle of aspirin and an ice pack. Or at least, that's the conclusion Kylie had made after waking up, crying because of the pain.

"Trevor asked Maura out again," Lorelei announced as she dumped dirty clothes in the hamper.

Kylie nodded, not caring to hear news about Trevor or Maura.

"She's thrilled about going out with him tomorrow."

"Good for her," Kylie muttered, trying to lift her spoon of oatmeal. She normally refused food from Lorelei, but she had nothing else. Lorelei wouldn't let her have the food from Kevin's chef, so she was stuck eating whatever Lorelei made her.

Bitch should eat her own slop.

Lorelei sighed loudly. "Kylie, you really should be happy for your sister. She must really like this boy."

Kylie set her spoon down and glared as best she could. "Are you really telling me to be happy for her?"

Lorelei had the nerve to look shocked. "You should be happy that she's happy. The boy broke her heart, and that was all your fault."

"It wasn't my fault. He forgot about her." Kylie threw her spoon to the tray and leaned back, breathing harshly. Her chest hurt so badly. Fortunately, it didn't seem like anything was broken. This time. The blood had been from hitting her head when she fell. Head wounds always bled like you hit an artery. And as far as her moving around, she had grown accustomed to hiding pain. Well, hiding everything.

Now Lorelei was giving her the dirty look she was used to seeing on her face. "Well, perhaps if you had not distracted him, he wouldn't have forgotten. I recommended you to him so you could help him pass his classes. If he had less worries, he might see Maura is perfect for him. You know I want a nice strong boy to care for her."

Kylie attempted to roll her eyes, but she couldn't. It hurt too much, and she was starting to panic. If the bruise was still visible on her face, she'd have to really hide from Kevin. Normally, she went to the woods to sit alone or walk. Everything stayed hidden in there, which was where she needed to be. Except the weather hadn't let up. Where was she going to go?

There's always Logan.

She wanted to groan for thinking of him. He had been in her thoughts a lot while she recovered. Everything from replaying her time with him over and over—to, unfortunately, imagining him with Gloria, and to even envisioning herself pinned under him as he—

"Oh my God, Kylie. Stop it," she whispered to herself, rubbing her flushed cheeks as she continued to picture her hands running across his mouth-watering body, tracing her fingers along his tattoos and down his pants. "Stop!"

"What?" Lorelei spun around, her surprised eyes matching her pitchy tone.

Kylie blew out a huge breath, fanning herself. "Nothing. I was just feeling a little queasy."

Lorelei studied her before shaking her head as she made her way to the door. "Rest up. I want you walking without hanging onto the walls before tomorrow. You know very well it doesn't hurt as much as you are making it seem."

"It does hurt," she snapped.

Lorelei gave her a long look. "You know what I mean. And you could hurt worse."

Kylie nodded, closing her eyes as she pushed her pain—everything—away from her mind.

"Finish that food," Lorelei added, shutting the door.

Kylie couldn't help it, she giggled to herself and sank into her pillows because Logan's smile suddenly popped into her head again. She wanted to go back in time just to see if more would happen now that she'd had the time to realize a bad boy giving you any attention at all was nice. "He hasn't even touched me, and I'm already becoming a slut for him. God, I wish I could see him again." She sighed as she remembered exactly why she had walked away from him. "He just wants to fuck me."

Opening her eyes, Kylie looked down at herself. Her tank top was stretched tight over her bandaged chest. "I wonder what Logan would do if he saw me like this." Her eyes stung. "He'd tell me I was weak. Then maybe go get a blow job from Gloria."

She tried to hold back her tears. Every time she let herself think of Logan, she had to wake up to the reality that she was nothing to him. Logan had sex with whoever he wanted. Kylie struggled to keep herself together, but eventually, she sobbed out loudly and held her face, crying more from the pain radiating throughout her body then the fact she was nothing to him. Nothing to Trevor—to anyone.

Her shoulders continued to shake as she played out all sorts of scenarios of seeing him, of never seeing him—of him not even remembering her.

"Oh, Daddy," she cried, her voice hoarse and muffled. "Why?"

So much came out right then. She'd kept her sadness in for years. Now it was all coming out because her damaged heart was breaking over a boy. And she had no dad or mom to hold her while her heart was crushed for the first time.

8
DATING

Rain pelted the glass, leaving chaotic, glittery streams as the world passed by.

"Remember," Lorelei said, putting the car in park, "wait until after ten to come up. I'll make sure he's in bed by then."

Kylie breathed out of her nose slowly, trying to calm herself as she looked at the clock. It was only six. "Okay," she whispered, pulling her hoodie tighter as she prepared to open the door. It was raining hard now. She was going to get soaked.

"Here." Lorelei grabbed her shoulder as she turned to leave. Kylie looked to see she was being handed ten dollars. "For dinner."

Kylie took the money without saying thanks and exited the car. When she reached the awning, she turned, only catching a glimpse of Lorelei's taillights leaving the parking lot of the small shopping center.

Already, her teeth were chattering from the cold. Her hoodie was soaked, but she was happy she'd at least avoided the huge puddles. It would be awful to have wet feet the whole time.

She sighed, trying to warm herself as she walked to the food market she'd been left in front of. This wasn't her normal routine, but even Lorelei agreed that she should go somewhere indoors. Her reasoning was she could catch pneumonia, and with Kevin home, he'd notice and take her to the hospital. That, of course, wasn't something Lorelei could allow. So Kylie had to try to keep herself healthy.

"Thank God," she said, sighing as the heat blasted her cold skin. Kylie didn't let it soak in though. The market looked busy, so she walked inside, going nowhere in particular. She just had to bide her time until it was close to ten.

◆◆◆

Roughly forty-five minutes had passed, and Kylie was enjoying herself. The smell of different foods, perfumes, and cleaning items were so different from the damp woods. It even pleased her to people watch. Being forced to not have friends, she'd grown fond of the quiet sport.

"Hood?"

Kylie gasped and looked away from the different shampoos she'd been smelling and right into a pair of dark eyes. "Logan," she said, shocked. Her shock quickly morphed to happiness, then anger and sadness. Then fear.

He was glaring at her. "What happened to your face?"

Kylie trembled from his angry voice. He had managed to keep it low so no one but her would hear him. "Nothing. I just fell." Her eyes watered as panic set in. She frantically darted her gaze around him, trying to find an escape.

"Fell?" He was now right in front of her, hot rage radiating from his entire being. "Don't give me that shit. Who did this?" He reached up to touch her face, but she shoved him back.

He stumbled a bit but quickly recovered, balling his hands before he seemed to register her fear. "Shit, Hood," he murmured, stepping close. "I'm sorry."

"It's okay." Her heart was so happy to see him, but sad all the same.

He slowly raised his hand to cup her cheek. "Tell me what happened."

"I can't," she mumbled, struggling not to lean forward and hug him.

"Why?" His thumb caressed her bruised skin. "I've been trying to find out how to get in touch with you. I wish you stayed."

"I can't see you, Logan," she whispered, but stayed right where she was. "I—"

He cut her off. "I know what Chris told you. He's an asshole. He just thinks"—he shook his head—"never mind."

She closed her eyes, not sure if it was better to look at his handsome face or keep it from her mind. He wasn't calling Chris a liar, and that killed her. "I have to go."

"No, you left me once, and now look at you."

"It's not your problem, Logan," she said, reminding herself he only wanted to protect her with the payment of sex on her end.

"Don't say that," he said, giving her just as nasty a look as she was giving him.

She tried her best to not weaken under his angry stare.

"I offered to help you, and you're being stupid by not thinking it over."

"I have thought it over! All week." Her chest rose and fell quickly. "Your plan won't work." She hated herself for implying what she did. She didn't want Trevor anymore. She knew now he was a silly crush, because Trevor was not the Grimm on her mind. No, the Grimm boy she'd been imagining herself with all week was the hot, conceited man-boy in front of her.

"It will work, Kylie," he said, keeping his voice low. No longer did he have anger in his eyes. "I'll keep you safe. I'll help you get stronger for when I'm not there."

She didn't want this. She wanted him, but he would never put her in any category but the one he'd already placed her in. "And what about Trevor?" Her heart felt like it had caved in. She couldn't make out his reaction.

His face was blank as he responded. "He'll want you when he sees that I do. And when he does, and you're ready to accept him, I'll leave you to him and be on my way." He looked around, then back at her. "Like I told you, I just want to hook up. I won't force you, but I still want you. I know you do, too. You're just afraid."

Kylie's heart was being cut all over again.

"We'll go as slow as you want," he added softly. "I'll always stop when you say."

Her eyes burned from fighting her tears. She didn't want him to know he was hurting her. She didn't want him to know he'd already broken her heart. "I'm not a whore, Logan."

"I didn't say you were. You know protecting you is my priority." His voice gave no indication on whether he meant it or not. "Will you tell me what happened, at least? You look terrible, baby."

Her sad heart fluttered at the simple term of endearment, but she quieted its hope as she remembered him calling Gloria 'beautiful,' then pointed out she only fell in his apocalypse category. "I'm fine. I really just fell down." When she peeked up at him, he looked ready to lose it. He looked the same way he had before his fight. Like the Big Bad Wolf.

"Kylie?"

She gasped and spun around to see Kevin standing at the end of the aisle.

Fuck my existence.

"Hi, Kevin," she said, trying to make sure her hood covered most of her face.

He smiled and walked closer, darting his eyes to Logan, hardening a bit as they did so. "What are you doing out here, sweetheart?"

She could practically feel Logan's body tense up the closer Kevin got.

"Is Lor with you?" Kevin glanced around as if Lorelei would pop out somewhere. "I got an earlier flight. I was going to surprise her." He held up a bouquet of roses.

She shook her head, lowering her gaze to the floor. "No, I'm alone. I just came out for a while. She should be home. I'm sure she'll be happy to see you."

Kevin nodded, trying to look at her before focusing on Logan. "You are?"

Logan stepped up behind her, and she stifled her gasp when his hand pressed against the small of her back.

"Logan Grimm," he said, extending the other hand for Kevin to shake.

Kevin shook his hand, eyeing Logan's possessive posture. "Kevin Blackwood. I'm Kylie's stepfather. Your name is familiar, but I'm sure it hasn't any association with my stepdaughter."

Kylie shook as Logan's hand slid and hooked around her waist, settling there as if he had always held her in that position.

What is he doing? Her mind was frantic, but she didn't dare move or speak.

"Well, we just started dating this week," Logan told him. "Kylie wanted to wait a while to tell anyone, but I guess now is as good a time as any. Right, baby?"

What? she screamed internally.

Kevin looked at her at that point, and she almost peed. His surprise was clear, and he didn't look happy.

She was more afraid of Logan though, so she leaned against him and nodded. "I guess so," she whispered, "seeing as I can't get rid of you." Her hot cheeks likely made her look as though she was only embarrassed, but really, she was furious and terrified.

Logan, however, couldn't appear happier. He grinned from ear to ear as Kevin took them in.

Kylie almost fainted when Kevin's eyes lingered on Logan's tattoos that peeked out under his white tank top.

How had she not noticed him wearing that under his leather jacket?

Oh, God, I'm dating a bad boy. A leather jacket, tank top wearing, bad boy!

"Well," Kevin said, stepping back, "I expect to see you for dinner sometime in the next week, so we can get to know you."

Logan nodded, pulling Kylie closer. "Sure. I look forward to meeting the family."

She swore his body heated up at those words.

"Good," said Kevin. "I assume you will also get her home safely tonight?"

"She's safe with me."

Kylie grew annoyed with the way they were carrying on like she was invisible. She was ready to beat the crap out of Logan. How was she supposed to protect her heart now? He was probably going to ruin everything.

"Well, I will see you both later," said Kevin, smiling tightly at Logan. His eyes barely seemed to register her cheek, but he called her out on it. "Kylie, your cheek is still swollen?"

She tensed, but Logan began rubbing her back. "Yeah, that's my fault. We were playing around, and she bumped my elbow trying to pin me." He kissed the top of her head. "I don't know how she got it in the first place though."

Kylie realized Logan was suspicious of Kevin and stepped in. "Yeah, I wanted to show him he's not so tough."

Kylie wanted to roll her eyes at Kevin's obliviousness—it was his own wife who hurt her, not whatever Logan was claiming to be. It did remind her to make sure she didn't give away her other injuries though, and she stood a little taller.

"That's where I know your name," Kevin said, oddly wearing a smile. "You're one of my fighters. *The Big Bad Wolf.*"

Logan shook his head. "I don't claim that name. That's just something the crowd and my old manager started because of my tattoos."

Kevin nodded. "Yes, I remember now. The Reaper."

Logan nodded, his posture still tense.

"I hope your reputation with the ladies is in the past now that you're dating Kylie."

She choked on her spit. Logan chuckled, rubbing her back as she tried to compose herself.

"Yes, sir. It's in the past." He hugged her with one arm. "She keeps me on a tight leash."

"Good girl." Kevin looked happy with the arrangement now. Kylie was stunned. "Just tell me if he screws up, sweetheart. I retired undefeated, after all."

Logan gave a fake laugh. "Warning received, Mr. Blackwood. I know all about The Black Wolf's reputation. I'll take care of her."

"Terrific." Kevin smiled at them and turned away. "Have her home by midnight, Logan."

"Yes, sir."

Kevin nodded and left the aisle. It felt like forever before she could even breathe.

"Hood?"

"What the hell, Logan?" She moved away as fast as she could.

He sighed, relaxing his stance. "Calm down. All this means is that your dad thinks we're dating. Dating, Kylie. It's not like I told him you're carrying my baby or that I want to put a ring on your finger."

Her face burned from anger, humiliation, and hurt.

He cringed, reaching out for her. "I didn't mean it like that, baby."

"Quit babying me!" She slapped his hands. "And we're not dating. This means nothing. All I have to do is tell him I stopped seeing you."

"But you won't," he said, smiling confidently.

"We're not dating. I'm not going through with this. This isn't—"

He cut her off, "Come to dinner with me."

"What? Why?"

"Well, maybe I want to have one date between us before our relationship ends." He grinned at her glare. "You know I think you're hot when you're all angry with me, Hood."

Her cheeks burned, and not from her bruised skin.

"Blushing now," he said in a teasing tone as he pulled her to him. "I can't tell which look I like more."

"Shut up, Logan," she muttered, trying not to smile at him.

Damn him and his smile.

He chuckled, placing his hands on her hips. His touch made her knees tremble, and he smirked down at her. She knew she was pushing aside their earlier conversation, but she didn't want to think about it right now.

"Where do you want to eat?" he asked, lightly caressing her waist.

Kylie closed her eyes, cursing her heart for letting him back in so quickly. This was why she never wanted to see him again.

"We can just pick up something, if you want, and go back to the apartment."

"I'm sure you have plans, Logan," she whispered, feeling him pull her that much closer. His legs were brushing against hers now.

"You heard Mr. Blackwood. My bachelor days better stay behind me."

She wished he wasn't joking, but she knew he was just teasing her. "Logan." She sighed, preparing to push him away.

"No, don't even think about it. I get my date before you get rid of me. We'll just talk and eat."

She stared at his gorgeous face, hating that she was so soothed by just seeing him. This was stupid. Dangerous for both of them. He could handle himself, but she was worried that Kevin could ruin him. But she was so consumed by Logan. He looked so confident as he stared down at her. He knew she wanted to say yes, she could see it in his eyes. He was not expecting rejection.

"Logan," she said, closing her eyes to give her strength.

He gripped her hips harder. "Don't you say n—"

"I want a milkshake," she cut him off. Peeking one eye open, she grinned at his smile. She knew she didn't have a chance against that smile.

"Anything you want, Hood." He gave her a triumphant grin as he picked up the shopping basket she had been carrying as she pretended to be a normal person. There were just a few things, like strawberry lip balm, raspberry lotion, shampoo, and conditioner.

"Oh, I wasn't really buying this," she said, getting his arm over her shoulder instead of a reply.

He started walking them to the front of the store.

"Logan, really. I was just wasting time and didn't want to look like I was stealing."

"Quiet," he said, looking around.

"What?" she whispered, looking around, too.

"I'm trying to remember if I need condoms or not."

"Logan!"

He laughed and kept walking them toward the checkout lines. "Don't worry, Hood." He squeezed her to him. "I stocked up on Monday."

"You're disgusting." She tried not to laugh because she could practically feel his smile as he walked with her.

"It's pronounced sex-y, Hood. Come on. I know you can say it. Seeeexy."

Her face hurt from smiling, and she stayed quiet as he placed her basket on the counter, still laughing as he pulled out his wallet. She realized he only had one item for himself. Men's bodywash.

Oh, Lord. We look like we're going to shower and rub raspberry lotion all over each other.

"Is that all?"

Kylie didn't look at the old lady who checked them out. She was still trying to hide her blush.

"Yeah," he said, pulling out cash.

She stayed quiet, fiddling with her still slightly damp hoodie as he got his change and their bags.

"You didn't have to buy me this stuff," she told him as they walked side by side to leave.

"Oh, I didn't buy it for you," he said.

She whipped her head over to look at him.

He smirked. "These are to stay at my apartment. I'd hate for Mr. Blackwood to smell our sex all over you when I take you home. Best to wash you up, make you all pretty again."

She shook her head, smiling as he pulled her to him again.

His hold tightened when they passed a few guys from her school. "Thanks for letting me take you out, Hood."

She smiled because he had mumbled this against the top of her head. "You have one date, Logan. And I want fries. Lots and lots of fries."

Now she just had to make sure he didn't see how hurt she really was.

✦✦✦

"Logan," she said, giving him an irritated look. He was sitting across from her in their booth, wearing a devilish grin with a straw between his lips. Stupid sexy lips. "I'm not answering that."

He released his straw and slowly licked his lips.

Sweet baby Jesus.

"You have to," he said, stretching his hands over his head. The action revealed a small section of tattooed flesh above his jeans. He caught her gaze and winked. "See something you like, Hood?"

Kylie closed her eyes and covered her face when he chuckled. "You're a mean bastard." He just laughed softly as she groaned, "I can't believe you're making me answer this."

"It's only fair." He carefully pulled her hands down from her face.

It was like he couldn't not touch her. Opening her eyes, she blushed because of the question she was about to answer.

"You're the one who suggested we play this game," he said, reminding her that she'd brought this upon herself.

Kylie groaned, trying to pull her hands from his. He was right, after all. When he kept pestering her about them dating, she decided they should do what she read in books: play twenty questions to get to know each other. However, it had slipped her mind that this was Logan she was dealing with, and by that, she should've known his questions would involve sex.

"You suck," she said when he held her hands tighter.

Logan smiled, a wicked gleam sparking in his dark eyes. "Well, baby, the question was will you? But I'll be nice and give you a freebie and tell you that if it's your body my lips and tongue get to taste—the answer is as often as you'll let me."

Hot! It was like he'd lit a fire right between her legs, and now it spread over every cell in her body.

"Logan," she said, failing miserably at hiding how turned on she was.

His eyes fixed on her lips, darkening as he watched her. "Keep saying my name like that, Hood, and you'll be spread out on this table with my face between your legs."

She didn't know what to do. Her only knowledge of sex had come from reading . . . Her head throbbed, but she was easily distracted by his smile.

"You can do that to me?" She yanked her hands free to cover her mouth. "Oh my gosh! I didn't mean to ask that."

Surprisingly, Logan controlled himself and nodded slowly, taking her hand again to hold between them on the table. "Yes. It's basically the equivalent of you giving me head, but I do it for you."

"Please stop," she said, turning her face away. She was so embarrassed. Of course she knew guys did that to women. At least in books they did.

"You still haven't answered. And I've given you so many freebies."

Biting her lip, she turned back to him. "But this is embarrassing. I don't know what you're talking about. I have no idea how to . . ."

He started shaking his head and rubbed the back of her hand in a soothing manner. "I didn't ask if you know how, or if you're good at it—I just asked would you want to with me?"

"I don't know," she said automatically, her heart hammering inside her chest. She didn't even know why she was having this conversation. But for some reason, she was pulled in by him, participating before she even realized that she was.

"Well," he said, smiling, "that's not a no." He started rubbing his thumb across the back of her hand again. "Your turn, Hood."

"Um," she said, staring at his hands playing with hers, happy that her lame answer worked. "I, um, realized that I don't even know how old you are. So, how old are you?"

"Does that matter to you?" was his instant response.

"I guess not, but I want to know."

Logan nodded and answered. "I'm twenty-one. My turn."

"I don't want to answer any more sex questions, Logan."

Nodding, he said, "I won't ask another. But that doesn't mean we won't continue our discussion another time."

She smiled, shaking her head. "Whatever. Now ask your question."

"You have to answer, okay? No backing out with some excuse."

She nodded slowly, comforted by the hold he still had on her hand but worried because of the seriousness he suddenly spoke with.

"Good." He held her hand tighter. "Who hurt you?"

Panic set in. She could see this had been his plan all along. Of course she wouldn't cause a scene. "You tricked me!" Her eyes watered as she kept them on his firm look.

"This was your game, Hood," he said, not changing his determined expression. "And don't give me any of that shit about falling down. You may have, but I know for damn sure that you were pushed if that was the case. Now tell me. Who did it? I know it wasn't Kevin—you weren't afraid of him, and that's the only reason he didn't wind up on the floor of that store."

Her eyes widened at his statement.

"Who?"

"Please, Logan," she whispered, her vision blurring with unshed tears. "No one did this. Just drop it."

"Fine," he said, gripping her hand tighter, "we'll go have a chat with Kevin and your stepmom then."

"No!" She tried to pull him back down when he slid out of the booth. He didn't budge. Instead, he started to pull her from her spot. The pain that shot through her body was terrible, but she only let out a small cry.

Logan stopped his attempt to yank her up. He studied her for a moment, no doubt scrutinizing the way she held her breath and her sudden rigid posture. "Where else are you hurt?" His voice was frightening.

She shook her head, still trying to subdue the cries wanting to spill out of her mouth. He couldn't find out the truth. No one could.

"Goddammit, Kylie. We may not have known each other for long, but I'm trying to help. How do I get you to trust me?"

"It was Maura," she whispered quickly, turning to look out the window because she just ruined everything.

"What?" He had lowered his voice, but she still flinched at the angry tone.

"I said it was Maura." *Oh God, what have I done?*

He slid down next to her, still holding her hand. "Your stepsister?"

She nodded and continued to stare out the window. It was the stupidest move she'd ever made. She was finally telling someone, and not just anyone. She was telling Logan Grimm, a man she hardly knew anything about—a man who within minutes of meeting her noticed signs of abuse and offered help. It might be a very warped sense of help he was offering, but he was still there, holding her hand and trying to find out who was hurting her. The danger of revealing this to him was almost worth it because he was making her feel so good just by holding her.

"Does Kevin know?" His arm slid over her shoulder, and he pulled her to his chest.

She wanted to cry and nearly did when she pressed her face against him. "No," she whispered, whimpering a little when he reached up with his other hand, sliding it under her hood to hold her head in place.

"But your stepmom does."

She nodded, not surprised that he could form such accurate conclusions.

"How long?"

She sighed as his thumb rubbed her cheek. Her mouth opened without really knowing she was talking, but she was. She was saying everything that she'd wished to say for years. "Since my dad died when I was fourteen. I tried to fight back, but when Lorelei didn't help, and the teachers—and the police—believed them, I stopped. They all believed her and said I just wanted attention."

His hold tightened as he rocked her gently.

"Nothing can be done, Logan. I'm just waiting until I can leave. Please leave it alone. It's not as bad as you think."

"No, it's going to stop right now," he said, letting a fierceness coat his words. "We're either turning them in, or I'm going to take matters into my own hands."

"The police won't believe me," she blurted. "They didn't in my old town, and they don't here. Lorelei manipulates everyone. Look at Kevin—he lives with me and he doesn't know."

Logan made a sort of growling noise and said, "That piece of shit knows. He's a fighter. We see weakness—injuries. He knows, and he hasn't done shit. I should—"

"No," she said, reaching her arm out to hug his waist. Her action surprised even her, but she liked it too much to pull away. It was what she'd always wanted. "Please. I don't want everyone to know. No one even knows me. I won't be able to take the uproar this would cause. And Kevin would be ruined—he doesn't deserve that. He's only been around for two years, if that."

"He's taken on the role of your father; he should protect you."

Kylie closed her eyes, savoring the feeling of his arms around her, the sound of his heartbeat—his strong body and amazing smell. Her internal chaos was soothed with him holding her. "Just let me wait it out, please. I'll get my inheritance soon, and then I won't have to see them. I can have a new life, and I'll forget all about this."

"They can't get away with this," he said fiercely. "Look at yourself."

"I have, Logan." She took a shuddering breath. "And I'm just a girl everyone forgot. No one cares, and I'm fine with that."

"I care, Hood."

She smiled sadly and tried not to let his sweet-sounding voice pull her farther down the rabbit hole. She knew he cared, but it wasn't the way she wanted him to. "I know. Thank you."

He kissed the top of her hood. "You're welcome, baby. But I'm not letting this go."

She figured that, and she let him talk so she could savor this moment.

"I get why you don't want to go to the police," he added, "but I'm not going to let them hurt you anymore."

"Okay, Logan." She didn't really see how things could change; they *couldn't* change, but she wanted this to last a while longer.

"We're going to keep dating," he told her. She didn't reply, and he kept speaking. "I'm going to show them that I'm here now. They won't touch you then."

"Maybe if they see we're friends," she said, still wanting to protect her heart even though she wanted everything he was offering.

He was quiet for a moment, then asked, "Do you really have a problem with dating me? Have you heard about me at school or something?"

She could swear there was a hint of sadness in his voice, but she dismissed it. Logan Grimm wouldn't be sad over a girl not wanting to date him. Because if she wasn't in his 'girlfriend' category, then she didn't matter enough. With those thoughts, she made a final attempt to keep her heart safe. "I don't like you that way, Logan."

His body heated up, but his voice was cool. "Because Trevor is the boy you dream about. I get it, Kylie. It's fine. I told you what I want between us, a good fuck—many. When we're done, when you're safe and ready to fall into my cousin's arms, I'll be fine fucking the next girl to catch my eye."

Her heart bled from each cut he just delivered.

"That doesn't mean my intention to keep you safe isn't genuine," he added, but his tone wasn't gentle. It was bitter.

She felt numb. "Let me think about it, okay?"

He didn't say anything, so she went on.

"I'm tired, my head is hurting, and it's getting late. I just want to sleep." Leaning back, she looked up at his face.

He wasn't looking at her, just staring at the tabletop with no distinguishable expression on his handsome face.

"Logan," she whispered, and feeling a mixture of bravery, longing, and appreciation, she reached out to hold the opposite side of his face, leaned forward, and kissed his cheek. "Thank you for caring. For everything."

Those dark eyes looked down at her, keeping her from pulling back just yet. She wanted to scream at him to not be a jackass and to just genuinely give them a chance, that she wanted to be his, not a forgettable fuck. She wanted to slap his gorgeous face, then kiss him and tell him that Trevor was nowhere near her mind, that it was him she'd dreamed about all week. Then she wanted to slap herself because all of this was asking for trouble.

So she simply let herself have these extra seconds of warmth—of everything Logan.

"I'll take you home, Kylie."

She nodded as he turned away and slid out of the booth. Her lip trembled, and she started to slide out, too.

"Step into her punches," he said with his back to her. "Step into her punch, and she'll be forced to back up. An amateur isn't going to know what to do if they don't have room to swing. If she takes you down, you hold on to her as tight as you can and keep your chin tucked so she doesn't choke you out. Hang on and tire her out. Never just lie there for it, Kylie. Never give up."

When she didn't respond, he shook his head and walked away.

"She doesn't use her hands," she whispered, watching him push the door open.

❖❖❖

"Who is he?" Lorelei asked, standing with her back toward Kylie as she entered her room. She was staring out the window, where a view of the driveway was.

"His name is Logan," she said, feeling a stabbing pain with just the uttering of his name.

"I don't believe what Kevin said about you two," said Lorelei. "You've been locked in this house all week. No one is interested in you. No one cares about you."

"Logan does," she said without thinking.

Lorelei spun around, surprise clear on her face. "And how long has he cared?"

"Since Monday." Kylie didn't know what she was doing. She had practically refused Logan, and now she was telling Lorelei there was something to it.

"Monday?"

Nodding, she went with it. There was no point trying to take it back. She was in trouble regardless. "Logan is Trevor's cousin. We met then."

Lorelei gave her a patronizing smile. "I didn't think you could work so fast. I'm sure your father would be proud to hear his only daughter whored herself out to the first boy to come along."

"I haven't whored myself out." She wanted to cry because that was exactly what Logan expected of her.

Lorelei chuckled, staring at her like she was a puny insect. "Do you really think any boy could truly love you? Once he gets in your pants, he'll toss you out his door."

"And what do you care?"

"Excuse me?"

Kylie straightened her back and fixed her own unloving smile across her lips. "I'm done with you two treating me like dirt. I've never done anything you haven't asked of me. And you let your slut of a daughter use me for batting practice."

Lorelei's mouth fell open, but she quickly closed it. "You know why—"

Kylie cut her off, "I won't turn you in for what you've done to me. I'm fine with letting God judge you when your body grows old and rots!"

"You will stop this at once, Kylie." Lorelei stepped forward, raising her hand to slap her, but Kylie moved forward, just like Logan told her.

It worked! Lorelei was caught off guard, and she moved back.

"You won't touch me again," Kylie hissed, trying to put as much venom in her voice as possible. Her sadness had made her almost deranged, but she was embracing it. "Logan knows what you've done," she added, feeling braver by the second.

"What does he know?" Lorelei challenged her. "*Hm?* I've never—"

Her head throbbed, but she poked Lorelei's chest, hard, stopping her from saying anything else. "The only reason he isn't in here telling you to back off is because I won't let him. But if you, or Maura, so much as spit on me, I'll tell him to call the police, and I'll tell him he can do whatever he wants to you while he waits for them to arrive."

"How dare you threaten me? You know why—"

"Get out of my room before I yell for Kevin." Kylie let her lips quirk up before she added, "I'm sure those wrinkles I'm starting to see will make it difficult to find another new husband with a hefty bank account. Especially after a divorce from someone so important breaks news."

"You bitch!" It was Maura's voice, though, not Lorelei's.

Kylie whirled around, ducking down when Maura took a swing at her.

The movement hurt, but she wasn't going to get hit again. She turned, preparing to protect herself, but Lorelei stepped between them, grabbing Maura before she could lunge.

"Stop, Maura." Lorelei gave Kylie a dark look. "Your sister has found herself a bodyguard."

Kylie huffed, feeling like she might breathe out smoke. She was filled with adrenaline, and she was itching for a fight like she used to, ignoring the injuries hidden under her clothes.

"Who?" Maura asked, laughing as if the idea of Kylie having someone was ridiculous.

"Logan Grimm." Kylie gave her the cruelest smile she could. "Trevor's older cousin. He's hotter and he likes me."

"How?" Maura asked.

Lorelei covered her daughter's mouth. "Come along, Maura. Kylie wishes to have the evening to herself." Lorelei's expression gave nothing away as she dragged Maura to the door.

"Oh, and, Maura," said Kylie, smiling the sweetest smile she could produce as she marched up to them. "Trevor only asked you out because your mom asked him to."

Maura's mouth fell open.

"Good night." She shoved them out of her room, slamming her door in their faces. Kylie turned around with a smile spread across her lips. She felt happy, but her fight was dying. She clutched the center of her chest with one hand as her body slumped forward.

"Ow," she whispered, hobbling toward her bed, finally reaching it after several painful steps. "I can't believe I just did that." She was afraid and knew she had probably just done the stupidest thing in her life, but Logan's smile suddenly formed in her mind and she couldn't help but grin through her pain. "I guess I'm dating Logan Grimm after all."

9
ADDICTED ON THE FIRST TRY

Lifting her shaking, sweating hand, Kylie knocked three times. It felt as though her stomach was being tied in knots and then cut apart with a jagged knife. A completely nauseous feeling, really. Her oatmeal from the early morning hours was seriously at risk of being sprayed all over the door in front of her.

There was no going back though. She was here, staring at the bedroom door that was slowly being pulled open.

The door creaked and came to a stop as it revealed Logan Grimm. Her stomach clenched and her body began to tremble upon seeing him.

Logan hadn't even noticed her yet. He was looking down at his phone with a slight frown on his face.

Kylie couldn't help but admire him in the moment. It was ridiculous for someone to be so attractive, but he was more than that. Logan Grimm was drop dead sexy.

"Hood?" he said, sounding surprised to see her standing outside his bedroom door on a Sunday afternoon.

It was a bold move on her part to just let herself into his apartment, but she couldn't exactly go knock on the front door now. "Hey," she whispered, feeling stupid because she had probably been standing there gawking at him. He was probably used to that look from her by now anyway. "I wanted to talk to you, if that's okay?"

That signature smirk formed on his tempting lips as he crossed his arms over his chest and looked her up and down. The look made her squirm in place. No one had ever looked at her the way he did. It wasn't romantic, at all. After all, she was simply a girl he wanted to get in his bed. But in a strange way, she couldn't help but feel flattered that he put her in such an intimate category with himself. No one had put her in that category, not until Logan Grimm had set eyes on her.

"I didn't think I'd see you again." He slid his phone into his pocket. "Figured you were running away. Are you okay?" His eyes lost that lustful gleam and scanned her full length.

Looking away from his intense scrutiny, she played with the hem of her hoodie. "I didn't think you would either," she mumbled, realizing how crazy this all was. It still surprised her that she was going to go through with this. "Are you busy? I can come back—or maybe you've changed your mind. Or you're mad. Oh my God, I'm so stupid . . . You were playing with me!" Tears instantly threatened to fall. All her bravery, all her confidence was being yanked right out of her shaking hands while full-blown panic set in. Thoughts of his possible lies spun out of control in her head, along with the possibilities of him only messing with her the whole time.

All she could think was run. And unable to look at his confused face any longer, she quickly turned to leave.

But seeing that Logan was apparently descended from a god, he was too fast for her. He snagged a hold of her sleeve, letting out a low chuckle, and kept her still while she struggled to free herself. "Hood," he said, sounding as if he was trying to soothe a small child. Obviously, he was ready to laugh and make her realize just how stupid she was to ever have believed he was genuine in his concern for her.

It only threw her further down the pit of embarrassment. She was going to be a laughing stock.

"Look at me, Hood."

The seriousness in his tone caused her to stop fighting him and lift her head. His dark eyes were fixed on her face, studying her carefully.

"I'm sorry I came," she said, trying not to sound so pathetic, but she was embarrassed and had never felt more stupid than she did in that moment.

"Why?"

"Because I realize now you didn't mean anything you said before," she said, almost yelling as a traitorous tear escaped.

He frowned and reached out to rub her tear away. It wasn't like her books where she melted or felt sparks from a guy's touch. No, his thumb was a bit rough against her smooth skin, and his caress was more like an upset parent wiping away dirt from a child's face.

"How did you jump to that conclusion when I only asked if you were okay?" he asked, baffled.

She wanted to retort with some proof supporting her reaction, but she stayed quiet.

"I wasn't lying about anything yesterday." He searched her face. "Did you change your mind about us dating?" He seemed a little shocked, but his surprise vanished as he looked over her shoulder.

She felt someone watching them, and she shook a tiny bit because only one person should be in his apartment. Trevor. God, she'd completely forgotten about him. "I did." She swallowed nervously, prepared for him to start laughing and to toss her out.

"Good." He kept staring over her shoulder, then he smirked. "I hope you're not a screamer." Her eyes went wide as he grabbed her hoodie near her tummy and tugged gently. "Because it looks like we're going to have an audience." With that, Logan winked at Trevor and pulled her inside his room.

"Wha—"

He slammed the door and shoved her against it, pressing his hand over her mouth. It hurt a little because of her bruise, and thankfully, he lessened the pressure.

Still, she instinctively began to shove at his chest. A pointless effort on her part; he wasn't going anywhere unless he wanted to.

"Shh . . ." His mouth was by her ear now. The stubble from his cheek tickled her in a pleasant way.

Ignoring him and the giddiness that threatened to consume her, she tried to talk. But with his hand firmly in place, 'What are you doing?' came out sounding like an erotic moan.

Those dark eyes connected with hers, and he leaned back a bit. Everywhere else, though, stayed pressed against her, she realized, and she liked it even with the pain it added to her injuries.

He was so firm, and he smelled nice. Like soap and man. Logan-y.

My man-boy!

"That sounded sexy as hell," he whispered, smirking at her terrified look. "Do it again."

"*Whmmm?*" Again, she sounded like a dirty slut, and it only made him grin wider.

"He's listening." He lowered his mouth back to her ear. "Trevor," he clarified. "I can tell he's still out there."

She tried to push him away. Even if this was the plan, she didn't know if she could go through with it now. So much panic was still present. He always brought out so many confusing emotions she wasn't used to.

As if he could hear her thought process, Logan shook his head, pressing his whole body against hers to the point it really hurt. "We're doing this. Do you trust me?"

She didn't know, so she looked at him, letting herself become mesmerized by the dark depths of his brown eyes as he waited for her to respond. Something was there, not just darkness—not just his arrogance. She couldn't figure it out, but it was the reason she was here—the reason she was following him into the unknown.

So, stepping over the chains that had restrained her for so long, she nodded.

The most genuine smile she'd seen him wear yet spread across his lips. It was stunning, and her knees wobbled.

"Let's put on a show then," he said, looking a lot more excited than she expected. "I'm going to make you moan for real now."

She tried to shake him off. She needed to scream for him to stop. She wasn't ready for *it* yet!

"*Shh.*" His breath tickled her ear, and her heart hammered away in her chest as his lips moved against her earlobe. "Don't panic. I know you're not ready to fuck. Just trust me."

She relaxed against the door, tired of fighting him and relieved that she wouldn't be losing her virginity in the next ten minutes. They had a lot to talk about. He needed to hear everything, and she needed to apologize for pushing him away yesterday.

"There we go," he whispered, pulling his hand from her mouth and then sliding it along her jaw, rubbing his thumb across her tender cheek as his lips moved from her ear down to her neck.

Oh, wow.

"Just relax," he murmured.

Now she was trembling for an entirely different reason. A new sensation began flitting around in her stomach, making intimate parts of her body tingle. He wasn't really doing anything yet—just brushing his lips down her neck and breathing in deeply.

This was the closest she'd been to a boy, and this guy put others to shame.

"You smell good," he murmured as he reached the side of her neck.

An embarrassing noise sounded in the back of her throat when his lips pressed a kiss to the base of her neck. She tilted her head to the side, wanting him to do it again.

His lips turned up against her skin before he placed another kiss to the same spot. It shot an ache right to the pit of her stomach, and she struggled to remain standing.

With her eyes closed, she didn't see him reaching up to push her hood back, and upon feeling it slip over the top of her head, she panicked again. The hoodie was her security—her shield—and him taking it away was like a bucket of icy water, yanking her out of the sweet delirium he managed to suck her into.

"It's okay," he said, gripping her jaw. His other hand took hers as she reached to pull her hood back in place. "You don't need to hide from me." He kissed her neck before gently sucking the same spot.

"Oh," she moaned, shutting her eyes and forgetting her hood and fear altogether.

"There it is." He nipped the tender spot, making her jerk, before he licked his bite.

"Oh my God," she moaned louder.

His chest made a sort of rumble as he gripped the back of her neck. The hand that held her wrist brought it to his side, and her fingers quickly splayed out over his waist, itching to touch him.

"Feel me," he commanded before leaving a trail of heated kisses all along her neck, occasionally sucking and nipping her skin.

She nearly squealed at his offer to feel him up, but she merely groaned in satisfaction at both the feel of his firm body and the assault he was still leaving along her neck.

He had returned his attention to her ear and nibbled the soft lobe between his hot lips.

"Logan," she gasped, squeezing her hands as she held his sides. This was like the first time she had chocolate. Better than that, and she wanted more. She wanted the whole candy store!

"Fuck, that was sexy," he said, chuckling quietly as he nipped her earlobe.

His laugh made her smile, and she enjoyed trailing her fingers up and down his sides, then across his abs. He shivered, kissing her right below her jaw before moving his face back.

He was smiling at her. "This is going to be more fun than I thought." The sound of a door shutting echoed, and he leaned away, holding out his hand. "Come on. We have a lot to do."

She took his hand and let him tug her farther into the room after he locked his door. "I don't know if I can really do it though, Logan. And we need to talk about everything that's happened."

He shook his head and squeezed her hand before letting go to turn on music from his phone. He turned the volume up to a decent level so it would block out their voices if anyone were to listen in. "Don't worry about us fucking yet."

She bristled at his crudeness, just as she felt a little pain in her chest. "Do you have to say that word?" She started to pull her hood back up while he moved around his room.

"What word?" He didn't look up as he dug into a small refrigerator by his bed. "Fucking?"

She blushed again. "Yes."

He tossed her a water bottle. "Baby, once I get you in bed, your pretty little mouth is going to beg for me to fuck you again and again."

"I doubt I'll ask for it. And if I do, I wouldn't use that word."

"What word will you use then?" He pulled his shirt up over his head, revealing his sculpted perfectness. Why did he always take it off? "Making love, perhaps?"

Kylie swallowed and looked back up at his face.

"I don't do love, honey," he said seriously. "Understand that now. I really don't want to hurt you. I might act like a dick, but I know that for you, at least, I don't want you getting your heart broken over me. If you think that's happening, tell me now. I'll find some other way to help you, but I'm not looking for a girlfriend."

His words were like rusty razor blades slicing across her skin. She knew he wasn't trying to be mean; he was being honest. She wasn't girlfriend material.

"I'm not going to fall in love with you," she said to save face.

He stayed quiet, watching her.

"I won't. I promise. I love Trevor, remember?" She wanted to slap herself for that blatant lie, but she wouldn't let him see how she really felt. Trevor was her getaway car, and she'd use him if she had to. Taking it back would make Logan's offer unnecessary in his mind.

But everything was different now that he'd come into her life. She wasn't willing to just sit by and add more scars, more pain. There was no way she was going to the cops, but maybe she'd be in better shape when it came time to leave town.

She knew this was a shitty thing to do to herself, but she couldn't bring herself to care anymore. Not after that taste. She was addicted to him. "What's the water for?" She shook the bottle to give herself a reason to look away from him. It felt like he could see through her, and she didn't want him to retract his offer over not hurting her. He would leave if he knew how she felt.

"Take off your hoodie," was all he said.

"Why?"

His tone was slightly irritated now. "So you don't get it all sweaty."

She sighed, not wanting to make him angry, and began unzipping in front of him while he just stood there, waiting. "Do you have to watch everything I do?" Taking it off terrified her, but she obeyed.

"Hood," he said in a no-nonsense tone. It made her jerk her head up, so she was looking him in the eye. "You're beautiful. I just want to see you embrace your beauty." He stepped forward and traced her bottom lip with his thumb. His eyes moved up to hers. "You really have no idea how attractive you are, do you?"

"Only my father has ever called me beautiful. But all dads say that." Her eyes hardened, and she moved her face away from his hand. "Don't play games with me. I just want to do what you offered. Don't mess with my head."

A dark look crossed his face and he moved closer, lowering his face to hers. "I told you to trust me. That means when I tell you something, it's the truth. Don't question it." He shook his head and moved away, pointing to the floor. "Lie down."

"Why?"

He exhaled and threw a towel down. "We're going to work out. Now are you going to do as I tell you, or are you going to question every little thing I say? We'll talk about yesterday later."

Kylie finished removing her hoodie and set it on his bed, seeing nowhere else to lay it. Then, as she kneeled to where he pointed, she looked up. This was the first time anyone had seen her without her hoodie, and she couldn't tell what he thought about it. Thoughts of being found pretty didn't even come these days, but she wanted Logan to think it, even if she was telling herself to not fall for his flattering words.

"Spread the towel out and lie on your back."

Kylie bit her lip as she spread the towel out. Obviously, he didn't think too much over seeing her, but she just did as she was told and refused to think about how below his standards she was. She wasn't even his type—Chris had said so. "Like this?" She was straight as a pencil with her hands balled at her sides.

Logan shook his head and moved to stand by her feet. "Bend your knees and spread your legs."

"What kind of workout is this?" She did as he asked.

He was still giving her a hard look. "This is just a warm-up," he said, dropping to his knees between her legs.

Her eyes went wide as he leaned forward and placed his hands on each side of her head, keeping her from any chance of escape.

He wasn't touching her. His hands were about shoulder width apart, but he was so close. His body heat started to blanket her.

"What kind of warm-up?" She started to shake as he lowered his face.

"Push-ups," he murmured, then kissed her cheek before pushing up into another one, then another. He was doing push-ups right over her. Right between her legs. "You need to get used to me being close." He kept doing push-ups, not even sounding strained as he spoke. "People don't expect me to be with a girl for longer than one night. You're going to be the exception, and that will get everyone's attention. We have to look comfortable—like we can't keep our hands off each other. You can't look like a nervous rabbit running from a predator."

He grinned at her hot cheeks and her nervous breaths. "The girl I'd settle down for would be able to satisfy me. So we need to get you in shape."

"Okay." Her voice trembled.

He smiled, and as he lowered himself down, he stayed right above her, hovering over her lips. "Have you ever been kissed, Kylie?"

Unable to look into those deep brown orbs, she squeezed her eyes shut and tried to calm her erratically beating heart. "No," she replied, tasting his breath around her tongue.

He was still holding himself right above her face. "So you're willing to have me take it?"

Keeping her eyes sealed shut, she nodded, beyond embarrassed. What seventeen year old walked around without having their first kiss?

"Tell me you want me to have your first kiss, Hood." The huskiness of his voice made her tummy squeeze, just as it caused her legs to accidentally move inward, squeezing his hips.

"Ah," she said, panicked, spreading her legs apart again. She was shaking like a frightened bunny.

"Tell me that's what you want, Hood. Tell me you want me to be your first."

She felt his lower half press down on hers. "Oh my God."

"Hood," he said in a firmer tone.

"I want you to be my first," she blurted out.

"First what?" His nose brushed hers, so faintly, almost tenderly.

She knew she needed to stop thinking things like this if she wanted to stand any chance of hiding her feelings. "My everything," she said with an airy voice. "My first everything."

His lips instantly covered hers. Shock consumed her at first, but it was quickly replaced with awe and desire. The pressure of his lips pressing against hers was pleasant. Amazing. Perfect!

His initial assault was a hard kiss, but he pulled back almost instantly, making the kiss so faint it was almost non-existent. He kneaded her lips carefully, and it was sweet torture. He wasn't being forceful—more to the effect that he was asking her to take control if she wanted to. He was letting her be a part of this experience, not just taking what he wanted.

So, sighing, she did just that. Kylie hesitated but lifted her hands from her sides to hold his waist as she returned his kiss. As hard as everything about him was, his lips were soft. His skin was smooth and warm under her fingers. But there was a controlled, maybe possessive, way his lips touched hers as he settled his forearms on each side of her head.

While he apparently wanted her to initiate more, he was quick to take control back.

She had no idea what she was doing, and he must have sensed that. For the moment, though, she wasn't letting her inexperience slow her down. When he flicked his tongue across her lips, she opened her mouth, instantly rewarded with his tongue slipping in to meet hers.

Better than chocolate!

She let go of all her insecurities for this tiny moment to drown in everything that was Logan, and she took all that was being presented to her. He tasted like mint, and while his mouth felt hot on hers, the coolness from his earlier drink had left a slight chill on his tongue. It was heaven.

Each flick of his tongue, every nibble on her lip, she savored and copied—not at all caring whether she was doing her part right or not.

He chuckled, causing her to open her eyes and stop moving her hands. She had her whole body arched up toward his while she was doing everything in her power to pull him down more.

"Not bad for your first kiss," he murmured against her mouth.

Her face heated up as she tried to calmly release her grip on him. Logan lifted his face away by only inches as he stared down at her, slowly licking his lips. She watched the action in wonder. They were fuller now, a bit red even. And her embarrassment grew as she remembered biting and sucking his lip after he had done it to her.

He grinned, situating his hands back into a push-up position. "What's wrong, Hood?"

She closed her eyes and breathed out as he resumed his push-ups as if they hadn't just participated in a mini make-out session. Her first make-out session.

She stayed silent with her head turned away from his. That was until he lowered his mouth to nibble on her neck. Shooting her eyes open, she shoved at his chest. He laughed but moved away after her shoves grew weak. Really, she would give anything to have him put his mouth all over her body, but the pool of desire cooled its waters as he acted completely unfazed.

"Tell me what's wrong." He gave her a warning look as he resumed his workout.

His abrupt shifts in actions and words had her emotions all over the place. It was like running a relay just to keep up with him. After a few more seconds, she finally sighed and answered, "I feel stupid."

"Why's that?"

She wondered how many push-ups he had done but shook her head and looked him in the eye. "Because I have no idea what I'm doing, and you let me get carried away like an idiot. And I kinda feel like a slut."

He laughed, bringing his knees to rest on the ground between her bent legs while he placed his palms over her knees. "You're not a slut." He laughed again. "And you did fine. A little more practice and you'll be a pro."

She gave him a disbelieving look. "I did not do fine."

"Why do you think you did bad?" His hands slowly began to rub up and down her calves.

It was distracting and wonderful. She had to force her eyes to stay on his. "I don't know," she said, proud that she didn't stutter. All she could think about was how hot he was making her body feel.

"Believe me, the kiss was good. Much better than my first kiss. I remember I was nervous, so I picked a girl I didn't like—that way it wouldn't bother me if I was bad at it. I was good, even if she wasn't." He smirked. "Gave me confidence to go after the girl I did want."

"Gross." She was put off by that fact. Logan had been around, and he'd likely still be prancing girls in and out of his bed and locker room while they did whatever they were doing.

"Jealous, baby?"

"No." She smacked his hands, angry now. Yes, she was jealous.

He just snickered at her glare and gripped her legs harder.

"Let go," she demanded. "Let's just finish this workout or whatever it is. I don't want to talk about the stupid kiss anymore. Or how many girls you've kissed. I get it, I don't know what I'm doing. I'll learn. Even if I'm never as good as one of those girls that wait outside your locker room."

"Give me your hand."

"What?" She didn't understand how he could calmly demand something of her after her rant.

"I want to show you something. Give me your hand."

Slowly, she held out her right hand, which he grabbed in a firm grip.

He started lowering his face again, bracing himself with his free hand as he guided the one he held toward his stomach. "I told you to believe what I tell you. Trust me. I won't lie to you." He lowered his lips to just above hers again, making her a little dizzy with his scent and the promise of what could happen if those lips touched hers. "This." He moved her hand down over his pants.

She felt a hardness that wasn't there before, and it grew more when she gasped and involuntarily gripped the shaft.

He grunted and brushed his lips across hers. "This is what your kiss did to me."

She moaned low in her throat and wrapped her hand around him more, sliding it down his growing length.

He exhaled slowly, adding, "These lips are mouth-watering. I've wanted to taste them from the moment you spoke to me."

"Really?" Her voice was breathy, and her eyes closed as she moved her hand up and down. She didn't even know she was doing it. She was just so caught up by him. It was as if everything she would normally do vanished around him. He brought down all her walls—all her fear and anxiety.

"Mhm." He kissed her softly. "You're going to kill me." His hips jerked forward, which caused the back of her hand to rub between her legs.

"Ah," she moaned, never having felt such an amazing sensation before.

Logan groaned, thrusting into her palm, but he pulled away quickly. "Damn, this is going to hurt later."

Kylie snapped her eyes open at his withdrawal, finally realizing her actions, and let go.

He laughed and pushed himself back to his knees, starting to stand. "You're adorable, Hood. And don't pout."

She fixed her shirt as she sat up, hoping her hot cheeks weren't as red as they felt.

He chuckled and held out his hand to pull her up. "Believe me, I want to keep going too. But you're not ready for that, and I'm not going to dry hump you on my floor."

"Shut up, please." She groaned and rubbed her face.

"Have you ever masturbated?"

Kylie's eyes widened, and she moved away from him after she was standing. "What kind of question is that?" She crossed her arms over her chest, attempting to hide herself.

He shook his head after guzzling down a whole bottle of water, then gestured between her legs. She refused to even look at his. Would he still be hard?

"An important one. You're acting like you've never felt anything like that. How do you expect to pull off having sex with me if you've never had an orgasm? People can pick up on that kind of shit."

She was too horrified to respond to what he was suggesting. "Well, I figured your offer meant I wouldn't be pretending."

He laughed and tossed his bottle away. "Fine," he said easily. "I'm still not gonna let us fuck until I think you're ready though. And we'll have to wait until you're eighteen. I'm too sexy for prison."

"You're so conceited."

He smirked, and it made her tingle between her legs. "Baby, when you've got the goods to back it up, it's not conceited—it's just fact."

"Whatever," she muttered, knowing it was best not to get into a debate about his hotness.

"Good. Now, give me thirty jumping jacks." He plopped himself down on his bed while she stared at him like he was crazy. "Quit wasting time, Hood. You've got to get in shape. Go. I have to think about our little problem for a minute."

Problem? She wanted to hit him. It wasn't like she was the only girl to not have an orgasm at her age. A girl was usually a slut if she knew so much before she was eighteen. It couldn't be as big a deal as he was making it out to be.

"I'm waiting, Hood."

She eyed him, noticing how his jaw twitched with aggravation and his eyes strained just a tiny bit, hiding his anger. It clicked, and she knew exactly what he was trying to do. He knew she was hiding her pain, and he was pushing her to confess.

His eyes challenged her to come up with an excuse not to obey him, but she wasn't going to let him win. Not yet, at least.

"Fine," she said, glaring at his dark eyes, and lifted her arms.

It hurt. A lot. Every jolt of her body as she completed a single jumping jack felt like being stabbed and beaten.

Logan sat like a statue, watching her struggle, her face no doubt scrunched up in pain. She finally whined on her twentieth one before shedding a single tear.

"Are you done pretending you're not hurt?" He sounded calm, but he wasn't.

She tried to do another but only cried out. Maybe she was as weak as he thought.

"Enough, Kylie."

She stopped and tried to rub her tears, but the pain nearly had her collapsing.

"Come here." His hard voice was frightening, but she obeyed, stumbling until she stood in front of where he sat.

He watched her wheeze and struggle to ease her pain.

Shaking his head, he reached out and grabbed her waist. "You're either stupid or too tough for your own good." He tugged her gently to stand between his legs. "I'm going to take your shirt off so I can see how bad it is."

She started to shake her head and move away.

"Stop it!" His voice was like a knife, stabbing her until she stopped fighting. "I'm not going to hurt you."

"I know," she cried through her wheezing breaths.

His face softened. "Let me look." He gently caressed her hips. "I'll take care of you. Just let me see."

She was ready to let him help her. Had it been anyone else, she doubted she would let them. Logan just made her want to put all her insecurities and secrets out there.

"Good girl," he said as she nodded. "Lift your arms for me slowly. Stop if it hurts too much."

Kylie continued to let tears fall as she raised her hands.

Logan smiled softly and started to raise her shirt, wincing when she let out a strangled noise. "*Shh . . .* Oh, baby," he whispered once he saw her bandages and the discoloration around the edges.

She cried, so emotionally overwhelmed with the soft sound of his voice. No one had cared or bothered with her. But Logan Grimm, a stranger and total badass, saw through her guise within minutes of meeting her. He'd stayed persistent in pursuing her. Even if he had ulterior motives and didn't like her enough to make her his girlfriend, she was really trying to believe he cared.

And now he was whispering encouraging words between gentle caresses as he exposed her hideous injuries.

"There we go," he said, cooing his words and kissing her sweaty forehead the moment he stood and freed her from her shirt. "*Shh*, baby." He wiped the tears from her eyes, not yet taking in the sight of her. He was giving her time to calm down before they went further.

"I'm okay," she said and let her head fall against his chest, comforted by his instant embrace.

"You're not." He ran his hand over her head. Her bun was falling apart, but he didn't seem to mind. "But I'm going to make sure you are from now on." He kissed the top of her head, then sat back down. "I'm going to take this off now."

She was frightened, but she stayed still as he pulled her between his legs again.

"I have to, Hood. I need to see how bad this is." His fingers moved to her bandage, brushing her heated skin every few seconds. "Plus, I want to check out your goods," he added, smirking as his eyes zeroed in on her hidden breasts.

"Shut up," she said, wincing as she tried not to laugh.

"Two birds, one stone, baby."

She smiled despite her pain and closed her eyes. It was going to be worse to see his reaction, and she couldn't stand to see his disgust. She wanted to hide. It wasn't right to let a boy see her, but she didn't think of it as a sexual act between them. It was more like a doctor's visit. But the doctor was a hottie who wanted to get in her pants.

Jeez, I'm so messed up.

"Do you know if they're broken?" he asked as the wraps fell away.

She only had her bra protecting her now. She regretted not having the sexy ones that Maura did. All she owned were a few T-shirt bras, like the one she wore now because it had been too painful to pull on a tight sports bra, her only other choice in intimates.

Perhaps it didn't matter. All he was looking at were the purple, blue, and green marks painting her scarred skin. It was normal for her skin to split open from swelling. After all, she was hit with either bats, belts—sometimes she even had cuts from shards of glass.

She shook her head, still blind to his angry and pained face as he hissed at each of her flinches when his fingers prodded the dark bruises. "They don't take me in. Too obvious."

Logan nodded, never letting his eyes leave her many injuries. "You know they don't recommend binding broken ribs anymore," he murmured as his fingers trailed along each rib, raising goose bumps along the way. "You can get pneumonia that way."

"That's not why they're taped. They always make me tape my boobs."

His fingers stopped their path.

Feeling his stare, she slowly opened her eyes. His many questions were obvious as they raced through his head, so she clarified at least one. "I guess it's because mine are bigger than Maura's, and she doesn't like anything to be better than hers. Well, that's what Lorelei said."

Logan dropped his eyes to her breasts, not showing any distinct reaction as he looked them over.

"She tried to force me to have a reduction," she added, curious to see what he thought.

"What?" His shock was heavy in his voice and eyes. "Are you fucking kidding me?"

She shook her head. "I only got out of it because the doctor said it wasn't medically necessary. He said they weren't that big."

Logan's lip twitched, but he stayed angry.

She continued, "He told them I had to wait until I was eighteen to make a cosmetic decision."

His jaw flexed as he pressed his lips together. Kylie trembled as his fingers started moving along each rib again. The pain was fading, and she didn't know if it had to do with resting or his touch.

"Well," he said, "I haven't seen Maura, but she has every reason to be jealous." He smirked up at her, settling his hands on her hips after finishing his inspection. "These tits are gorgeous, Hood. And I haven't even seen them. They're like a Christmas present I'm dying to unwrap."

"Shut up," she said, smiling as he pulled her closer.

A mischievous look stayed on his face as he slowly dropped his lips to the top of her left breast, never removing his eyes from hers. "I'm serious, honey."

A startled gasp escaped her as his lips kissed her softly, right above her bra.

His lips were hot. "They're lovely. And I'm going to worship these girls"—he moved to her right breast, kissing it just as tenderly—"every chance I get when you're better."

Trembling with desire, she struggled not to beg him to rid her of her bra and take her nipple into his mouth.

"Mm," he hummed and sucked her skin hard, still right above the edge of her bra, and left his mark. "Fuck, it's killing me to not have you."

"Logan," she whispered, reaching out without thinking and gripping his head. "Oh . . . I," she moaned when one of his hands reached up to massage her left breast as he still kissed around the right.

"What?" His tongue slipped just under her bra.

"Ah," she cried out, throwing her head back and tangling her fingers in his thick hair. God, it was so soft too. "Oh, please, Logan." She didn't even know what she was asking for. Only that he was torturing her and only he could end it.

Logan moved the hand holding her waist down to her butt and squeezed.

"Logan," she whispered, out of breath.

He looked up but didn't say anything. Instead, he just grabbed her hand, led her around the bed, and gently pushed her down. "Lie on your back," he said as he lifted her feet.

She wanted him, but she shook from fear and pain.

"Don't be scared." He leaned over her and kissed her cheek. "I'll never hurt you. I will always take care of you, Hood." He smiled and kissed her nose. "Do you trust me?"

She searched his beautiful face, calming her nerves and soothing her tortured heart. "I trust you, Logan."

He smirked and put his lips back on hers, carefully climbing on the bed. Kylie forgot everything and let him push her legs apart as he settled his body between them. She was too caught up in his kiss to stop him, but she did notice how gentle he was being this time.

"Slow down, baby," he whispered against her mouth, smiling when she lifted her head off his pillow to try to reach his lips again.

She was a chocolate addict, and he was the most delicious bar of chocolate ever to be made. "I love this," she whispered, not opening her eyes, and she moaned into his mouth while one of his hands slid up and down her jean-clad thigh. "Oh my gosh, Logan."

He smiled, moving his lips along her jaw. "You're going to be a sex fiend, aren't you?"

Her body shook and erupted in goose bumps as he left wet kisses down her jaw. "I don't care." She felt so crazy, but she needed this. She needed him. The pain wasn't even in her mind anymore. Just Logan. Only Logan.

"Baby steps, Hood," he whispered, lightly biting her bra.

"Logan, please." She tilted her head down to see him grinning with the edge of her bra in his mouth. She didn't know why she ever pushed him away. This was amazing.

"I don't want to hurt you." He kissed the skin above her bra before he moved his lips to the bruises.

She closed her eyes and threw her head back while those hot lips and his skilled tongue nursed her wounds. "I don't feel it anymore," she said softly, keeping her eyes closed.

"Good." He kissed over a rather large scar at the base of her rib cage, a strange rumble sounding from his chest as he repeatedly kissed around the edges. "No more."

"No, I need more," she told him, in case he was talking about them continuing. She was like a kid who didn't want to leave the candy store. She was stuffing her pockets full of candy.

"Baby, look at me."

Kylie opened her eyes, not sure when he had made his way back up to her face. She frowned at him.

Logan, however, grinned and nipped her lips. "No pouting. I just want you to know something."

"What?" She lifted her hands to touch his beautiful face.

He turned his lips to kiss her palm. "I won't let them hurt you anymore."

She smiled. "I know you won't." *You'll only destroy my heart.*

He smiled and cupped one of her breasts in his hand. "These are lovely." He gently applied pressure with a careful squeeze. "But I'm not unwrapping them until your ribs are checked."

"Logan," she whined, but he lowered his mouth over hers, shutting her up. "*Mmm.*"

"I said I would make you feel better," he said, lightly trailing his fingertips away from her breast, down to her stomach. "And I meant it."

The button on her jeans popped, and her eyes flew open.

He was already watching her. "Ready for me to take another of your firsts?" His hand slowly slid over her jeans, between her legs, but he waited for her to respond.

Not even waiting to think it over, she nodded and pulled his mouth to hers. "Gimme more."

10
EXPOSED

Kylie's uneven breaths and whimpers filled the silence before a new song began to play.

Logan's lips smiled against her neck, his breathing heavier as he held himself up with one forearm resting close to her head. With his face nuzzled in the crook of her neck, he leaned over her as much as possible, one muscular thigh draped between her now jean-free legs.

"Oh, my . . ."

The light touch of his bare chest as it brushed the side of her heaving breasts had her shaking. It was too much but not enough at the same time. God, he was still drawing slow circles inside the tingling folds between her legs. Beautiful torture. That's what this was. He'd given her a glimpse of heaven, and now he was lowering her to Earth once more.

It was no wonder he liked sex so much. If this was just his hand . . .

"Fuck, Logan," she said, trying to push him away. "Stop."

He chuckled as her hips rose to meet his hand anyway.

Whining because she didn't know whether she wanted him to stop or continue, she kept shoving his shoulders even as she lifted her hips, begging for more of what he'd just given her while occasionally squeezing her legs around his thigh.

She needed to rub herself against him as much as she desperately needed him to stop. "I can't take it," she whispered when he leaned away. She stared into his eyes as they drifted over her slightly sweaty face, which took turns between relaxing and scrunching up from her post-orgasmic bliss.

He looked pleased with himself if the slight upward curve of his swollen lips was anything to go by. The way he had kissed her, murmuring dirty words in her ear which he always managed to follow up with something endearing, told her he enjoyed giving her this.

This being her very first orgasm—all courtesy of Logan Grimm's talented fingers.

She wanted more. She would make sure he gave more—but for now, fatigue grew too great and she closed her eyes, sighing when his hand slid away from the once most untouched part of her body. Although his hand was sliding along her thigh and other parts of her body that he obviously felt like exploring, she could still feel his almost phantom touch swirling between her legs.

"How do you feel?" His deep voice induced a throbbing between her legs.

"Sleepy," she said, a weak smile lifting her lips.

He chuckled, his body vibrating next to her.

"Thank you."

He gave her a soft, brief kiss. "You're welcome, Hood."

She kept her eyes closed, still wearing a drowsy smile while her breathing became more relaxed. "*Mmm*," she hummed, still blind to what he was doing but aware nonetheless of his fingers gliding over her skin. "I'm going to have to shave my legs again if you keep that up," she whispered, shivering as goose bumps broke out across her legs for the hundredth time.

Logan laughed softly and rested his hand on her hip. "I was going to tell you they feel a bit prickly."

"Shut up." She opened her eyes, squinting as if she was seeing the light again for the first time in hours. "I don't think you had to take my pants off all the way." Kylie glanced down at herself, surprised she wasn't freaking out about lying there with nothing but her bra on. But she had only felt comfortable under his soft gaze when he asked if he could de-pants her. And that's how she stayed once he had her exposed—well, almost exposed. He had insisted that her bra stay on because he didn't trust himself to not get a little rough.

"Well, your panties were already ruined."

Fire engulfed her cheeks as she remembered him revealing to her that she was so wet for him. "Oh my god," she groaned, covering her face with one hand.

Logan kissed the top of her breast. "Relax. I told you not to be embarrassed."

"It's gross." It was humiliating!

"Did I look grossed out?" He pulled her hand away and turned her face to look at him. His eyes were lighter for some reason, his face completely relaxed as he waited for her to answer.

God, he's so perfect.

"No," she whispered.

"No, I didn't." He rubbed his thumb across her bottom lip. "I told you my dick never wanted to be buried inside a pussy more than he did yours at that moment."

"Logan," she moaned as he pressed his leg against her still tingling center. She couldn't care less that she could almost taste herself.

"Damn, baby." He gripped her jaw and kissed her hard. Not waiting for her to respond, he pushed his tongue in her mouth, claiming her tongue as his victim, forcing her into submission.

The little mewling sounds it brought out of her seemed to please him. He let out a possessive growl and pressed his hardness against her.

She moaned, rotating her hips up to create that pleasant friction between her legs. "Logan, I need it."

He growled, sucking her bottom lip before releasing her—closing his eyes in the process and moving his hips away.

"Not yet." He gave her a quick kiss before moving his leg away completely. "Sorry, Hood. If we start up again, I'll fuck you before I can stop myself."

"But I want you to." Her eyes widened at her words. It was like he'd made her into a completely new girl, a girl who wasn't afraid to say what she desired. Which, at the moment, was Logan. Inside her.

"I know you do. But not yet. I need to wait until you're at least eighteen, and I want you to be ready for me."

She groaned, making him laugh, but he quickly sat up when she coughed and grabbed her ribs. "Oh, ow." She hissed, breathing in painful pants.

Logan leaned over her, holding his hand over hers. "*Shh*. You have to relax."

She coughed, each one causing more spasms of pain.

"Hood, relax." His stern tone made her watery eyes grow wide, and she held her breath. "There you go. Breathe out, slow and steady."

Kylie let out whiny, blubbering sounds. Logan stayed quiet, keeping one hand over hers while the other gently caressed her hair.

"Better?" he asked, rubbing his hand along the purple bruise. The caress felt electric, and it warmed her skin, soothing her pain.

"Yeah," she breathed.

"Good." He leaned down, dropping a kiss on her forehead.

"God, that was probably the most unattractive thing you've ever seen," she said, still panting a little while Logan laughed. "Can you gimme my clothes, or cover me?"

Logan reached down toward the foot of the bed where his covers had been kicked and began pulling them over her. But not before kissing all the way up the inside of her leg. "Baby, you couldn't be unattractive to me if you tried." He nipped the tender skin of her inner thigh.

She reached down, pushing his head away from *there*. "Logan, I can't take any more."

He chuckled, his hot breath blowing across her moist skin. "Next time, kitty," he cooed to *it*.

"Did you just talk to my—" She couldn't even say it! She blushed, still pushing his head. He kissed the inside of her thigh before making his way up her hip and stomach.

"Say it, Hood," he murmured, licking her bra.

"No, Logan," she said, still pushing him. In all fairness, she wanted nothing more than for him to keep up his assault, but with the mood gone from her coughing fit, she realized she was throwing herself at him—her bruised, disgusting self.

"Say it."

"Say what?" She glared at him when his face came to hover over hers. She was thankful that he had at least followed her original orders by covering her up.

"Pussy." He smirked down at her.

"I'm not saying that word."

Grinning, he kissed her chin. "You will soon enough."

She smiled, turning her face away, though he continued to kiss and nibble along her jaw until he sighed and moved to climb over her.

"Where are you going?" She pulled the blanket tight against her chest as he faced away from her. Again, she blushed when she realized he was rearranging himself.

"Nowhere. I just need to finish working out." He turned, smirking as he caught her eyes zeroed in on his crotch. "Soon, Hood."

"Can you give me my clothes?"

"No." He snickered. "I'll give you a pair of shorts to wear. Your panties are soaked."

"God, Logan. You really know how to make a girl—"

"Wet?" He laughed and sat on the floor. "Oh, believe me—I know."

She groaned, pulling the blanket over her head. His scent intensified, and she paused, sniffing his blanket. Oh, it smelled like him but also like fabric softener. *Heaven.*

"Did you just sniff my blanket?"

"Yes, I did." She lowered it enough to see him.

He laughed and began doing some sit-ups.

After about fifty, he said, "Baby, I want you to come to the gym with me in a bit."

"Why?" She loved that he called her baby. Him calling her 'Hood' was even growing on her, though she found it a little strange that he called her by her last name. That seemed like more of a friend way to address someone.

"I want my trainer to take an X-ray."

She tensed up but stayed quiet.

"Don't worry about him reporting anything," he added. "He's cool. I just want to know if they're fractured or not."

"Are you sure he won't tell? No one can know."

He sounded a little winded as he did each set faster. "Yeah. He won't say anything." His breathing got even heavier. "He can probably give you some good painkillers, too."

She smiled and rubbed away the moisture in her eyes. All she ever got was a bottle of aspirin and instructions to ice up.

"Do you need something now?" he asked. "I shouldn't have forced you to show me that way. I was just pissed because you're so stubborn."

"I'm fine." She yelped when he yanked the covers back.

He was sweating, and he looked magnificent. His muscles were fuller, his veins pumping with fresh blood as he breathed heavily—showing off his lickable abs.

"Shit, Hood. Does it hurt bad?" He sat next to her and reached out to rub her side.

"I'm fine." *More than fine.* "It's just achy now."

He didn't look like he believed her, but she smiled at him, trying not to ogle him.

"I'm used to it."

The anger returned to his face, so she reached out, rubbing his arm while it flexed and twitched. It felt so natural to touch him, but still, she surprised herself with her boldness each time.

As she continued trying to calm his anger, she pushed back her own sadness from the terrible truth of her past. Seeing him so affected by her pain warmed the cold pieces of her broken heart.

"Let me get you some painkillers," he said after a few seconds. "Then I'll shower and we can drive to the gym, okay?" He reached up to play with her hair, which had come undone.

"Okay," she said.

He didn't say anything else and started pulling the loose pins from her hair.

"Oh, let me fix it." She tried to sit up.

He shook his head. "Stop. I want to see it down."

"I'm not allowed," she whispered, trying to stop his hands.

He glared, almost snarling, "Dammit, Kylie. I told you—no more hiding."

She flinched away from his hand and felt bad when he looked a little hurt.

"Just let me see." He sounded bitter. "If I tell you I think you look bad, you can put your fucking hood back up."

She knew he wasn't really angry at her, that he was just angry over the fact she was forced to hide, so she sat still and let him finish.

After getting poked a few times, receiving angry mumbles of apology in response, he leaned over and deposited the handful of bobby pins on his nightstand.

She reached up, trying to smooth out her hair, but he shoved her hands away and began doing it himself. He was silent as he ran his fingers through her long, waist-length blond hair, unraveling it.

Biting her lip, she waited until he was satisfied, staying quiet as he let his eyes run over her.

He twirled a lock of hair around his index finger, looking at it carefully before he leaned forward and kissed her lips. "Fucking beautiful."

Smiling, she received another kiss from him.

"No more wearing your hood up. Okay?"

"Okay."

He kissed her a few more times until the loud laughter of several guys filtered in from the apartment.

Logan exhaled and leaned back. "Trevor must have invited his teammates over." He stared at the door for a long time, the muscle in his jaw ticking while one of his hands played with her hair.

She loved her hair, but she never saw it down for longer than a few minutes before she rolled it up into a bun. It made her happy to have someone admire it again.

"Baby?"

"*Hmm?*" She was staring at his fingers, following the veins on his forearms that led to several tattoos. Her eyes had been drawn to one of them, a half-moon hidden behind tree branches. He moved before she could see what scene lay below the moonlight, but she wasn't complaining because he presented her with his back. His sexy, sexy back.

"Will you scratch my back for me?" He tilted his head to the side, smiling as if he wasn't angry just a moment ago. "I can't reach it."

"Oh, yeah, I can do that."

He held out his hand and pulled her up slowly.

She grimaced but nodded that she was good. "Where?" She placed her hands on his shoulders, almost moaning because of the heat and strength he radiated.

"My back turning you on?" He chuckled when she smacked his shoulders. "Oh, yeah. I love the rough stuff, Hood."

"Do you want me to itch your back or not?"

"I think you mean scratch."

Her face heated up. "Don't make fun of me. You know I meant scratch."

He smiled over his shoulder. "Sorry. Yes, I do. Just drag your nails straight down. I hate when people go all over the place."

"Well," she said, dragging her nonexistent nails straight down, "maybe you shouldn't be such a demanding asshole."

"Harder."

"Like I said—demanding."

"Hood, do you even have nails? Scratch."

"But I'll mark your skin." She stared at his tanned skin, wanting to trace her fingers over the skull tattoo hidden among his ink.

"Just do it. I'll be fine."

Sighing, she dug her nails in at the top of his traps and dragged them straight down. Logan groaned loudly, making her face warm because it sounded like he was getting off on it.

"Fuck, that feels good," he said, groaning louder when she did the action again.

"*Shh*," she whispered. "You're being so loud."

He only got louder. "Fuck, baby! Oh, yeah–just like that."

"Logan!" She smacked his red, somewhat bleeding back. "Oh my God!" she screamed. She felt terrible. He was bleeding. "Oh, Logan!"

She rubbed around the blood smears, tears pricking her eyes.

"Ah," he yelled. "Fuck!"

It startled her, and she yelled out, thinking she had hurt him more. "Oh my god." She tried to climb off the bed, but he stood up and walked to his dresser before she could. She stayed kneeling on the edge of the bed, watching him, waiting for him to flip out on her. But he simply dug around in a drawer until he produced a pair of drawstring athletic shorts and a red shirt.

He walked back to her, wearing a huge grin, and handed her the clothes. "Thanks, Hood." He pecked her lips. "You got just the right spot."

"Are you sure?" She studied him, noting that he still had sweat glistening on his perfect body.

"Positive, baby. Put this on. I'm going to go grab you some painkillers. Then I'm gonna jump in the shower. We'll go to the gym, then eat when we're done."

"Okay," she whispered as he walked to his door, unlocked it, and left the room.

She was confused by his behavior and jumped when a roar of cheers and whistles sounded from the living room. She distinctly heard Logan's sultry voice among the other voices, and he certainly didn't sound upset as whatever he said was welcomed with more cheers.

"Hood," he said, walking back in, slamming the door behind him. "Got your pills."

"What's going on out there?"

He shrugged and handed her the bottle of water she had earlier. "They're just playing video games." He waited for her to swallow, then took her water and helped her pull her shirt on.

"Why were they cheering when you went out there?"

"They always cheer when they see me."

Kylie rolled her eyes. He could never go too long without showing how big his ego was.

Despite his charming cockiness, because she wouldn't lie, she adored that about him—she knew something was up. He avoided eye contact with her whenever she tried to look at his face. "You're being strange."

"I'm just worried that I hurt you more," he said as he pulled her up to her feet. After she had slipped on the shorts, he grabbed her face between his large hands and said, "Evander will check you out, and then I'll feel better."

"Oh." She inhaled slowly. He was so close, his nose almost touching hers. "It's not your fault. I actually knew you were trying to get me to confess."

"Really?" He shook his head, smiling before he let go of her face. "Then you're too tough and stupid."

"Hey!"

He snickered and pulled her body to his. "Fucking with you, Hood."

"You're a jerk."

He began running his fingers through her hair. "I like your hair down."

She smiled, admiring the locks of hair he was rubbing between his fingers. A cut was in order, but she was just happy to see her hair the way it used to be.

"Thank you. I've missed wearing it down."

Instead of replying, he pulled her by the small of her back until they were pressed together and slid his other hand behind her head. He grabbed a fistful of hair to tilt her face up. He didn't hesitate to claim her mouth, and she didn't fight him. She loved his kiss.

"I think I'm going to like us dating," he murmured, nibbling her lip.

Kylie smiled, but this reminded her that Logan was just playing a game. "I want chocolate," she blurted out the first thing she could think of. Anything was better than remembering they weren't really together—that they'd never be together.

Logan laughed. "Well, I want a sandwich." He grinned and squeezed her butt. "Get your cute little ass in the kitchen and make me a sandwich—and when we're out, I'll buy you two chocolate bars."

When he gently shoved her toward the door, she snapped, "What do I look like to you? I'm not your mom."

Logan dropped his playful look. "You're my little hood."

She frowned, not understanding him.

Logan walked to a different door. "Just make me a sandwich. I'm fucking starving." And with that, he walked through the door to his attached bathroom.

"Whatever," she muttered, glancing down at her attire. "Shit." She looked around, but she realized her clothes were missing too. "That bastard took my clothes!"

She stopped herself from screaming as she yanked the door open and stomped her way down the hall. Her fury over being treated like this vanished the moment she turned the corner. Fifteen pairs of eyes were on her.

Oh. My. God.

Trevor was right in the middle, staring at her with the same dumbstruck look the other fourteen football players were wearing.

"Um," she muttered before hurrying across the room. Breathing out and pinching her side, she leaned against the refrigerator. Her ears perked up, hearing animated whispers from the guys in the next room.

"Dude, that chick was fucking hot."

"Logan always gets the hottest ass."

"That was Kylie Hood."

The last voice belonged to Trevor, and she gasped.

"The girl who wears the hoodie all the time? I thought you brought her home a week ago."

Trevor didn't respond.

"I thought that chick was a leper," someone else said. "Why would she cover up? Did she look like that for you, Trev?"

"Since when does Logan go after your seconds?" someone asked as a few guys laughed.

"I wasn't with her like that," Trevor snapped. "I already told all of you to stop saying shit about her."

"Whatever," someone muttered.

"I'm surprised he hasn't tossed her out already."

"Logan probably forces her to hide under that hoodie. Bet he doesn't want anyone tapping what's his."

Kylie rolled her eyes at that one, even though she was blushing like crazy because these boys thought she was pretty.

"I can't believe weirdo Kylie Hood is fucking your cousin, man."

"Never woulda thought he'd go for a younger girl after—" The sound of someone getting hit cut off whatever that person was about to say.

Her eyes went wide, and though she tried to hear them continue, they must have lowered their whispers. "Shit, shit, shit," she chanted as she pulled out ingredients for a ham sandwich. They knew who she was—even without her hood. Trevor knew who she was. But then she remembered he had seen her go into the room with Logan earlier. Wearing his clothes suggested they must have had sex. "Oh my God," she whispered, placing lettuce and tomato on top of the ham.

It all made sense. The back scratch, him wanting her to leave marks, him walking out in front of them with his bloody, clawed back on display, him yelling out the way he did . . .

Logan Grimm set her up, and without even realizing, she was already the girl that Logan had in his bed. He had managed to expose her not only to himself, but to the world.

"That sexy son of a b—"

"Kylie?"

Fucking girly-balls!

She turned slowly and smiled. "Hi, Trevor."

"I can't believe it's you," Trevor said, stepping closer. "You look so . . ."

A shaky smile formed on her lips as she stared into his big blue eyes.

"Wow," he finished.

Though her cheeks were probably red as tomatoes, her tummy wasn't doing the little flips it once had. Actually, she felt a little sick to have him so close. "Thanks, I guess," she said, taking a small step back. Only, her butt met the counter, allowing him to come closer.

He was only a foot from her now. The smile on his lips that once made her sigh dreamily did nothing for her. It only reminded her she was lying to Logan, using him. Using him and Trevor.

Trevor cleared his throat and took a step back. "Um," he said, cringing a little. "I'm sorry if you heard the guys just now. They were just—well, just being guys. I told them to stop with the rumors that started when you came over."

"I heard. Thank you." She nodded. It wasn't the first time she had overheard boys talking about another guy's conquest—because that's what she was, Logan's latest conquest. *Bastard.*

"I would have stopped them," he said, "but I was kind of in shock. I mean, I thought it was you outside his door, but that didn't make sense. But here you are." He gestured to her with his hand. "And you're wearing Logan's clothes."

Kylie grimaced, but she also remembered Logan's plan. He was under the impression that she loved Trevor, and this was his attempt to make her noticeable.

He certainly accomplished that.

She couldn't wait to slap him around. He could have at least told her what he was doing! "Well, yeah," she said, swallowing. What was she supposed to say? 'Yeah, your cousin just made it seem like we had sex because he thinks I love you, and this is him trying to make you jealous. But I don't like you anymore . . . I sort of like him, and I just want him to rip my clothes off and finish what he started.'

"I shouldn't have introduced you to him," Trevor whispered, his eyes fixed on her face. "Has he hurt you?"

She shook her head, frowning. Logan wouldn't hurt her, right?

"Thank God. Let me take you home then." He reached out for her hand, but she pulled away.

"He hasn't hurt me."

Trevor backed up. "Okay. But you don't know him, Kylie. He's a bad guy. He's probably already forgotten that you're here. He doesn't keep girls, and sometimes, it's pretty bad the way he kicks them out. I would hate to see him hurt you in front of all these guys from school. I can't stop all the rumors."

She felt a little sick to her stomach as she imagined Logan taking girls to bed, then throwing them out like trash.

"He won't do that to me," she said, not sure if she was completely confident with her statement. But what was there to be sure about anymore?

Trevor sighed. "Listen, he will tell you anything to get you. Shit, I feel terrible. If I had stayed that night—or just did my project. Just let me get you away from him. You're too nice of a girl to get caught up with him. I'll try to make sure the guys don't say anything that will make you sound like one of his whores."

"Just because I came out of his room in his clothes, I'm one of his whores? Am I not good enough to actually be someone he'd be interested in?" She knew she sounded stupid, because really, that's what she was to Logan, but that's why it hurt. She wanted to be good enough for him. The fact she wasn't made her want to scream and destroy everything.

Trevor shook his head. "I didn't say that. I don't want people making up things about you just because you—"

"Because she what?"

Kylie and Trevor both turned to see Logan enter the kitchen. His face held no sign of emotion, but his eyes raged with hate.

She just didn't know if he was angry with her, or the fact she was there with Trevor. Or maybe it was both?

Trevor backed away from her, moving to stand by the sink as Logan glared at him and took a step into the kitchen. She knew she should be yelling at him for what he did, but she could only stare at his hair. It was wet, making it even darker. And he did that thing where he jerked his head to make the hair move out of his eyes. It was insane how he could make the simplest things look downright sexy.

"I was just offering to take Kylie home," Trevor told Logan.

Kylie glanced at Trevor, then at Logan. She bit her lip when the latter turned to smirk at her.

"Why would you take the girl I'm dating home?"

Kylie breathed out a small sigh of relief as Logan walked toward her.

"What?" Trevor's shock was clear, and Kylie could practically see his eyes bulging out of their sockets when Logan gently grabbed her by the back of her neck and leaned down to kiss her.

Heaven. Chocolate. Muscles. Logan!

Too many words—too many sensations overtook her. She didn't think she would ever grow tired of feeling his lips on hers, and she knew she was in trouble. He was going to get away with everything if he kissed her like this. It was like he was giving her a box of Chocolate Logan Kisses, and she was ripping them open before he could say sorry.

Sighing against his mouth, she reached out to hold his waist. He was wearing a shirt now, but that didn't make the feel of his hard body beneath her fingers any less pleasant.

"Hey, baby," he murmured against her mouth, both his hands now cupping her face while his towering frame blocked any view of Trevor.

Her initial reaction was to sigh, but she remembered her anger and opened her eyes to glare up at him.

The man had the nerve to smile against her lips, then peck them again.

"I'm angry with you," she whispered but gasped as he brushed his lips back and forth over hers. He was sort of sucking her breath in his mouth, but she also reveled in tasting his minty breath on her own tongue.

"I know," he whispered, still smiling and still pressing tiny kisses to her lips. "I'll explain later. And I'll let you punish me."

"Asshole," she muttered, making him laugh. "And I made you a sandwich like an idiot."

He chuckled and kissed across her cheek before coming back to her lips. "I saw. Thank you, Hood."

She should have pushed him away, but really, who would push him away?

Sexy man-boy messing with my hormones.

"I should have spat in it," she hissed, but she kissed his lips hard instead of slapping him like her brain was telling her to.

Logan chuckled and held her tighter, kissing her harder until she could only submit to him. And why wouldn't she? Whoever was opposed to being dominated by a man clearly hadn't experienced the raw dominance Logan displayed.

Trevor cleared his throat, making her pull her lips away from Logan's. Instead of Logan stepping back, though, he reached down to her hips and lifted her onto the counter. She barely had time to reach out to steady herself before Logan had stepped between her legs to where her thighs cradled his waist. It made things . . . tingle. And she had to force herself not to scoot her butt to the edge just to be closer.

Logan reached for his food, and didn't turn as he addressed his cousin. "Did you need something, Trevor?" He lifted his sandwich to his mouth while one hand stayed on her thigh, under the athletic shorts he had given her. "*Mmm.*" His thumb caressed the inside of her leg. "Delicious, baby."

"You two are really dating?" Trevor asked, clearly annoyed with the fact they had basically made out in front of him.

Kylie didn't dare answer. She didn't know what Logan's plans were, but speaking up and saying something that didn't make their stories match would only make her look like the idiot.

Logan stared at her, running his hand up and down her thigh in a soothing motion before he answered. "I said that, didn't I?" He took another bite, winking at her as he chewed.

Kylie's giddiness over his attention died. He was putting on a show.

Trevor hadn't responded, but Logan kept talking to her as if another person wasn't in the room with them.

"Do you want a sandwich too, baby? Or do you want to wait till we go out?"

"I'm fine," she said, squirming when he slid his hand higher on her thigh. It felt like a trail of fire was being set by his fingers. It meant nothing to him though.

Trevor finally spoke again. "She's seventeen, Logan."

Logan's grip tightened around her thigh, and for some reason, she put her hand over his.

He turned his hand, linking their fingers. "Not that any of my relationships have ever had anything to do with you, but I know she's seventeen. It's no big deal. She'll be eighteen soon."

He finished his sandwich and turned to look at Trevor. There was no room for her to slide off the counter because he leaned back against it, his muscular back brushing against her chest when he crossed his arms.

Trevor stood still, watching everything happening between them. Those slate-blue eyes of his were darker, like staring into a deep abyss. "But she's not eighteen yet, and you've already gone and fu—"

"Finish that sentence, and I'll knock your ass out," Logan said, moving to take a step toward Trevor.

Scared to see them fight, she grabbed his shoulders and pulled him back against her. Logan let her, though she felt his muscles ready to unleash a whole lot of hurt on his cousin. Not really thinking any of her actions out, Kylie's legs went around Logan's waist, her fast breaths sliding between them as she held on tight. "Logan, stop," she whispered in his ear. "He didn't mean—"

"Like hell he didn't," he yelled, his hands coming up to grip her calves, ready to pull them away from his waist.

"It's statutory rape," Trevor told him.

Logan made a sort of growling noise and began to pry her legs off, but she tightened them. She was torn between wanting to stop them from fighting and being angry that this was all an act for Logan. Still, she didn't think she could stand the sight of Logan beating up Trevor.

"*Shh*," she cooed into his neck while his chest heaved up and down.

"Did I say we had sex?" Logan yelled. He was really good with his acting, because she almost believed his anger.

"It's obvious," Trevor yelled back.

Several of the guys peeked into the kitchen. A few even went to stand beside Trevor, trying to calm him down.

"Relax, Trevor," one of the guys said when he shook their hands off him. "It's just Logan. No one will say anything."

"No," Trevor yelled. "He tricked her into having sex with him. She's a minor!"

"Dude," another guy yelled at Trevor. "We're all like the same age. Don't worry about it."

"Fuck you, Ricky. You just banged a fifteen year old." Trevor moved to stand right in front of Logan.

Kylie hung on as tight as she could, all while Logan kept his hands over her legs, ready to rip them away if they were to fight.

Trevor continued, "She's a nice girl. A normal person would be ashamed for tricking someone like her, but it's hopeless to expect you to do anything with a girl that doesn't involve fucking them. You can't even stop yourself from destroying someone as innocent as her."

Logan laughed, but it was a dark and cruel sound. "I don't know who you're trying to fool with this shit, but what I do with Kylie is our business, not yours. If I want to see her, I'll see her. And she's right here. You don't need to talk about her like she's a child who can't think for herself."

"You're not dating her," Trevor growled, his eyes burning into Logan's.

"Why don't you ask her?" Logan rubbed her legs.

Every boy in the room zeroed in on the small movement.

"Go ahead," Logan challenged Trevor. "While you're at it, ask her if we fucked."

Every pair of eyes went to her. Squeezing her arms around Logan, she hesitated, shaking. She did not expect this to happen. Her plans had been to come, talk to Logan, agree to dating, and to apologize. Not have her first kiss. Her first make-out session. Her first orgasm! Now she was preparing to have two boys fight over her.

"It's okay, baby," Logan told her, his palms sliding softly along the front of her legs. "Not that it's any of his fucking business—and Trevor loves getting into my business—but go ahead and tell him what we were doing."

"The truth?"

He chuckled, nodding. "The truth."

She looked over at Trevor. "I got wet."

Logan's head went down as he laughed silently. There was no way she was admitting why she was really wet.

"I mean, sweaty," she corrected. "We were working out, and he gave me this to wear. We didn't have sex."

"So you guys are really dating?" Ricky asked, looking at Logan like there was something else he wanted to say.

Logan narrowed his fierce gaze on Ricky. "Tell him, Hood."

"We're really dating," she whispered.

One of the other guys turned to Trevor. "See, man, nothing to worry about."

Logan straightened himself and gently pushed her legs away, then glaring at Trevor, he said, "Get over whatever your problem is. She's mine. You had your chance, and you left her to me."

He smirked at Trevor while Kylie's heart jackhammered against her chest. Surely, it would explode any minute now.

Logan continued, "To make things clear, though, I'll go ahead and explain what we've been up to. I came out without my shirt on because I took it off to work out. You guys asked who I had in the room, and I told you—the most beautiful blonde I've ever seen."

Kylie's breath hitched, her chest hurting because of how hard and fast she was breathing. Her poor ribs were really taking a beating today. She just wished this was how he really felt.

"When you asked if I was going back for seconds, I told you I was getting her medicine. She had a headache, you morons. I had the bottle of aspirin in my damn hand."

The boys all had red faces as they looked back at her.

"Like I said," Logan went on, "I don't need to explain shit to you, and I won't do it again. I'm just doing this for Kylie. But"—he looked at all the guys—"talk about her like this again, and I'll break every one of your faces."

"Sorry, man," one of the guys muttered. "I mean, we were only messing around. But the marks, and the yells coming from the room kind of made it seem like you were having some wild ass sex."

Logan shook his head and turned to lift her off the counter. "If any of you idiots got some real action"—he put his arm over her shoulder and pulled her close, kissing her forehead as she hugged herself to him—"you'd know that a girl usually digs her nails into your shoulders or arms. Fuck's sake, she can't even get her arms in a position to drag them straight down." He scoffed and began to pull her out of the kitchen. "Fucking amateurs. I had an itch—she scratched my back."

Kylie blushed along with the boys. Trevor still looked ready to fight, but he just pushed his way out of the kitchen. A few of the boys followed, but most of them moved to get refreshments from the fridge.

"Sorry again, Logan."

Logan stopped with her, nodding to the guys left behind.

"And we're sorry, Kylie."

She gave a smile but turned her face into Logan's chest. Being so exposed was worse than she ever thought it could be. The attention was nothing like she remembered . . .

"No more hiding, Hood," Logan murmured into her hair as they walked back to his room.

After he shut the door, she pulled away from him. "This is all your fault." She glared at him, rubbing her eyes so she wouldn't cry. "You knew they would think that about me. You should have told me what your plan was!"

Logan sighed as he sat on his bed. "Baby, I'm sorry. It played out a little differently in my head. And I didn't think Trevor would come in there to play white knight with you." His eyes darted away from hers and his hands balled up.

"They think I'm a slut." This wasn't supposed to happen. She wasn't supposed to come off as a whore.

He shook his head. "Hood, they're just a bunch of dumb jocks. And now they know you're mine. That's all I meant to accomplish. I wanted to stake my claim."

She stared at him in disbelief. "Your claim?"

He rolled his eyes. "Do you really think I'd share you with anyone?"

She stayed silent. Wasn't that the point? To get her ready for Trevor?

"I'm a dick, Hood. These guys all know that, or they've seen me with other women, women that are more than happy to climb in bed with the next guy they see because they know they're not returning to mine. I'm not oblivious to the fact Trevor and some of his friends have waited around for my seconds. I was doing what I thought was best to make it clear that you're different."

He reached out and grabbed her hand, pulling her until she stood between his legs while he looked up at her. "I admit, the back scratch was low of me. But I did sort of want them to think maybe we had already slept together. It's expected. But this way, if it ever came up with a cop or something, we'd still be able to say we haven't had sex." He shrugged and put his hands on her hips, pulling her even closer. "I'm sorry." He wrapped his arms around her waist, grinning when she couldn't take her eyes away from his face. "I should have prepared you, but I thought you would chicken out if you knew what you were walking into. You did great though. I'm proud of you."

She sighed, placing her hands on his shoulders. "They still think I'm your slut. They said you'd throw me out. Is that normal?"

"I'm not throwing you out." He chuckled. "And they don't think you're a slut. Trust me." He laid his head against her chest, closing his eyes as he hugged her tighter. "You're not like the girls I've had here."

She frowned and absentmindedly began running her fingers through his damp hair. "Because I'm blond?"

"What?" He leaned away a little, opening his eyes.

"Chris said you like brunettes." Kylie tried to decipher the anger in his gaze, but she had no idea what to make of it.

Logan exhaled, closing his eyes again as his warm breath seeped through her shirt. "Chris is an asshole. My point is I've never reacted to those guys insulting chicks I've had here. And I've never said that any of them were mine. Like more than a fuck, you know? You're mine."

"But I'm not yours."

He kept his eyes closed and smacked her butt. "You are. You just don't want to believe it."

She smiled softly and hugged his head, enjoying his pleased groan as he held her tighter. "I wish you wouldn't say things like that."

"Like what?" His voice was adorable all muffled.

She bit her lip, unsure how to say anything without giving her feelings for him away. "Saying I'm yours when I'm just a project for you."

Logan's grip loosened.

"When you're just preparing me for Trevor."

Stupid, Kylie! Stupid! Stupid! Stupid!!!

Logan let her go and pushed her back. "Put your clothes back on." He stood up and walked to his door. "They're on my counter."

Kylie's eyes watered, staring at his back as he left the room without even looking at her. "I'm such an idiot," she whispered to herself as she walked into his attached bathroom. "A stupid wimp."

11
I'M SORRY, IDIOT

If being on the opposite end of Logan's fists hurt, receiving the cold shoulder from him had to be worse.

"And you'll keep this between us?" Logan asked his trainer.

Kylie looked up, hating that he no longer held her close. He only looked at her when asking her a question.

"Sure, man."

Kylie let her eyes drift over to the man Logan had introduced her to. Evander.

"I'll keep my lips sealed," Evander said. "I won't even put her name on them."

"Thanks." Logan shook his hand, then turned to her, a harsh gleam in his eyes. "Kylie, go with Evander. He'll take your X-ray, then I'll meet you in his office."

Again, he didn't wait for her to respond and walked out. She jumped when Evander spoke to her, distracted by Logan's retreating figure,.

"You ready, sweetheart?" He held up his hands in a surrender gesture. "Easy." He smiled. "Don't worry. Logan will meet us. It will only take a few minutes anyway. Let's go."

She started following him down a hall. It was quiet, but she realized they weren't really in the gym area. This was all medical and rehab-therapy rooms.

"I don't have to take my shirt off, do I?"

Evander chuckled. "No, sweetie. Logan would probably kill me if I asked you to." He held a door open that had a Radiology sticker stuck on the outside. "After what happened with Chris, I think everyone knows to leave you alone."

Kylie frowned and went to stand where he motioned for her to. "His manager, Chris?"

Evander nodded while he moved around his equipment. "Yeah, he's doing better now—still trying to apologize and get his job back, but I don't see Logan forgiving him anytime soon. Especially since he still has you around."

Kylie didn't understand what he was talking about, but she stayed quiet to gain information.

"That in itself proves Chris got what he deserved." He looked up after preparing his machine with a smile. "He's pulled worse stuff on Logan anyway—it was coming to him. Ready?"

♦♦♦

Kylie tried to sink lower in her chair. She knew why Evander kept glancing at her. She knew why the frown on his face only grew more prominent as he studied her radiographs.

He could see it all.

Every broken rib. The scar tissue that had built up. He was seeing what four years of abuse had left behind. But she didn't care what Evander thought. The one person who she wanted to care hadn't met them like he said he would. An hour had passed, and not one word had come from Logan.

"Uh, Kylie." Evander's voice had that sympathetic undertone to it. The one she remembered hearing right after her mother died when she was only seven—then again, when her dad died just before her freshman year.

"Yeah?"

He smiled, a pitying sort of grin. "Logan just texted me. He's on his way."

She nodded and looked back down at her lap.

"He decided to get a massage. I guess he needed a full one—that's what's taking him so long."

She didn't look up. She knew that Evander had no idea about how she felt toward Logan. Not that it mattered anyway. The man's words were purely informative. He was too busy analyzing every detail of her chest X-ray.

She wondered if the X-ray showed her broken heart, wondered if he could see the crack Logan had already started—and if they were retaken just now, would they show it being ripped apart by a Spanish beauty?

"Sorry," came Logan's voice as the door opened.

Kylie didn't look up, though she felt him; his presence was unique to her already.

"I needed to do something."

She shook her head as the door shut, breathing a sigh of relief when he didn't come near her. He stood beside Evander instead.

"It's fine," Evander told him. "I hope Gloria got out whatever knots you must have had."

Logan was slow to respond, but he eventually muttered a simple, "Yeah."

Kylie reached up to rub her eye. She wanted to cry, but she wouldn't give him the satisfaction. Sure, he could do what he wanted. After all, she was the dumb idiot still pretending to love Trevor. But he knew she was bothered by his relationship with his masseuse. Did he get another blow job? Or did he decide to find out if she was better in 'the sack'?

"Well," Evander started, business-like tone present, "I really wasn't expecting any of this. If the police come, Logan, I have to say I took these."

"They won't come," he said quickly.

Kylie turned her head to stare at the wall. She didn't want to hear what Evander found. She knew. She'd felt every blow. She knew exactly how it felt to be hit with an aluminum bat versus a wooden one. She knew getting kicked left her winded, while blows from baseball bats did just as much damage as falling down the stairs.

"Fine. But I think you both should consider going to the police. This is serious, Logan. It's not just a black eye."

"Just tell me what you found," Logan snapped. "Are there any fractures right now?"

Evander sighed. "No. I haven't seen what she looks like, but by the way she's carrying herself, I can tell she's in pain. I'll give her something, put it in your name."

"Thank you." Logan's voice was calmer now.

"Okay. So I guess that's the good news. I can examine you, Kylie, but really, I can't do much for bruises. Just take the medicine I prescribe, take it easy, and don't receive another injury."

She nodded but kept her head down.

"You have so much damage done, I'm surprised you haven't punctured a lung. And that no one's stopped this. This is like looking at an amateur fighter's chest *after* he's retired from underground fighting."

"Evander." Logan was getting irritated.

So was she. She didn't need to listen to this.

"Right. Sorry. I don't think she wants to look, but come here; you can see for yourself."

She listened then as Evander explained the four fractures she'd obtained over the years. He broke down each one for him, how they occurred from what he thought was two or three different incidents. Then he explained how he didn't doubt other fractures would be revealed over more of her body. None of it mattered to her. She had already lived through them. And if she and Logan kept up their charade for the next few weeks, she would never experience them again. Everything could stop.

"Do you have any questions, Kylie?"

She snapped her head over to see Evander looking at her. Logan was staring at the monitor where her X-rays were displayed.

"Um, no," she whispered. "Thank you for your help."

Evander gave her a sad smile and nodded. "Just stick with Logan, sweetie. He'll keep you safe."

She nodded, unsure if Logan even wanted her around anymore. He hadn't said anything to either of them.

"All right," said Evander. "You can come to me for anything. Don't hesitate. I'll be back—I need to go call in your prescription."

She swore the room got smaller when Evander left.

Logan didn't move. He stood there with his arms crossed, his face unreadable as he looked at her X-rays.

"Logan," she whispered, hoping he would just say something.

He didn't.

She didn't know what he could be thinking. Her own thoughts were jumping from one of today's events to the next. She tried again. "Logan?"

Still, he stayed quiet. Kylie was tired of it. She was upset over her own foolish choice to lie to him about Trevor, and having him ignore her only added to her inner turmoil.

"I don't need the pain meds," she said, standing up. "I'll go tell him to forget it. I'm going to head home though. Thanks for today, I guess. And, well, I guess just trying to help. But you don't need to worry—I'll figure things out on my own. I'm used to dealing with it, and it's fine. It's the way I want things." She smiled in his direction, though she felt like he wasn't even listening. "Bye, Logan."

The pain from those words stabbed her heart, almost making her cry. Still, she turned to leave her man-boy behind her.

With her hand outstretched toward the doorknob, Logan finally spoke.

"Kylie."

She hadn't heard him walk closer, but as soon as she turned, he was there, placing his hands on her cheeks and smashing his lips to hers.

A shocked cry fell out of her mouth, but he swallowed it and the happy-emotional sobs that followed. There was no way she could hold in her tears now. She let him take her cries inside him—let him hold her up. This was all going to go to hell, but she didn't care. She wanted this.

"I'm sorry," he murmured and resumed kissing her as he rubbed her tears with his thumbs. "I'm so sorry."

She nodded as best she could, squeezing herself closer as he began to kiss her tears.

"I wasn't with Gloria," he whispered against her cheek.

This relieved her, of course, but she didn't understand him, and she knew he wouldn't explain. So she just kept still as he brushed his lips across her skin.

"It's fine, Logan," she whispered.

"No, it's not, Hood." He nuzzled his nose against the side of her neck. "Forgive me. I shouldn't have pulled any of this shit with you today. And I shouldn't have gotten angry earlier." His words were muffled, and she sensed he wanted to say more, but he only added, "Just please let me be here for you. I want to be the one who protects you. You're not alone."

It wasn't some declaration that he had the same feelings she was developing, but he was telling her he genuinely wanted to be there for her. He was sorry, and she was an idiot. But it felt right.

"I want you here with me," she told him, smiling when he grinned and attacked her lips again.

He pulled back and carefully rubbed her tears. "Good. You're not getting rid of me. Just do one thing for me, Hood."

"Sure."

His dark eyes scanned her face while he rubbed the pads of his thumbs over her wet cheeks. She sighed, loving that he was holding her again, and closed her eyes to wait for his demand. "Promise me that when you're with me, Trevor is nowhere near your mind. And his name is definitely not one we speak when you're in my arms."

Kylie smiled, earning her one of Logan's breathtaking grins. "Trevor who?"

12
THE BAD KIDS

Kylie pressed her lips together as she pushed her hood off her head. Her hair was already down, hanging over her shoulders. Everyone at home had seen it spilling out from the hood she always wore, but this was her first time taking her hood off.

Kevin's stare wasn't uncomfortable, but she felt it taking in her change in appearance as he drove her to school.

He cleared his throat when the building came into view. "I think I like the influence Logan Grimm is having on you."

She felt her cheeks flush. "He's pretty great."

"I hope so, sweetheart. Just be careful. Don't let your heart get too attached." He turned into the school drop-off lane. "I really hope you have a good experience with him, but your first boyfriend usually isn't your last."

"What do you mean?" Her heartbeat sped up as she watched the Godsons walking past her window. Janie Mortaime was in the center of the group, holding Ryder's hand while she held Tercero's arm, speaking to him. Ryder seemed to ignore how wrong it looked for his girlfriend to be all over his brother while he was right there. Kylie frowned at the sight, but she was more drawn to Ryder's hold on Janie because it reminded her she wouldn't have *her* bad boy there to hold her hand during the day. In fact, her bad boy wasn't a real boyfriend. He cared about her, but that wasn't the same as being real boyfriend and girlfriend.

"I mean," Kevin said as he drove a bit closer to the drop-off zone, "first loves rarely last more than a few months, and Logan has probably had a long line of relationships. This thing you've started is nothing new to him. He has a job, a life that doesn't involve school, and he is surrounded by women. I was a fighter—I know what kind of life he has. And it is full of women, not innocent girls trying to keep their grades up in high school."

Her mouth went dry. First, it was still hard to picture Kevin as a fighter. He was her stepdad and a businessman. Seeing him the way she'd seen Logan fight was just weird.

Kylie shook her head to rid herself of even imagining Kevin shirtless. "Logan hasn't had a girlfriend before."

He gave her a pitying look. "Sweetheart, I'm sure he has had a few girlfriends. Worse, I know he has a reputation when it comes to women. I'm not saying he's playing with your feelings—he seemed genuine about dating you when I met him—but I'm concerned you'll invest too much in him. Once it becomes clear to him you're still very much a young girl putting school first—which I hope is the case—he might realize he's not ready to have a relationship with you."

Her eyes burned as she watched the Godson brothers staring at a group of girls dancing in the courtyard. Archer took out his phone to record them, but they were all watching the show the girls were putting on. The only one not looking was Ryder, but that was because he was busy kissing Janie on a bench nearby.

The thing that had her heart on the verge of breaking was the realization that *all* the Godson brothers had girlfriends—not just Ryder. Yet they were whistling as the dance team shook their asses and blew kisses at them. They were the definition of bad boys, just like Logan, and no girlfriend, especially one for show, was holding them back from other girls.

Kevin was right. Logan was a guy who had women throwing themselves at him all the time. He would forget about her whenever she wasn't there to kiss him.

Kevin patted her knee. "Just guard your heart, okay? I'm here if you need anything. And I'm his boss, remember? At least that should keep him in line."

"I will. Thanks, Kevin." She smiled as best she could. He was right, after all. Logan had no idea she liked him or that she no longer wanted anything to do with Trevor. But that was the plan for Logan. He was being a sort of guardian angel while he gave her experience to go after Trevor. He was making Trevor jealous to force him to make a move.

Kevin finally made it to the drop-off zone, and he smiled as he unlocked the door. "Have a good day."

"You too." She clutched her bag and got out of the car. She didn't know if it was her imagination, but it felt like everyone was watching her as she made her way toward the door. It was hard not to pull her hood over her head, but she promised Logan last night she wouldn't hide under it anymore. She felt like he would know if she'd worn it the next time she saw him, so she was determined to keep her hood down all day.

Wolf whistles filled the courtyard, and she grinned at the attention, only to feel humiliated when she turned to see it was merely Archer and Savaş whistling at Janie. The girl was giving Ryder a lap dance, probably because the dance team had planted themselves across from where Ryder was sitting.

Kylie didn't know what she was feeling as she watched Ryder hold on to Janie's hips with a big smile on his face, or when Archer quickly ran over and shoved dollar bills into Janie's shorts, which resulted in Ryder snatching his brother's arm as he got up.

The girl didn't get offended at basically being viewed as a stripper. She merely laughed as she pulled Ryder's face to her breasts to keep him from attacking his brother.

The crowd roared with laughter as Archer made a run for it, and they cheered when Savaş walked toward the group of dancers and started slowly pulling his shirt over his head.

"Take it off, baby," Janie cheered as Ryder carried her past him. She even started making the dollar bills Archer had given her rain down in Savaş' direction.

"Miss Mortaime," Principal Prince shouted, marching toward them.

Janie turned, winking at the principal as Ryder glared at him.

"Hi, Nick." Janie held out a dollar. "You gotta take it off before you get paid, big boy."

Mr. Prince actually smiled as he snatched the dollar from Janie's hand. "Get to class."

Ryder snatched the dollar right back. Mr. Prince strolled forward, shooing away the girls who were trying to shove dollars into Archer's and Savaş' pants.

As people pushed their way toward the doors, Kylie realized one thing.

No one was looking at her. No one.

She was just as invisible as she'd always been under her hood.

She sighed as she turned, only to stumble back. "Trevor."

He smiled at her before glaring at Ryder, who roughly knocked his shoulder as he passed him.

Kylie noticed Janie peering over Ryder's shoulder with her eyes locked on Trevor's. She felt pathetic over the fact that even Trevor was staring at the girl, but then he muttered 'slut' and turned to face Kylie again.

"Can I walk you to your first period?" Trevor asked.

Kylie was in shock. "Are you talking to me?"

He chuckled, patting some jock on the shoulder as he moved closer to her. "Yeah. I wanted to check on you—make sure you were okay."

"Oh." She couldn't help the butterflies that fluttered in her stomach. "I'm good."

He gave her his gorgeous Trevor Grimm smile, moving to the side as the dance team walked by. Many of the girls looked at him, then her, muttering 'Who's that?' as they went inside.

"Good," he said, holding the door open for her. "So, can I walk you?"

"Yeah." She noticed people were looking at her now. "Thanks, Trevor."

Again, he gave her a big smile. "Sure. You look nice, by the way. I like your hair down. It's pretty."

"Thanks," Kylie whispered, smiling. She could barely concentrate on her steps as her racing heart sped up even more when she realized students were watching them. Once again, she was the girl Trevor Grimm made important to everyone, and she didn't mind at all.

◆◆◆

Kylie slouched down in her chair, trying to hide her tears as a group of girls giggled a few rows behind her. Being noticed wasn't what she had hoped for. In fact, she'd been teased and bullied by a group of Grimm fan girls for most of the day. She had to hide in the bathroom at lunchtime to escape their taunts, and now she was in English class, she had to face even more ridicule. All because of the football team.

Those dumb jocks let it slip she was dating Logan, and apparently everyone at school knew who Logan Grimm was. He was a legend throughout the town. She felt like a fool for not knowing about him and worse because everyone thought he was too good for her. They all thought it was a joke.

"She's not even pretty," said one of the girls in the back row.

Kylie closed her eyes, only to jump when something smacked her forehead. She ignored the laughter and looked down to see a wadded-up piece of paper had been thrown at her.

"What a weirdo," someone whispered.

"She must be a really good fuck, or she's paying him to fuck her," someone else muttered.

"No, I think it's because her stepdad is Kevin Blackwood—he owns the fighters. Logan's only dating her to butter up her daddy."

Kylie glared at her desk, refusing to look up as people filed into class. How did everyone even know about Kevin owning the fighters? Then again, she was sure she saw Kevin's name on the building when she went to the fight.

Philip Miller sat behind her, and he tapped her on the shoulder. "Hey, Kylie."

"What?" She looked over to see his friends laughing.

"How much?" he asked.

She knew she should've stayed quiet, but she couldn't. "How much for what?"

"How much to suck my big dick?"

His friends roared with laughter.

"Leave me alone," she snapped, her blood boiling as something else was thrown at her.

"Aw, don't be like that," Philip said. "There's no way Grimm isn't getting his dick sucked right now—you might as well learn how to do it properly if you want to keep a legend like Logan Grimm interested in you. Don't you know he used to date—"

His words dried up, and the laughter from his friends ceased.

It became clear why when she noticed the Godsons in the doorway.

Ryder guided Janie to her desk, but his violent gaze was on Philip. "Got something to say, bitch?"

Philip leaned back in his seat, clearly not ready for another beating from the bad boy.

Archer chuckled, snatching one of the balled-up pieces of paper from Kylie's desk as he passed by. He threw it right at Philip.

"Archer," Mrs. Demoness shouted. "Sit down, or you will get detention for disrupting class."

Archer flipped her off and took his seat.

Philip and his friends didn't bother Kylie for the rest of the class.

Thank God for bad boys.

"You think you're so hot, don't you?"

Kylie stopped walking. She'd been focusing on the floor since people were still picking on her, but now she realized she was surrounded by six girls. The one who had spoken was the school's version of a queen bee—Melody Sokolav. She was the head cheerleader, and she also happened to be Maura's best friend. Well, Maura liked to say they were best friends, but Kylie was certain no one really liked Maura.

Speaking of Maura—Kylie locked gazes with her dreaded stepsister. This wasn't going to go well.

Melody's lip curled up in disgust as she looked her over. "I asked you a question."

"I'm not trying to be anything, Melody," Kylie whispered, looking around to see that a few people were coming to watch the confrontation.

The girls laughed at her as she stared back with wide eyes. All she could do was stand there.

"Look at what she's wearing," someone said, laughing. "She wears the same thing every day."

"I heard she gave the whole football team blow jobs," another person said.

"Yeah, that was after she finished a three way with Trevor and his hot cousin."

"The whole team had to go get tested for herpes."

"She gave Ray crabs."

Tears welled in her eyes as the crowd grew. Many were laughing while others just watched without helping her.

"They said she was begging for more. What a whore."

"None of that's true," Kylie said, fighting with all her might to keep her tears at bay. She refused to cry.

They laughed at her pathetic attempt to defend herself.

"Maura," Melody called, "didn't you say you caught her trying to seduce your stepfather?"

Kylie shook her head at Maura, begging with her eyes to end this.

"I caught her completely undressed on his bed when my mom was gone," Maura told the group.

"That's a lie," she shouted. Her head throbbed as she tried to look for a way out, but they had her trapped between them.

Maura grinned evilly. "Just like it was a lie that you had to have an abortion for your real dad's baby when you were twelve?"

Kylie gasped. Others started screaming out that she was sick. A murderer. A whore. The world spun around her as their insults became louder and more hostile.

"Well," a new female voice said from outside the circle, "climbing into bed with older men was always Melody's fantasy. Y'all sound jealous."

The crowd moved to reveal a group of four girls with Janie Mortaime smiling at the front.

"Isn't that right?" Janie smirked as she placed herself between Kylie and Melody.

The whole hall went silent, waiting for someone to say something. Kylie darted her eyes around and saw Ryder Godson and his brothers leaning against some lockers a few feet away.

"So," said Janie, a wicked little grin on her lips, "how's business these days, Suckthemoff? Earn enough to pay off that boob job yet?"

Melody's mouth closed in a tight line as the three girls behind Janie snickered.

"It's Sokolav, Janie, and you know it," Melody spat.

"All I know is that you suck them off for a little green." Janie smirked, adding, "But you swallow for free."

Monica, Tonia, and Elise—the girlfriends of Ryder's brothers—all laughed.

"I hope they gave her a discount," Monica said, tilting her head to the side as she observed Melody. "The left one looks a little lopsided."

Several laughs sounded around them. Kylie still wasn't sure what was going on. These were the bad kids. While she didn't think Ryder and Archer had been defending her in English class earlier, there was no denying Janie was putting herself between her and Maura's friends.

Speaking of Maura, her stepsister was trying to distance herself from the confrontation, like a coward.

"Maura Payne." Janie turned a cruel smile toward her. "How's it been? I see mommy dearest paid for your nose to get fixed after I broke it."

Maura glared at Janie, though the fear was still present.

"Looks good," Janie said, taking a step toward Maura. "You should refer Melody to your doctor. Who knows, maybe he'll give you a discount so you can get your tits big enough to fill out that padded bra you're wearing. "

Kylie distinctly heard Ryder and his brothers laughing among the crowd.

Maura's face flamed with embarrassment, but she still had the guts to fire back, "That's not what your boyfriend said last night."

Janie laughed, glancing over at Ryder. "Babe, I'm curious—where'd you manage to hide Maura and her huge tits last night?"

Ryder slowly slid his eyes down Janie. "I was wondering the same thing, baby girl. You know exactly where I was."

Kylie was sure his eyes were glowing as they settled between Janie's legs.

Archer was the one to say something to Maura. "They live together, dumb bitch. She's in his bed every night."

"You would know, brother," Tercero said, smirking. "You tried to squeeze in with them before Ryder threw your naked ass out into the hall."

Laughter filled the halls; the crowd was even larger now.

Janie focused on Maura again. "Did we ruin your Ryder-Loves-Me fantasy?"

"Go to hell, stupid cunt," Maura said.

A strange smile touched Janie's lips, almost amused, but something else too. "I've already been crowned queen there, silly. Now tell everyone you're fucking my boyfriend again. But I'll warn you"—she leaned forward and whispered—"you're nothing to him. Not a damn one of you means shit to him."

Maura screamed like a banshee. "You bitch!"

Janie threw a punch, hitting Maura right on the nose. Kylie gasped with the crowd, and all hell broke loose. Melody went for Janie, but her friends shouted, tackling several of the girls with Maura.

The crowd cheered, causing more and more students to rush over. Janie was still punching Maura, but her group was outnumbered and it wasn't long before Melody broke free from the melee and grabbed Janie's hair to pull her off.

Monica grabbed Melody's ankle, yanking her down.

Melody smacked the ground face first, then cried out as Monica began dragging her off Janie, and in doing so yanked Melody's leggings clean off.

"WOOOOO!" Tons of boys started to cheer, but they died off quickly with sounds of horror and disgust at the sight of her panties. They were big, and clearly not Melody's regular pair.

"Oh, shit, it's laundry day," someone yelled, making the crowd lose it.

Ryder and his brothers were the loudest again, and Kylie found herself laughing with everyone until she saw Tonia, Archer's girlfriend, being pinned down. Before the girl could punch Tonia, Elise, Tercero's girlfriend, tackled her. Boys made cat noises while others filmed everything. Then a shirt suddenly went flying through the air.

There was silence for a few seconds.

"Oh, yeah," a bunch of guys yelled, realizing that in the wrestling match, the girl Elise had tackled lost her shirt. "Take her bra off!"

Kylie couldn't stop smiling, but her heart raced painfully fast because a flash of steel caught her eye. Maura had a knife. "Maura, no!"

Janie turned just in time to miss the knife being swung at her back. The crowd gasped while Ryder and the boys sprang into action, pushing people out of the way.

"Showing off all your crazy today," Janie said, grinning at Maura instead of running like she should.

"I hate you," Maura screamed, still holding the knife up. It wasn't big, but it was still a knife.

"Doesn't everyone?" Janie smiled, not looking afraid. "Come on, we're both crazy. Be original if you're gonna threaten me."

People started yelling that teachers were coming, but the bad girl kept her eyes on Maura, tracking her like she was the predator, not the prey. Her posse had abandoned their victims and stood off to the side.

"I'm not crazy!" Maura let out a wild cry and charged Janie.

Janie stepped forward and blocked the attack, grabbed Maura's wrist, and twisted it behind her back.

Maura screamed out in pain, but Janie wrenched her arm up higher.

"Drop it," Janie said, not letting Maura go. The knife clattered to the floor, and Savaş pocketed it before it could get kicked out of the way.

Ryder spoke calmly, but his eyes were ablaze. "Leave her, babe. She's had enough."

Janie looked ready to argue, but the crowd started breaking up, everyone running away to avoid punishment.

Unfortunately, Maura was stupid enough to say something else. "I might be nothing, but you're still a lying, cheating bitch. One day you'll be nothing too."

Kylie had no idea what Maura was talking about, but judging by the fury on Janie's and Ryder's faces, some of it was true.

"You don't know anything," Janie growled as Ryder tugged her.

Maura cradled her arm, her green eyes shifting between Janie and Kylie, but it was Janie she spat at.

Oh, no.

Janie was being dragged away, but even Ryder paused, taking in that Janie was wiping off her arm. He stood no chance of stopping the kick Janie sent to Maura, nailing her right between the legs.

"Dammit, woman!" Ryder lifted Janie up as Maura dropped to the floor, crying. Then he stomped past Kylie with the others rushing after him.

Kylie was in shock. She couldn't believe everything that had just happened. She could only stand there and take in the sight of Maura sobbing with her hand between her legs as kids continued running in every direction to escape the teachers.

"Blondie!" Ryder's entire group had stopped, and they were staring at her. Ryder had Janie over his shoulder, but he was staring at Kylie. "You're coming with us. Hurry up."

She didn't move, but when Janie lifted her head and narrowed her teary, hazel eyes at Kylie, she took a step back.

Janie shook her head. "Get your little ass over here."

"Babe." Ryder smacked Janie's butt but also squeezed and rubbed it as though he was soothing the sting. "Hush."

Teachers yelled for students to stop running while others helped Maura's damaged pack.

"We won't hurt you, Kylie." Janie's hazel trained on her, and lost the violent, taunting gleam. "I promise. Just come with us, or they're going to pin some of this on you."

Kylie looked around, noticing that teachers were grabbing students for questioning. She saw a boy had stopped to help Maura, and she shook her head. Maura would turn this around on her, blame her for it. So she ran after them and followed them to the parking lot.

"Hanging with the bad kids now, Kylie Hood," Janie said, her voice teasing as she rubbed under her eyes. They were red, and she had some swelling on her cheek like she'd been slapped.

Kylie's face warmed as the group continuously sent her stares before breaking off toward different vehicles. She kept up with Ryder, figuring he meant him when he told her to come.

Janie smacked Ryder's ass. "Put me down—I'm driving."

"No, you're not," he told her as they approached a black SS Camaro.

"But it's my car." Janie started squeezing his butt cheeks.

"I know it's your car." Ryder muttered out a few curses while he dug through his girlfriend's bag. "Where are your God d— Oh, here they are. Stop squeezing my ass."

"I can't help myself," Janie said, squeezing more.

Ryder sighed and pulled open the passenger side door. "Get in, Blondie. Now."

Kylie yelped and ran to jump in the back seat as Ryder placed Janie down on her feet. He was instantly kissing her, and Kylie looked away, unease tugging at her stomach.

"Are you okay, baby girl?" He didn't sound like the cold-hearted guy she knew he was. "Damn, you took a few good hits."

Kylie looked back to see they were done kissing, and Ryder was inspecting any wounds Janie had sustained, even the girl's bruised knuckles.

"I'm fine," Janie whispered as Ryder sweetly kissed her fingers.

It surprised Kylie when blood stained his lips, but he licked it and went back to checking over Janie's face.

"You've gotten sloppy, babe. And soft," he said, checking the parking lot quickly. "I warned you to keep your head together."

"Whatever," Janie muttered. "And it was her head that was the problem—hard as a rock."

He gripped her chin, staring into her eyes. "You okay?"

A forced smile was Janie's response, and Ryder sighed, kissing her one more time before he situated her in the seat and rounded the car.

Janie didn't acknowledge her. She just started inspecting her reflection in the mirror.

Ryder got to the driver's side, but as soon as he went to sit down, he said, "Dammit, woman, I've told you to scoot the seat back when you park."

"My car," she said as he fiddled with the seat control to move it back so he could fit inside. "I can do what I want."

"I bought it," he deadpanned as he got in. "I want to be able to drive it if I need to." He roughly pushed up the visor and started the engine.

Kylie had never sat in a car that actually made her butt vibrate, and it was a little terrifying. "Um," she said to get their attention because they weren't even bothering with her.

Janie turned to look at her. "Why didn't you take up for yourself?"

Ryder shook his head, but he didn't say anything as he drove through the parking lot.

"You can't let people treat you like that," Janie went on, her gaze running over Kylie's face and taking in her hood.

It was like she'd never seen her before, and now she was sizing her up. *Great.*

Janie's eyes met hers. "They won't stop if you just stand there crying."

"I wasn't crying," Kylie whispered. She wanted to, but she never would. "I'll never cry in front of them. I just didn't know what to say."

Ryder sighed when a strange look danced across Janie's face and raised Janie's hand to his mouth, kissing it. "Don't, babe."

Kylie held her breath as Janie kept staring. Surely, she hadn't said anything wrong.

A sort of manic smile appeared on Janie's face, like she'd flipped a switch in her head. "I can't stand your stepsister, but I fucking hate Melody. She never fails to spread lies to her minions about me. I should've hit all of them."

Ryder gave his girlfriend a soft look. "Babe, you know they're full of shit."

"I know." Janie sighed as she moved into her seat again. All Kylie could see was the girl's profile, but she managed to catch the lost look on Janie's face. Maybe the girl was envisioning how the fight should've gone.

It made Kylie wonder if bad kids just loved getting into fights. Ryder certainly made a game of it with the amount of fights he got in.

Or maybe she was thinking about the things Maura said, about her cheating—maybe the cheating was why he got in fights. Maybe they both just loved hurting people.

Ryder tenderly caressed Janie's swollen cheek with the back of his fingers. "Don't let any of their words get to you. We know the truth, okay?" Janie didn't respond, and he added, "They can try to tear us apart but it'll never happen. . . . I love you, angel. Longer than always."

Holy shit, that was the sweetest thing Kylie had ever heard, and definitely not something she expected Ryder Godson to ever say.

Janie certainly seemed to think so too as she smiled dreamily at him. "That was romantic as fuck, babe."

"I know." He grinned at her, and it was a totally playful look that Kylie had never seen him wear before. "Are your panties about to come off?"

Janie laughed, then winked at Kylie before focusing on him again. "Who said I'm wearing any?"

Ryder glanced in the rearview mirror. "Blondie, I'm throwing your ass out the window at the next stop."

"What?" Kylie saw them approaching a stoplight.

Ryder laughed, reaching over to Janie's lap. "I want to see if you're lying. Show me." He smirked, looking back at Kylie. "Close your eyes and ears. She's gonna start moaning in a sec."

Her eyes bulged. Was he really trying to take his girlfriend's clothes off with her in the car? Was he going to finger her or something dirty?

Janie giggled again, pushing his hand away. "Stop being horny."

"With you? Never." He smirked at her. "Let's ditch the blonde. Our cabin in the woods just got stocked. All our toys are there. We can forget the world—everything. Just us, like we're supposed to be."

It was the most Ryder had ever talked around Kylie, and she was entirely stunned that he was actually sweet and well-spoken. He mostly spoke with his fists and with simple statements that made you want to piss yourself and cry. But this Ryder was like a totally different person.

Janie smiled at him like he was the best damn thing in the world. "Not yet, my love."

My love, Kylie thought. *What, are they from the eighteen-hundreds or something?*

He sighed, removing his hand to shift gears. "Not yet."

Kylie put aside the peek into Ryder's world and found the courage to speak up again. If she didn't, she feared they would forget about her and really go camping in the woods. "Where are you taking me?"

Ryder's emerald eyes met hers in the rearview mirror. "To the gym."

Janie twisted around to face her. "We're taking you to Logan."

Kylie's mouth fell open. "You know him?"

A severe frown transformed Janie's face. She didn't answer. No, she simply scrutinized every inch of Kylie's appearance before shaking her head and turning forward to stare out the window.

Kylie shifted her attention to Ryder.

He was already watching her through the rearview mirror. The way he stared might've been exciting if it wasn't for the unemotional expression on his face. She felt utterly exposed on the receiving end of his attention and lowered her eyes to escape.

Only the low hum of what Kylie realized must be classical music filled the silence.

After what felt like an hour but judging by the clock was only fifteen minutes, Ryder said, "Logan is Janie's ex."

13
HIS PAST

"Babe?" Ryder reached out with the back of his hand to caress Janie's cheek. "We can just drop her off—you don't have to talk to him."

Kylie stared down at her lap as she tried not to become visibly upset. They were in the gym parking lot, still in the car, and Ryder was pampering Janie while Kylie was trying not to have a damn meltdown because, of course, it had to be Janie Mortaime who had some claim on the only guy to ever notice her. She was obviously the brunette Chris had warned her about. How could he have meant anyone else?

Hell, even Philip had tried to warn her. He had started to say Logan dated Janie, but fear of Ryder had shut him up.

"I'll be fine," Janie said as she rubbed her chest. "I want to see him. You know I just . . ." She didn't finish whatever else she meant to say. She climbed out of the car, leaving the door open for Kylie.

Ryder muttered out a few curse words and jerked his chin toward the open passenger door. "Out."

She jumped when he got out, slamming his door. Janie was already out of sight, walking into the gym, and Ryder was marching after her.

Every bone in her body hurt as she climbed out and shut the door. She saw Ryder glance behind him before the car alarm sounded.

"Hurry the fuck up," he hollered at Kylie as he shoved the gym door open.

She didn't move. All she kept hearing in her mind was that Logan was Janie's ex. It made her want to vomit all over the place—all over the car Ryder *bought* for her.

Her whole stomach cramped as even her fingers went numb. She needed to run. She was going to run. Hell would freeze over before she followed them because she knew what she'd see—Janie would be all over Logan like she was with Ryder's brothers.

"You better do as he says."

Kylie stumbled back. The rest of the Godson brothers and their girlfriends had arrived.

It was Monica who had spoken, and they were all slamming doors to each of their vehicles. Monica and Savaş got out of a red Hummer as Archer exited a classic white mustang, and Tercero locked his gorgeous matte black Audi r8. It always boggled Kylie's mind that Ryder didn't drive a crazy car like his brothers, but she didn't give a damn about any of that right now.

"It's not a secret Logan wants Janie back," Monica told her, bringing back the swirl of fire in Kylie's gut. "That's why he doesn't date," the girl added. "You better get in there if you want him to remember you."

"Mon." Savaş gave Kylie a quick once-over. "I think she's just finding out about them."

Archer chuckled. "Monica, darling, you have an even bigger mouth than I do."

"Whoops." Monica snickered, hanging onto Savaş's massive arm. "Well, she's about to see how he gets when he sees the only girl he's ever loved. Even I feel jealous with the way he looks at her."

"Hurry up," Tercero muttered, walking ahead of the others. "Savaş, Archer."

"Yeah." Archer threw down a cigarette and ran toward the door.

"What's happening?" Kylie whispered as the girls all sighed.

Tonia answered, "Oh, they're just here to make sure Ryder and Logan don't fight."

"What?" Kylie darted her gaze over to the gym. Ryder was no longer at the door.

Monica shrugged. "They fight over Janie sometimes because Logan wants her back, and Janie wants to keep their friendship. Seems like a lot of drama, if you ask me, but who can really blame Janie for not giving up Logan Grimm?"

"Yep, they all love Janie," Elise commented dryly.

Tonia and Monica shrugged like that wasn't a big issue.

But Kylie's heart fell to the floor. The fight Ryder had lost had been to Logan. To win Janie somehow.

Monica grinned again. "He's completely hard up for her. You should be careful with him—they're not what they seem."

"Monica," Tonia said, pushing her friend toward the building, but Monica's voice still carried to her.

"What? I would want to know what I'm about to see between them."

Elise was still standing by her. "They're just really old friends."

Kylie stared down at the pavement. "He told me he never had a girlfriend."

"He lied," Elise said bluntly. "Come on. It's not like this means Logan doesn't like you now. I think you're prettier than her anyway."

Kylie tried to smile at this, but she was feeling way too many things to be happy about the compliment.

When they made it inside, loud yells and sweaty men greeted them, but there didn't appear to be a massive fight between Logan and Ryder.

"Oh, bummer," Elise said, coming to a stop by the others. "I was hungry for a sexy guy fight. At least Logan is shirtless."

Ryder grunted, crossing his arms as he stared ahead.

Kylie followed his line of sight and sighed. There he was. Logan Grimm. He was indeed shirtless, and he was beating the crap out of a punching bag on the ground. She bit her lip as she watched him, his muscles flexing and glistening with sweat as Mark coached him and a few other guys who were all doing the same thing.

"Grimm," Janie yelled from where she stood at the gate of the octagon Logan was working out in.

He snapped his head up, eyes locking with his ex-girlfriend. And he smiled that heartbreakingly beautiful smile of his. For Janie.

"Hey, honey." Mark opened the gate and pulled Janie into a quick hug. "I was wondering when you were ever going to come back."

Janie beamed up at the man. "Missed me?"

Mark laughed, inclining his head toward Logan. "I'm not the only one. He never shuts up about you when you're gone for too long. Put him out of his misery so I can have my fighter in top shape, please."

Kylie had enough of this; she took a step forward.

Ryder made a growling sort of noise, halting her. "Uh-uh, stay put. They have some shit to talk about first."

She fumed while the blood in her veins sang with rage. Janie shouldn't have anything to talk about alone with Logan. Kylie's eyes were damn near about to spill over with angry tears because Logan was smiling at Janie the same way Ryder did.

"Baby doll," Logan said loud enough for them to hear. He tugged her to him, hugging her tightly. "Fuck, I've missed you."

Janie didn't shy away. She squeezed him just as tightly as he was her, allowing him to lift her off her feet. "You're sweaty."

"You always liked it when we got sweaty together." Logan chuckled, kissing her cheek as he lowered her to her feet. "You staying with me a while?"

Janie's reply was too soft to hear, but it was like a blow to the chest as the truth became clear; Logan wasn't going to keep away from any woman while he was with her. She was a damn joke.

She bit her cheek and watched Logan settle his hands on Janie's hips as they talked softly to each other, Kylie's mind replaying his words. What the hell did he mean 'when they got sweaty'? Why was he touching her to begin with? Why wasn't she pushing him away? Why would he ask her if she was staying for a while? Why wasn't Ryder stopping this?

Finally, Janie moved his hands down, and Logan actually looked disappointed.

"Fucker still can't help himself," Ryder muttered, shaking Tercero's hand off his shoulder.

"Brother," Tercero said in a warning tone.

Ryder shook his head. "I'm in control."

Archer chuckled. "At least he didn't grab her ass this time."

Kylie balled her hands and shoved them into her pockets. Why was she watching this?

Logan's sudden anger regained her attention, but she realized it was only because he noticed Janie's injuries. Janie seemed to be explaining how she got hurt, and that's when he turned toward them.

At first, he glared at Ryder, but soon dropped his eyes down to where Kylie stood. His expression went from shock to guilt, but he didn't come over. No, he returned his focus to Janie, and his words to his ex were easy to make out: *What is she doing here?*

"Don't worry about them, Red." . . . Archer, Kylie realized.

She jerked her head around and gave him the nastiest look she could manage. "I'm not worried."

He smirked and continued in a teasing sort of tone. "It's all right to be jealous. We all get a little jealous of them."

"I'm not jealous." She wanted to scream; why were any of them jealous of Janie and Logan? This was freaking insane.

Archer gestured to her hands. "Your fingernails digging into your palms say otherwise."

"Leave her alone," Ryder said, not looking at any of them.

"Why?" Archer grinned at his brother's glare. "Are you jealous as well, brother?"

Ryder cut him a dark look. "Shut the fuck up."

Archer laughed, ignoring the worried look his girlfriend wore. "Don't be pissy. You're the one she picked."

Ryder didn't say anything, but he punched Archer on the shoulder. Hard.

"Ow." Archer chuckled off the attack but still moved so that Savaş was between them.

"I'm hungry." Savaş gave Ryder a bored look. "If you're not going to fight him, I'm leaving."

"She just left me feeling fucking happy earlier." Ryder smirked mischievously, adding, "If he grabs her again, give me ten seconds before you stop me."

Savaş simply nodded and pulled out his phone.

Kylie looked down and stared at her feet when Janie and Logan laughed together.

"Aw, don't be sad, Kylie," Tonia told her. "They're just friends. He's known her since she was born."

They were making it worse.

"Janie's head over heels for Ryder," Tonia went on. "Totally in love. And, well, Logan is just the guy she loves."

What? Kylie glared at the girl. "Isn't that the same thing?"

"No," said Monica in a duh tone. "Being in love is completely different from only loving someone."

"They were in love," Elise said, covering her mouth when Ryder glared at her. "Sorry."

Monica kept talking. "Anyone can love another person—or thing. Like I love Ryder's ass, but no way in hell am I in love with him."

Savaş glanced down at his girlfriend. "Mon, shut the fuck up about my brother's ass."

Monica grinned wickedly at him. "Would you like me to talk about his dick?"

Archer and Tercero laughed. Ryder ignored them.

Savaş smiled. "If you're going to enlighten everyone that you think mine's bigger than his, don't bother. We already know it is."

Ryder slid his eyes over. "I'm bigger. And better."

Savaş glared at him. "We measured, bitch."

A superior smirk formed on Ryder's face. "And we did the math. Dick to body ratio with our heights, my dick is ten percent bigger than yours. And you're not that much taller than me."

Monica didn't comfort her boyfriend. She was staring at Ryder's crotch. "I wish I was good at math."

Kylie looked away from them. All she could wonder was if Janie knew the difference between Ryder's dick and Logan's.

"How long have you been fucking Logan?" Monica asked.

Archer snorted. "She doesn't look like someone he's been fucking. No offense, honey. That's a compliment."

Kylie snapped her mouth shut. She didn't know how anything he said was a compliment.

"Are you guys actually dating? Or . . ." It was Monica again.

"We're dating," she said defensively. "He said girls are never just friends."

"At least he's being honest for once," Archer said. "It's true that girls are never just friends, but Logan and Janie are best friends. Therefore, not *just* friends."

"What?" She stared at him, shocked and furious. "You said they were exes. Exes are not best friends."

Ryder chuckled, moving a step closer to the ring. "You have no idea what you've got involved in."

"They were best friends," Tercero said, "before he decided to make her his girlfriend when she was, what?"

"I think she was fourteen," Tonia said, smiling sadly. "First for both."

"First?" Kylie was panicking. "She was his first girlfriend? How many has he had?"

Archer frowned, eyeing Logan and Janie for a moment. "She's been his only girlfriend. Do you know anything about him?"

She wanted to cry and scream. They were looking at her like she was a moron.

Elise patted her arm. "Don't stress out. They were together, but after Logan fought Ryder, and well, a lot of other things, they broke up."

Kylie stared at the side of Ryder's face. "You fought him for her?"

He chuckled. It was dark, like the laugh of an ax-murderer in a movie. "You don't want to know the truth.

But, yeah, we got in a fight because Logan's a bitch, and he felt threatened because he knew I was better than him."

"You're not better than him." She glowered, feeling stupid because Logan was making her look like an even bigger fool.

"Like I care what you think." Ryder's gaze was so cold she wanted to hide. "You didn't even know they were a couple—and I'm assuming by the way you were about to break down in tears when you found out, he lied. Surprise, Logan lies all the damn time."

Logan was not a liar. He was blunt and honest, and she hated them for trying to make Logan look bad. "So Logan beat you up and she what . . . cheated on him?"

While the others gaped at her, Ryder wore a cruel smile and said, "She's not a cheater. I stopped fighting back because he's a dumb fuck, and I didn't want her hurt because I would've destroyed him. And, no, she didn't feel sorry for me. She felt like shit for watching me take a beating because Logan was a jealous, insecure fuck."

Kylie flinched at his harsh tone.

"He lost her on his own," he continued. "I was just lucky enough to find her after everything."

Tercero shoved Ryder forward, muttering things to him as his body seemed to shake.

Archer shook his head. "Do you really not know anything about them, or what happened after they broke up? Fuck, even the teachers still gossip about it."

Kylie stared at Ryder. He looked ready to go over and pummel Logan, but Tercero was holding his shoulder. She glanced at Logan and Janie. Logan wasn't smiling as much, but he was still looking at Janie in a way he hadn't looked at her.

Monica scooted closer and whispered, "He means did you not know she was raped after they broke up?"

"Raped?" Kylie asked, disbelief coating her voice.

"Damn, clueless as fuck." Archer walked to Ryder's other side.

Tonia sighed. "They don't talk about it with us, but almost everyone in town knows, so I'll tell you what we know. After Logan graduated—and the breakup—Janie was struggling. She and Ryder weren't together yet. And, well, she got in trouble at school one day, and when she left after-school detention, two boys grabbed her." Tonia gestured to Ryder. "That's why he's so protective all the time. So is Logan—he blames himself. All our guys felt bad for it happening right under their noses. We weren't close with her then, but I know it messed her up."

"Of course it did," Monica said, almost protectively.

Kylie whipped her head around to Ryder. He was glaring at Logan, and Logan was cupping Janie's cheeks as he spoke to her.

"What?" Janie yelled.

They all looked up to see Janie push Logan's hands off her cheeks and slap him across the face. It wasn't a light slap either, it was a full-on bitch slap.

How dare she hit him!

Logan's head turned to the side, and he kept his face turned as Janie began to verbally attack him.

"Logan," her next word was whispered in a hissing voice so that no one else could hear, then with her initial angry voice, she yelled, "Grimm."

"Ooh, full name," said Archer.

"What's his full name?" Kylie asked, not sure what to do. She felt nothing. She felt empty.

"I think only Janie and his family knows," Monica answered. "It's a Grimm thing. They're . . . secretive."

Kylie frowned, noticing the others nodding. "Is Trevor the same?"

"Why do you care about Trevor?" Ryder asked, peering over his shoulder.

Kylie swallowed, darting her eyes away from his fierce gaze.

"I don't care," she whispered.

Savaş snorted. "Do you think we're idiots?"

She looked at all of them. "I just don't care about Trevor."

"Then why do people think he's into you?" Monica asked. "You know that's why people were talking about you today, right? Everyone's talking about how lovesick you looked when he walked you to class. They think you're fucking both Grimms."

Ryder turned, facing Kylie. "You pretended to like Trevor to get closer to Logan."

Archer laughed. "I'm pretty sure Logan's looking to smash."

Tercero shook his head at Archer. "Have some manners."

Ryder kept watching her, and a dangerous smirk formed on his lips. "Do you love him?"

"Of course not." She crossed her arms, wondering all the while why Ryder and Logan sounded so much alike. "I didn't use Trevor to get close to him. I only met him at their apartment. But that's not why we're dating."

"Listen, honey," he said—again, sounding an awful lot like Logan. "I'll give you some advice. Although, I doubt you'll be smart enough to use it."

"Excuse me?" She put her hands on her hips.

"I'm going to give you advice," Ryder said, not at all fazed by her anger. "Whether you use it or not matters little to me. But because I love my girlfriend, and she has a ridiculous attachment to that fucker, I'm going to be nice and help him out."

"Babe, do you hear that?" Savaş nudged Monica. "Ryder's going to be nice."

"Shut up," Monica said, slapping her huge boyfriend's hands from her waist. "I want to look at Logan."

Tonia and Elise giggled while Savaş glared at her.

Monica was practically drooling. "He's like the sexiest thing to ever walk the Earth."

"Monica," said Ryder, glaring at the girl who was swooning over another man in front of her own boyfriend. "Will you shut the f—"

"Oh, shut it, Ryder," she said, moving away from Savaş. "We all know God made you the ultimate eye-candy—I just want to look at one of the runners-up."

"You're cut off from any dick tonight," Savaş said, walking away.

"Wait!" Monica ran after him. "Baby, don't be mad."

Ryder shook his head before focusing on Kylie. "I don't know what game you two are playing. Obviously, Janie is hearing Logan's side, and by the way she's reacting, I'm going to say you and Logan have done something really stupid."

"Uh." She was silenced when he shook his head, glaring a bit as he did so.

"Don't try to make up some lie to cover your tracks—I see them, and you're not Logan's real girlfriend." Ryder's expression darkened. "Now, whatever dumb idea you have concocted together, drop it. It won't work, and everyone will get hurt. And if this is some dumb plan for him to get Janie back, I'll kill him—and you for helping him."

Now she understood his line of thought, and it was complete bullshit. "What I do has nothing to do with your girlfriend. There's no game."

Ryder snorted. "Yeah, and Logan looked at you and completely got over Janie."

Tercero covered his eyes, sighing. "Brother, some sensitivity might be useful."

Kylie's eyes welled up with tears, and she hated it. She wasn't sad—she was mad.

Ryder narrowed his eyes at Kylie. "Just tell Logan you want him and get over whatever it is that made you come up with your little plan. Maybe he'll see a reason to let go and start something new."

Kylie's anger collapsed, and she let her sorrow show. "He doesn't want me the way I want him. He's just helping me out because I have my own problems. It has nothing to do with her."

"Logan's into you," Tercero said, lowering his hand.

Archer spoke up next, "Our big brother just likes to find reasons to kill Logan. You'd be a distant memory for

Logan if he didn't like you. Definitely not some girl he's letting rumor spread that he picked to replace Janie."

Ouch.

She rubbed under her eyes. She wanted to tell them Logan wasn't doing any of this to get Janie—that they were all assholes, but she was more consumed by the fact they were trying to help, even if they were mean. "Why do you care about me?"

Ryder frowned. "I don't care about you."

Archer snickered, which only made the importance she'd felt rising with them vanish. They were just mean, and they wanted to praise Janie instead of accepting she was the one Logan was with.

Tercero settled his black eyes on her. "Janie and Logan are friends—she wants Logan to be happy. We care about seeing her happy for him."

"It's not her business." Kylie dropped her gaze when Ryder gave her a piss-inducing glare.

"Yes, it is," Tercero said, grabbing his girlfriend's hand. "Take Ryder's advice and maybe he'll stop looking at her like he is. And you have a lot to learn about him—he's not who you think he is."

"Good luck, Red," Archer muttered, grabbing his girlfriend's hand too.

They walked away, leaving Kylie with Ryder. He just kept watching her before holding out his hand behind him.

Kylie wondered what he was doing until Janie appeared and grabbed his hand.

"Sorry. We had to talk about something private," Janie said softly. Her eyes were a little red, like she'd been about to cry.

There shouldn't be anything private between them.

Janie smiled sadly at her. "He's a good guy. He just needs to remember that."

Kylie wasn't ready to see the way Logan was looking at his ex, because his ex wasn't looking at him like an ex-girlfriend with a boyfriend of her own should.

Ryder wrapped an arm around Janie's shoulders. "Come on, baby girl. I'll buy you a shake and fries, and you can show me if you're wearing panties or not."

Janie chuckled, looking away from Logan. "Bye, Kylie."

Good riddance. Kylie was torn between rage and sorrow. She could only nod.

"And don't hurt him"—Janie gave her a big smile—"or I'll kill you."

Ryder chuckled and started dragging her away to where the group waited.

Kylie stared after them, watching Ryder kiss her head. Nothing was sweet about it now.

Janie suddenly jerked out of Ryder's hold and shouted, "Don't think I haven't noticed you spying over there."

Everyone looked at where Janie was yelling. Gloria.

"Stay away from Logan," Janie went on.

Gloria looked frightened as Ryder kept a hold on Janie, keeping her from walking over.

"Yeah, I know your skanky ass is still chasing him," Janie hollered. "Go learn how to give a proper blow job, then maybe you'll find some poor fool who wants you. Stupid cunt."

"Come on, babe," Ryder told her, pulling her back to him.

Janie grabbed a towel off the ground and chucked it. It landed nowhere near Gloria, but it was obvious Janie had a lot of hate for Gloria. Kylie felt the same rage when she saw the pretty woman walking away, but she didn't like Janie acting like she had any say in Logan's life.

"Kylie, you better kick this bitch's ass if she tries anything. Or I'm fucking both you hoes up!"

Ryder pulled her to the door as the others laughed.

A low chuckle behind Kylie made her jump.

Logan gave her a soft smile. "She's really not that mean."

Kylie took a deep breath. "But she's the girl you said you never had."

Logan sighed, running his hand through his sweaty hair. "Yeah . . . She told me what happened at school," he said, smoothly changing the subject. "Are you okay?"

"Yeah," she said. "Janie started the fight before anything more could happen."

"But they still hurt you." He moved closer as he trailed his eyes over her. "She told me what they were saying all day, and what those girls said about you."

Kylie looked down, not wanting him to see how pathetic she had been.

"I know none of that's true, if you're worried."

"I'm not," she snapped. None of that crap would be true.

"I should have thought about how people would react." He got even closer. "Girls did the same shit with Janie when we got together. And again when she took up with Ryder."

"I really don't want to talk about your ex, Logan." She gave him a dark stare, hoping he would back off. "It was bad enough hearing all this from her fan club."

Something sparked in his eye when she looked up at him. Whatever it was, he seemed pleased and nodded. "Right. Well, we have other stuff to talk about anyway. Those girls aren't going to let this go." He held out his hand. "Come on, Hood. We have shit to do."

"You're not even going to apologize for lying?"

He lowered his hand. "Sorry I lied. I had a girlfriend when I was seventeen. We were together until just before my graduation." He shrugged. "I don't like to talk about her with people I don't know, and we don't know each other. I figured you knew about us since you go to the same school."

"I only started there last year." Kylie sighed, drifting her eyes over him as she thought over everything that had happened today. She feared retaliation from Maura. She felt pathetic because she felt inferior to a girl who had once held Logan's heart in the palm of her hand, and she was sad because he probably still loved that girl too much to ever consider having more with her.

"Baby," Logan whispered, sliding his hand into hers.

Kylie got lost in his eyes as his other hand came up to hold her cheek.

"I'll do everything I can to keep you safe, okay?"

She didn't say anything and closed her eyes when his lips touched her forehead.

"And I'm sorry I sort of lied about not having anyone before. It's all in the past."

"It's fine, Logan. It's not a big deal." It was a huge deal. She leaned away from his lips to stare up at him. She had to build up her walls again. "I was just embarrassed, I guess. Meeting the ex when I'm supposedly dating you is a little shocking, you know? And it's not like you really had to tell me about your past. I'm not your girlfriend."

"Right. Come on, Hood," he muttered, grabbing her hand. "I need to change, and you're not standing out here for all these guys to stare at." He dragged her away, down the halls she was growing familiar with.

A tiny smile made its way onto her lips because he was holding her hand in front of people. It was a small thing, but after her day, having him just acknowledge her at all was nice. He wasn't interested in talking about Janie, so that had to be a good sign.

14
PLAYING

It should be a crime to look that good.

Kylie shook her head and looked away from Logan as he pulled a shirt on.

"Did you get a chance to have lunch, Hood?"

She returned her attention to him. "I kinda didn't go to the lunchroom today."

"Why?" He started gathering his things.

"Because everyone was laughing at me."

He glanced up, his expression unreadable as he studied her face. "Because of me? Or because Trevor was all over you this morning?"

Her mouth fell open. "All over me?"

"Janie told me what everyone was doing and saying at school." He went back to packing some of his things. "And she mentioned he walked you to class, which I guess started everything. Why was he walking you?"

"Can I not get walked to class?" Her heart pounded away. Why was he asking her about Trevor and caring so much about what Janie had said?

"You can." He sighed, not giving her a single glance. "Let's go eat, and then we'll get you a phone."

"Are you mad at me?" She didn't know why she blurted out that question, but she felt like he was mad she'd found out about his lie.

"Mad at you?" He snatched up his bag, heading toward her.

"Yeah." She watched him, her hands shaking because he probably wasn't going to like what she was about to say. "Because I found out about Janie. And because I came here with her? I didn't know they were bringing me here, and I didn't know she was your ex until we were almost here."

Logan exhaled as he sat beside her. "I'm not mad you came here with her. I've actually been thinking about how to introduce you to her, but I haven't talked to her for a few weeks."

Her chest ached, but she didn't know what she was really feeling. It was true, then—he and Janie were still close. That could either mean he intended on lying all this time, or he hadn't planned on keeping her around long enough for her to find out.

He took her hand. "I'm sorry you had a bad day. I know exactly what you went through, and if there was something I could've done to protect you from those fuckers, I would have. Which is why I'm glad she stepped in. She's going to be fine but she got hurt, and that bothers me because I hate seeing her hurt. But I'm glad you had someone there."

Everything he said was hard to swallow. A part of her had been so happy to have someone helping her, but she wasn't thrilled about it being Janie anymore. She didn't give a crap that Janie was dumb enough to fight and get hurt.

Kylie found herself getting angrier. "They were pretty brutal with those girls," she told him, curious about his reaction to his ex-girlfriend beating someone.

He leaned away. "You're worried about them fighting the girls who would've beaten you up?"

"They wouldn't have hit me."

"Hood, your stepsister beats you—of course they would've hit you."

"No, they wouldn't have." She pressed her lips together as he turned his head away.

His tone became harsher. "What did you want to happen then? Do you want to get beat up in private and then made fun of with no one stepping in? Does verbal abuse not bother you? I don't say this to be mean given what you've been through, but, for me at least, words are a lot more painful than any punch. For Janie, seeing you get talked to like that is horrible."

Fire burned in her lungs. "Verbal abuse is wrong, and I don't want to get beat up anywhere. I'm just saying Janie punched Maura just for calling her a cheater, and because she bragged about Ryder cheating too. That's no reason to punch her—or anyone."

He let out a dark laugh as he focused on the floor instead of her. "You think she's okay with being called a cheater? Or being told her boyfriend is cheating? You expect her to just take that in silence?"

"This was about me, not her." Kylie didn't know what she was saying anymore, but she couldn't stop.

Logan let go of her hand. "How do you figure her being called a cheater is about you?"

She glared at him, hating that she already missed his touch. "Those girls surrounded me. I'm not mad someone helped me—I'm just saying beating up a group of girls for talking mean is wrong. They ripped their clothes off and Janie kicked Maura in the vagina. That's too much. I'm probably in trouble now."

"So being verbally attacked is fine? Having girls say you were pregnant with your dad's baby is fine?" He let out a sarcastic laugh as her heart thundered in her chest. "Do you know Janie and Melody used to be best friends until Melody turned every bitch in school on her? All because Janie became my girlfriend." He shook his head like he couldn't understand how wrong Janie's behavior was. "You have no idea what they put her through. Maybe she wanted to stop that from happening to someone else. Damn, why are you focusing on her fighting and not that your sister almost stabbed her?"

"I yelled out when I saw it," she retorted, frustrated that he was so protective of Janie and angry with her for being logical. "Why don't you care about me? You're only worried about Janie getting hurt."

"I am not." He stood and glared down at her. "Fuck, Kylie. I don't even know why we're fighting about this. Would you rather she'd walked away when she saw them bullying you?"

Honestly, she wished Janie hadn't butted in, because now Logan was only concerned about his ex. It was almost like if Janie hadn't interfered, she never would've been the ex-girlfriend Logan was still in love with.

He grabbed his bag. "Would you be like this if another girl had taken up for you?"

"Another girl wouldn't have taken up for me."

"Then what's your fucking problem with the one who did?" He wasn't looking at her like a girl he cared about now. It was almost disgust. "Would it have been fine if it was Trevor who stopped them?"

The problem is she's your ex! Her eyes were stinging, but she refused to cry or yell out her jealous thoughts. "I doubt he would beat up a group of girls just for talking crap. You're missing the point. They would've eventually left me alone, but now all this has happened."

"No, the point is you're mad I had a girlfriend before I ever knew you," he said bluntly. "They were harassing you, and she protected you. Trevor used you, and you're fine with his help but not hers. And lay off her. They shouldn't have said shit to her."

"She shouldn't have used her fists." She breathed heavily. "And it's not that you had a girlfriend—it's that you lied."

He searched her face for what felt like a long time before finally talking, his tone gentle but still laced with annoyance. "I'm sorry I lied. But what do you want? You want me to lie to you and tell you I never dated her, never loved her?"

The air left her lungs, but by some miracle, she managed to look him dead in the eyes. How could he say that to her?

"I get omitting I'd had a girlfriend was a shitty thing to do," he said like he was trying to explain something to a child, "but I don't like talking about losing her. I just don't understand why any of this even matters to you. You said it yourself—we're not really together."

If it was possible to get stabbed in the heart with words, she'd be dead.

"We both know what this is," he muttered, "and it's not like this changes anything. I'm still gonna help you, and it's not like I'm going to treat you like you're just an extra fuck."

"Aren't I?" she asked before she could stop herself.

He ran his hand through his hair. "I've told you what you are. I don't know why you're so upset with me over this." He was staring at her like she was the one in the wrong—like she was the liar.

She felt so pathetic, and she absolutely hated it.

"Let's just go." Logan shook his head like he couldn't believe he was still there with her. "I'm not in the mood to fight about this. Janie is my ex, but she's my best friend too."

"You said girls are never just friends."

He shrugged a shoulder. "She's not just a girl to me— never has been. She's her own category."

"That's nice." *What an asshole*, she thought, standing too. "I just don't understand why you're playing me."

"How am I playing you?" He chuckled, and it wasn't that sweet sound that sent shivers down her body. It was like burning knives being stuck into her skin "I told you I cared about what happens to you, and that's the truth. You want to be with Trevor, Hood. Is that a lie?"

Her eyes went wide. There was no way she could tell him the truth—any of it. He'd walk away.

"Whatever." He held out his hand for her to take. "Let's go. I'm starving, and you need to eat."

They walked hand in hand down the hall, but she had never felt more alone.

Logan held the door open for her, and he surprised her by putting his arm over her shoulder. "Hey, I'm sorry for lying."

She sighed, melting against him. "It's okay."

He pressed a kiss to the top of her head. "You look really pretty with your hood down. I'm proud of you."

How could he do that? How could he make her forget he was breaking her heart? Maybe there was hope, and he'd get over this thing with Janie and leave her in the past like real people did. She wouldn't be able to bear it if she was only a tool for Logan to get Janie back, but damn, it made sense. He was telling her she could use him for Trevor. *Oh, God . . .*

"Logan, do you want her back?"

"Don't do that—don't pick a fight with me over her." His body was tense as he led her past vehicles. "Our breakup sucked. I loved her. I wanted a future with her—we were planning our future together. But shit got fucked up, and she's with Ryder now."

"What if he breaks up with her?" She peeked up at him. "What if she comes running to you—will you take her back? I don't see how you could want her back after she left you for him anyway, but would you?"

"Just stop." He dragged a hand down his face, frustrated. "The only people who know what went on with her, Ryder, and me are the three of us, so don't talk about her like you know anything. She's a part of my life no matter who comes along for me. That's not going to change, and that's my choice."

Well, this wasn't working out. "Fine, I won't ask about her."

"Thanks." He let out a deep breath. "What did you think of the Godsons? Have you met them before today?"

The change of subject was good. She could even see if he cared about her around other guys. "They were moved into my class last week, but today's the first time I've ever spoken to them. I always thought they were interesting, but I think I prefer the distance I had before."

He laughed, tightening his hold on her. "Distance is probably best when it comes to them."

"Do you know them very well?"

His head bobbed. "My family is involved with theirs for . . . work. Same thing with Janie's family."

She didn't want to hear about Janie's family. "So do you and Ryder fight all the time?"

"Not all the time." He smirked. "Worried about me?"

She shook her head. "You're the professional."

"Yeah, but that's a drawback in real fights. He's the only guy I know who can beat my ass." He waved toward the gym. "Mark wants me to befriend him so he'll come here to train. He did when we trained Janie after some shit happened, but he hasn't been back."

She saw the pain and guilt he was trying to hide. "I heard she said she was attacked or something."

"Raped," he said as he came to a stop. "She was raped."

Kylie swallowed as she watched his eyes darken. "I'm sorry. That must've been awful for you."

He frowned as he stepped up next to a black motorcycle. "Let's get you on."

"Where's your car?" She stared wide-eyed at the sexy but scary machine he was pulling a helmet from.

"At my apartment. I prefer my bike. Do you like it?"

She did, but she never thought she'd be riding one. "It's nice."

He grinned, holding up the helmet. "You need to wear this. I'll drive safe, but you still need to wear it."

"What about you?" she asked as he moved closer.

"I'll have to do without until I get you your own."

Her own? Kylie's cheeks hurt from smiling.

He smirked, pushing her hair away from her face. "Blushing, Hood?"

"It's just hot out here." She tried to control her expression as he leaned forward.

"It's seventy degrees." He gave her a quick kiss. It felt like fire, and she wanted to burn in an inferno instead of just the quick spark of a match.

"No more fighting today," he murmured, cupping her cheek. "We'll focus on you from now on, okay? We need to figure out how to get you through the rest of the year, and come up with a plan to get you healthy and in shape."

She knew she had a dumb dreamy smile on her face, but instead of saying something sexy, she teased him. "Are you calling me fat?"

Logan chuckled as he slid his hands down to her waist. "I was talking about your stamina. You don't look like you can keep up with me yet."

"Keep up with you?" She was surprised she'd managed to keep her voice steady. His hands were so firm. Strong. And they were tenderly sliding along her hips.

"In bed, Hood." He winked, swinging something around her back. "You're not ready for me yet, but I'll get you there. Carrying my backpack is your first workout."

"That's not a workout." She hoisted it onto her shoulders as she tried to hide her excitement over him still thinking about her in bed.

He watched her for a moment. "Is it too heavy for you? It doesn't hurt, does it?"

"No." She grinned as he lifted the helmet over her head. "I'm strong."

Those brown eyes paralyzed her. "I know you are. Never forget it's okay to be fragile though. Everyone can use someone to lean on from time to time. Lean on me, baby."

"Look at you, trying to be all sweet now."

He swung a leg over his bike and pulled it into position as he started it. "I don't have to try. If I want to be sweet—I'll be sweet. And for you, I want to be sweet . Now get on."

Kylie focused on adjusting the straps on both the helmet and backpack before climbing on behind him.

"Hang on, okay?" He shivered a bit, making her grin as her hands settled against his stomach.

"Just don't go too fast," she said, squeezing her legs.

He patted her hands, laughing quietly. "Just relax and enjoy the ride."

She did. After the initial takeoff and the many turns it took for them to reach the highway, she found herself smiling and resting her body against his. She especially enjoyed the moment when he grabbed one of her hands from his stomach to hold in his as he rested them on his thigh. She'd passed Ryder and his brothers as they rode their motorcycles on her way to school once, and Ryder was doing that with Janie. It had been on her bucket list ever since. Now Logan was checking off everything she'd always wanted.

The longer they drove, the more she thought over her situation with Logan. Maybe it was unfair to hold his lie against him—he just hadn't wanted to reveal that his first love broke his heart. After all, he believed she was only using him for protection and to get Trevor. It was such a stupid plan. Yeah, it had been his idea, but she was the one who kept feeding the lie because she didn't want to get hurt.

There were only two options: go along with the plan and eventually see him leave her heartbroken while he went off with another girl, or she could tell him the truth about her feelings for him.

After all, she was a clean slate for him. She just had to show him she was nothing like Janie, and how that was a good thing.

"Chinese sound good?"

Kylie jumped a little, getting a squeeze before he lifted her hand back to his stomach.

"Yeah," she said, her voice muffled under the helmet.

Logan took the exit they needed, and she realized he had taken them to an outlet mall in the town over.

"I normally don't eat out, but I'm starving," he said, parking and cutting the engine. "Here." He held out his hand for her so she could steady herself as she climbed off.

Her legs felt fuzzy and weak.

Logan grinned as he walked closer to her. "Did you like it?"

She nodded after he helped pull the helmet off, and she smiled like an idiot when he fixed her hair, then threw his arm over her shoulder and walked them to the entrance.

"Good. I like having you wrapped around me. Gets me excited for the day I get to be in you."

"Logan." She laughed.

"Baby, I know you like feeling me up. And don't deny you can't wait for us to fuck."

That hurt a bit to hear, but he was thinking about being with her, so she loved it. "You're so full of yourself."

"Don't worry, you'll be full of me too." He chuckled and moved out of her range when she swung at him. "Easy," he said, grabbing her hand. "You're just too much fun to rile up."

She rolled her eyes at his smiling face as they entered the restaurant. An old woman greeted them before leading them to a table in the corner.

"This reminds me of when I was little," she said, grinning at the paper menus that showed the different Chinese years. "My mom used to take me to a restaurant like this, and I would get the tea and Egg Drop Soup. I felt fancy because my tea was hot. I would pretend to be a princess."

Logan watched her looking at the different animals as he ordered them waters and a tea. "You felt fancy?"

"Yes." She stuck her tongue out. "I had a little tea set at home, but no one would play with me."

Logan frowned, but she ignored it and continued her story.

"Daddy and my mom were always working. They were both doctors, so it was rare to see them, but I remember this. I think she was always visiting a friend. I can't remember all the details—but we would go quite a bit, and I would sit by myself while my mom sat at another table with whoever she was seeing. The waiters were always nice to me." She frowned, wondering why she never thought about how strange her memories of her mom were.

"She wouldn't even eat with you?" Logan reached over to hold her fingers when she began tapping them.

"Yeah, I guess that's a little weird. I was just realizing that."

Logan squeezed her fingers. "Is there anything else you remember?"

"Not really. Maybe there was more, but I was only seven when she died. Sometimes I think I dream of her, but I usually forget it after waking up. I'm glad I forget because sometimes I dream of Lorelei in my mom's place, and she's nothing like my mom. She married my dad right after my mom died."

He nodded and looked over the menu. "My mom died when I was eighteen. Cervical cancer. My dad went to prison when I was sixteen."

"Oh." She wanted to know what his dad was in prison for, but she didn't ask. "I'm sorry you had to go through all that."

"Thanks, Hood." He squeezed her hand again. "I wish you had the chance to know your mom more before she died. And your dad."

Their waiter came to take their order, and they went quiet after he left.

Logan looked up, frowning. "Listen, I know I said we'd focus on you, but I want to talk about one thing Janie said."

She bristled at the name but tried to keep calm. "I didn't really talk to her—what did she say that you want to talk about?"

"Well, it was what Maura did." He eyed her. "The knife she pulled on her."

"Oh." She shrugged, thankful this wasn't really about Janie. "She's never pulled one on anyone before. That I know of, at least."

"You're sure?"

"Well, yeah. She's never done anything like that to me. She normally uses bats, but she'll hit me with anything as long as it will hurt."

Logan's nostrils flared and his hands began to shake. "She hits you with a bat?"

"Yeah," she said, her hand shaking in his. "Lorelei stopped her the one time she punched me, but she just went back to hitting me with a bat. I think she just didn't want Maura hurting herself." Her head throbbed, but she smiled at his enraged glare. "It's kind of hard to fight back against a bat."

"You're not going back there." It was such an abrupt, no-nonsense statement.

Kylie sighed and looked away. "I have to."

"She'll kill you, Kylie. I'm not going to let some crazy bitch beat the shit out of you until you're not able to wake up. What the fuck is wrong with her?"

"She won't kill me." Kylie's heart pounded. "Janie just pushed her too far."

He scoffed. "Yeah, she told me Maura is obsessed with Ryder."

"Obsessed is a bit of a strong word. Everyone stares at him."

He leaned back in his seat. "Including you?"

"No." That was a lie. A big fat lie.

"Yeah right." He sighed, tapping the table.

"I don't." God, she couldn't tell him Ryder had been her favorite fantasy after Trevor. He'd leave for sure. "I think he's a complete jerk. And as far as Maura goes, I think she just wanted to humiliate me today. I found out she likes Trevor." That wasn't true. She'd always known Maura liked Trevor. It was how she first noticed him. The fact Trevor seemed oblivious to Maura had been one of his best traits. "I think it just made her mad that I'm dating you and he talked to me. If I have any attention, she flips out." She rubbed her throbbing head.

"Do you have a headache?" He reached for his backpack. "I have pain meds. Just over-the-counter stuff."

She sighed, holding out her hand for the pills. "Thanks. It must be allergies or something. I keep getting them lately."

He felt her forehead. "You don't feel like you have a fever. We can talk to Evander if they keep bothering you."

"I'll be fine." She swallowed the pills, closing her eyes. "I think they just come and go with the seasons."

"All right." He sighed, taking her hand. "But we can go to the hospital if you need. You never know, maybe she hit your head too hard and something is wrong. Plus, it might help if you talked to the police."

She snapped her eyes open. "My head is fine, and I don't want the police involved. I'll be fine with Maura. I think she just wants me to go back to being a nobody. Anyway, she won't hurt me with you around."

"She won't," he said fiercely. "And you're not hiding anymore."

"I know. I'm just saying I think it was to bully me, scare me. I really don't think she'll hurt me anymore."

Their waiter appeared with their order, and after asking if they needed anything else, he left them alone again.

They ate in silence, but then he looked up and said, "You're getting more than a phone if you're going home. But I still think we should go to the police—it won't be too hard to at least get you out of the house. I can make a few calls."

"They won't believe me, Logan," she said, slightly panicked. "They never have."

He sighed, eating again. "Then I'll get you protection. I'm not letting you take the chance of being defenseless."

Kylie stared at him, her mouth hanging open before she spoke. "Logan, I can't have a weapon."

"We'll get you self-defense stuff." He grabbed her hand again. "Janie said the girl is completely mental, and I'm not going to ignore her opinion. We'll get you simple stuff you can carry all the time, but you're also going to learn how to fight."

"Logan, I can't fight."

"You can learn to protect yourself. I'm sure if she didn't use a bat on you, you could take her." He glanced off to the side. "I was going to ask how you'd feel about Janie helping me train you."

Her smile dropped. "No."

His gaze softened. "She's not going to hurt you, Hood. She's just going to help because she's trained to do all sorts of combat."

She'd seen Janie fight before, and she always looked crazy—not like a fighter. "Why would she be trained in combat?"

He sighed, balling his fist. "After she was raped, we decided to train her. That's all she did every day for a year with us. She doesn't practice much now, but she knows different styles and weapons."

"I get training her after whatever she went through," she said, frowning, "but I really don't see how me getting beat up by her would help. I've had enough of a mean girl beating me up."

He rubbed her hand. "Hey, she's not going to beat you up. I'd like it if you had someone at school looking out for you, and she would be a great person to have on your side. If you start training with her, it'll be easier for you to be around them."

"I don't want to be around her. Or any of them," she added, hoping she didn't come off jealous. "They're bad kids."

"They're not bad." He chuckled, squeezing her hand. "Just think about it, okay? It'll make me feel better."

She huffed. He wasn't going to let this go. "How do you know she even wants to do this? She threatened to kill me."

"When?" He looked at her like she was insane.

"See!" She darted her eyes between his. "You don't even believe me. She threatened that if I hurt you, she'd kill me."

He laughed instead of getting angry. "Baby, she's my best friend. That's just what people say sometimes. Haven't you heard a best friend say that?"

"I've never had one," she spat bitterly. "And I've only seen that in movies. I doubt you said that to Ryder and his brothers."

"I did," he said, straight-faced.

"You threatened to kill them if they hurt her?" She couldn't believe he'd threaten to kill anyone for Janie.

"Yes." He laughed. "It's what you say to make sure they don't hurt your friend. I don't mean it. And Ryder won't hurt her anyway."

She sighed as she played with her hair. "It's so hard to picture you with her—even like friends. I won't be friends with her. She's just too—I don't know."

Logan's eyes seemed to dim. "I don't expect you to end up being close. It's just that she can train you and back you up when I can't be there. It would be different if you fought back, but you don't."

He looked stressed. "I don't know any other girl at your school who would help you."

"I don't need help," she said harshly, hoping he'd drop it.

He sighed, closing his eyes for a second. "I didn't mean it like that. Why can't you see I just want you safe? Your sister has been beating you, your stepmom allows it, and Kevin hasn't even picked up on what's going on. You are refusing to get proper help, and I can't be there all the time. I swear she has no intention of hurting you. She acts tough, but she's honestly the sweetest girl I know."

God, he was just making it worse and worse.

He doesn't know you really like him, idiot.

The sudden thought surprised her, and she could barely keep her face relaxed as he watched her.

"Don't be afraid," Logan said. "I'd worry if the girls at the gym trained with you, but not her. She'd be all about letting you build on your strengths and patient with you in a way I'm not even sure I could be. Plus, I wouldn't mind watching you two go at it." He winked at her baffled look. "Catfight, baby."

"You perverted—"

Logan laughed as the waiter smiled and gave him their check.

"Thanks," he said, pulling out his wallet. "What?" He still grinned at her glare. "I'm a guy, Hood. Two hot girls fighting, grabbing each other and no doubt saying dirty words. Someone's tit is popping out, and I'm hoping it's yours."

Kylie swatted his hand away when he offered it to her to pull her out. "Dammit, Logan. I'm—I'm telling Ryder. Yeah, I'll tell him you want his girlfriend's boob to pop out in a catfight."

He laughed louder. "Go ahead. He's a hornier bastard than I am."

"Yeah, well, I doubt he's over there wishing for his girlfriend to flash everyone." She looked away, realizing she was sort of saying Logan should consider her his girlfriend.

She prayed he wouldn't laugh at her, so it caught her off guard when he muttered, "I didn't think of that. Okay, I still want a catfight—lots of hair pulling, maybe kiss her or something. But I'll put a sports bra on you to keep your tits safe. Those girls are all mine."

"You're a pig."

He chuckled and pulled her to him, hugging her as he kissed her hair. "You like it."

"Whatever," she said, elbowing him one last time. Even though she was beyond annoyed he'd throw Janie into his little fantasy, she was completely giddy because he didn't laugh in her face about the girlfriend slip.

"How are the ribs?"

She leaned against him as they walked past different stores. "Fine. I hardly feel it when I walk now."

"Good. It looks like you're feeling a lot better. Oh, here, let's grab you a phone." He pulled her into a mobile phone store.

15
LIAR

The sports and outdoors shop Logan had taken her to was boring, so when he struck up a conversation with some salesman, Kylie took the chance to explore the new phone he'd bought for her.

She didn't know what apps she should get just yet, but she was too absorbed with the contacts Logan had already put in for her.

He had added himself, of course, but also Janie, Ryder, Evander, the gym, and some friend named Than Messor, who was a police officer they could trust if things got messy. He'd hinted this guy could look into her abuse, but she declined, and thankfully he dropped it.

Kylie grinned as she came across the contact he'd created for himself: *Logan Stolemypanties Grimm.*

"Hood," he called, not looking up from the counter. "Black or red?"

"What?"

Logan held up two keychains that resembled spades, with handles on the end to go between your fingers. "You hold it like this"—he closed his hand, leaving the pointed end of the heart sticking out—"and punch."

"I don't think I need that."

"You're getting one, so pick."

"Fine," she said, sighing when he grinned in triumph. "The black one."

"He's bringing your mace out," he said, still looking at the items laid out in front of him. "He said the triple action stuff has OC pepper and tear gas. I figured that's better."

Kylie smiled, watching him frown as he inspected a little expandable baton keychain.

"Logan," she said, watching him flick the baton out a few times.

He didn't look up. "*Hm?*"

"I'm not in love with Trevor." *Oh, God, what am I doing? Not being a liar...*

Logan stopped playing with the baton and slowly looked over at her as she wondered why she was even thinking like this. She'd had a plan, and now she was . . .

Her heart pounded in her chest. She could make something up. Anything.

She had nothing. All she could think about was Ryder telling her to come clean about her feelings. She didn't know how he knew she was lying to Logan, but he did. Would the truth be worse than letting this lie go on for however long she managed to pull it off—with Logan always thinking she was using him to get Trevor? But he was stuck on Janie. She felt lightheaded.

"Are you going to elaborate or just stand there?" He didn't look angry, but he also didn't look happy.

It hurt to breathe. She had to say something. It might be better to scare him off now rather than fall completely in love with him.

"Hood?"

"I thought I loved him," she blurted, pausing to see if he'd say anything. He didn't, so she kept going. "But I realized it was just a silly crush."

He didn't move. He didn't blink.

"I'm sorry I lied. I really don't know what I was thinking. I guess it was just that Lorelei and Maura were about to hit me again, and I blurted out you were protecting me, and all I could think was you'd keep me safe. I wanted to tell you the truth, but I was afraid. And I thought if I kept reminding you—kept reminding myself—that it was just to get Trevor, then I wouldn't be lying. But I hate saying anything about him to you. I feel terrible for using you both."

She swallowed, her eyes misting with tears. "The truth is, I don't have feelings for your cousin. I have feelings for you."

He stayed quiet, and she began to shake as fear took hold of her.

"I know you don't want a girlfriend, and that you don't want to hurt me, but I can't lie anymore. I like you. A lot."

She rubbed her face when a tear fell. "I know you only care about my safety, but I needed to tell you. Just don't think you have to stay with me. I get it if you want to cut me out."

Oh, she wanted to scream for him to stay, but she didn't. She kept going. "I get it if I've made this awkward, but I need you to know. I need to tell you what I want."

"And what do you want?"

She swallowed, startled at his sudden question. "I want us to really date."

He showed no reaction.

"I want this—whatever is happening between us—I want it to be real. No games. No tricks or lies. I don't care about your stupid categories—I want you."

Logan stayed quiet, then smirked. "I thought you weren't going to fall for me, Hood."

Now it was her turn to stay quiet.

"Didn't you say, 'I won't fall in love with you, Logan. I don't like you that way, Logan'?"

"I didn't say I'd fallen for you," she whispered, shaking because he had started walking the few steps it would take for him to stand in front of her. "And I'm telling you I like you now."

"Really," he said, grabbing her chin and tilting it up. "Well then"—he lowered his lips to brush across hers—"I guess I better up my game."

He kissed her before she could really comprehend what he'd said—what he meant. But she didn't care. She threw her arms around his neck as he held her close and kissed him back, loving that he always managed to show her his dominance with just a kiss.

He pulled back but only so he could kiss down her neck. "You know what this means, don't you, Hood?"

"We're really dating?" She sighed, gripping his shirt to keep him close.

Logan nodded, smiling against her neck as he pressed more kisses there. "And"—he kissed his way back up her neck—"we need to stop at the lingerie store. I'm buying sexy shit for you to wear so I can rip it off after every real date I take you on."

"You're a pervert." She was melting.

"A pervert you like. A lot."

"I can take it all back, Grimm." She really couldn't.

He shook his head and lowered his mouth to hers for a short kiss. "Not happening," he said, leaning back when the salesperson returned. "I already told you—you're mine."

16
CREEP TO FREAK

I'm such a creep.

Kylie couldn't stop that thought because the smile on her face wouldn't go away. She giggled to herself as she rolled onto her stomach, thankful that Logan hadn't come into his room yet. Of course, this probably made her seem even creepier because she sniffed the sheets on his bed. But she couldn't care all that much—she was happy.

And even though it was there in her mind that they weren't a full-on couple yet, she was floating. They were really dating. Sure, they might not be boyfriend and girlfriend yet—at least she didn't think they were. She didn't know if dating was just dates until they decided they wanted to be exclusive, or if dating meant they were already together. Maybe she should've asked. It was too late now, though. She didn't want to freak him out by asking him to label them further. God, this was complicated.

But he was worth it, and she was determined to make them official.

Her smile faltered as she thought about Janie. Well, not just Janie—all his girl-toys. Would he still see Janie? Would he carry on with other women until he decided to put her into the official girlfriend category?

I can't go crazy-girlfriend on him and make demands.

She wanted to. She wanted to tell him his Janie days were over, but that probably wouldn't go over well. Surely, he'd understand having a girl, especially an ex-girlfriend, while he was with her wasn't going to work.

"Ugh," she groaned, not wanting to go down this line of thinking. She wanted to focus on the fact Logan Grimm—the man-boy who had once said he didn't do love—was trying to start a relationship with her. He'd even announced that he was trying to win her love. That had to mean something. That had to mean he wanted to call her his girlfriend.

Kylie closed her eyes as she rolled onto her back. She hadn't slept much the night before, and their day and these incredible new feelings were all wearing on her. She needed to get some real sleep, but that was going to have to wait.

It was five o'clock, and they had just come back to his apartment. Logan wanted a little more time with her before taking her home, and he said he needed to shower. Things were about to get messy because of the fight between Janie and Maura. Kylie wasn't expecting Maura to let it go. Logan wanted to do everything possible to show he was keeping an eye on things and that they really were seeing each other.

"Yeah, I'll make it up tomorrow."

Kylie opened her eyes to see Logan entering his room with his phone to his ear. He hadn't looked at her yet. He was setting his stuff on a dresser.

"She's better," he said to the person on the phone. "Yeah. I talked to her about Janie—she's going to think about it. Ryder is going to start with me. Well, maybe, but he agreed to come by this week. I think he's just looking forward to fighting me without her getting mad at either of us."

Kylie frowned when she realized he must be talking to Mark about her training up at the gym. Logan had gotten a call from Janie when they were looking around the outlet, and he'd moved away to talk to his ex. He promised it was just because he didn't want her to feel bad when he told Janie she wasn't ready to start training with her, but it still annoyed her that he wouldn't talk in front of her.

"We won't let it get out of hand," he said, turning to smile at her as he dangled a lingerie bag in front of him. He walked up to her and kneeled on the edge of the bed after spreading her legs apart. "Just count it as sessions with you if I do fight him. He's a bigger challenge than the others anyway."

Logan placed a hand by her head and lowered his lips to brush against hers as he listened to Mark talk. "Okay," he said, sliding his cheek against hers, making her sigh and hope he would end his call.

Maybe she could make him. Kylie smiled, then lifted her hands to his sides, making him pause whatever he had been saying. At this point, she couldn't even remember what he was talking about. She was too busy slipping her fingers under his shirt, almost moaning because he felt that amazing. "Oh, I've missed this," she whispered, her voice airy as she turned to kiss his neck.

Logan tensed above her, but he tilted his head so she could kiss more of his neck. Mark was still talking away while Logan grunted replies. It was funny and kind of cute, but she was tired of it. She felt like she had tried to fight her craving for Chocolate Logan Kisses all day, and now she was ready to binge.

"Logan," she said, breathing his name on the side of his neck while continuing to slide her hands around his sides.

He pushed himself up onto his knees, his hand on her leg because she had been trying to wrap them around his waist. "Mark, I'll see you tomorrow." He didn't wait for a response and tossed his phone on his bed. "You're in trouble now, Hood."

She squeaked, smiling like a fool when he lifted her and tossed her to the middle of the bed. Kylie bit her lip when he didn't come to her right away, but she wasn't disappointed.

Logan stayed at the edge of the bed, smirking at her no doubt needy look, and started pulling his shirt over his head.

Crap yes!

She wanted to laugh at her thoughts, but she was too busy enjoying the show he was giving her. There was no way to stop her eyes from roaming all over him. Her body was on fire simply because every one of his beautiful muscles flexed from the tiniest of movements.

"Your body feeling okay?" He kept his eyes on hers as she forced herself to look away from the masterpiece that was Logan Grimm.

She nodded, breathing out a, "Yes."

He smirked and undid his pants. "Good."

"Logan," she whispered, all sorts of tingling spreading throughout her body. She wanted him to touch her everywhere. God, she wanted to touch him. Taste him.

"We're not having sex," he said, making her chuckle because he looked disappointed by his own decision. "I'm leaving my briefs on."

He laughed at her pout, then he finished pulling his pants off.

Magnificent. Just everything. Him, all of him. He was perfect.

His gorgeous face and dark eyes—his muscular thighs and calves. And his six-pack. Oh, his six-pack! Christ, she'd touched every inch of them already, and she still wanted more. She especially wanted to slide her hands down the dip on his waist that created the delicious V that disappeared under his boxer-briefs.

She couldn't decide what she wanted to touch first. Not when she let her eyes take in his inked arms, chest, and back. *Gimme.*

"Don't worry, baby." He kneeled on the bed again as he started removing her shoes. "I'm going to take care of you, okay?"

"Okay." Her breath was a little shaky as he slid his hands up her jean-covered legs, squeezing her thighs and hips before he moved to brace himself above her.

"Did you miss my touch?"

"Yes," she whispered, reaching up to hold him to her.

Logan grinned before kissing the corner of her mouth. "I've missed feeling you beneath me." His voice was low as he slid his mouth across her jaw to kiss her neck.

"You just touched me yesterday." She moaned as he sucked her neck. It amazed her how him touching her in one place could make her whole body come alive.

"That's too long," he whispered in her ear.

Kylie lifted her hands to grab his face, the slight stubble on his jaw tickling her palms. "Oh, good," she said, trying to pull his lips to hers. "I thought I was being needy."

He chuckled but gave her what she wanted, dipping his mouth down to hers.

"Mm," she moaned, moving her fingers to the back of his neck while she slid her other hand down his chest, over his abs and down to his . . .

"Fuck." He pulled her hand away from his waistband, linking their fingers before holding their hands above her head. He kissed her harder. "I won't stop if you do that."

Kylie wanted to beg for him to let her, but she wasn't ready. "I'm sorry."

Logan grinned as he shook his head. "Don't be sorry. I just want to do things right." He smirked as he carefully lifted her shirt to expose her breasts. "Well"—he lowered his lips to the edge of her bra and kissed her sensitive skin—"a little bit right."

Her lips pressed together, muting the whimper escaping her as he left a trail of kisses down her stomach until he reached the button on her jeans.

"Because I've never been the good guy," he murmured, snapping her button open. "But I'm trying to be better"—he kissed her stomach—"for you."

Kylie smiled at his mischievous grin.

He grabbed the sides of her jeans and started pushing them down. "But I'm still me, baby." He stuck one hand under the small of her back to lift her, then yanked the rest of her jeans off and tossed them on the floor.

"I like you the way you are." She arched her back as he started kissing, licking, and nipping her skin on his way back up.

"Well." He slid his hand up her thigh, tugging it so he could settle himself between her legs. "I am pretty fucking amazing, Hood."

"Don't ruin the moment with your big head," she said, laughing at his arrogant grin.

"But no girl enjoys a small head."

She frowned but then moaned when he lowered his hips to hers. He was already getting hard. He was the first guy to be with her like this, but he was big, and he was hitting a spot that made her cry out in ecstasy.

"Moment still ruined?" His husky voice sent shivers through her body.

"Nuh-uh," she whispered before pulling his lips to hers.

Logan took over from there, tasting her lips before rewarding her with a breath-stealing kiss. "I think it's time for my presents." He kissed her neck before pulling her shirt off.

She was a little marveled that he did it so quickly but was too busy squirming and moaning to comment.

"I want to unwrap my girls," he murmured, licking her cleavage.

Kylie could only nod, still lifting her hips to meet his slow movements.

Logan chuckled, his breath moistening her heated skin. "Oh, my beautiful Kylie." He sneakily slipped one hand under her when she arched her back because he moved away for just a second. They locked eyes, and Logan smiled as his expert fingers popped the hooks of her bra.

Kylie moaned, trying to keep her eyes open as he looked away, sliding his hand out from under her and around to cup her right breast.

"Oh, fuck, they're perfect," he whispered, giving a gentle squeeze before peeling her bra off completely.

She panted, struggling to keep her eyes open so she could watch him as he massaged her right breast.

"Please, Logan," she whimpered, watching him lower his mouth. Her whole body clenched up in anticipation. "Oh!" She clutched the back of his head the moment his hot tongue flicked her nipple. "*Mmmm*. Oh, dammit."

Now she couldn't even look. She wanted to, but she could only close her eyes and enjoy what he was doing to her.

His hands never stopped moving. His lips and tongue never stopped tasting, sucking–kissing. His hips. Her hips. Both of them, constantly moving, grinding, teasing the other.

She squeezed her eyes shut and tugged his soft hair. "Logan, I need you."

He swept his tongue over the top of her breasts, murmuring, "You have me, Hood."

She shook her head, whining. "I need . . . I don't know. Give it."

Logan chuckled, kissing and nibbling his way up to her lips. "What do you want me to give?"

Kylie moaned, lifting her hips to feel him. He was so much harder now. She wanted to touch him, wrap her hand around him. Stick him inside . . .

"We can't yet." He groaned the more she rubbed herself against him. "Oh, fuck." Logan leaned down and rolled so he was on his back and she was straddling him. Kylie blinked, opening her eyes, steadying herself by placing her palms on his chest.

"What are you doing?" She sighed, shaking when he brought his hands to her hips and rocked her.

"Get yourself off on me." He squeezed her hips and thrust his.

"Wha—"

He kept one hand on her waist while the other reached up to tease her breasts. "I want to fuck your brains out right now." His voice was just as rough as his hands were becoming. "But we can't. And I won't let your first time be a hard fuck." He cupped her cheeks, gentler this time. "If you stay under me, I'll rip your panties off." He chuckled when she probably showed she welcomed that idea. "Baby, don't make me do something you'll hate me for later."

"Okay." She sighed against his mouth.

"This is dry sex," he said, slowly pulling her hips back and forth. It felt . . .

"Fuck yes," she yelled.

He was rocking her again, but he groaned when she grinded against him. "I want to see you lose yourself." He thrust up, matching her movements perfectly. "I want you to use my dick to make yourself feel good."

She closed her eyes, digging her nails into his chest when he began massaging her breasts.

"He wants to be inside your sweet pussy, but he can't—
"

"Oh, God, stop talking." She bent over him more, rocking her body harder. Faster.

He shook his head. "I'm going to taste her. I'm going to worship her."

She whined, the heat becoming unbearable and necessary all at the same time.

"I'm going to bury myself inside you."

Faster. Harder.

"How's this feel, baby?"

"Good." The heat, the need took over all thoughts and actions.

"Oh, fuck, there you go." He grabbed her hips hard, rocking her against his hardness. He was smiling as she dug her nails into his skin. "Come for me, Hood."

"I am," she cried out, her entire body warming, shaking. Tingling. There were just too many sensations to describe the explosion of pleasure she was experiencing. Every part of her clenched up and jolted as waves of the most incredible feeling rolled through her.

Logan pulled her face to his, and Kylie sighed against his mouth as he slid one hand down the back of her panties, squeezing her butt cheek. His other hand gripped her hair, and he kissed her long and hard. "I'm never going to get tired of watching that," he whispered, rubbing his nose against her cheek. "You okay?"

She nodded, feeling a little sleepy.

"I'm gonna go shower then, okay?"

She nodded but realized he was still as hard as before. "Oh, what about you?"

Logan grinned as he sat up with her. One of his hands went straight for her breast as he kissed her cheek. "I was just going to take a cold shower." He kissed her neck while he played with her hair.

"Does that work?"

"Not really." He pecked her lips and started to lift her off. "But I'm not going to go jack off with you sitting out here. It's fine."

She watched him stare at her body as he began to move off the bed. He was fighting himself, she could tell. He wanted her as badly as she did him, but all he cared about was pleasing her.

"Logan," she said, biting her lip once he was standing. His body was constantly flexing, ready to attack, to ravage.

"Baby, I can't look at you much longer without taking your panties off and finishing what we started. Let me go shower."

She reached out, grabbing his hand before he could leave. "Let me shower with you."

"What?" His eyes went wide.

Kylie was sure his cock twitched, and she bit her lip as she crawled to the edge of the bed. "You made me ruin another pair of panties anyway," she whispered, standing right in front of him. "And you've seen all of me without even letting me touch you." She lifted her arms around his neck.

"Kylie." The warning was clear, but he grabbed her waist and pulled her against him.

"We're showering together." She kissed his chin, allowing this boldness to take control of her.

Logan groaned as she carefully palmed his hard-on.

She'd never wanted something as badly as she wanted him in her at that moment. "And you're going to come for me."

Logan chuckled before effortlessly lifting her up. He pulled her legs around his waist and carried her to his bathroom. "I've turned you into a freak."

He lowered her to her feet when he seemed to realize he'd need both hands to turn the shower on. Luckily, her hands and lips were free to do as she pleased.

Mm . . . Muscles.

Kylie leaned forward, pressing her lips to Logan's chest while she kept her hands glued to his sides. She pressed kiss after kiss to his chest while he leaned partially into the shower to adjust the spray. His free hand cradled the back of her head—she'd never felt more cared for.

She had no idea what she was doing. She was just doing what she wanted.

"It's a good thing we already have your shampoo and shit," Logan said.

Kylie pulled her lips away just as he placed his hands around her face.

He kissed her softly. "We still can't fuck, all right?"

She nodded, running her fingers along his back and shivering from the cool air.

"You have to help me with that. 'Cause once we get undressed, I'm going to want nothing more than to thrust my dick inside you."

Dear God, the tingle that surged between her legs was unbearable. "I'll try to help."

Logan chuckled. She couldn't believe she was standing there, hugging him with her bare breasts pressed against his body.

Logan's eyes flickered down to her chest, and he smirked. "Cold?"

She smacked his back, smiling, and kissed his chest again. "Shut up and warm me up."

"I love seeing you like this," he murmured against her mouth.

She smiled, moaning when one of his hands fell from her face to cup her left breast.

"So free—so comfortable with your body." He placed a kiss to her collarbone, his thumb teasing her nipple. "So beautiful."

She loved what he was saying, but if she thought about it much longer, she'd chicken out from what she wanted to do. "Logan," she whispered, moaning and throwing her head back as he started to lower himself to one knee, his mouth never leaving her skin. "I need your clothes off now."

He smiled, then lightly bit the inside of her left breast. "So needy."

"Logan." She opened her eyes and stared down at him. "Please."

"Don't beg me, baby," he said, sliding his hands up her legs to settle on her hips. "Just take. It's already yours."

She didn't know what to think about his statement. Her mind was clouded with lust. And the fact he had pushed his hands inside the back of her panties to squeeze her butt, and was now sliding them down, pushed all other thoughts out of her mind.

Logan kept his fingers in constant contact with her trembling body, occasionally squeezing where he seemed to not be able to help himself. She watched him, mesmerized by the look of awe and adoration on his face as he studied her.

"How bad do you want me in you?"

She snapped her eyes to his.

"In here." He gently spread her legs, and with one hand holding her waist, his other slid up between her legs.

She moaned, shaking and gripping his head as his fingers parted her lips, allowing his middle finger to draw a teasing circle around that sensitive bundle of nerves.

"*Hmm?*"

She nodded, whimpering because the ache was so beautifully torturous.

"I mean it when I say take what you want. But right now"—he pushed his middle finger inside, making her breath hitch as her body tensed up—"this is as far as I can go." He twisted and pumped his finger as he brought his mouth lower. "But if you let me, I can give you something that feels just as good, if not better. I did promise your kitty this last time."

"Wha—" she cried out as he flicked his tongue against her. "Oh, Logan."

He made a humming noise as he continued to lick and suck, and that only sent more shocks of ecstasy through her body and over her skin. At some point, he'd pushed her against the corner where the glass door of his shower met his wall. And when he lifted one of her legs over his shoulder, she shot her hands out to hold herself up, one against the glass and the other gripping a towel rack.

It was painful but lovely.

Kylie bucked her hips without having any control over her body or the sounds she was making. Logan was forced to abandon the attention he was giving her with his hand so he could keep her legs apart. She was nearly kicking him away while also attempting to bring herself closer to his talented mouth.

Luckily, Logan wasn't a pushover, and when she bucked and pushed, he held her tighter and kept her where he wanted her.

"Oh, shit," she said, panting. "Fuck me."

Logan let out a small chuckle. The vibrations from the sound almost made her explode.

Licking. Sucking. Nibbling.

Faster. Slower.

She didn't know what to do! She just wanted him to get her where he was taking her. She needed it like it would be her death if she didn't have it. "Oh, Logan. Yes! Stop. Keep going!" She moaned. "Oh, yes."

He growled, lifting her so he was practically serving her on a platter to himself.

Panting and writhing, she felt the tug more intensely than she had when he used his hand. She moaned, cried, begged for him to rip her apart. She needed him to break her.

And he did.

Screaming out his name, she shattered. Shaking and clenching, she fell apart. And she swore his lips were smiling as he kept giving her torturous flicks with his tongue.

"Stop." She bucked and kicked, hating and loving how amazing the pull that started from her abdomen was. It only got stronger. His kisses, nibbles, and licks were too much. "Oh, please, stop. I can't take it." She loved it though.

Logan smiled, rubbing his cheek against her thigh.

"I hate you." She didn't hate him at all. She didn't even know if it was possible to hate him.

He laughed and kissed her thigh before carefully removing her leg from his shoulder. "You don't hate me, Hood." He grinned up at her before dropping his lips to her hip.

"I do," she said, trying to pout but sighing because her skin burned and tingled still. "And this was supposed to be for you."

"This is for me." He kissed her stomach and looked up at her.

"But I wanted to please you."

Logan smirked and stood up, kissing her lips before taking a step back. "Then please me, baby."

She pried her fingers off the towel rack, swaying a bit on her shaky legs, and took a step toward him. He didn't say anything, didn't reach out to touch her when she lifted her fingers to his chest.

Another step closer, and she bit her lip, unsure of her actions as she looked up at him. His expression would have alarmed her if she wasn't so turned on. The room was filling with steam, the chill in the air long gone as they both took heavier breaths.

She was so scared but so comfortable with him at the same time. So keeping her eyes on his, she let her hands slide down his chest until they reached his waistband.

He hissed when her fingertips just barely slid inside, and when he broke eye contact to look down at her hands, she did too.

Her breath shook with his as she pulled the elastic band away. He was straining against his briefs, and when she pulled more, she watched him start to spring free.

"Fuck, Hood. You're killing me."

After clearing enough space, Kylie parted her lips, awed by his magnificence, and started to push his briefs down.

"Will you help me?" she whispered, tracing her finger around the tip. It was so smooth, so enticing.

"Help you with what?"

She looked up, smiling because of his pained voice when she slid her fingers around him. "If I do it wrong."

"What are you talking about, baby?" He reached up to cup her face, obviously wanting to kiss her, but fighting himself.

She wrapped her hand around him, not able to completely close her hand. *Wow.* "I want to use my mouth."

His eyes went wide and darted between hers. "You sure? You don't have to. You can just use your hand."

She shook her head, turning to press her lips against his palm. "I want to taste you too."

"Damn," he whispered and pulled her lips to his.

She mewled into his mouth as she pumped her hand, and her anticipation increased when he grew harder and bigger in her palm.

He still hadn't answered, and she was growing anxious.

"Logan," she whispered. "I want to try, but I don't want to do it bad."

Shaking his head, he pecked her lips. "You won't do bad. I'll love anything you do to me." He groaned, thrusting a little in her hand.

"Okay." She kissed his jaw, smiling when he groaned and tilted his head so she could reach his neck. "Just tell me though."

"I will, baby." His hand, which had been loving her breast, fell away and reached out to the glass. His other had slid from her face to her hair as she kissed down his stomach. "Oh, shit, this is the best already."

His words gave her confidence like they always did, and when he tugged her hair because she had made sure to slide her breasts against him as she got on her knees, she was ready.

They locked eyes, her hand slowly moving up and down before she ran her thumb along the rim. He squeezed his eyes shut then and exhaled sharply, telling her that was a sensitive spot and somewhere to focus on.

Licking her lips as she gazed at the drop of moisture on his tip, she leaned forward and licked it. Logan muttered out a curse and tightened his grip. His whole body was tight, flexing when she placed a kiss to the soft skin and swallowed his essence. It amazed her that she liked the bittersweet taste.

Again, she flicked her tongue out, twirling it around the head once before she decided to travel the full length of him. That's what girls in books did, and they must be right because he let out a satisfied growl.

She knew the wait was killing him. So, kissing and licking her way back to the tip, she gripped his shaft with one hand. Her other cupped his balls, like she'd heard was a good thing to do, and she took him completely in her mouth.

◆◆◆

"You know that was the best I've ever had, right?"

Kylie smiled, leaning her back against his wet chest. Her eyes closed as he rubbed bodywash all over her stomach, never waiting too long to return his attention to her breasts.

"I tried my best," she murmured. "*Mmm*." She hummed, remembering how much he seemed to love the sound when she had her lips wrapped around him.

Logan chuckled, hugging her to him as he kissed her neck. "It was amazing, baby."

She nodded, agreeing with him because of what he had given her.

After he kissed her a whole lot more and ran his hands over every inch of her body, he sighed and turned off the chilling water. "We need to get out. I have to get you home."

Kylie groaned but nodded at him. Logan reached out, pulling two towels in for them. She didn't hide the way she let her eyes scan his gorgeous body, or her blush when she realized he was semi-hard again.

"I can't help it," he said, laughing at her embarrassed look.

"But didn't you like–" She made a weird exploding motion with her hands, which made him laugh again as he fixed his towel around his waist.

"I did." He pulled her towel around her body and pecked her lips. "But just having you near me gets me hard. And I have incredible stamina." He winked and hugged her, dropping a kiss to her shoulder. "We're going to go at it for hours when you turn eighteen. Fuck, let's get dressed. This is torture."

He kissed her lips, then exited as fast as he could, leaving her giggling as he cussed out her sexiness on his way to his bedroom.

Still smiling, she peeked out to see him already wearing a pair of jeans.

"Such a tease," he muttered, shaking his head with a smile. "Your lotion is on my dresser. And just pick out a pair from the stuff we bought today. You're leaving the rest here."

She smiled when she picked up the lotion. "Have you been using this?" She laughed when he blushed. "Are you blushing?"

"Shut up, Hood." He marched over to her. "I had to use something that smelled like raspberries." He smirked and kissed her quickly, then reached for her bag.

"What do you mean?"

He winked and pulled out a pair of black, lacy panties and a matching bra. "Do you think I didn't get myself off after yesterday?"

Her mouth fell open as she realized what he meant. He chuckled and returned to his drawers. She forgot his perverted ways and internally screamed as he made room for her stuff alongside his.

His phone rang, and he went to retrieve it from his bed, only to realize it had fallen on the floor during their moment there earlier.

"Stop standing there naked," he said, preparing to answer his call. "We really can't do any more today, no matter how badly I want to."

She nodded and dropped her towel, smiling when she heard him cussing softly to himself.

"Hello," he said, making her giggle because of just how angry he sounded. "Who?"

Kylie decided to end his torture and pulled up her panties, smiling in the mirror when she fixed her bra.

"Yeah, she's with me," he said, sounding serious.

Kylie spun around, seeing him lift his finger to silence her question.

"She came to the gym because she was upset. I've kept her with me. No, I don't know where they are . . . Yeah, we were just about ready to head to you."

Kylie walked up to him, getting his hug as he listened to the person on the line.

"Yes, sir. We'll be there shortly. Okay. Bye." He looked at his phone for a second and then sighed.

"Who was it?"

Logan tilted her chin up and kissed her before answering, "It was Kevin."

She let out a small gasp while he dropped his hands to her waist to keep her close.

"The cops want to talk to you. Apparently, Maura was hysterical and hurt bad earlier. They're talking about pressing charges, and your stepsister is blaming you, saying you pulled a knife on her. She and her friends are claiming they were just defending themselves from Janie and the girls after you instigated them all into a fight."

"What?" She let him pull her close as he kissed her hair.

"Don't worry. I'll take care of it. They'll know she's lying."

"But," she said, thoughts of being thrown in the back of a police cruiser then a jail cell popping into her head.

"*Shh.*" He kissed her hair again and hugged her tight. "Let me make a few calls and then we'll go."

"Who are you calling?"

He kept his arm around her as he scrolled through his contacts. "Ryder first. Kevin said the cops are looking for them." He hit the call button and lifted his phone to his ear. "Ryder's older brother is better friends with my guy on the force. He'll keep Janie protected at all costs."

She wanted to smack him for thinking about Janie, but he was talking again.

"Then I'm calling her brothers."

"Brothers? Logan, what about me?" *What the hell? Kevin calls, and he's making sure Janie is okay?*

"Yeah, I didn't want to talk to your dumb ass again today either," he said, presumably to Ryder. "The police want to question Kylie. Maura's trying to pin it on her, but they're looking for Janie too." He was quiet, then he responded, "I said I hadn't seen any of you."

Logan moved away, bending down for her clothes as he listened to Ryder. "Yeah, I need you to get him to call Than to find out what's going on."

Silence.

"Well, just deal with it," Logan told him. "He keeps her out of the trouble she gets in."

Kylie followed his silent order and started pulling her clothes on.

"Whatever. Just get him to include Kylie in his protection. I don't want her going anywhere near the station. She didn't do shit anyway, but her family is crazy. They won't protect her."

Finally, she smiled, realizing he'd been thinking about her all along. She sat on the bed as he finished getting his stuff together.

"It's not like that," he said, "but this wasn't Kylie's fault. It'll come back on Janie, so you need to do it."

There was a loud retort, and Logan tensed up.

"I have to go." He ended the call and held out his hand for her as he thumbed through his contacts again.

Kylie jumped up, running to take his hand and getting another quick kiss before he pushed call.

"Don't worry, Hood. I'll take care of you."

"Okay," she whispered, letting him pull her out of his room.

"Gawain," he said when the person must have answered, "it's Logan. Yeah, she's gotten into shit again. She hurt some girl at school."

The person on the other end yelled out, and it sounded like he was yelling for others on his end.

"I need you all to take care of the kids at school," he told this Gawain person. "Okay, but you need to make sure they're clearing my girl—she's the one Janie was protecting. Her name's Kylie Hood." He nodded, listening to the person on the other end as they reached his car. "All right. Yeah, Ryder is calling Than, but he won't call *him*." He was quiet and tense. "Yeah, come to the gym after you're done. Okay. Later." Logan pulled the door open for her but kept her from sitting down.

"What's happening?" she asked, leaning her face against his hands when he cupped her cheeks.

He took a deep breath, releasing it as he stared into her eyes. "Ryder is going to have his older brother pull his strings with the police. They'll get you under their protection as well. They're practically untouchable because of their dad."

"Why would they help? It's not Ryder who's in trouble."

Logan smirked and pecked her lips. "Janie has lots of admirers."

Kylie frowned, not sure it was a good idea to rely on Janie and Ryder, and not thrilled to hear that Janie apparently had some sort of magical pussy that called to men.

"Don't stress out, okay? This is going to work."

"But you said the Godson family is one to stay away from. What about Janie's parents just calling and saying she was, like, doing it all in self-defense?"

"Janie doesn't have parents. She mainly relies on her stepbrothers because her stepdad is kind of a hard-ass. Plus, he's not around very much. Her brothers, though, they're kinda legends around here."

"Yeah, I've heard rumors." She'd never bothered listening to them because no one wanted to hear about how great the Mortaime girl was, but she knew they were supposed to be a big deal.

"See? With all of them, you'll be fine." He seemed very happy with getting their help. "They can get pretty much anything done because people either fear or worship them. They'll make sure no one talks about Janie or you. If the police can't get witnesses to back Maura's story, they have nothing. It's Maura's fault anyway, but I don't know how far her and her friends' claws go with kids at school. This is just insurance."

Kylie sighed but nodded, trusting his plan. Logan took another quick kiss, then helped her inside the car.

As she pulled her belt on and glanced at the clock, she realized they had spent two and a half hours fooling around. "This night has turned into a freaking mess. I can't believe Maura is pulling this crap. And how the hell am I now mixed up with the Godsons and the Mortaimes?"

Logan chuckled and started the car. "Not the Mortaimes—Janie's mom died when she was a baby. My mom and dad helped her stepdad raise her because he only knew how to deal with a bunch of boys."

Kylie nodded, understanding his relationship with her a little more now.

He smiled at her and reached out to squeeze her leg. "Don't worry about anything. And don't let it ruin our amazing night. I loved it and can't wait to be with you again."

She smiled and linked their fingers when he took her hand.

"Everything will work out, Hood. You have me, and soon, you'll be under the protection of the Godsons. And the Knights."

17
SUPER FREAKY

Kylie turned away from the window to look at Logan when he pressed a kiss to her trembling fingers.

"I'm going to be with you the whole time, okay?"

She nodded, still afraid because she remembered how the cops had been. They'd stared at her as she cried and relayed everything, then they listened to Lorelei, and they'd told her that, this time, she would get off with a warning for fabricating a story to get her stepsister and stepmother in trouble. They'd walked out the door after shaking Lorelei's hand, and they never came back.

Logan was on her side, but he couldn't force the officers to believe her. If they wanted to, they could throw her in jail.

"Oh, baby." He kissed her fingers before he reached out to wipe away her tear.

She didn't even know it had fallen.

"I promise I won't let anything happen," he said softly. "Even if they question you, I'm staying with you. You need a parent anyway. I'll talk to Kevin and make sure he knows I need to be there too. I won't leave you."

"Okay," she whispered, realizing they were entering the gated community she lived in. Her mind was running rampant with all sorts of horrible scenarios, absolutely hating that the wonderfulness that came out of what started out as a shitty day was now being yanked away.

"Shit," Logan muttered before pulling off to the side of the road and yanking his phone from his pocket. "Hey," he said, listening to the person talk while he reached out for her hand again. "Where did she go?" He listened again. "Well, keep her by your side at all times. It's not safe for her to do that. What did Than say?" Again, he listened for a minute, sighing at whatever he was hearing. "Who cares? Every other asshole is into her and you don't care."

Kylie realized he was talking to Ryder, and she almost rolled her eyes. Would she ever get away from hearing about Janie?

"I can't believe I'm having this conversation with you." Logan laughed, shaking his head. "Stop being a pussy—no one is going to take her from you. I'm the only one you'd have to worry about anyway."

Ryder yelled an insult back.

Logan chuckled. "I'm not trying to get back with her, idiot. I have a girl. I'm just fucking with you."

Kylie couldn't stop her smile, so she turned to look out the window.

"All right. Call him, and don't forget about Kylie. She's the one in trouble right now."

There was a quick reply from Ryder.

Logan's tone darkened. "You will give a fuck because this is Janie's fault."

"Like hell it is!" was clear as day from Ryder.

"Janie knows to keep a low profile and she messed that up, didn't she?" Logan's hand started shaking as he listened to Ryder talk. "No, she doesn't know anything about that."

Kylie frowned at the fake smile he gave her.

"What happened then has nothing to do with what's happening now," he said. "I know it's the reason why the cops need to stay away, but you're supposed to keep things quiet. She should know better." He sighed, nodding. "You know I'll do what needs to be done. We're in this together."

There was a snappy sort of response from Ryder, but it was unclear.

"I said she doesn't know, and she's not going to. Just drop it." Logan exhaled as he let go of her hand to rub his eyes. "I'll call you when I'm done, all right? We're almost at her house." He hung up and stared out his window without saying anything.

"Well," she said, getting no reaction, "that was a strange conversation."

He chuckled nervously. "Yeah. Sorry. Ryder gets a little panicky when shit happens with Janie. He doesn't like the cops snooping around."

"By the way you were whispering about 'what happened then has nothing to do with what's happening now', I'm going to take a wild guess and say that Ryder and Janie have done something illegal, and you got pulled into it somehow. And he doesn't want her questioned because he's protective."

Logan stared out the window. "What the fuck am I doing?"

Kylie's heartbeat sped up. She wasn't really trying to pick a fight. It just seemed clear that Ryder was some sort of criminal—maybe a drug dealer—and something had happened in the past. She just wanted the fight situation sorted out. She wasn't the one who did anything wrong. "Logan—"

He sighed, rubbing his face. "Listen, I'm not going to lie—Ryder is dangerous, but he's not exactly bad. And the shit he's worried about is serious. I'm involved."

"You're kinda scaring me."

He grabbed her hand. "Don't be scared. Nothing with us will affect you, but he's going to be angry until I can sort things out. I just need his help, and I need to make sure you and Janie are cleared of this. She doesn't need this."

"Well, I don't either." She didn't understand why he was so concerned with Janie. The girl had her own boyfriend.

"I know." He lifted her hand, kissing it. "Just trust me, okay? Everything I'm doing is to keep you safe."

"You won't blame it on me so she stays out of trouble, will you?" She didn't like how he was making it clear Janie was his priority.

"No." He gently squeezed her hand. "I just know they're blaming you because they're afraid of Janie and the Godson family. Once it's clear you're not at fault, they'll go after her."

"Well, Ryder has money, so I'm sure it'll be fine."

"You don't understand, baby." He closed his eyes. "Just let me do what I need to do to get you both out of trouble."

Warning bells sounded off in her head. There was just something about Logan's posture while talking to Ryder; he was afraid. Something big was going on there, and she wanted to find out what it was. "Who's the brother you were talking about?"

He eyed her. "He's older than them, and he's very powerful."

A fifth Godson? One that made Logan more worried than he was about Ryder. "Like strong?"

"He's physically strong, yes," he said, "but it's the shit he's involved in that makes him powerful. He's not like the other Godsons. He rebelled against their dad, and he runs this underground kingdom type of thing."

"Oh." She was intrigued but terrified. Logan legitimately looked worried about this older Godson brother. Whatever the Godson family did must be more dangerous than she ever thought. "So why are you asking Ryder to call him?"

He tapped his fingers on the steering wheel. "Because he's able to do just about anything—and he'll do anything for Janie."

She looked away, sighing as he pulled onto the road again. This was still about Janie. Logan knew it would come back to smack Janie in the face, and he was making sure his precious ex wasn't in trouble.

"Try not to think about him," Logan said. "You probably won't meet him, but he can get both of you out of this mess."

She should've kept her mouth shut, but she was too annoyed, and curious about this mysterious brother. "Why does he do anything for Janie? Don't tell me he likes her."

He didn't pull his attention from the road as he replied, "Like isn't the right word. But, yeah, he has a thing for her."

"Doesn't everybody," she muttered.

"No." He chuckled, patting her leg. "Don't act jealous. Trust me, you don't want a single Godson interested in you in any way. I know girls practically throw their panties at them—I've seen it happen—but they're not a family to mess with. And Janie—well, it's not what you think with her. They have reasons for being in her life. It's complicated."

"Whatever." She crossed her arms. It didn't make sense that he wanted her to stay away and not know anything about them while he was asking for their help.

"So here's the plan," he said. "Tell them exactly what happened. But maybe change that you saw Janie throw the first punch. Just say it wasn't clear from where you stood—there was too much chaos. If they ask about the knife, tell them what actually happened, but leave out that they took it. Just say you saw it fall, then you ran because you were scared and upset.

"Say you left school because you were worried about Maura doing something else to you. If they ask why you didn't just call Kevin, tell the truth; you don't know his number because you don't have a phone. So we were waiting until we felt he would be home because you were afraid of Lorelei's reaction."

"How did Kevin call you?"

"I guess he got my number through the gym." He frowned, tapping his thumb on the steering wheel. "He must have figured you'd be with me."

She nodded, feeling her stomach twist when they pulled up to her house. There was a black car she didn't recognize parked outside, but no one was around it. It didn't look like a cop car until she saw a flasher light near the rearview mirror.

"All right." He put the car in park, then grabbed hold of her hands. "I'm here. I won't leave."

She tried to smile at him, but she knew she looked terrified.

"Come here." He sighed, pulling her face to his and kissing her softly.

She reached up to keep his hands on her, not wanting to leave his embrace. "Thank you, Logan."

He playfully nibbled her lip before kissing her cheek. "You know"—he left a trail of kisses down her neck—"I know we have to deal with serious shit, but right now, all I'm imagining is having you slip off your pants so you can climb on my lap and ride my d—"

"Logan." She pushed him away, but only because she was annoyed he had turned her on.

He laughed and opened his door when she opened hers. "What?" He walked around to where she stood with her arms crossed, trying her best to look annoyed. "We're going to do a lot in this car, baby. Just wait." He placed his hands on her hips and pulled her to him. "You're only turning me on more, Hood." He smirked and gave her a quick kiss. "Better get that sexy, angry look off your face before I walk in there with a massive hard-on for Kevin and the cops to see."

She kept glaring and glanced at the car, speaking before realizing what she was saying, "Well, I guess I better learn to swallow then. I don't think Kevin will approve of me coming home with your cum all over me, because I'm definitely giving you a blow job the next time you drop me off." She smiled at his stunned face and pushed herself up on her tippy toes to peck his lips before sauntering her way to the front door. She remembered something like this before—maybe a book—and she couldn't believe it was what popped into her head. He was probably going to laugh.

"You know that doesn't help my boner situation." He jogged up behind her.

"I know." She giggled as he grabbed her waist to keep her from opening the door.

"I thought you liked your *pearl* necklace," he murmured in her ear, hugging her from behind.

She grinned because she felt him getting hard against her butt. "I loved it."

He nuzzled her cheek as his fingers caressed her stomach. "Good, because I like giving my girl presents."

Her eyes shot open, and she turned her head to the side. "Logan, what do you mean when you say, 'my girl'?" She was so unsure of how things worked in relationships. She'd told herself she wouldn't make him clarify, but he continued to call her my girl, and that had to mean more than the two of them simply dating.

"What do you think it means?"

She swallowed, ready to ask if he considered her his girlfriend already. "Am I your—"

The front door was yanked open. "There you are."

"Hi, Kevin," she said, trying to pull herself away from Logan, but her man-boy didn't let her get far.

"Kevin," Logan said, nodding to her stepdad before sliding his arm around her waist to pull her back to his side. "Sorry we took so long."

Kevin lowered his eyes to Logan's hand placement as he rubbed his thumb up and down her side.

"It's no problem." Kevin held the door open. "Thanks for bringing her. She'll call you tomorrow." He held his hand out for Kylie, dismissing Logan's obvious intention to enter with her.

Logan pulled her closer, shaking his head. "Yeah, she's not going in without me."

Kylie's breathing sped up, and she darted her eyes between the two men. For the first time, she realized how powerful Kevin's presence really was. He was just as tall as Logan, maybe not as bulky, but a guy you wouldn't want to piss off. Then again, neither was Logan.

"This is a family matter," Kevin told him.

"I realize that—but your family matter involves Kylie, and anything involving her will have my full attention. So I'll be staying with her until she tells me to go."

A patronizing smile touched Kevin's lips. "I appreciate your concern, kid. And while I gave my consent for you two to date, I'll remind you that she's a minor, and I'm her guardian. I can forbid her from seeing you."

Logan grinned in an unfriendly way while keeping his hold firm. "One, I didn't ask for your consent. We're together, and there's nothing you can do about it."

Kevin looked ready to breathe fire.

"And two, she's not a child. She's a beautiful young woman—one who will soon be a legal adult, and one you've neglected since assuming the role of her stepfather."

An icy glare overcame Kevin's face. "You have five seconds to get your hands off her and back in your car."

"Logan," she said, grabbing his sleeve after he pushed her behind him and took a step closer to Kevin.

He didn't acknowledge her and continued speaking to Kevin. "If I leave, she comes with me. You don't get to pull the daddy card just because the police are poking around. Don't pretend you've never noticed what they've been doing."

Kevin opened his mouth, but a new voice silenced him.

"Actually, Mr. Blackwood." Footsteps sounded behind Kevin as a man wearing a police uniform stepped out.

Kylie looked him over, stunned by the smoldering look he gave her and his swoon-worthy tousled chocolate brown hair as he smiled at Logan. "Since Mr. Grimm appears to be the initial cause of all this mess, I'd like him to stay."

Logan stepped back, placing his arm around Kylie as his tense posture relaxed.

"Of course," the man continued, "if you have a problem with Mr. Grimm entering your home, Kevin, we can have them follow us to the station."

"No." Kevin held the door open again. "Here is fine. I'm sure Kylie wants to be somewhere comfortable."

Logan scoffed as the officer turned to her.

"Let me introduce myself, Miss Hood." He smiled, though there was no kindness to it. "I'm Police Chief Messor." He stuck out his hand. "But you can call me Than, if you'd like."

Kylie recognized the name and realized this was Logan's guy, so she relaxed and shook his hand. He wasn't kidding when he said he knew people. "It's nice to meet you."

He nodded and released her hand, gesturing for them to come inside. Kevin, she realized, had already walked off. They quietly followed the chief.

Logan turned and pressed a sweet kiss to her temple just before they came to the opening of the room where Kevin waited. Kylie lowered her eyes from his fierce look, but she noticed a woman sitting on their couch where the chief was heading.

Than cleared his throat and gestured to the woman. "This is my lead detective, Kali Parvati. Detective, this is Kylie Hood and Logan Grimm. I insisted, after gathering the information we learned earlier, that Mr. Grimm stay in case you have any questions for him."

The detective smiled as she stood and held out her hand. "Hello, Kylie." They shook hands before Kali turned to Logan and shook his hand too. "Mr. Grimm. If you both will take a seat."

Logan took her to the opposite couch as the detective, chief, and Kevin returned to their spots.

"I'll try to make this as easy as possible, Kylie," Detective Parvati said.

Logan took Kylie's hand in his while the detective pulled out her phone.

"And please," Detective Pavarti said, "don't mind Police Chief Messor's attendance. We were having a private meeting outside of work when I received the call regarding Miss Payne's assault. Seeing that Mr. Blackwood is a prominent member of our community, and both yours and Miss Payne's stepfather, the chief insisted on joining me."

Kylie shook her head, muttering, "It's no problem."

She noticed the smirk on the chief's lips as his breathtaking blue eyes zeroed in on Logan's hand, but she returned her attention to the detective, realizing just how striking the woman was.

Kali shifted her near waist-length, sleek black hair away from her flawless, oval face. Her dark brown eyes nearly matched the color of her skin, and they were focused right on Kylie. "Excellent. Now, I assume you have no problem with your stepfather and boyfriend remaining present?"

Kylie blushed and shook her head, feeling her face grow even hotter when Logan removed his hand from hers, only to place it around her shoulders in a more intimate hold.

"Great," said Detective Parvati. "I've already spoken to your stepsister and most of the other girls with her. They all gave me near-identical stories that could put you in some serious trouble."

"I understand." Kylie swallowed, leaning against Logan for strength. "But whatever they told you is a lie. I did nothing but stand there while they surrounded me."

The detective nodded, messing with her phone as she took down notes. "Then give me your side. I'll just listen, and if I have a question, I'll stop you."

Kylie nodded, then told her about the rumors and teasing that had been going on—then how she found herself surrounded by Maura and five other girls.

"And how did Miss Mortaime come into this?" Detective Parvati asked.

"She just showed up," Kylie said, her nerves shot. She was about to puke. "I didn't ask her to help me—she just stood between me and them. Her friends were there, too.

And then it turned into an argument between Janie and Melody, then her and Maura. They don't like each other."

Than Messor smirked, his gaze taking in Logan as his detective made notes.

"How do you know Janie?" Detective Parvati asked.

"I don't, really." She tensed up. "I just know she fought Maura once."

The chief leaned over, whispering in Detective Parvati's ear.

Logan gave Kylie a gentle squeeze, but she didn't know if it was to comfort her or to tell her not to bring up Janie's violent past. She was just telling them what she knew.

"Ah, I see." Detective Parvati smiled. "Than has informed me there is a report filed about the fight between your stepsister and Miss Mortaime. I'll look it up when I return to the station. Now, you say the verbal attack Maura and her friends aimed at you shifted to personal instances with Janie Mortaime?"

"Yes." Kylie wrung her hands together. "They just started insulting each other back and forth—I have no idea what they were really getting at, but then there was total chaos. They were just fighting."

"Do you know who attacked first?" the chief asked. His fierce blue eyes made it hard to look away from him.

"No." She took a shaky breath. "I was behind them through the whole thing, and kids were shoving and cheering. Then, I don't know, I looked at Maura and saw her pull a knife out of her bag. I screamed because I assumed she was going after Janie. I guess Janie knows how to defend herself though, because she caught Maura's arm and twisted it until the knife fell."

Than made eye contact with Logan, a small smirk playing across his lips before he controlled it and looked back at his detective—well, at her chest.

"What happened to the knife?" Kali looked up after asking her question, then glared at Than until he chuckled and looked away from her breasts.

Kylie shrugged. "I don't know. Kids started screaming that teachers were coming, and everyone started shoving and running to get away. When I looked back, Maura was crying on the ground and the others were gone. I panicked and ran too."

"Why did you panic?" The detective watched her, continuing when she didn't respond right away. "From the story you've just told, you've done absolutely nothing wrong. Why not go to the teachers?"

Logan rubbed her arm, soothing the anxiety the detective caused in her. Because she had no idea if this Kali Parvati person was someone Logan trusted.

"I don't know," she muttered. "I was just upset. It was too much to deal with after everything else that had happened. I just wanted to be somewhere else."

"You walked almost ten miles until you reached the gym where Logan was?"

Kylie nodded. "I'm used to walking. He's the only person I feel safe around."

"You don't feel safe with your family?" It was the chief who asked.

She tensed up, watching Than, Kali, and Kevin all narrow their eyes at her. "I just meant that I know Maura has a problem with me getting attention, and that after her fight, she might take it out on me. I mean, she had a knife, and she pulled it on someone. I had no idea if she meant to use it on me originally, but I didn't want to find out. I knew Logan would keep me safe, so I went to him. We were just getting ready to come here when Kevin called."

The detective looked at the chief, neither saying anything until someone's phone rang.

"That's me." Chief Messor stood up, grinning when he realized who was calling him. "Excuse me, I need to take this."

They nodded, watching him walk out. Kylie couldn't help but snoop, and she peeked at his phone as he lifted it up to his ear. The contact read: *L. Godson.*

"I figured you'd be calling me." His voice faded as he left the room.

"Well," Detective Parvati said, regaining Kylie's attention, "at the moment, I don't feel it necessary to place you under any custody. Right now, it's just a case of she said, she said, and you weren't the one to assault anyone.

"We'll finish questioning Miss Payne and the other girls, and Miss Mortaime. I will likely have questions for you after I do get a chance to talk to her and her group of friends. They all disappeared, but we'll find them. For now, I expect you to stay out of trouble. Your stepmother is insisting Maura stay at the hospital for observation, so you shouldn't have to worry about a confrontation until tomorrow." She then turned to Logan. "Mr. Grimm, it's been a pleasure. Please call us if either of you have additional information you feel might be useful."

Kylie and the others stood while Detective Parvati gathered her things. Logan kept his arm around her waist, quiet as the detective went to shake hands with Kevin.

"Did I do okay?" Kylie whispered, turning in his arms.

"You did great, Hood," he said, hugging her. He looked over at where Kali still spoke with Kevin, then back at her. "You kinda made it clear you're not friends with Janie, so that looks good for you—she won't buy that you instigated Janie and the girls into attacking Maura."

Kylie pressed her lips together. She couldn't tell if he was upset with her because she wasn't praising Janie like a hero. Beating up mean people didn't make you a hero.

"I don't want to leave you here with Kevin," he muttered, relieving her because he obviously wasn't angry with her. "But I have a feeling he's going to keep me from you as soon as they leave."

"Then take me with you." She hugged him tighter.

"I don't think I can without him causing a scene. And with the way that fucker acted with me outside, I'll probably end up in jail for fighting him."

"Then what do we do?" She knew he wasn't talking just to talk. Kevin had pissed him off, and she knew neither one was ready to back down.

He rubbed his hand up and down her back and lowered his voice. "Keep your phone hidden from everyone. Call or text me if anything happens. Anything."

She nodded, already knowing she would. "But what if he tells me I can't see you?"

Logan scoffed. "I might not feel like getting locked up, but that's only because I can't protect you from jail. I'm seeing you no matter what. How do you feel about me sneaking over tonight?"

Kylie's mouth fell open. "Like spend the night with me?"

He nodded, smirking as he added, "And I'll tell you what I mean when I say my girl."

"Okay." She smiled like an idiot.

He chuckled and kissed the top of her head before sighing. "He's coming over. Call me when you're alone, and we'll figure out what we're going to do."

She nodded and got a quick kiss on her lips before Kevin cleared his throat.

"Kylie, I think you should escort your friend out, and then you and I will talk at dinner."

Kylie didn't want to be clingy, but she didn't want to be alone with Kevin. "Can he stay for dinner?"

"Some other time when my evening isn't ruined because my stepdaughters are fighting over a boy." Kevin glared at her before doing the same to Logan.

"Okay. Um, I'll just walk him out."

"Make it quick." He turned to leave the room without sparing Logan a glance.

"Prick," Logan muttered as he started walking toward the front door. "Which way is your room?"

She pointed to the stairs. "I'm the corner room. There's a big tree right outside my window."

He smirked. "Convenient."

"It's not like I planted it for you."

He chuckled, his eyes lighting with mischief that made him look adorable and sexy at the same time. "Yeah, yeah. I know you can't get enough of me. You probably knew all along you were coming to Logan Grimm's town and thought, 'I better have a tree for this bad boy to climb.' Go on, tell me you planned this."

"I did not." She smiled, shoving him even though she wanted him to hold her tighter. "That's the most ridiculous thing ever."

"This is Blackwoods we're talking about. Grimm, Knight, and Godson territory."

"What?" She looked up at him, confused. "This is Kevin's town. His family founded it in the 1800s."

He scoffed. "You really don't know how legendary we are then. Blackwood was just the family who did the paperwork. Our families don't need documents to know what belongs to us."

"Okay." She shook her head. "That's probably the freakiest thing you've said."

"You're the freaky one." He snickered, hugging her. "I would have never thought it. Hood's a super freak, super freak."

"Shut up." She laughed, covering her face as she prayed Kevin wasn't listening.

He didn't stop. "She's super freaky, yowww." Logan cut off his surprisingly good interpretation of Rick James' *Super Freak* when the door suddenly opened from the outside.

"Logan." Than Messor smirked as he looked between them. "I'm sure Miss Hood would love for you to continue serenading her about how kinky and freaky she is"—he winked at her—"but I'd like to get our little conversation over with quickly. You're not the only one who wants to sneak off with his super freak." Than's eyes slid to where Detective Parvati waited.

Logan chuckled, hugging Kylie, her mind blown by the police chief's words.

"Younger than you usually settle for, Than?" Logan sounded completely relaxed now they were alone.

Than shrugged and looked back at the detective. "She's your age. Top of her class." He looked back at Logan. "A goddess in bed, that one."

Logan chuckled and asked, "He call you?"

Than nodded. "Hurry up—we're meeting at Ryder's. I don't think he's very happy with you. Be ready for that." He nodded at Kylie again and left them to pull the door open for Kali, not hiding the ass squeeze he gave her when she leaned over to move his jacket off her seat.

Logan laughed softly and hugged her again as he lowered his lips to her neck. "I need to go."

She sighed and enjoyed every little kiss and lick he gave her.

"Call me if anything happens, yeah?"

She nodded, smiling because he slipped his hand under her shirt to caress her side where she still had bruises.

"And send me a text when you're alone."

"Okay," she whispered, her body shaking in a way only he could make it.

"All right, I'm leaving. Lock the door to your room. I don't want Kevin sneaking in because everyone is gone."

Kylie smiled and nodded.

"Oh, and you might want to get a nap in before I come over."

"We're not messing around like that, Logan."

He laughed and kissed her cheek over and over. "You sure?"

"I'm sure," she said, laughing when he started trying to reach for her bra. "Stop!" She smacked his hands and shoved him. "We're going to talk and sleep. No"—she moved her hand in a shaking motion.

Logan lauged and grabbed her hands. "What—no shaking up cans of soda?"

She blushed, smiling even more when he reached up to hold her face.

"Okay," he murmured, kissing her softly. "Just talking. I want to hear who asked you for a blow job so I can beat the shit out of him."

"Don't beat anyone up." She was giddy to have him protective of her.

"I'm at least scaring the fuck out of the little shit." He grinned, kissing her forehead. "See you in a few, baby."

"Yeah." She felt like she was floating.

"But leave your bra off." He let go and walked down the steps. "I'm using your tits for my pillow."

18
ALWAYS THE ONE

A low laugh pulled Logan's attention from the image of Kylie he had on his phone. He looked up and pushed himself off the hood of his car to meet Than in the driveway.

Than scanned him, shaking his head. "Do you really have it that bad?"

Logan shoved his phone in his pocket and frowned. "What are you talking about?"

They started walking along the pea gravel path toward the Godson family mansion.

Than grinned, pointing to his pocket. "The girl. I didn't think it was that serious. Ryder just said you were sort of seeing the girl this was all about. I thought he was joking."

"I doubt Ryder can make a fucking joke," Logan muttered. "But, yeah, I guess I'm with her."

They started up the huge stairway that led to the front entrance.

"You guess?" Than chuckled.

"Fuck you."

Than laughed at him.

Logan sighed, rubbing the back of his neck. "Don't give me shit. You're the one banging your new young detective."

The police chief shrugged. "At least mine is legal. You're not fucking this one, are you?"

"Not yet." Logan panicked. He knew the laws were strict in Oregon because he was obviously older than Janie. Back then, he'd made sure they could be together, but he wasn't sure if things had changed. "Can I get in trouble with her? She's not eighteen."

There was a mischievous gleam in Than's eyes as he spoke, "I know she's not eighteen. Kali looked up your age difference right away. She was ready to shut you down, but you're in the clear because you're within the three-year gap."

He released a big breath. "I can't believe I didn't even double-check. I never really planned on fucking her. Well, not until she was at least an adult."

"You said you weren't fucking her." Than chuckled, patting his back. "Maybe wait, yeah? She's got too much shit going on, and you need to focus on getting her out of trouble and fixing the mess you started."

Logan rolled his eyes, but his heart ached from the truth of that simple statement. He'd started it. "He wasn't going to take care of shit."

Than hummed. "You know better than to jump to conclusions when it comes to Ryder. Or any of us."

"Whatever," Logan said, dismissing further talk about the subject. "Before we go in, what do you know about Kylie?"

Than sighed and pulled out a cigarette. "I know you're protecting her from her family. Which one is hurting her? If it's Kevin, I'll bury him where no one will ever find him."

Logan chuckled, shaking his head. "I would've already done it. It's the sister. Her mom covers it up."

"That's odd." He shrugged. "But I guess the other daughter is her blood."

"Right." Logan was nervous about bringing up Kylie's past because she really needed to be the one to talk to the cops, but she was too stubborn or afraid. If Than found out, he could start building a case. "It's been happening for a long-ass time—since her dad passed away. Kylie thinks Kevin is clueless, but he knows. She could hardly walk without limping the first day I saw her. She's tough, and she hides her pain, but we're fighters—he had to notice it at some point. And I know he's seen that bruise on her cheek. The first time I saw them together, he acted completely clueless about it. I thought it was him until I realized she wasn't afraid of him."

Than nodded, blowing out some smoke. "I noticed it. It looks about a week old."

"Yeah, she covers it up well. She used to wear her hood up—I guess she was going for the shy teen look. I get him not seeing everything, but she was limping."

"I'm assuming she refuses to seek help?"

Logan nodded. "Said that she's tried to get help in the past. I guess in her old town, because she only moved here her junior year. She doesn't like to talk about shit, though. I think she's terrified of being called a liar."

"Well, you know all about that." Than took another drag. "Lorelei Payne-Blackwood, her stepmom, is gorgeous. It wouldn't take much on her part to get the cops to lay off."

Logan grunted, but he could easily see that happening.

"Cops are corruptible, Logan, especially in this world." Than smirked. "But we're already watching her family."

Logan whipped his head around. "What for?"

Than tossed his cigarette and stamped it out. "An anonymous tip came in last week. They didn't offer much—just that we should consider the circumstances surrounding both Dr. Oliver Hood's and Dr. Scarlet Hood's deaths."

"What have you found?"

"Oliver was having an affair. And Scarlet found out." Than rubbed his wrist.

"So what does that mean? Her mom died when she was what? Six or seven?"

"Seven," said Than. "She was communicating with someone. About what, we don't know. All we know is that she met someone over the course of six months. We're considering exhuming their remains to do autopsies. It appeared neither of them had one performed because both deaths were ruled accidents."

Logan's mind started spinning. "Kylie said her mom used to take her to a Chinese restaurant—that she was always meeting someone. She didn't seem to know more, but I guess that makes sense because she was so young."

Than considered this information. "Well, that sort of helps solidify that Scarlet was seeing someone. You're sure Kylie doesn't know who her mom was meeting?"

Logan shook his head. "No, she said she doesn't remember much of her mom. It seemed like she only had dreams to go by. What are your theories?"

Sighing, Than said, "Only that Oliver was cheating—with Lorelei."

Logan's eyes went wide. "Really?"

Than bobbed his head. "And now we know that Scarlet may have been considering divorce. Or perhaps she was cheating as well."

"Damn."

"You sure know how to pick them." Than chuckled, his eyes drifting up to the moon. "Do you want me to take her out of that house? I'll do everything I can to ensure they're punished, but with the new circumstances, it will take time for the courts to convict. Especially since it looks like they're leaving her alone with you around. It's always hard to prove unless someone goes in right then, or they've thoroughly documented evidence throughout their abuse." He waved toward the house. "With this shit about the girls beating up the sister, it might come out they're just having a sibling spat. Violent as hell, but it could be more trouble for Kylie. More than likely, her sister and mom will walk."

Logan looked down, then said, "Let me talk to her first. I want them to pay, but I'm leaving it to her on how. I was going to ask her about moving out when she turns eighteen."

Than shook his head. "I already dug around. There's a block on her inheritance. Lorelei has full control until Kylie finishes college or until she's twenty-one. It was something her birth mother did to ensure she wasn't reckless, I suppose." He shrugged. "She has several odd stipulations that suggest they worried she'd blow through it all. In the event of Kylie's death before then, Lorelei gets everything."

Logan frowned, wondering what her parents must've been thinking. "You're sure it wasn't Lorelei?"

Than nodded, looking away from the moon. "Both wills were solid, except Oliver's wife changed on his when he remarried."

"That sucks." Logan sighed, his gaze drifting to the moon too.

"She's real, you know," Than said quietly. "Asleep, but real. Living and breathing. Waiting for her prince to take her home."

Logan smiled as he took in the little half-moon. "You know I wasn't raised to fall in love with the fairy tales."

"Because your mother wanted you to be hers. And that didn't stop you, did it?" Than patted his back, knowing Logan wouldn't reply. "You may not have been raised to join us, but you're a Grimm. Soon enough the stories will be too hard to resist—you'll see what I do."

"Yeah." He closed his eyes, refusing to think about everything his mother had done that ruined so much of his life—so much of his baby doll's life.

"Are you doing better with her and Ryder?"

Logan could always count on Than to keep him in check, to maintain peace between everyone. "I didn't think I was. She's always been the one, you know?"

"Yeah, I know, kid." Than gestured to the door. "Let's get this over with."

"All right." He rang the doorbell, running his hand through his hair.

"You didn't tell Kylie who Janie is, right?"

Logan smiled to himself. "Of course not."

"Good." Than rubbed sanitizer on his hands. "Kylie doesn't need to know our secrets. No matter who she ends up becoming to you, she's not your destiny, and you know what's at stake if you open your mouth."

His fists started to shake. "I won't."

"Good boy."

He should've stayed quiet; his guilt was crushing him, but he felt the urge to defend Kylie. "Janie shouldn't have done what she did."

Than looked away from the door. "She was just trying to help. You know what those girls put her through, and you haven't been around lately to know she's emotional as hell. Of course she snapped and attacked them for that shit. But you wouldn't know that because you've been balls deep in ass and pussy."

Logan lowered his head. Than was right. He always got carried away with pussy around a fight because he wanted his baby doll beside him, and she was with Ryder. Even if they weren't together, it stabbed her in the heart to see him that way again, so they would stop talking, then Ryder would bring her around after so they could make up.

"Don't get in too deep with this girl." Than sighed, rubbing his wrist again. "You have major shit to work out before you go falling for someone else. Especially someone you know nothing about. She's not one of us."

"I'm not talking about this shit with you." He could hear someone approaching the door.

Than's reply was as sharp as a blade, "Then don't blame Janie for your fucking mistakes."

"Hey," Savaş greeted, opening the door.

"Hey, you big bastard. Took you long enough." Than knocked his shoulder as he stepped in first, patting Savaş on the back.

Savaş grinned, gesturing for Logan to enter. "Had to get dressed."

Than rolled his eyes. "You're not supposed to have the girls around when shit is going down."

Savaş shut the door before leading them through the foyer. "They helped us find her. Head up to the media room. We're still waiting. Want a drink?"

Than nodded. "No alcohol. Keep Logan clean, too. He needs a clear head."

"Pussies." Savaş laughed, walking away.

"Can you stop acting like my father?" Logan glared at Than.

"Stop acting like a child, and I'll stop treating you like one." Than shook his head as they ascended the stairs. "You know he's going to be pissed. If something happens to her, we're all screwed."

"Well, that's why we're all in this mess," Logan muttered and turned into the media room where loud shouts, insults, and just random curse words were being thrown back and forth between Ryder's brothers, Tercero and Archer.

"Whatever you say, Logan. You know what really happened."

Logan didn't respond to Than's comment, but he followed him over to the empty couch as he scanned the room. The only people there were Tercero, Archer, and their girlfriends. Both Janie and Ryder were missing.

"Hey, idiots," Than said, both of them sitting at the same time. "Where's Ryder?"

Neither brother looked away from their game, but Archer responded, "Fucking Janie."

Than looked at Logan, but he ignored his stare, keeping his eyes on the game to hide the usual pain of knowing Janie was with Ryder.

"They've been going at it nonstop ever since he talked her into coming home," Archer added.

Than spoke up. "A little more information than we wanted, but do one of you want to go tell him we're here?"

Tercero was the one to answer. "We were specifically told that if we interrupted them, we'd be dead. So, no. He was panicking—he needs to be with her right now. Sorry, Logan."

Logan shook his head. "It's fine."

"Knew he was into the new chick," Archer said, grinning at Tercero before focusing on Logan. "Are you gonna wait to claim that V-card?"

"What the fuck are you talking about?" Logan glared at him.

Archer smirked, not fazed by the beating that would come to him. "She wasn't exactly giving off Logan Grimm fucked me vibes."

"Mind your business," he snapped. "And keep your traps shut about me and Janie when you see her."

A malicious smile formed on Archer's face. "Thought you could keep your baby doll a secret? I'm surprised she didn't already know, but making her think she's the only girl . . ." He tutted as though he was chiding a child. "Bad Logan."

Logan moved to knock his ass out.

Than grabbed his shoulder. "Enough. Both of you."

He shook Than off and closed his eyes, trying to push down the rage building inside of him.

After a few more seconds, Archer spoke up again. "Are you still fucking around while you're with her? Or is she keeping you satisfied?"

Logan stood up quickly, as did Than and Archer. But a voice stopped him from shoving the police chief off so he could kill the smart-mouthed Godson.

"Logan, stop."

He turned to see Janie enter the room. She wore an oversized shirt and an unmistakable head of sex-hair. Ryder came in after her, wearing only a pair of low-sitting track pants, carrying a gallon jug of water in one hand, and a protein shake in the other.

Ryder stayed quiet, watching Janie walk closer until she was standing right in front of Logan.

Logan only looked away from his rival when her soft fingers slid across his forehead.

She gave him a smile before hugging him. "Archer, I won't stop him from beating the shit out of you if you keep it up."

Logan hugged her but held her at arm's length. It went against his instincts to pull her closer, but knowing Kylie was so upset with his and Janie's relationship had him feeling guiltier than he already felt. He owed it to them both to be better, but it was Kylie who was waiting for him. Not his baby doll.

A teasing smile spread over her lips as Ryder walked up behind her. "I just wanted to see," she said, giggling before turning to look at Ryder. "I told you."

Ryder rolled his eyes before addressing whatever secret they were sharing. "Yeah, you proved your point, but you didn't have to hug him, babe. You're not even wearing a bra. Go over there before I fuck him up just for feeling your tits on him."

"Like he hasn't felt them before," Archer muttered.

Ryder's stare was deadly. "Shut the fuck up."

Than laughed and sat while Logan looked between his ex and her boyfriend.

"Hey," Ryder said, sounding a little more relaxed now that Janie had plopped down on the oversized chair, her eyes lighting up at the game Tercero was still playing.

"Hey." Logan sat back down.

"Up," Ryder said, staring at Janie while she messed with a game controller. She got up without looking at him and sat on his lap after he took her spot.

Ryder chugged his protein shake before taking a long drink of water, then sat his jug on the floor. "Your girl back home, or she get taken in?"

"She's at home," Logan told him, looking away from Janie's horrible attempt to run and shoot properly on the game.

"*Donna, così mi ucciderai!*" Tercero muttered as Janie laughed.

"Tercero," Janie sang as her avatar caught up to his, "you know I get all tingly and want to follow you into battle when you speak Italian."

Logan watched Tercero send her an amused look, ignoring his girlfriend's glare from across the room.

"It is I who follows you, *tesoro*," Tercero said, winking at Janie. "I've told you before, think of me—for I am yours to bring."

Logan glanced at Ryder. His rival was watching his brother like a hawk, but then he chuckled when Janie's player ran into a melee.

"*Morte*," Tercero muttered and chased after her.

"Stop flirting with her and save her ass," Ryder told his brother, kissing Janie's neck.

"Babe, I can't fight good when you do that." She giggled as Tercero did his best to keep her alive.

Logan glanced at Than, who was watching them as well, but he also took in the anger radiating from Tercero's girlfriend. Was this how Kylie felt when he was with Janie earlier? He felt so much rage when Janie was with Ryder, and she wasn't his girlfriend anymore. *Dammit*.

Elise, Tercero's girlfriend, stood and stormed out of the room.

Archer chuckled, his eyes almost glowing as they settled on Janie. "Vicious little queen."

"No one fucks with my boys." Janie leaned forward to where Tercero was sitting on the floor and kissed his cheek. "And I'm sorry."

"There is nothing to be sorry for." He returned a kiss to her cheek. "And I meant it—I am yours in your darkest hour."

She nodded, nuzzling his cheek a little too intimately before situating herself on Ryder's lap again.

Logan sighed, irritated because there was real meaning behind what they were saying to each other, and he didn't like thinking about what it meant. Not to mention, he didn't like thinking about how close Janie was with Tercero—well, all the Godsons.

The tense atmosphere had nothing to do with their cryptic conversation though; something must've happened with Tercero and his girlfriend, and Janie was playing dirty. He smiled to himself. She was protective as hell. He could only imagine if Kylie did anything to piss her off. He didn't want to see them fight, but he wasn't sure how he was going to keep things peaceful because Kylie was too innocent to handle Janie.

"Sweet girl." Ryder kissed Janie's hair before shifting his attention to Than. "Did you tell him the shit you're working on about the girl?"

Than nodded. "I filled him in when we got here. I'm a little worried about her being alone with Kevin, because Logan's right, he should have noticed she was being hurt."

Ryder looked at Logan, then over at the girls sitting at the table, talking. "Girls, get out. And don't snoop. This isn't your business."

They all looked at him, annoyed, but got up and left as Savaş entered with a plate loaded with sandwiches and drinks. Monica snagged one of the drinks before muttering insults about Ryder being a jerk as she kissed her boyfriend goodbye.

"And make sure her cheating ass is gone before you leave," Ryder shouted.

That explained it. Logan grimaced, wondering how the hell anyone was stupid enough to cheat on one of the brothers. The girl was lucky Janie didn't skin her alive.

"What are you talking about, Logan?" Janie had abandoned her game and turned her focus to him. "I know Maura's a bitch, but I didn't think anything more of it—just that maybe they'd had an argument about Trevor."

"Just tell them," said Than, elbowing Logan.

Logan glanced at him before answering Janie. It wasn't right to talk about Kylie like this, but he knew Janie might be her best support. "Maura's been beating the shit out of her since her dad died. I tricked her into showing me how hurt she was. She was covered in bruises and scars. I thought maybe her ribs were broken, so I had Evander check her out. An X-ray showed four old fractures and tons of scar tissue from them being re-injured."

"Damn," Savaş muttered, then started eating.

"I'm sorry, Logan," Janie murmured, her eyes going to Than before focusing on him again. "I thought it was weird that she kept her hood up, but you know I don't really bother with girls at school anymore."

"I know." He smiled sadly because he knew why she didn't bother anymore.

She grinned. "We'll take care of her. I'm glad I fucked Maura up now."

Logan shook his head. "You know you're supposed to keep a low profile."

She shrugged and curled into Ryder's hold. "I screwed up. I always screw shit up, and then you guys try to keep me from getting hurt. You should just let me get in trouble so I won't ruin everyone around me. I already hate what I've caused you all to do."

Ryder kissed her cheek and whispered words they couldn't hear into her ear.

"I know." Her lips quivered.

The others all looked around like they were busy, but Logan watched them. He knew she would do this. That was why he hated himself for even dumping this on her.

"Baby doll," he said, getting her attention and Ryder's glare, which he ignored. "We keep you safe because we want to. And because the shit that happened shouldn't have. It was our fault. I'll always be here for you—both of you—but that doesn't mean you go and put yourself in these kinds of situations. You have to realize it puts more than just you in danger."

Janie sighed as she played with the hem of her shirt. "I didn't mean to. That bitch was asking for it."

Logan leaned forward, resting his forearms on his knees. "You already know Ryder isn't cheating, and he knows you're not. You need to think shit through and not let them get to you."

Her eyes lit up like fire. "You're one to talk!"

Ryder tucked her head under his chin as he rocked her.

Logan looked away. That was a low blow on his part, one that hit a nasty wound.

"Why don't you just go talk to the detective," she spat, fighting Ryder's hold. "Get them to pull the tapes and put me away so I won't be a bother to you. I deserve it, don't I?" Her pretty eyes welled up with tears as the gold and green within them roared like flames. "I was the one who did it, right? I'm always the one, aren't I? Aren't I?" she yelled. "I did all of this! I'm why we're here. And I fucked it all up."

"Stop," Ryder yelled, pinning her hands down as she tried to break free.

Logan squeezed his eyes shut. He knew the others were watching him. They knew the truth, too. They knew this would come to pass, and it was his fault. Not hers.

"No," she screamed. "It's all my fault. Just put me out of my fucking misery because he'll always think it's my fault."

"Well," came a different voice from the hallway, "we are here because of you, but *this* wasn't your fault."

Logan looked up, his blood running cold at the sight of two silhouettes.

"I know for certain you were not the one who went after anyone. Isn't that right, boys?"

Janie settled, wiping her tears as she sat straighter. "Hey, Luc."

19
MY GIRL

Kylie stared at the pasta on her fork, rolling her eyes as Kevin let out another frustrated breath.

"Are you refusing to answer me?" he asked.

She looked up, doing her best not to glare at him. "I'm not having sex with him, Kevin."

He looked relieved and returned his attention to his plate. "I don't think it's a good idea for you two to see each other anymore. At least not while we're trying to clear up this matter with your sister. Perhaps not until you finish school."

"No," she said before she could stop herself.

Kevin glanced up, surprised. "Kylie, I just want what's best for you."

"So does he." She believed in her choice to be with Logan. No one was going to take him from her, not when she'd just gotten him.

"You barely know him, sweetheart. Look what dating him has already caused. Your sister is in the hospital because his ex-girlfriend got angry. What is going to happen to you if she decides she wants him back? Don't ask me to sit back while my daughters get bullied over a boy who is more than likely filling his bed with other women."

"He likes me, not her." She was so angry she nearly cried. "We're going to be together forever."

Kevin set his napkin down, a disbelieving laugh leaving his lips. "I have never heard you sound more like a silly girl than you did just now. Do you really think he intends on staying with you after you give him what he wants?"

Kylie's heart hurt, and she looked down at the table, letting the words tumble out. "I might be a silly girl, but I trust Logan. And I know I'm more than that now."

Kevin took a drink of water before staring her down. "You're not seeing him while you live here."

She gasped. "You can't stop me."

He held his hand up. "Just listen to me. I've never tried to be a father to you—I'm sorry for that. I just thought it was wrong under the circumstances. It's different with Maura because she's Lorelei's blood. But you were just . . . Well, I'm sure you understand what I'm getting at."

He looked at her like she would accept his reason for not stepping up as her father. "It was a bad decision to be distant with you; I see that now. But you have to let me fix it. Let me try. I don't want you going down the path Logan will take you. I tried to stay out of it, and I was going to, but this incident with your sister only proves that I need to step in and protect you. He's trouble, and he has already caused a rift that we still need to mend. Christ, Kylie, Maura said you pulled a knife on her!"

Kylie let out a sarcastic laugh. "And you really believed her? She's crazy! Did you even listen to what I told that cop?"

"I listened to every word." He sighed, rubbing his forehead. "My point is, you two have never been this way before. I thought the Trevor boy was the reason for her drop in mood. So when I saw Logan, I figured the anger she'd developed would end. Clearly, I was wrong."

"You're wrong about a lot of things," she muttered, "and you're blind if you think this is the only time Maura has had a problem with me. It's laughable, really—I don't know why I've stayed silent. But I'm not going to bother relying on you. You're still sitting there thinking this is over a boy. You can't even see what's really been happening, and that's all because you're so absorbed with your wife.

"Well, you can go play house with those two crazy bitches because I don't want you to be my dad. I don't want you to pretend you suddenly care. You had the chance to take care of me, and you failed. And guess what? I found someone who saw that I needed help, and he's been trying to help me from the moment I met him. I'm going to keep seeing Logan, and you can't stop me!"

She didn't wait around for his response. She slammed her hands down and pushed herself up from the table, throwing one final glare at Kevin before storming out of the dining room. Her blood was boiling. Her heart was racing as it pounded away in her still slightly sore chest. She couldn't believe the nerve of him. He had no right to come along now and act like he wanted to be her father.

Kylie stomped her way upstairs, her legs shaking so much she feared she'd collapse. She felt like she was going to explode. She felt like she had to fight and run all at the same time. He wanted to take Logan from her!

"Not happening," she said to herself, slamming and locking her bedroom door. She let out a growly scream, knowing full well she sounded psychotic, but she needed to let her rage out. It had been so easy to get attached to Logan. So fast. So powerful.

Of course, it had a lot to do with the fact he was the first person to really notice her. The logical part of her knew it wasn't normal to become so attached so quickly. In fact, she used to scoff at the stupidity of girls claiming they were in love after just becoming a couple, but she couldn't help herself from craving exactly that with Logan.

"Maybe I'm being crazy," she whispered as she fumbled through her pockets to pull out her phone. She had his contact pulled up before she knew it, her trembling fingers hovering over his name: *Logan Stolemypanties Grimm.*

"Maybe Kevin's right, though." Her eyes burned as her emotions made her start to crack. "Maybe Logan will leave right after we have sex. Maybe Janie will snap her fingers, and he'll go running to her."

She sat down on her bed, staring at his contact. She wanted to believe in the words she'd said to Kevin. She wanted to believe in Logan, in what they could become. But what if she was being a silly girl? What if she had been driven mad over everything that had happened to her? What if she was just a crazy girl with an out-of-control crush? Obsessed? God, she could hardly believe she'd just been hoping to brush up against Trevor two weeks ago.

The notification light began blinking, and she almost dropped the phone. Her breath hitched as she slid the lock off to read the message.

Logan Stolemypanties Grimm: I'm almost done baby. Just checking to see if ur ok.

She laughed out a slight sob and started her response, a smile on her face as she struggled to contain her happiness. She had to keep faith in him. She was hurt, not crazy. She was just reaching out to grab the hand being held out to her. She wasn't becoming obsessive.

I'll be better when you come, she replied.

Logan Stolemypanties Grimm: What's wrong? Did something happen?

She smiled, shaking her head even though he couldn't see her.

I'll tell you when I see you. I'm fine.

Logan Stolemypanties Grimm: Are you safe?

I'm fine! Just an argument with Kevin. It's fine.

Logan Stolemypanties Grimm: He didn't hurt you?

NO!

Logan Stolemypanties Grimm: Calm your tits woman. I just wanted to make sure you were ok.

Logan Stolemypanties Grimm: Did you take your bra off yet?

Her heartbeat sped up, and her smile stretched wider.

Logan.

Logan Stolemypanties Grimm: Panties?

LOGAN!

Logan Stolemypanties Grimm: Scream my name again, baby. I'm almost there.

She laughed and started pulling off her shoes.

You're disgusting.

Logan Stolemypanties Grimm: We've had this conversation already.

What conversation?

Logan Stolemypanties Grimm: I'm SEEEEEXY Hood. Sexy! Aren't I?

She couldn't stop smiling.

You're an idiot. And aren't you supposed to be doing something?

Logan Stolemypanties Grimm: Not doing anyone til you're 18.

She rolled her eyes.

Are you coming?

Logan Stolemypanties Grimm: No. Why? Are you naked? I might bust a nut just thinking about you.

"Fucking pervert," she muttered, smiling.

You're sexy.

Logan Stolemypanties Grimm: Be there in 20.

Logan Stolemypanties Grimm: Kylie, Kylie, let down your hair.

Kylie rubbed her sleepy eyes as she read the message. It was already near midnight, and she'd given up on Logan coming over.

She sighed, texting back, *What? Are you finally here?*

Logan Stolemypanties Grimm: Open your window.

She went to her window. Peeking out, she saw Logan sitting on a tree branch a few feet away.

She grinned and pushed her window up for him. "Why did you want my hair?"

"I was trying to be romantic."

She didn't know how that was romantic. It gave her the creeps.

He rolled his eyes. "Forget it, Hood. Just move so I can climb in."

Frowning, she stepped back and held her curtain so he could get through. He lifted himself in quite easily. She tried to stay calm, but when he turned to lower her window, she pounced. She wrapped her arms around his waist and pressed her cheek to his back.

Logan chuckled as her arms squeezed him from behind, but when he turned, his smile fell. "What's wrong?" He placed both hands on the sides of her face. "Baby, what happened? Did he hurt you? Is Lorelei here?"

She frowned, happy but overwhelmed. All her fears over what could be coming finally began to hit her. "I'm just happy you're here," she said, her voice cracking as she tried to pull him closer. "I thought you changed your mind."

"I didn't change my mind. I just got held up." He pulled her head to his chest as she hugged him tightly. After a few seconds of just savoring his hug, she sighed and lifted her head.

Logan didn't waste time and pressed his lips to hers. And, finally accepting that he was there and holding her, she smiled against his lips and wrapped her arms around his neck.

"I swear I need these lips more every second," he said, kissing her over and over.

Kylie smiled with him. He made everything better.

He backed her up to the bed. "Did you follow orders?"

She giggled as his hand slid under her shirt to find no bra.

"Good, little Hood."

"Ew," she said, smacking his hand when he tried to squeeze her breast.

"Ew?" He frowned and lowered his hands to her hips just as the bed met the back of her knees. As her eyes widened a little in anticipation, Logan smirked, then lowered his lips to her neck and eased her onto her back.

"You sound like a creepy old guy." Her head ached, but she tried to push the pain away, as well as her nerves. That was hard, considering Kevin was downstairs.

Logan brushed his lips over hers. "I'm not that old. And I think you mean freaky, not creepy." He wiggled his eyebrows. "Super freaky."

She glided her fingers across his chest before holding his face between her hands. "Kevin said I can't see you anymore. I told him I was going to see you anyway, and he can't just start acting like my dad now."

Logan relaxed and settled himself on his forearms. "So I've made you a freak and a bad girl. I like it."

"I am not a bad girl." She didn't want to be associated with being bad, at all. She was better than that. "Maybe you've made me a little bit of a freak, but I'm not a bad girl."

He chuckled and played with her hair as he glanced around the room. "You know, I've never snuck into a girl's bedroom before."

"Really?" She didn't know if he was joking or not.

He kept looking around before looking back at her. "Really," he said, settling his eyes on a picture of her with her real parents.

In the position they were in, it probably wasn't a good time to bring up his ex, but she was super curious. "Not even with Janie?"

Logan looked away from the family picture to frown at her. "What?"

She sighed and leaned upward to kiss his neck. The way he'd tense and tilt his head to give her more access made her think he would spill his secrets. "I asked if you ever snuck into Janie's room."

"Are you trying to kiss me into answering?" He chuckled and dipped his face to take the kiss she was aiming at his neck.

Turning her head, she giggled as he performed his torture on her neck. "I was just curious," she said, moaning when he slid his hand up her shirt.

"Are you happy that you're my first sneak-over?"

"Surprised." She sighed, closing her eyes as he kissed her chest.

He grinned when his lips kissed her shirt, just on top of her nipple.

Kylie peeked her eyes open to see him smirking at her. He darted his tongue out to lick her through the soft fabric. "Jesus," she hissed, squeezing her legs against his sides.

He leaned forward to kiss the spot he licked before moving to gift her other breast with equal attention.

She sighed, running her fingers through his thick hair. "Fuck, I'm so wet and . . ."

Logan started laughing, almost a little too loudly, so she pulled his face between her boobs to muffle the sound.

"*Shh,*" she tried to hush him.

He kept shaking from laughter. His hot breath created more moisture where his mouth was pressed against her shirt.

"Dammit, Logan."

He laughed but overpowered her, pushing out of her hold. "I'm sorry," he said, grinning as he rubbed his wet lips. "You just talk so dirty now. It's funny."

She glared at him.

"It's not funny?" He genuinely looked confused.

"I was talking about my shirt, Logan."

His eyes went to the two wet circles over her nipples, then he smiled.

"Don't smile."

"It looks like a smiley face though." He snickered, lowering his face to her chest.

She smacked his arm, stopping him.

"Do you want to punish me with your tits again? 'Cause I can be a bad boy if you want me to."

"Just answer the question."

He exhaled and moved to put his head down on her stomach. "Why do you want to talk about my relationship with her?"

"I don't." Lie. She wanted to know everything, and she didn't like that he didn't say ex-relationship. "I just want to know this one thing."

"No," he said, annoyed, "you want to know everything because you're a girl, and girls can't just keep shit simple."

Breathing became difficult, like sucking air through a straw. She hated he was so defensive about Janie but quick to snap at her. "Don't get angry."

"I just don't want to fight. There's nothing for you to worry about. I'm with you, not her."

Kylie knew it was stupid to talk about Janie. But for this instant, at least, she was just excited to be his first at something. She needed details. If she was his first, she felt almost like she'd won some sort of battle over the other women Logan had been with. "I only wanted to know this. It's not about her. It's just—is this really the first time you've snuck into a girl's room?"

Logan lifted his head and smiled. "Yes, baby. I've done a lot of stupid shit with women, but I've never stayed the night at one's house. I've never climbed through her window, or snuck inside any other way. You're my first."

She grinned, too happy to contain her giddiness.

He chuckled and kissed her stomach, snappy attitude forgotten. "That makes you happy?"

She nodded, still smiling.

"Well, good"—he pushed himself up to hover over her before giving her a soft kiss—"'cause you're my first and last sneak-over buddy."

Her stupid smile slipped. "Buddy?" Her mind hadn't even registered the first part of his statement.

Logan stopped his kisses and shrugged. "You know what I mean. My girlfriend."

Her breath audibly sucked in, and her body trembled. "I'm your girlfriend?"

Logan nodded. "Hood, I told you from the beginning; you're mine. My girl."

She was almost in tears as he kissed her cheeks, her nose and chin, then finally her pouting lips because she was trying so hard not to cry from everything he was making her feel.

"Aren't you?"

She nodded quickly, wondering if this was his way of officially asking her out. Obviously, things with Logan weren't going to follow the traditional rules she'd read about in her novels. But being his was not a question for her. "I'm yours, Logan. Only yours."

Her lips trembled as he brushed his back and forth across them. It wasn't quite a kiss, but it felt like he was taking her breath away all the same.

"And I'm yours, Hood." He caressed her cheek, smiling. "I know I told you I wasn't looking for a girlfriend, and I wasn't, but I still considered you mine."

"Now you're being romantic," she said, reaching up to pull him down.

He didn't disappoint her. Just like every kiss he'd given her, he led the way but made sure she stayed with him—teasing her, though, by making her think control was hers before dominating her again. She didn't care. He was her boyfriend! He could dominate her all he wanted.

"Did you lock your door like I told you to?" His low voice was huskier than it had been before, and she felt his excitement begging for her attention.

"I locked it," she whispered, dropping her hands to grab the top of his jeans. He let her snap the button but pulled her hands away before they slipped inside.

"Does he have a key?" he whispered, his gaze darkening.

She blinked through her lusty Logan daze and nodded. "Lorelei has a key. I'm sure he has one too."

He pushed himself up to get off the bed they had worked their way to the center of.

She fixed her shirt and sat up to watch him look around the room. It was dark, but there was still enough light from the moon to see most of the objects around them. A wooden chair by her desk gained his attention, and within seconds, he was carrying it to her door.

After he pulled out his phone to give himself some light, he quietly slid the back of the chair under her doorknob, moving it a few times until he seemed satisfied, and walked back to her.

"I don't like that he has a key to your room," he said, pulling his shirt over his head.

The sight, even just in the moonlight, left her speechless.

He's so sexy. And he's mine!

Logan turned to sit on the edge of her bed and bent over to take off his shoes. "We're getting you out of here as soon as possible."

Watching his muscles flex under his skin and tattoos was sort of lulling, and when Logan turned, she could barely hold her eyes open.

"Hood? You sleepy?"

She nodded, smiling.

He tugged his jeans off and placed them by his shoes. "I forgot you have school tomorrow."

"It's okay," she whispered as he leaned over to lift her up and pull her blanket out from under her.

"No, you need to get some sleep. You're still healing. I don't want you getting in trouble for falling asleep in class." He got her situated before he climbed in beside her. "We can talk after school tomorrow." He slid one hand under her shirt to rest against her stomach and pulled her close.

"This is another first for me, baby," he whispered, kissing the back of her neck.

"You mean cuddling?" She kept her eyes closed but smiled as he placed a few more kisses along her neck, his hand never pausing its exploration under her shirt.

He chuckled, the low tone soothing to her sleepy state. "Just being in bed with a girl without fu—"

She tried to buck him off her before he could finish what he was going to say, making him laugh again.

"Sorry, Hood." He reached up to pull her face toward his. "I like this." He kissed her, smiling against her lips. "Let's sleep, honey." There were several more kisses and nibbles to her cheek before he moved back into place behind her.

"Night, Logan."

He kissed her hair, murmuring, "Night, baby." Then he smacked her butt. "And don't back this ass up again unless you want me in you balls deep."

"What?" She tried to turn around, but he just kissed her head and held her still.

"Go to sleep."

She stared into the darkness, trying to figure out what he was saying until she got it. Gasping, she tried to smack his hand. "Logan, that's so nasty."

He smacked her hand back and hugged her tighter. "I'm horny."

"When aren't you?"

"Go to sleep. I'm tired too."

They settled into silence, a sleepy smile on Kylie's lips as he continued giving her a light massage wherever his hand could reach.

"Are you going to sneak out before I have to get up?" Her eyes were closed and her words soft.

"I'll wake you up before I go," he murmured, kissing her head. "I'm just going to run down to where I parked and come back to get you. Kevin can suck my left nut if he thinks he can keep you away from me."

She smiled, falling even more into the sleepy bliss that Logan gave her. After a minute, she said, "Just don't get into a fight with him. I feel bad for yelling at him before. He's just worried, I guess."

"Not worried enough. And the bastard is itching to fight me. Don't worry about anything though. I'll handle it. I'll take care of you."

She wanted to talk more, but with his body weight pressed against her and his strong arms hugging her tight, she was asleep in no time.

20
REMEMBER THIS

"What are you doing, man?"

Trevor looked away from Logan's drawer to see Ricky standing outside the bedroom door.

"Just keep an eye out," Trevor told him.

Ricky looked nervous as he glanced over his shoulder. "I don't think you should sneak around in here, man. He goes nuts about the slightest thing. What are you even looking for anyway?"

Trevor shrugged. "I know he's fucking Kylie. I'm just trying to find proof to burn his ass."

"I think he really likes her," Ricky said. "Maybe you should let it go."

"He doesn't like her. He's using her like he uses every girl."

Ricky took a small step back, shaking his head. "I don't think so, dude. Janie even helped her yesterday. And if

Janie's on her side, that means Ryder and all his brothers are with her too."

"Stop being a pussy." Trevor sneered.

"I'm not. It's just—the rumors that went around after Janie got raped."

"She wasn't raped," Trevor snapped. "She made it up—just like the pregnancy."

Ricky hesitated but said, "I believed her. You saw how depressed she was when school started up again, and she was wearing all those baggy clothes after cheating with Ryder. Then the Knights were all over the place, and they let those boys off."

"So?"

"So, you saw Logan with Ryder, and then Leo and Lycius vanished. So did their families, including the old police chief."

"What's your point?" Trevor looked up but then started digging through Logan's drawer. "He bought her lingerie. That proves it!"

"Dude," said Ricky, gaining Trevor's attention again, "that doesn't prove anything. And do you realize what can happen if you try to take him on? Those guys disappeared. Their families just vanished from town."

"So what? They moved to get away from the rumors that whore started."

"Stop calling her a whore, man." Ricky glared at him.

Trevor laughed, shaking his head. "You're such a dumb fuck, Hermes. Janie will never look at you."

"It's not like that," Ricky snapped. "Just stop calling her that."

"Whatever." Trevor took photos of the lingerie. "Just keep your mouth shut, and I won't let it slip to Logan you saw her naked when he was—"

Ricky shoved him. "I didn't mean to see!"

Trevor pushed him back. "Get out of here. And keep this shit to yourself."

"Fuck you." Ricky brushed past him, leaving Trevor alone in the apartment.

"Idiot," Trevor muttered, pausing when he saw a picture of Janie at the bottom of Logan's drawer. He shook his head, closing the drawer.

◆◆◆

So fucking gorgeous.

Kylie knew she probably looked like a stalker or something with her face inches away from Logan's as he slept, but she couldn't help herself. He was lovely. There wasn't anything about his appearance she'd change.

She smiled because, for once, she was waking up happy, and it was all because Logan, her official boyfriend, had her pulled against his bare chest with a possessive grip on her thigh, which was draped over his waist. She stifled her giggle when he mumbled something and tightened his grip on her.

"Oh, my," she said softly. The boy was hard in his sleep, and simply knowing that part of his body was surging with blood caused a tingle to grow between her legs.

"Baby?"

Damn that husky voice of his. She had to squeeze her legs together just to keep from climbing on top of him so he could thrust inside her. *I have serious problems.* She really hoped the wetness that started to soak her panties would go unnoticed. "I didn't know you were awake."

He kissed the top of her head. "I've been awake for an hour."

She tried to hide her face in his chest as he laughed. "I wasn't being a weirdo."

"Staring at me with your face just an inch from mine while I sleep isn't weird?"

"No, I read it's how couples greet each other in the morning."

He chuckled but quieted himself quickly. "Well, I guess tomorrow morning you can expect my face hovering over yours when you open your eyes."

"Shut up." *Tomorrow?* She had never been so embarrassed or giddy before. "I wasn't trying to be creepy."

"Stare all you want, baby. I know I'm sexy. No one will blame you for it."

"You're so full of yourself." She pushed herself out of his arms even though she wanted nothing more than to stay right where she was.

"You're just jealous because you're not," he said, letting her go. "Yet," he added, winking.

"Do you always have to talk about us having sex?"

"Yes," he said, completely serious.

"What?" Her happiness smacked a brick wall. Was that really all he wanted? Still?

"Kidding, Hood." He tilted her chin up, smiling tenderly. "But I am imagining the fact that all I have to do is slide your panties over to sit you down on my co—"

"Dammit, Logan!" God, every time he was sweet, he followed it up with something dirty. It made it so hard to believe this still wasn't just sex for him.

"What? I'm horny."

Her happiness deflated even more. "But we just did stuff yesterday."

He stared at her, confused. "So?"

She was nervous about having the sex talk. Of course, she couldn't stop her thoughts from imagining how it would feel to have him moving in and out of her, but it was still insane. She really didn't know much anyway. There were those few erotica novels last year she'd been so embarrassed over reading, but was that how everything worked? So far, those naughty chapters she'd once stared wide-eyed at were all the instructions she had to guide her. Logan hadn't laughed at her efforts; she was always a bright student. But how did guys work? Did they need more? "How often do you—you know?" She pointed to his bulge.

Logan chuckled. "Hood, I'm hard several times a day. Since meeting you, it's been a little more than normal. But that's because the moment I laid eyes on you, I imagined stripping you right there in my kitchen and bending you over my table."

"What?" She couldn't believe he was imagining that the first time he saw her.

He shrugged. "I'm a guy. We're always horny. And having a hot woman close by, especially one I get to hold and kiss—I'm going to be walking around with a boner until I can at least jack off."

"Does it hurt?"

He chuckled, nodding. "It's uncomfortable."

"I'm sorry," she said, looking away from him. "You won't go . . . to another girl, will you?"

Logan didn't answer her. Instead, he pulled her face to his and kissed her. The knowledge that they hadn't brushed their teeth barely had time to bother her.

"Let's take a shower," he murmured, still kissing her as he began to pull them both out of bed. "Then you'll see I don't need another girl."

That wasn't very comforting, but she was ready to do anything to keep him. "But what about Kevin?"

Logan began kissing her neck. "He better not come in when he thinks you're showering."

She grinned at his angry tone, moaning as he sucked her neck. "No, he never comes to wake me for school. I think we're good as long as we keep it down."

"Good."

"*Shh*," she whispered when he placed her on her feet. "Let me brush my teeth." She wiggled out of his hold, glancing at his massive hard-on before she raced to her sink.

"I already kissed you. You taste good."

She chuckled, putting her toothpaste on her toothbrush while she looked around for a spare. She knew she'd chucked one of those dentist's bags around here somewhere. While she searched for it, Logan took the initiative to warm the water up before she watched him approach her in the mirror. They kept their eyes locked as he wrapped his arms around her waist and dipped his head to kiss the side of her neck.

"I found a spare toothbrush," she mumbled, holding it out for him.

"Do I have bad breath?"

"Yes," she said, lying flat out to his face. It was unfair how perfect he was, and all the more reason to show him she could be perfect too.

He pouted but let go and opened his toothbrush. "You're a mood killer, Hood."

She smiled as he started brushing his teeth, giving her time to rinse her mouth and move away from the sink so he'd have room. She had no intention of killing the mood. After making sure the water was warm, she walked to where he could see her reflection next to his. After receiving a wink from him as he brushed away, she started pulling her shirt up over her head.

His brushing ceased during those few moments she was stuck under her shirt, then when she finally looked up, she was blessed with his full attention.

"I don't want you to think of another woman, Logan." She didn't look away from his reflection.

He didn't say anything. His eyes kept darting between hers and her body.

Kylie reached for her panties, still watching his face in the mirror. "I want to be the only woman you think of—the only one to bring you pleasure." She pushed her panties down to her ankles before kicking them away. When she looked at him, his toothbrush was barely hanging from his mouth. "If you're in pain, and I'm not with you, you think of me—of what you see right now." She had no idea how she managed to make her voice sound so smooth, seductive, but she knew she was returning the mood he'd clearly wanted her in. "Can you remember this, Logan?"

"Yes, baby."

"Will you need another woman to satisfy you, even if we can't be together?"

He shook his head.

"Will you wait for me?"

He nodded.

"And when I'm not able to touch you, will you think of me when you have to touch yourself?"

Logan leaned forward and rinsed his mouth out fast before walking to her, not even pausing before he lowered his mouth to hers. One hand was in her hair while the other pulled her against him.

She didn't notice how quickly he pulled his briefs off, or when he managed to pull them both under the water. All she had in her mind was his lips, his tongue—his strong arms holding her against his perfect body. And just for a moment, a tiny escape from reality, she lost all connection to the world around her and began to become one with Logan.

"Aah!"

He had her lifted, pressed against the shower wall. Her eyes were wide as her mouth opened. She panted as only the tip of his dick started to press inside her. She wanted it. He was there, and he felt amazing.

He growled, and she tried to pull him in.

He still wasn't inside enough—it was only the tip. She wanted him deeper, and she finally began to feel her warmth stretch around him.

"Fuck!"

Then he wasn't there.

"What?" she whispered, confused.

He set her on her feet and pushed her against the wall, silencing her with his fierce expression when she looked up at his face.

"We can't, Hood." He grabbed a hold of his cock and started stroking himself. "This is all I ever want to see." He reached for her hand with his free one, the other still busy sliding up and down his shaft in steady strokes.

She had never been more turned on, and that was saying something, considering he had been able to take her to ecstasy and back several times now.

Kylie squeezed her wet legs together to try to relieve the ache between them, moaning as he groaned and kissed the inside of her wrist. She could still feel him. Just that teasing caress he had given, and she knew it wouldn't leave until he was completely inside her.

The squelching sound of his hand mixed with their heavy breathing bounced of the tile wall.

"Touch yourself, baby."

She barely noticed that he had lowered her hand and was guiding it between her legs. He stepped closer, the tip of his throbbing dick brushing across her belly. All this occurred as he kept his strokes firm and steady.

"I don't know how," she said, tilting her head up so he could kiss her.

Within seconds, she was moaning into his mouth because he began rubbing circles with his fingers before sliding one inside her.

"Like this," he said, grunting as he pleased them both. "You try it. I want to watch you."

She nodded, too consumed by everything she was feeling. Her chest arched into his palm. She could hardly tell that it was her hand between her legs now. He pressed one of his thighs against her hand to give her even more friction to rub herself against.

Kissing her, he promised she was all he wanted. "Wait for me, baby." He grunted, jerking himself faster.

"Harder, Logan," she said, her breath almost gone as she watched him follow her order. He was so beautiful—and damn, she was ready to ask him to take her.

"Ah, fuck." He grabbed her head, his fingers tangling in her hair and tugging. "Come."

21
I AM TRUTH

Kevin was cooking. Kylie didn't even know he could cook.

"What are you doing?" she asked, staring at his back while he stood there pushing a spatula around a skillet filled with scrambled eggs.

He turned his head, frowning but not stopping his task. "I'm cooking breakfast. I know Lor says you don't like the cook's food, and she isn't here to make it for you."

She continued staring at him, unsure of what to say as she wished she was back with Logan. He had snuck out ten minutes ago to go get his car, promising to be there as soon as he could to take her to school. But what she wasn't expecting to find when she came down to wait for him was her stepfather acting like a stay-at-home dad.

"Sit down." He nodded toward the stool by the kitchen island. "I want to talk to you before I take you to school."

"Logan's coming to pick me up."

He switched the burner off and turned with the skillet in hand. "I'm taking you."

She shook her head. "He'll be here any minute. I want him to take me."

"We talked about this last night, Kylie. You will not see him. He's turning you into a delinquent."

"A delinquent?" She let out a sharp laugh as she took a step back. "I can't believe you. I get bullied, and I'm the delinquent?" She shook her head again. "Logan cares about me. He's the best thing to ever happen to me. He's the one who tries to take care of me after I've been left all by myself. Even his friends, or whoever they are, are better people than Maura and Lorelei. They didn't have to help me, but they stepped up when those mean whores—"

"Enough!" He slammed his hand on the counter. "I've had enough of you talking back to me like this. You've changed so much, and you can't even see it. Your looks, your smart mouth, and I don't doubt he's already trying to have sex with you."

She screwed her face up in disgust. "I have changed, but it's in the best way. And don't talk to me about what I do in my relationship. I'm almost eighteen. You haven't even been here for me anyway. Don't you dare tell me to stay away from the first man who has."

"I'm trying now," he whispered.

She stared at him in disbelief.

"Please, Kylie." He braced himself against the counter. "I'm just trying to help. You don't know Logan. He's dangerous, and you have no idea about the families he's close to. I'd hoped they were only rumors, but last night I realized the girl involved in the fight yesterday is the same girl who—well, I'd rather not say. Just trust me—it's best to end things with him before you get hurt."

She was dying to know what he was about to say regarding Janie, but she was too angry that Kevin was trying to take Logan from her. "I'll only hurt if you make him leave me. And he won't let you."

Kevin sighed and shook his head. "You don't even know him. You met a little over a week ago. You're being a foolish child because he's the first boy to take an interest in you."

His words hurt, but she was still too fired up to stop. "But he's already healing the wounds I've had for years."

The doorbell rang.

"He's here," she said, looking over her shoulder. "I'll eat with him."

"Stop." The furious spark in his eyes made her halt. "Stay put."

She stayed still and watched him walk away to answer the door. She kept quiet and listened to him telling Logan that she wasn't going to school today. Her heart raced so fast she felt almost dizzy, but fire consumed her when Kevin started to tell Logan they were no longer allowed to see each other.

"No," she yelled, running to the door.

Logan looked furious, and she knew he was seconds away from throwing a punch.

"Don't you dare pull this shit." She ducked Kevin's arm when he reached out to keep her back and ran right to Logan's side, where she was instantly engulfed in a hug.

"Get your hands off her," Kevin snapped.

Logan moved quickly, carefully shoving her behind him before he had his hand wrapped around Kevin's throat. And before she could scream, he had Kevin pinned against the nearest wall.

"Logan." She ran up behind them.

He didn't even look at her. "Stay back, Hood."

Kylie froze upon hearing his dark tone.

Kevin wasn't afraid. He was merely staying still, waiting.

"I'm not hurting him," Logan said, his voice low and raw.

"Let me go," Kevin seethed. "I'll call the police, you worthless punk. I'll keep you from ever fighting again."

"And I'll call the police on you," Logan said, inching his face closer. "You're not the only rich bastard with connections, Blackwood."

Kevin laughed. "What could you possibly say about me, kid? I didn't put it together at first, but I know now exactly who you consort with."

Logan smiled evilly. "Then you know not to fuck with me, and you know I'm not going to let this abuse you've turned a blind eye to continue."

The dark look in Kevin's eyes dimmed. "What are you talking about?"

"Logan," she whispered, her heart thundering. She almost felt like she might pass out. What did Kevin know about Logan? And what was Logan doing?

"Relax, Hood." Logan still didn't look at her. He kept staring at Kevin, scrutinizing him. "Don't try my patience—I have almost none. You've seen her limp. You've seen her flinch. You've ignored her hiding the bruises and cuts. And she runs for safety into those damned woods because the fucking wolves are right here."

Kevin stared at him, darting his eyes to Kylie, then back to Logan. "I don't know what you're talking about."

"Yes, you do," Logan yelled, slamming Kevin back hard, "and it makes you just as guilty as them. You don't have to be the one beating her with a fucking baseball bat to be responsible for the wounds she's received." He made a sort of growling sound before shoving Kevin away and pulling her under his arm. "Stay the fuck away from her. She's not coming home tonight—she'll be staying with a friend of mine until she decides whether or not she wants to be in this house. And don't you dare try to come after her. I already have someone looking into shit, and they're more powerful than you."

Logan picked up the backpack she'd dropped and grabbed her hand to pull her out the door.

"Kylie," Kevin whispered, making them stop at the steps. "I swear I don't know what he's talking about. Please stay. Let's talk about whatever it is he's insinuating."

Kylie shook her head. She was furious Logan was going behind her back—he wasn't supposed to tell anyone—but she was more enraged with Kevin trying to stop her from seeing Logan. So she looked at him and said softly, "Kevin, deep down, I think you've always known what they've done to me."

He started to shake his head.

"Don't," she snapped, her panic wrapping her up. There was no way she could stay here now. "I'm going with him, and I'm not coming back. You can call Logan if you want to get in touch with me. I know they're coming home today, and I'm not going to sit here anymore while they try to kill me. Let me go, or I will make sure your name is ruined in this town. And don't threaten Logan again."

When Kevin stayed quiet, Logan kissed the top of her head and pulled her to his car.

◆◆◆

Sighing, Kylie put her binder in her backpack and closed her locker.

"Kylie." Trevor jogged over to her. "Hey, you need a ride?"

"No," she said, walking around him. He was drawing so much more attention to her than she already had, and when she looked down at her red hoodie, she contemplated pulling her hood up again.

"I want to talk to you though."

She sighed and stopped walking. He took the chance to move closer, so they were just a few feet apart.

"What do you want to tell me?" she asked. "I don't really have a lot of time. I'm supposed to meet my ride outside." She wasn't lying. Logan had called her at lunch and said he would be coming to pick her up.

He frowned, scanning her appearance. "Who's giving you a ride?"

"Logan, of course." It made her feel so giddy to say that.

Trevor sighed, stepping even closer. "He's using you. I don't know why he's so into this play with you, but he's tricking you. And you can get in trouble for having sex."

She scoffed and took a step back. "He's not playing anything. And we're not your business."

"I'm just trying to help," Trevor said with a sad, guilty look in his eyes. "I introduced you to him—put you on his radar. Now he's destroying you."

"Wow." She shook her head and walked away.

"He has sex with girls as bets," he rushed out before she could pass him. "Ask his friends. Well, the guys at his gym. No one is really friends with him."

She looked at him but didn't know how to feel.

"Did he tell you he broke his manager's arm?" he asked softly. "You were a bet, Kylie. Chris saved you. Logan lost it and attacked him."

"You're lying." Her heart thundered in her chest. It couldn't be true. "Chris was just trying to get me to leave."

"He was trying to keep you from getting hurt. I promise you, as soon as you guys have sex, because I know now that must be the case, he'll dump you. And just like Chris said, another girl will be in his bed before you know it." He touched her shoulder, bending to stare into her eyes. "He's probably hopeful he'll get Janie back. He keeps a picture of her in his dresser—probably to jack off. I saw he had the lotion she used to like. He always talked about how she smelled like raspberries."

Her heart cracked. "No."

"And what about you, Grimm?" Ryder Godson walked out of the dark hallway. "What sort of twisted shit do you engage in?"

Trevor tensed and, surprising her, fired back, "Fuck off, Godson."

A deadly smirk lifted Ryder's lips. "Isn't that your job, pretty boy? And I know damn well he never told you how she smells or tastes, so enlighten me on how you know what lotion she uses."

Kylie looked between the two of them, sort of happy to see the wicked gleam in the bad boy's eyes as he glared at Trevor. If Ryder was denying this, then there was hope. No way would Ryder allow Logan to have anything of Janie's.

Trevor didn't back down. "Are you gonna tell her the truth about them?"

Ryder shrugged a shoulder. "I don't give a fuck what she thinks about them. Grimm can pine after my baby all he wants. He's not getting her back."

Kylie whimpered, darting her eyes between them.

Ryder's gaze slid over to her before settling on Trevor again. "And he gave Janie their pictures, so stop starting shit between them."

Trevor's nostrils flared and his jaw clenched as he spoke through gritted teeth. "I'm warning her. He wouldn't have a picture of her naked in a drawer full of lingerie this morning if he was over her. He's using Kylie, and I won't let it happen."

"Maybe he kept a picture so we have more reason to fight." Ryder chuckled, tilting his head. "But it's not your business what he and Janie had together. Now get the fuck out of my sight. I'll let you live in fear for a few days just because you've seen her naked."

Trevor's eyes flashed as he appeared to debate saying something.

"Run along." Ryder made a shooing gesture. "I'm not in the mood to deal with you anymore today."

Trevor glared at him but walked away without looking back at her.

"Come on, Blondie," Ryder ordered her.

She didn't move.

"Check your phone," he said, annoyed.

After sliding her finger across the screen, she realized she did indeed have a text from Logan.

Logan Stolemypanties Grimm: I'm in a meeting with some guys about a fighting contract right now. Ryder will bring you here.

"Ready?" Ryder asked, glancing at his own phone. "Piece of shit."

"I'm sorry." She didn't know what she did to piss him off so much.

"Not you, dumbass." He lifted his gaze from his phone. "Your boyfriend is gonna get his ass beat if he still has a picture of her."

Her eyes watered as she shook her head. "Does he really have it just to fight you? And it's my lotion."

He stared at her. "Trevor is just trying to get you to hate Janie like everyone else already does. If there is a picture, I'll take care of it." He turned, walking away. "Hurry the fuck up."

Even though her heart was cracking, Kylie jogged to catch up with him. "Thank you, Ryder. For taking up for me, and for the ride."

"Thank my girlfriend. I told Logan to suck my left nut and come get you himself." He gave her a dismissive glance. "Stop staring at me like a fucking puppy. I wasn't taking up for you. I was protecting my girl."

Kylie dropped her gaze. God, he really could make you feel like you were nothing. She just wanted him to be a little nicer. "Why not the right one?"

"What?" He shoved some poor football player who was getting something out of a locker.

She watched the guy drop a bottle of pills.

Ryder stepped on them. "Oops."

The football player stared at Ryder in absolute fear before scrambling away.

"That was mean." Kylie watched Ryder squish the pills.

He leaned down, picking up the bottle and the only intact pill, inspecting it. It was a small white tablet. "Do you know what this is?"

She shrugged. "I don't know. It's in a prescription bottle. He probably needs it."

Ryder shook his head as he crushed the pill between his fingers, making the powder fall to the floor. He started kicking the powder around before noticing a soda in the locker. He opened it, pouring it on the crushed pills, and started walking without bothering to clean it up. "It's a roofie."

Her jaw dropped as she hurried after him. "For real?"

"No, I just get kicks out of destroying medicine." He gave her an annoyed glare. "Yes, for real." He held up the bottle. "Unless his name is Guadalupe and he lives in Juarez, Mexico, this isn't his. Most of the team took a trip there to smuggle this shit back. They've been dealing them to sick fucks who've been drugging girls at parties."

She rolled her eyes. "I doubt that's happening. This isn't some lame movie."

He shoved the doors open. "Do yourself a favor and shut the fuck up when you don't know what you're talking about."

"I was trying to joke," she said, trying to keep up with him.

He stopped walking and stared at the pavement as he spoke in a low but deadly voice, "If you're making jokes about girls getting raped, you can walk your stupid ass right off a damn cliff."

Her heart hammered away. "Sorry. If you're serious, why not call the cops?"

He lifted his head, exhaling loudly as he started walking again. He didn't answer her.

It was so humiliating to be in his presence, but she couldn't deny she wanted him to keep talking to her. So she blurted, "You said he could suck your left nut. Why not the right?"

He didn't acknowledge her and kept walking through the parking lot.

She felt so embarrassed. She never ever thought she'd even talk to Ryder, and when she did she asked him why not his left nut?

Ryder cast a glance over his shoulder at her, a mischievous smile on his gorgeous face. It stunned her, but he spoke, breaking the daze he almost put her in. "Janie owns it. The right one—no, actually, they're both hers. But the right is her favorite."

"Oh my God," she whispered, grossed out but giddy as hell to have him actually joking with her.

"Nope," he said. She almost asked what he meant but he continued. "Seems like you got your own pair."

"My own pair of what?" Kylie kept her eyes glued to his profile, waiting for a reaction besides his normally cold expression.

"Balls."

Her mouth fell open. "Whose balls?"

Even though he looked annoyed with her, he kept talking to her, "I didn't think you'd take my advice and tell him you liked his ugly ass."

"Oh," she said, smiling. "Yeah, I guess I did. Do you think it was stupid to tell him?"

"If I thought it was stupid, I wouldn't have suggested it."

She bit her lip before rushing out, "Do you think it's stupid to like someone so quickly? I mean, my stepdad keeps talking about me being dumb, and that Logan's dangerous and so experienced—"

He pulled a set of keys from his pocket. "I fell for a girl after staring into her eyes once. She was in a serious relationship with Logan, and don't get all emotional about that—it's not your business."

"I didn't say I was emotional about it." She was. She totally was. And it was so her business.

"Yeah, right." He chuckled, checking something on his phone. "I fell for Janie. Hard. Everyone told me she was set up with him, that he was just waiting for her to finish school, but I didn't care. I didn't go looking to steal her, but what point was there in denying I wanted her? I knew I could be more for her, and I could—believe me. Logan treated her like shit, so I knew I was better for her than his bitch ass."

As much as Kylie wanted to argue on Logan's behalf, she wasn't about to say Logan and Janie should've been left to live happily ever after.

"So I made a choice." He pocketed his phone. "I didn't sit there like a pussy and cry because she was taken, or come up with some dumb plan just to get close to her. I took a chance. I told her how I felt. There's stuff that makes our relationship more intense—theirs too—but I was better for her. I knew she was mine, and I could love her better than he ever could."

She bit her lip to keep from saying something nasty. It stabbed something painful inside her to hear someone love another girl. It wasn't fair to be unwanted for so long while someone else was being cherished like a princess. Especially one that was cared for by Logan while *she* had been suffering.

"If you keep your real feelings to yourself," Ryder went on, "how the fuck is anyone else going to know what you want?"

Words came flying out of her mouth before she could stop them, "Did she cheat on him with you?"

He glared at her. "I already told you she doesn't cheat. She didn't then either."

She was terrified, but she still asked, "Then why do people think that? I even heard someone say you got her pregnant." She'd paid attention to the whispers today because Janie wasn't at school. People were saying she was arrested, shipped out of the country by her stepdad, or on the run. But it was the rumor that she'd gotten pregnant after cheating on Logan that piqued her interest. There was no way Logan should want Janie after she had done such a thing.

He paused, breathing hard as he closed his eyes. "People say shit like it's their business, especially when they don't know what the fuck happened. I suggest you forget what you heard."

"Sorry," she muttered.

"I don't care if you're sorry." He opened his eyes and started walking again.

Kylie sighed, gripping the straps of her backpack. "Did anyone tell you you were stupid for falling in love with her like you did?"

"Not to my face. My advice is don't give a single fuck if someone tells you it's stupid. You might be dumb as fuck for loving that person, but you don't have to give a fuck what anyone says. If you're both honest and that person makes you happy, fuck the world."

"I've never heard anyone use so many f-words before."

He shrugged. "I'm impressive at everything I do."

She shook her head as they approached a light gray Camaro. It wasn't the same one she rode in the other day. It gave off a sense of dread, which was made worse by the license plate: SORROW. "Is this yours?"

"Obviously," he said, opening his door and sitting. Before she could sit, he turned it on, the roar louder and more powerful than the one she rode in last time. "The other car was the one I bought Janie. She loves Camaros. Hers is an SS, 6.2 Liter V8 Di engine, 455 horsepower and 455 pounds of torque." He revved the engine a few times before taking off. She literally jerked in the seat, her head slamming against the headrest. "This is a ZL1. It's a Supercharged 6.2 Liter V8, 650 horsepower and 650 pounds of torque."

She grabbed the edge of the seat with one hand while her other held the door. "Okay, I get it, it's faster. Slow down."

"I want to see my girlfriend. So, no."

She glanced over at him. He didn't look any different, but she could see the strain in his green eyes.

"Why did she help me?"

"Who?" he asked, not sparing her a glance.

"Janie. Why does she care so much? Logan is her ex, and I'm no one to her."

He flicked his eyes over to her, then back to the road. "She loves him, and that's all there is to it."

Her lungs burned. "Does she want him back?"

"Are you seriously asking me that?"

"Sorry." She rubbed her chest, startling herself because she forgot her breasts weren't taped.

"Like I said—don't care if you're sorry. Or about anything you say or think."

God, he was so mean.

"But her feelings for him have nothing to do with you or me," he said. "Same thing with him. You just have to accept that they're close if you want anything with him. We did something stupid, and she kept me and Logan from paying the price. She still does. But it was our fault. And it'll always tie us together—especially the two of them. Their relationship is destined."

She frowned, pressing her palm harder against her chest. "Destined?"

"Yeah."

"How do you deal with it?"

He shrugged. "They love each other, and I hate it, but that's just how it is. I want my baby girl, and she comes with a mutt I can't tell her to toss back on the street."

Kylie looked down at her lap as her heart started to bleed. Logan was officially her boyfriend, but she was starting to believe there was never going to be a time when she really had him to herself.

"They're each other's first love." He sighed, shifting gears. "You don't ever get over that. In their case, they won't just drift apart. That's not how any of *us* work. I'm not going to explain why—just accept there's more to all of us than you think. I told you, you have no idea what you got into with him."

"I've never believed people don't get over first loves," she muttered, staring out the window. Whatever he was trying to hint at was probably something absurd, and she wasn't going to listen.

"Because you haven't had one." He didn't look at her. "Janie happens to be mine. I just got there second."

"But you guys seem made for each other." As much as that irked her, it was true.

"That's the fairytale way of viewing it." A slight smile touched his lips before vanishing.

"I just want that. I want to matter."

"I'm not your friend, so stop blabbing to me. I'm giving you a ride because Janie asked me to."

Her stomach cramped as she told him, "I don't have people to talk to."

"Maybe because you don't try to talk to anyone." He rolled to a stop at a red light.

She clasped her shaking hands together on her lap. "It's not that simple. I was forced to be a loner."

"I doubt that." He glanced out his window. There was a patrol car beside them. He flipped off the officer.

The cop just looked forward as Ryder chuckled and took off again.

Fury sizzled in her veins from his comment, and she couldn't stay quiet. "Are you calling me a liar?"

"I'm saying I see everything." He sounded bored. "And I never saw anyone holding a gun to your head, forcing you to not talk to the people around you."

"You never saw me before the fight," she spat. "And you have no idea why it wouldn't take someone holding a gun to my head to make me hide."

He slowly slid his gaze over to her. "I said I see everything. Sometimes it takes me a while to make sense of what I'm looking at, but I always do when it's time. And you, Blondie, you were the only one keeping yourself hidden under that hood. Try to use the excuse of being afraid of some retaliation all you want. If that were true, you would have run when Trevor approached you. Everyone knows Maura is in love with him, but you had no problem showing your face for him—no problem letting her see it happen either."

Her breathing quickened. "I showed my face because of Logan."

"Sure you did," he said calmly, focusing on the road again.

"You don't know anything." She tried to sink deeper into the seat. The air inside the car felt too thin, and she hated that he got to her.

"I know you've been getting the shit beaten out of you," he said like it was common knowledge, "and you let it go on until you had a Grimm to act like a knight in shining armor. I know you wanted Trevor until he shattered your little fantasy of him being a dream guy, but you didn't care much, did you? Not when Logan Grimm was there, whispering sweet shit in your ear. He probably said you were special—that you were the only girl he wanted—that you weren't like the others and he wanted to protect you."

Her breath hitched.

He smiled, and it was the cruelest thing she'd ever seen. "I know he wanted to fuck you, but he slowed down because you're not eighteen. He checked, by the way—you're not at risk of getting him locked up because you're within a three-year age gap. So if he fucks you now, it's because he's not scared."

Her eyes watered, and the air in her lungs was no longer hers. Ryder was taking everything from her.

"I know he saw a bit of Janie when he looked at you," he added. "He saw a girl who needed a hero. He saw a second chance." He almost sounded concerned, but she knew better now. "But the only chance he's hoping for—that he needs—is for a pair of hazel eyes to look at him like he's the greatest man in the world again." He stared at her. "What color eyes do you have, Blondie?"

"You're an asshole." She turned away from him.

"The truth hurts. Don't say I didn't warn you. I am truth. Logan is a lie."

22
DOUBT

Kevin stood in the foyer with his arms folded over his chest as he watched Lorelei and Maura enter the house.

"Where's Kylie?" Lorelei asked, setting her purse down.

"With her boyfriend," he said, watching the two women look at each other. "Her boyfriend who told me she would not be coming home until she felt safe here. Her boyfriend, who is affiliated with the most powerful families in the world, threatened to call the police on me for not protecting her from being beaten with a baseball bat."

Lorelei gestured to the stairs. "Go to your room, Maura. Do not come out until I say."

"But—"

"Do as I say," Lorelei snapped, walking to where Kevin stood.

Maura looked between her mother and stepfather, then slowly ascended the staircase until she was out of sight.

A door slammed upstairs, and Lorelei stared into Kevin's eyes as she reached for the zipper on her dress.

✦✦✦

"Ow," Kylie muttered, rubbing her elbow where the door Ryder had just walked through hit her. She didn't even know why she was following him. She should have been walking home. What she was doing was stupid. She was following Ryder even though he'd just ripped her heart out. All she wanted was for him to be a little nicer to her, and he proved he didn't give a shit about her.

"Lost your way, babe?"

Kylie stopped walking, her eyes widening when a guy stepped out in front of her. He might've been a decent looking guy at one time, but his cauliflower ears made him look disgusting, and she cringed when he gave her a broken smile. *God, how does Logan stay so good-looking?*

"I said, you look lost. Need some help?"

She shook her head.

He took a step closer. "Come on, cutie. Don't be like that."

"I'm here to see my boyfriend," she whispered, trying to move away when he continued to advance. "Logan Grimm."

"Grimm?" He laughed and kept walking until she was backed up against the wall. "The Reaper doesn't do girlfriends. Just a half hour ago he had his little hottie Mortaime in his room and her screams bouncing around the whole gym."

Kylie's lungs collapsed as he laughed again, driving a rusty knife into her heart.

"Now stop playing hard to get," he said. "Grimm's not interested in anything but a hard fuck, and he looked more than satisfied with that little brunette of his."

Kylie's lip trembled and tears welled up in her eyes.

"Hey," came a different voice.

The man turned around to see who had spoken, only to have Ryder's fist slam into his face before he could say anything.

Screaming, Kylie covered her ears to keep from listening to the sounds of Ryder's hits against the limp guy's face.

"Babe!"

Kylie peeked her eyes open, not realizing she'd closed them or crouched down against the wall, as Janie came running toward them. Ryder threw a final punch and stood up, not looking away from the broken guy.

Janie touched his shoulder. "Ryder, look at me."

Kylie's chest hurt as her heart pounded fiercely. Not from fear as it had just done, but from anger now that she had her eyes on Janie.

"Where is he?" Ryder asked, growling as he turned to glare at Janie.

"Who?" Janie walked closer, worried as she looked over her enraged boyfriend, but not afraid. "Babe, what happened?"

"Logan," Ryder snapped, his eyes narrowing on his girlfriend's confused face.

Kylie was too afraid to move.

Ryder was pissed, and he was ready to explode again. "Did he touch you?"

Both Kylie and Janie flinched from his harsh voice.

But Janie's frightened look shifted into one of anger and disbelief. "You know better than that." She stepped toe to toe with him, tilting her head to look up at him as he stared down at her with the most terrifying glare Kylie had ever seen. "Is that what this was?"

"Why the fuck does he still have your picture?" he growled.

"What picture?" Janie's gaze stayed angry as she glanced at Kylie.

Ryder didn't answer, he just kept taking deep, angry breaths and clenching his bloody hand.

Janie focused on Ryder again. "Did that piece of shit say I was fucking Logan while I waited for you? Really, Ryder? We're doing this shit? You know I can't handle you being angry with me right now."

Ryder growled out something before smashing his lips to hers. Janie kissed back just for a moment before punching his chest and trying to shove him off.

"I'm sorry, baby girl," he said, his voice still hard but soothing in a strange way. He kept trying to hug her. "You know shit's just getting to me."

Janie kept trying to shove him away, her face scrunching up, heartbroken. "I know, but you should trust me."

"I do." He kissed her face all over because she pressed her lips together, refusing to kiss him back. It was pathetic and infuriating to watch him acting all sappy after being such a jerk to her. "Forgive me," he begged Janie. "Please. I've just been worried about you all fucking day."

Kylie didn't know how to feel yet. Part of her was still shaken up from being cornered by the fighter and the unforgiving beating Ryder so effortlessly delivered, but another more hurt and enraged part of her was ready to claw Janie's eyes out. She was done with this girl. She was nothing but trouble. And every time she needed comfort, it was Janie who got it.

"It hurts me," Janie whispered as he kept kissing her cheeks and hugging her.

Kylie might have thought it was cute once, but now she could only see Logan with his arms around Janie, her stupid fucking hazel eyes staring up at him.

"I know. I'm sorry," Ryder told her, still leaving kisses on her unresponsive lips, her cheeks, nose, and chin.

"What happened?" came Logan's yell from down the hall. He came marching over, throwing Ryder a fierce glance before he took in Kylie's crouched figure. "Are you okay?"

She flinched away from him when he tried to grab her. It was just an automatic reaction, and all she could see was the smile Logan had given Janie when they came to the gym yesterday. God, Ryder was right. Logan hugged Janie—he even kept his hands on her until he was forced to let go. Janie was going to steal him from her.

"Hood?" Logan caressed her cheek.

Kylie stared at his dark eyes, her heart losing its rage and crumbling at the thought of how Logan and Janie must have been. What second chance did Logan really want? Was she just there to get him to a point where he'd win some part of Janie back?

"Baby, what happened?" he asked, looking frustrated. He glanced at Janie, making Kylie turn to see Ryder carrying the bitch down the hall as she kept up her pouting like she'd been the one hurt instead of her. Ryder, the asshole he would always be, was apologizing like a little boy. He'd broken *her* heart with everything he'd said, and now he had the nerve to pamper Janie right in front of her.

"What happened?" Logan was angry now, taking in the moaning guy and her glare toward Janie and Ryder. "Kylie!"

"He said you were with her," she said, cutting her gaze to him, ignoring a few guys who came to check on the man on the floor. "The guy he hit. He said you were with Janie."

Logan frowned, searching her eyes. She had green eyes, not hazel. Was that all he was seeing? That they weren't the eyes he wanted staring into his?

"He said you didn't do girlfriends," she clarified, her anger returning, "and that you were fucking Janie half an hour ago. Said he could hear her screaming."

"And you believed him?"

She didn't answer, dropping her eyes from his now furious stare. She didn't know what she believed, but she certainly feared it.

"Whatever," he said, standing up.

She blinked to soothe the stinging in her eyes and watched him mutter under his breath while he ran his hand through his hair.

"Fuck," he yelled, punching a door.

She flinched as she stood and took a step back.

"It wasn't like that," he shouted, hitting the door again. "She was screaming because I was fighting with her brothers. We were wrestling." He paced away, then walked back, trying to soften his features, but he was clearly angry she doubted him. "I haven't even touched her since yesterday. And that was just a hug."

A hug was too much in Kylie's mind, but she tried to allow his confession to pick her heart back up. She tried to focus on how confused and hurt both Logan and Janie were at the accusation. There was no guilt in either one of their expressions, and all the times she'd seen Ryder and Janie together in the past, she'd always felt they were completely devoted to one another.

But that didn't change the fact Logan loved Janie, and he'd wanted her back. He'd said they were over, not that he didn't want her. Then there was the picture, and the lotion. Logan said he'd used it, but now she didn't think it was to remind him of her. He was thinking of Janie.

Trevor had to be telling the truth if he knew about the lingerie, but she didn't know when she could confront Logan about it.

"Did this guy touch you?" he asked.

She shook her head. "He just had me cornered."

"Ryder heard him say that shit to you? That's why he did this?"

She nodded. "I thought he'd walked away, but I guess he came back when the guy kept talking. He just hit him."

"I wasn't with her like that," Logan said softly. "I swear."

"Okay," she said, looking down, unsure if she could really allow herself to trust this relationship he had with Janie. After all, Logan was pretty much a mystery; they barely knew each other. They'd only met eight days ago, and she'd spent very few of them with him.

She wondered if she was really being as foolish as her stepfather claimed. She'd heard groups of girls talk in the past—all telling each other that someone was moving too fast when they claimed they were in love, or if they went beyond kissing after just a few days together. Christ, she'd let Logan give her an orgasm the third time she saw him. He'd eaten her out, showered with her. He'd spent the night and jacked off on her!

It was all so fast when she thought about it that way. He was just so addictive. Nothing else mattered when she was in his arms. Maybe that was all it took to make the lie work.

"You don't believe me?" Logan asked.

"It's just hard." She looked up to see him watching her. "You were so happy to see her yesterday."

"Listen," he cut in, "I'm not going to be unhappy to see her just because, at the time, we were pretending to date. I hadn't seen her in a while, and things were tense with us. So of course I was happy when she showed up.

"Things have changed though. I'm with you. You can't go and believe everything some asshole says about me and her. If I wanted her—or anyone else—I would have kept things the way they were, or bailed on you when you told me how you felt."

What he said made sense, but she didn't like how he still emphasized how much Janie was a part of his life. If Janie cheated on Logan, she could cheat on Ryder after all.

"I'm sorry," Logan said before blurting, "I never fucked her."

Her heart seemed to beat again, and he continued, "I was her boyfriend, but I didn't try to be special for her. We were just us." He smiled, but he didn't look happy. He was angry. "I'm trying to be deserving of you. I won't fuck around on you."

Hope filled her wounded heart. Janie didn't have all of Logan, and he'd almost had sex with her this morning. She meant more. She smiled up at him. "I'm sorry for thinking you would be with her."

"You don't have to be sorry," he said. "Just have a little faith in me. I'm probably the shittiest boyfriend a girl could have, but I'm trying."

She didn't know how he managed to weaken her anger. "You're not shitty. And I'm sorry for even thinking—"

"Can I kiss you now?" He moved close to her, his gaze tender. "Please? I've been thinking about you all day."

"Oka—"

Logan didn't let her finish. He told her with his kiss how much he wanted her faith in him, in them.

"I'm sorry," she mumbled against his lips. "He was just scary, then he said all that stuff and Ryder—"

"I wasn't with her like that." He gave her a breath-stealing kiss before pulling back to rest his forehead against hers, his hands cradling her face. "I mean it."

"What if she wanted you back?"

"I wouldn't want her," he said, rubbing his thumbs across her cheeks. "Listen, Hood. I care about you a lot. I did pretty much as soon as I saw Trevor taking advantage of you. I'm not good at expressing how I feel." He frowned and shook his head a little, worrying her again. "All right, this isn't really what I want to say, but it gutted me every time you brought up Trevor."

"Really?" Her voice was soft, and she almost sighed when he smiled.

"Really." He gave her a long, sweet kiss. "Will you have a little more faith in me?"

"Yes," she said. *Fuck Ryder.* "I'm so sorry."

He leaned away to stand up straight. She wanted to tell him something amazing, but she couldn't find the words. After all, he still wouldn't say what she wanted him to. That he liked her, not cared for her or wanted her. Like led to love, and she knew she was already traveling that path with him. Nothing amazing popped in her head, yet somehow words still spilled out. "So her legendary brothers are here?"

Logan nodded, looking relieved that they were done with their fight. "Just two of them. She has eleven."

"Eleven?"

"They're all adopted."

"Oh," she said, still pondering over Janie having such a large family. The girl had everything, it seemed. "So you fought them?"

Logan grabbed her hand. "We were just fucking around and ended up in a mock-brawl. They said I needed practice because I arranged a sparring match with Ryder later today."

"But he's so mean, and he looked ready to kill that guy just a few minutes ago." She wanted to be as far away from Ryder and Janie as possible. She wanted Logan to never see them again, too. "He was so angry thinking you were with her. Are you sure it's a good idea?"

Logan watched the man being helped up before leading her down the hall. "I can handle a fight with Ryder. It'd be nice if you didn't think I was such a pushover next to him."

"No," she said, panicked when she saw his muscles tighten. "I know you're not a pushover. It's just—you said he's a good fighter, and he's pissed. He thought the same thing I did about Janie."

"He knows better than to believe she'd cheat." He sighed, squeezing her hand. "It's sparring anyway. We're not gonna fight like we hate each other—we've done it a few times before. It'll be fine. Will you cheer for me, or is it going to freak you out to see me fight?"

"I'll always cheer for you," she gushed.

He grinned, kissing her hand. "That's my girl. Forget all this shit out here. Be my good luck charm, okay?"

"Of course." She beamed up at him. "And I didn't mean to make you think I doubted your fighting skills. You're the toughest guy I've ever seen. You're going to kick his ass, I know it. I can't wait to watch him go down."

Logan laughed, pulling her in the direction of his personal locker room. "A little dark, Hood."

Her eyes widened. "What do you mean?"

"Yesterday, you said violence was wrong, but today you're ready to see me destroy Godson." He stopped walking, scanning her. "Did he hurt you?"

"Not exactly." She pressed her lips together.

"Then how exactly did he hurt you?" His eyes darkened as he waited for her answer.

"It's nothing." She rubbed his chest before hugging him. He did care. "He's just not very friendly, and it was another rough day at school."

"Oh." He sighed, all his tension rolling off him. "I should've sent someone else to get you, but he was already there."

"It's fine." It wasn't. "Thanks for making sure I had a ride."

"I'll try my best to be there next time," he said. "If it was just the Knights here, I'd have gone, but I had a possible fight to discuss. Mark would kill me if I missed those meetings."

Her gaze drifted around the building. Logan was a grown-up. He had a job. God, Kevin was right. He knew this life. "Um, you can focus on your work. I can walk. I can even go home again. I think Kevin will keep an eye on things now."

"You're not going back to that house." He gave her a nervous look. "And I kinda already asked Janie if you could spend the night with her."

She nearly screeched, "What?"

He dragged a hand down his face. "Just come in here for a second, and I'll explain."

"There's nothing to explain," she snapped. "I don't want to stay with her."

He sighed, shoving his door open. All the sweetness in his touch was gone. "Just listen to me."

"I already said no." She was ready to run to the woods. To the dark. Where she belonged.

Logan let go of her hand as he went to a locker. "You're part of my routine now, Hood."

She jerked her head up to see him wearing a small smile.

"I'm happy to see where we go," he said, "but I have responsibilities. I have a job. Kevin's my boss. He could fire me, leave me practically homeless and ruin my reputation. So I have to do shit here. I'm already getting pressure from the team and Mark. He understands things are hectic with you, but you needing rides from school isn't an emergency."

"I said I can walk." She wasn't doing this.

"I don't want you walking—it's dangerous." He clenched his jaw. "Listen, I don't want you going to your house when it's not safe, but I can't move you into my apartment. Kevin's my boss. It could cost me my job—everything already could cost me my job, but I don't want to push him further."

She swallowed, feeling so stupid for yelling at Kevin this morning. Now she had nowhere to go because Logan didn't want her with him.

"Her brothers already said it was fine." He ran a hand through his hair. "You don't have to become friends with her. Hopefully, I'll be leaving by the time you're ready for bed, and I'll be there when you wake up." He hesitated, searching her face. "Are you already back to hating her?"

Her eyes widened. "What?"

"Hood, I know it's stupid to expect you to like her, but she's—"

Kylie cut him off. "It's fine. I'll go to her place tonight, but I'll be going home tomorrow."

"What?" He put down a roll of tape he'd pulled out.

"I said I'm going home tomorrow." She trembled and her head throbbed. "I get that you want to keep me safe, but I would rather be in a room with Maura than her."

He looked like he'd been punched in the stomach. Breathing out, he closed his eyes and muttered, "Please think about this. She's not a bad person. She's just misunderstood, and she's willing to help."

Kylie shook her head. "I don't want to be around her. I can't stop seeing you smiling, holding on to her. And I can't take hearing everyone say you want her back."

"Hood," he said, looking at her again. This time there was an angry spark in his dark eyes. "Don't listen to what people say. And we already talked about how I was with her.

You and I weren't really together when you saw that. I'm not doing anything wrong now."

The door to his room banged open and Ryder walked in with Janie.

"Babe, you can knock." Janie gave her a small wave. "Hey, Kylie."

Feeling Logan's stare, she tried to smile back, but she wasn't sure what her face looked like as she nodded at Janie.

Ryder met her stare and scoffed before guiding Janie to the couch. It was then Kylie realized he was shirtless and wearing a pair of black fighting shorts like Logan. *Holy cow.*

He had tattoos, not nearly as many as Logan, but she didn't get to see them because he sat, pulling Janie to stand between his legs. He closed his eyes and rested his head against her stomach, seeming tired.

Janie sent her a shy smile as she ran her fingers through his hair. "Oh, Kylie, I brought you clothes to train in."

Ryder lifted his head and pushed Janie's shirt up a little, only to begin kissing her stomach.

What the hell?

Janie didn't seem bothered by it and kept talking. "I left them in my locker."

Her locker? Kylie glanced at the locker Janie pointed to. It was open, and the inside was covered with photos. Logan was easily visible in them, and he was smiling at her in each one. Ryder was in most of the pictures, and so were his brothers, which, strangely, infuriated her more. How many guys did this girl need?

Again, images of Logan and Janie kissing, laughing, and just being them filled her mind. What naked picture had

Trevor seen? When did Logan receive it? Did Janie take a nude of herself and send it to him? Did he take it himself?

Kylie knew she needed to chill out so she didn't go insane, but she couldn't stop all her doubt about Janie wanting Logan—of Logan wanting Janie back. She pushed against the door that kept out all the nasty things that wanted to torment her—that kept *everything* out—but her arms shook, ready to give up every time she looked at Janie.

"Yeah," Logan said, making her stop her internal fuming, "I changed my mind, baby doll." He winced, shaking his head. "Um, she's not ready to train just yet."

"Oh," Janie said, nodding at the locker. "Well, you can still take the stuff I bought. I think everything should fit."

Logan smiled sadly, and Janie stared at him like she could read everything from that smile.

Hazel eyes began to drift her way, but Ryder got up, dragging Janie out of the room before they could connect with hers.

Logan went to the locker and pulled out a pair of black leggings and a red pullover with a hood. "She thought you might be comfortable in this."

Kylie stared at the clothes he held out. A different sort of pain shot through her. She couldn't remember the last time someone, besides Logan, had really thought of her as they picked out clothes. Why did it have to be Janie?

"Just take it with you so you have something to change into tonight," he said. "If you can't get past things with her, I get it. I'll go with you to talk to Kevin. If he'll put a stop to it, then it's up to you if you want to stay. I'm just trying to make sure you're safe."

Her head ached again. "You made her think I was going to train with her?"

"I just hoped if you saw her it would make you want to try." His features softened, and he suddenly seemed exhausted. "I wasn't lying about wanting you to learn to defend yourself, or about her being a good sparring partner. Her brothers even came to meet you."

"Me?"

He nodded. "She asked them if you could stay." He acted like he was going to touch her, but lowered his hand. "Her stepdad isn't home, and they came to straighten shit out for her at school. They're in meetings with the parents of the other girls all day tomorrow. Hopefully, all this shit will be sorted after that."

Kylie rubbed her fingers across the red fabric. "She bought this for me?"

"Yeah." He went to his locker again. "If it bothers you to have something from her, just leave it here. I can run you to the store to grab a few things after I'm done."

It would've been so easy to stay quiet, to let this argument fade into the darkness, but she didn't think she could.

Until she looked up at him. There was a fierceness returning to his handsome face, but his eyes, they were dimming of all light.

"You really want me to get along with her, don't you?"

His Adam's apple bobbed. "I want you to give her a chance to show you it's possible to come out of darkness. She's been through hell, and she's my only friend. She wants me happy, and I want her to see me happy."

Somehow she managed to smile and turned to take her top off so she could change clothes.

His arms were around her in an instant, hugging her as he kissed the top of her head. "You don't have to do this."

"I do." She squeezed his hand.

He smiled against her hair. "I swear you'll enjoy training. Well, when you actually get to the fun stuff."

"Okay," she whispered, sighing as he moved her hair away from her neck and pressed his lips to her racing pulse. A hand soon grabbed her breast and she sighed. This was better. She had this with Logan—Janie never had.

Gasping, she opened her eyes and froze at the sight of the ugly reflection staring back at her. A smile of acid and scars and bruises spattered across her skin. "Oh my God!"

"What?" He looked at her, starting to let go.

She pointed at the mirror before shoving him away. Her smile was gone, but she could still see the damage it had hidden. "I'm a monster."

"What?" He tried to stop her from pulling her shirt on.

"Don't touch me," she screamed. It was his fault. He made her see.

"Baby, what are you talking about? You look fine. Beautiful."

"No, I'm not. You're a liar. I hate you!"

He moved away like he'd been slapped. "What's wrong with you? I haven't fucking lied."

"How could I have forgotten so quickly?" she whispered, looking around the room, but there was nothing there. She gasped, her eyes watering. He was a masterpiece, and she was a creation of Hell. She was nothing compared to Janie in his eyes.

"Forgotten what?" he asked.

She looked over each of her pale scars, wondering how she could have gone from hiding to being naked in front of Logan so easily. She never looked at herself when she was with him because he made her believe the lies. He made her feel special, but she wasn't. "That I'm disgusting," she spat, hating how pathetic he made her feel. How pathetic all of them made her feel. "That I'm just a girl you want to fuck. I'm just on your *fuck* list. Maybe it's because you want to fuck a broken girl because you never got to fuck the one who just walked out that door!"

"What the fuck?" he yelled, throwing the tape he'd been holding, knocking everything off the desk. "How can you say that?"

"Because it's true," she said, her hands shaking as her breathing became so fast it hurt. "You're only with me because I'm broken like her."

He stared at her for a few seconds before finally speaking. "You're not broken—you're hurt. The marks you have are going to heal—they've already healed a lot." He took a harsh breath and added, "And don't you fucking say she's broken—you know nothing about her."

She could barely breathe; he was defending Janie? "Oh, forgive me for speaking the truth. You wanted to fuck her, and Ryder beat you to it. Now you're settling for the first damaged girl you've seen since."

His eyes went ablaze. "Watch what you say. I mean it, Kylie. I'm not going to deal with you saying this shit about her. If you want to talk about what's got you acting like this, fine. But don't bring her into it."

Heat burned her cheeks, and she fired back. "You just want her back! That's all this is for you."

"What the fuck are you talking about?" he shouted, throwing his hands up. "I'm with you. Not her."

Kylie didn't say anything. She let the darkness that always surrounded her wrap her in its embrace. She let those wicked words that were always whispered in the dark grow louder. Their dirty claws dug into her heart as their menacing grins promised she would never be loved—that the man she was giving her heart to would only desire another.

"You know what? Fine." His harsh tone made the air freeze in her lungs, but all she could do was stand silently as he walked to the door. "Keep making up shit. Keep refusing my fucking support because you don't like my only friend—attacking her because she used to be my girlfriend."

"Sorry I'm not perfect like her," she screamed.

He put his hand on the doorknob and stared at it before speaking again. "Do you know what Ryder was doing when he was kissing her stomach?"

She didn't answer him. She just stared at his blurry reflection in the mirror, her heart pounding harder the farther he moved away.

"He was kissing her scars. She's covered in them. She's not perfect." He yanked the door open. "But she believes him when he tells her she's beautiful. She lets him heal her wounds. She lets him help her get stronger."

"There you go again," she croaked, "praising her like everyone else."

He let out a bitter laugh. "Fine, Kylie. She's the best fucking girl ever and you're nothing—that's what you want me to say, right? So there you go. I'm done. Sit here and make up more shit if you want. I've got shit to take care of. And, no, it's not fucking my ex-girlfriend." He walked out, slamming the door so loud she shrieked.

She stared at the door, her breaths becoming harder and harder to take as she sobbed, eventually falling to her knees. She hid her face in her hands, gasping for air while the hate-filled whispers grew louder.

They laughed at her tears and howled in victory over their wounded prey.

Doubt had won.

23
THE PADAWAN

How could it feel like she'd been beaten? How could words hurt more than the physical blows she'd endured all these years?

"Ow." Kylie sobbed as she tried desperately to pull oxygen into her burning lungs. "Ow." Tears escaped, sliding across the bridge of her nose and onto the floor she was lying on. He'd left her. And the pain—so much pain. She didn't know what was happening. All she knew was that it felt as though her heart had been ripped right out of her chest.

Her life was ending. She couldn't breathe. She couldn't escape. There was only pain, and she was all alone.

Time lost all relevance. All she knew was that in every instance she'd ever thought about death, she had never imagined it would take so long to pass.

"Oh, Kylie." The soft voice didn't sound real, and it wasn't Logan. "Shh . . ."

"It hurts," she told the voice, not caring who it was, only relieved that someone was finally there. Maybe she really was dying, and this was an angel come to take her away.

"I know." A hand lightly caressed her sweaty forehead. "You're going to be okay. It will pass."

She shook her head, sobbing and sucking in huge but empty gulps of air. The hand moved to her hair and began stroking her head in a soothing motion.

"It will. I promise. It always passes."

Kylie recognized who was speaking, and it wasn't who she wanted. Now she wanted to die.

Janie sat behind her and rubbed her back, right behind her heart as she continued talking. "It hurts right here, doesn't it?"

Kylie didn't respond, she just kept trying to breathe, kept crying, gasping, because she didn't know what else to do.

Janie continued, "You're having a panic attack. It's going to be fine. It will go away soon."

A panic attack? Kylie kept crying, confusion, pain—sadness and relief all overwhelming her as Janie rubbed her back, right where it felt like her heart was being stabbed and torn apart. But it was pounding so fast. As if it was trying to beat a whole lifetime's worth of beats before it stopped.

"Slow down," Janie told her. "You have to try to slow it down." Her hand ran through her hair again. "I hold my breath. It's probably not the right thing to do, but try to hold it for a few seconds, then let it out slowly."

Kylie continued sucking in air, sweat drenching her body as she felt herself clenching up from the pain. It was crushing her, and the ringing noise in her ears made it hard to concentrate. Was she supposed to call 911? *No, just let me die. I deserve to die.*

"Do it," Janie said. "You'll pass out if you keep breathing like this."

She didn't know if she should trust Janie, but she obeyed as the girl cooed soft words of encouragement beside her, never stopping the pressure on her back, never showing impatience or hysteria.

"There you go." Janie's voice was a sweet melody in the chaos. "Let it out slowly."

Kylie breathed out, whining when the pain did not dissipate. She'd never felt so much pain before.

"Again."

Kylie followed the order. She'd hold her breath for a few seconds until she was told to let it out. Then, after what felt like hours, she went limp from exhaustion and the pain faded.

"It's over." Janie tucked Kylie's hair behind her ear. "This time, at least."

Kylie cried as she felt a tissue being dabbed on her cheeks. She hated crying and didn't want to in front of Janie, of all people. But she couldn't stop.

"Stupid boy," Janie muttered, shaking her head.

"He left me," Kylie croaked.

"He's just with the boys." Janie produced another tissue and wiped along Kylie's forehead. "I told Ryder to make sure he stayed away. He said you decided to stay here. I heard you screaming and let myself in."

Kylie tried to take calming breaths while her boyfriend's ex-girlfriend took care of her. This was the last thing she expected. If anything, she'd imagined Janie would be falling all over Logan while Ryder let her.

"Did you fight?" Janie asked, her voice soft, concerned, nothing that Kylie wanted to associate with the girl ruining her life.

It seemed impossible to lie now. "Yes. He left me."

"Did he say that?"

"He said he was done," Kylie whispered, closing her eyes. She wanted to scream at Janie for being the cause of it all, but she was so tired.

"Well," Janie said, "speaking as someone who's been in a relationship with Logan Grimm, that's not a breakup." She smiled tightly. "Trust me. You might get into a lot of fights, but you'll know when he breaks your heart."

Kylie didn't understand why Janie would say that; she was the one who broke Logan's heart, after all.

"Is this your first attack?" Janie asked.

Kylie closed her eyes again. She didn't want to talk, didn't want Janie to comfort her. But she felt this strange compulsion to answer, so she did. "I don't know what happened."

"Yeah, they're terrifying," Janie murmured. "I've had other things in the past, but these are different. Logan's dad found me on the floor of his bathroom the first time I had a full-blown one. I thought I was dying. They always feel like that, but don't worry, you're not going to. It just feels like it."

Kylie sighed, keeping her eyes closed. She'd certainly never experienced a panic attack before, but knowing that she had just had one, and that Janie had apparently had them more than once, she wanted to hide. She was nothing like the girl Logan found perfect, and the negative similarities between them reenforced her fear that Logan was using her because she was broken and easy. Despite all of this, though, because of a strange urge to speak, she muttered, "Thank you. I'm sorry you had to see this."

"Don't be sorry," Janie said. "I'm glad I could help. It's harder when you have them around people who don't care, or they don't know what to do. I actually have anxiety whenever I have to go places where I've had one before. I usually hang all over Ryder or have one of his brothers with me to feel brave."

She stayed still, steadying her breaths with every passing second. None of this made sense. Janie was a mean girl. She was a flirt. Not a girl who suffered from mental disorders.

"Do you want to talk about it?" Janie asked.

"No." Kylie's tears slid into her hair, but she refused to look up.

"Okay," Janie murmured. "But just so you know, keeping it in doesn't always help. I get you're used to being alone, but it's okay to let other people hold you through bad times. I'm just offering you the comfort I didn't always have."

"You just said you have everyone helping you," Kylie said before she could stop herself.

"I have people around me, Kylie, but that doesn't mean I didn't feel alone—or that I let them help. It took a long time for me to get here. You can be surrounded by loved ones and friends, but unless you let them in, none of them know what's happening inside you."

A chill made Kylie shake, but she stared ahead, her eyes fixed on the door. Panic tried to rise, but the fatigue engulfing her was unlike anything she'd ever experienced. "Why would *you* ever go through this alone?"

A sad smile formed on Janie's lips. "Because I thought I was hurting them by just existing. I wanted to protect them, so I tried to keep it all hidden. No one wanted to hear how bad things were, so I stopped telling them. They liked it that way." She gave her an even sadder smile. "People like the lies because the truth, for me at least, is too much—too dark. Too sad. It would've been better if I was gone forever, is how I saw it."

Her breath hitched. She'd had the same thought before—the truth hurt, so she stayed silent. "Logan would be devastated if you weren't around," Kylie whispered bitterly. "They'd all be sad."

Janie shrugged, not affected by the slight bite in her tone. "I didn't believe that then. Nothing is what I thought I deserved. I was a monster. No matter what I did, I destroyed them. When I tried to get better, I failed. Repeatedly. So I let the pain consume me, and I shut them out. I would love to say I've had Logan wrapped around my finger, because it would mean all the pain I suffered from him not being there would be gone, but I didn't. He wasn't there when I needed him most. Still isn't."

"I don't believe you."

"You don't have to. But I'm telling the truth. It helps, you know? Sharing pain. It helps the person telling and the people listening. It's how people relate to someone." Janie kept running her fingers through her hair, her voice even softer now. "I know Ryder and the others told you about the rape."

Kylie could only nod, startled that Janie would blurt this out.

"Did they tell you the boys got away with it?"

Kylie wasn't expecting that. "How?"

A humorless laugh passed Janie's lips. "Because I didn't fight back? Because they wore condoms? Because they knew someone in the police department? Because I was a sad girl? I don't know, really. I had no one to back me up. All I had was my word against theirs, and they walked."

Kylie sat up slowly. "What about Ryder?"

Janie's chin wobbled. "I'd already told him to leave me alone. I hated myself because I'd fallen in love with him while I was supposed to love Logan."

Janie wiped a tear from her cheek. "I wanted to die because that was so wrong, and I'd lost my Logan because I couldn't not feel everything for Ryder. I didn't deserve either of them. So even though Ryder was trying to help me, I told him to stay away. I just wanted Logan back; I'd hurt him."

Kylie watched a few tears fall from Janie's eyes. "What about your family?"

Janie smiled and nodded. "They thought I was just a stupid girl with a broken heart."

"So what happened?" Kylie didn't realize she had grabbed Janie's hand and was now the one doing the comforting, and about her breakup with Logan of all things.

"I started this," she said, gesturing to her stomach with her free hand. She let go of Kylie's and lifted her shirt enough for Kylie to see white scars.

"You're a cutter?" Kylie blurted.

"No." Janie stared at a particularly jagged scar before lowering her shirt. "I wouldn't really classify myself as anything but a screwup. I'd gotten a nasty cut during my rape, and I just saw it every time I looked in the mirror. I'd, um, hold a knife over the scar—I guess to finish the job they started—and I usually ended up cutting myself."

Kylie shook her head, not believing what she was hearing.

Janie slid a finger across her stomach. "Those were the better days. Those were the days when I still knew I existed, and I just wanted to die. But the days I was really in danger were the days I was empty. On those days, it no longer mattered Logan had abandoned me, that my family would've preferred to just put me on pills or in a mental institution. It no longer mattered that a boy loved me so fiercely that he was ready to destroy everything just to keep me. Nothing. I felt nothing, and I would see how much pain I caused Logan and his mom. How much of a disappointment I was to my family, and how I would never be what Ryder said I was. So I just did it. No tears. I just swallowed all the pills and went to sleep and waited for Death to take me home."

Kylie had no idea why she was even listening to this, but it was like she had to know how much Janie had suffered. "What happened?"

Janie sniffed, rubbing her nose as she smiled. "Ryder. Earlier that day, before I overdosed, my stepdad asked me in front of the principal and police if I was really raped, or if I just regretted having sex with those two boys like I did with Ryder. I didn't know it was possible to die inside when I already felt like I'd left my soul in the woods. But their faces—I'll never forget how they looked at me, how my own stepfather could say such a thing. Ryder got pissed. I didn't even know he was carrying me or that I was crying until he put me in his car and took me to my house to pack my stuff.

"When he packed, I went to my bathroom. I looked in the mirror, felt nothing, and took everything in my medicine cabinet. I never felt the pills go down. I didn't gag. I took everything, and then I went to my brothers' bathroom, and I took all the pills and bottles of medicine they had too."

Kylie stared at her, her mouth open as she watched Janie stare across the room like she was seeing it all happen again.

"He didn't know I'd done it," Janie said softly. "He'd been arguing with my brothers, so when he took me to his house, I was already slipping away. He put me on his bed to rest while he set up a room for me, and I fell asleep. I don't know for how long, maybe an hour, but something woke me. I could barely move, but for once, there was no pain. I pushed through the drugs in my system until I stumbled into his bathroom. Then I took everything he had.

"I couldn't stand anymore. I just lay on the floor and closed my eyes. There was light. Just light . . . Then he was there." She rubbed a spot on her chest, below her heart and to the side. "I thought he was an angel. He was shouting at me, but he was so beautiful. I told him I loved him, that I was so sorry for not telling him sooner."

The girl smiled sadly and continued, "It's all blurry in my memories, but I know he carried me to his car and that Archer drove while Ryder tried to make me throw up. I think I did throw up on him and Tercero, but they kept trying to make me puke more.

"And Ryder, he told me he loved me more than anything. I thought I was already dead because that was the greatest thing I could ask for. Someone still loved a disgusting monster like me, and he was begging for me to fight—to stay with him. I realized he believed me. He didn't doubt anything I'd said. Everything I'd done to him—blamed him for—he let me do it because he loved me.

"So, when it got too dark, I listened to the voice that said, 'grab his hand.' I held it as he prayed; I listened to his brothers shouting at doctors to help. I stared at emerald fire, and I let it engulf me when he said, 'Live, Sweet Jane'." She grinned. "It's a legend with our families."

Her smile grew brighter. "I knew God sent him for me, and I just let go and grabbed hold of him. He holds me every chance he gets and reminds me it's not time to go, that he won't let me die. No matter how many times those thoughts come, he just holds me tighter, tells me 'not yet,' and I stay."

"I'm—" Kylie didn't know what to do as Janie let out a pitiful cry. She didn't know if she felt sorry for her or if she believed everything. It was strange that the girl would spill such personal stuff to her, but something tugged at her gut when Janie spoke. Like a pull that guided her to comfort her enemy. "I'm sorry this happened to you," Kylie said, surprising herself. "I—you're so. Oh, gosh." She couldn't think of anything to say. If Janie knew everything she'd just screamed at Logan about her, she'd probably get her ass beaten by Ryder. No wonder the asshole was so violent. "I feel kinda bad, I think," she muttered. "I hated you so much."

Janie chuckled through her sniffling. "I knew you and Logan fought because of me. I just didn't know it would be so bad. I thought he was smarter than this."

"We don't have to talk about me," Kylie rushed, her chest tightening as panic seized her. "I didn't mean to say I hated you."

"Oh, hush." Janie waved her hand through the air. "It's totally fine to not like me. Really, who likes the thought of their boyfriend's ex?" She gave her a teary smile. "I would totally hate me, too, if I were you. I'd lose my shit if Ryder had an ex that he talked to. Seriously, if roles were reversed, I would've probably punched you in the boob."

"What?"

Janie giggled until Kylie laughed with her. "Boob punches. They hurt. I would have punched you so hard."

Kylie watched Janie stare at nothing. It was hard to push down her hatred for her, but she saw something in Janie that Logan must have. Janie had already been through so much, and he was just trying to help the girl he lost. It would be sweet if she wasn't the other girl in his life. He was so protective of Janie but not her. How did Ryder deal with it all?

"Logan wants me to be like you," Kylie blurted.

Janie sighed, looking older than her eighteen years. "No, he doesn't. Trust me. A part of Logan really hates me. I wish that were easy to understand, but this is us—there's no letting go of the other. But you, he doesn't want to see you destroy yourself like I did. He's just being stupid because that's what boys do. They don't know what to do, so they take it out on us.

"Right now," she continued, "I guarantee he's hating himself for walking away. The boy is cocky as all hell, but he's insecure when it comes to believing he's a good guy. I bet it's hard for him to see someone stronger than me struggling and refusing him."

"I'm not stronger," Kylie argued.

"You are." Janie dropped her eyes to a tattoo of a half-moon on her wrist. "But you can fall just like I did. He thinks you need him the way I needed Ryder. You aren't like me, Kylie—I see it. And you don't have to be. I pray no one's ever like me.

"I got lucky. I needed someone to pull me back because I leaned too far over the edge. I went so far, I slipped until a hand grabbed mine. I doubted what I meant to my family and friends. I sat in the dark room in my mind and listened to those terrible words. I believed them and let them destroy me. I became that monster—the one who hurt them.

Janie shook her head. "Don't be like me. If you need a hand, grab the one Logan's holding out for you. But be honest; let him see the real Kylie. The game you tried, that's only going to make things worse."

"He told you about the plan with Trevor?" Kylie wanted to be furious, but she was still stuck in a place where she felt almost numb to her anger.

"Yeah." She patted her leg. "Don't beat yourself up. Hell, it would be one of those teen-romance stories they turn into movies, but try to focus on the moment you decided to be honest with him instead. How amazing was that? I bet it was better than any cliché story I've ever read."

Kylie remembered the sports store, then their time at his apartment.

Janie laughed, pointing to her cheeks. "Naughty Kylie Hood."

She covered her cheeks. "How do you know something naughty happened?"

"'Cause this is Logan Grimm we're discussing." Janie chuckled, rubbing under her eyes. "Isn't it so fun to start learning about each other? Like all relationships in the beginning are so addicting. I still daydream about Ryder with me—after the bad stuff . . . Just be careful. You don't want to ruin it by learning a few months later that all the important stuff was a lie. Like Ryder and I had so much bad shit, but if we'd hidden things, it might've all fallen apart. I can't imagine not having him." She shook her head. "So even though you hate me, listen to me."

Kylie looked down at her lap, ignoring the pain pulsing in her head.

"Above all," Janie said, "remember the boy doesn't fix you. A lot of guys struggle with that. Even Ryder does sometimes."

"I can't believe we're having this conversation," Kylie said, looking around the room. It felt strange to see it lit up. She'd felt like she was in a dark cave this whole time. "I mean, we just fought about you, and I wanted to claw your eyes out."

"Well, I'll let you get a few hits in, but my peepers are my money maker." Janie giggled. "They're really all I have going for me besides Ryder and my car."

"I don't think the guys who like you are interested in Ryder or your car."

"Oh, I know." Janie flashed her a cheeky grin. "It's a secret though."

She frowned. "It's a secret why guys like you?"

"Oh," Janie said, frowning before smiling again, "they don't all like me. But there's an actual reason why so many are drawn to me. It's like magic."

Conceited, but okay, Kylie thought. She started to stand as Janie got up. "I'm sure it's just guys think you're beautiful. I know Logan thinks you are."

Janie held out a hand. "He definitely thinks that about you." She walked to a cabinet. "And who cares if a few guys think about my looks? It's not like it's anyone's business what someone thinks about another person, and it's not a crime to be beautiful."

Kylie had never looked at it that way. Pretty girls were envied by other girls, and that somehow made them villains when they had admirers.

Janie went to her locker and dug around. "I'm suiting up."

"Suiting up?"

She held up a Superman shirt. "Logan is a Batman fan. I'm Team Superman. He'll understand I'm trying to be something he wanted me to be. It's private."

"I guess you have a lot of private things with him. I don't know anything about him." Kylie stared at the shirt she was holding, the swirl of doubt trying to gain strength with that confession. "He knows everything about you. And you know him."

"Well, yeah—we grew up together." Janie shrugged. "But he wants to know you. He wants to discover every little secret there is inside your head."

"Really?" She looked up as Janie pulled on the tank top and started braiding her hair on each side of her head.

"Yep." Janie winked. "Just give him a nice peep show. He doesn't need to know everything. And remember to be patient—these things take time. Now clean your face up. We have to go show that boy he doesn't just walk away when his girl is crying. I swear boys never learn. Don't they get that every time we say we need to be alone, we want them to stay? And when we run, we want to be chased?"

Kylie smiled and took off her shirt to replace it with the red pullover Janie had bought. "Thanks for the clothes. I'll pay you back."

Janie smiled sadly at her. Her gaze had lingered on the marks across her stomach. "You're welcome, Kylie. And don't worry about paying me back. I used Ryder's money."

Kylie chuckled, wiping away more of her tears. "I don't know if that's good or bad. He might end up shaking me upside down, asking for his money."

The girl's face flushed. "If he says anything, I'll just distract him with a blow job."

"What?" Kylie covered her mouth.

"He's actually more of a pervert than Logan." She covered her red cheeks.

Kylie rubbed her arm as she pushed away the image of Janie doing that with Ryder. "I didn't tell Logan to leave me alone, though. He left on his own. I really think he broke up with me."

Janie sighed and walked over to her. "Whatever happened, he just panicked. He would've kicked you out if he was breaking up with you.

"He's trying to help, and if he can't figure out how to, he blows up. It's how he is. It's how a lot of guys are, actually. It's like watching them put together the most complicated piece of furniture. They have the instructions if they just sit down and read them—talk to you—but they try to wing it. And when it doesn't work, they yell and throw you away.

"Logan just tried to fix you without your instructions. All he saw was me put back together. He remembers what it took to get me here—mostly just Ryder being there to hold me together. So Logan's panicking because, with me, he only knew his mistakes after it was too late. With you, he's rushing to pick you up, but you're still in pieces. He's trying to hold them, but his hands are full.

"You both need to step back and learn to communicate. Just get to know each other, because you really don't know anything about him or our world. It isn't just me and him. There's a lot more to us."

"Like?" Kylie didn't understand why they all kept making it seem as if they were superheroes with secret identities. Or spies. Maybe Ryder was a mafia boss.

"I don't think you're ready for that," Janie said a little cautiously. "I'm just saying that getting to know the man Logan is, and showing him who you are, is really what you need to focus on right now. Things could work out, but"—she clicked her tongue—"you might inflict some permanent damage on each other if you're not careful. Plus, you have your own shit to cope with. I think your sister has serious problems, and her having a knife on her is pretty messed up. It wasn't a kitchen knife."

"What do you mean?" Kylie had forgotten all about Maura.

"It was a combat knife," Janie said. "It was dirty, like it'd been in the ground, but it wasn't a regular ole knife."

Kylie swallowed, remembering Janie had chosen to come between her and the girls that day. "I guess I sorta forgot you put yourself in danger."

"Oh." Janie stared at her, like she was waiting for her to say more. When she didn't, Janie smiled. "Well, you're welcome."

There, Kylie thought; she had made some effort to be pleasant. She still felt pathetic regarding Logan though. "How do I fix this with him? He wants me to just trust all of you, and I'm not used to it. I'm definitely not used to how mean Ryder is. Then I feel so ugly for Logan, and he wants me to go out there where everyone can laugh at me."

"First, Ryder's not really nice to anyone but me—don't let it stress you out. And you're not ugly. No one's gonna laugh at you either—not when they know we're behind you." Janie really took her in. "Stop worrying about what Logan wants from you. Don't get better for him. You build yourself, Kylie Hood. Otherwise, you'll fall apart when you really need to stand on your own. But if you want that boy to use his toolbox on you"—she wiggled her eyebrows—"you need to point him in the right direction. Show him the steps he needs to take."

"You sound like that alien—the green guy." Kylie covered her mouth, mumbling, "I'm sorry. I just meant you sound wise, but you're so young."

"Quit apologizing. Now, hurry up, my young Padawan. Your boy Grimm we must get."

"Huh?"

Janie rolled her eyes. "You're going to go fight for your boy. It's time to show him who Kylie Hood is."

She rubbed her temples. "I can't fight now. I mean, I can try, but I'll look like an idiot."

"Do or do not. There is no try." Janie pushed her to the door. "Just come on. You're going to show him he can't walk out like this. He needs to sit down and read your manual, or you're going to smack him over the head with it."

"But he thinks I need to be like you." *And I still kinda don't want to be around you yet,* she silently added.

"There's only one Janie Mortaime, doll face." Janie winked. "But you don't want to be that crazy bitch anyway. And that's my point—learn from my failures. I'm like Anakin Skywalker. You be Luke, okay? No dark side for you. Trust me—that's my kingdom." Janie fluffed Kylie's hair and wiped under her eyes. "Who are you?"

Kylie didn't know if Janie had lost it or what. "Kylie Hood?"

"No, no, no. You're Kylie fucking Hood." She lightly poked her chest. "Bring that hoe out here. I heard she was checking out my boyfriend."

Kylie's eyes widened; she totally had checked Ryder out. "I wasn't."

Janie snickered. "Don't worry. I drool over him, too. I just want to see the girl who poured her heart out in the middle of a sports store and caught herself the sexy Logan Grimm. Guts, girly. I have a feeling you're not the shy girl everyone thinks you are. That's okay. You got huge balls. It's time to smack Logan in the head with them, 'cause you're about to show him yours are bigger than his."

Kylie laughed nervously as they walked down the hall together. There was a strange connection forming between them. She didn't like how it felt. It was like Janie really did have some ability to draw everyone to her, and it only frustrated Kylie to feel it happening to her.

But maybe it wasn't so bad. Maybe she could figure out some way to navigate the unorthodox relationship Logan had with his ex. She didn't have to like her. And really, how involved would Janie be in Logan's life now that she was there?

24

BROMANCE

"Get the fuck off me," Logan said calmly. He wouldn't make a bigger fool out of himself than he already had. It was pure surprise on his part that allowed Ryder to get the drop on him so easily. If he hadn't turned his back on the bastard to stop Janie from going and pissing Kylie off even more, he'd have never gotten forced flat on his stomach with his arm wrenched behind his back and his ex-girlfriend's huge-ass boyfriend sitting on him.

Ryder chuckled, adding more of his weight. "You're surprisingly comfy, Grimm. Just like Kylie looked comfy sitting in my car. You know every fucking woman can't resist me. And your little blonde—she stares all the fucking time."

"Whatever, asshole," Logan said, smirking even if what he was about to say could get him killed. He just couldn't help himself. "You know where Janie used to be more than comfortable."

"Enough talking about my sister and girls in general, all right?" said Gareth, one of Janie's eleven brothers. "Come on, Logan. You can get out of this."

"I know I can," Logan said, lying out of his ass. Ryder was going to snap his arm if he tried to escape the hold. Of course, Ryder applied the slightest pressure to remind him. Logan glared up at him. "Get off."

"Like you do with pictures of *my* girlfriend?" Ryder gave him a deadly glare that would send guys of all ages to their grave.

Sighing, Logan glanced at Gareth and Gawain Knight. They'd known him longer than Ryder, but never went up against their little sister's boyfriend. They wouldn't interfere unless he allowed it anyway. Not that he'd ask for help. "I don't get off to anything of hers."

"What picture do you have?" Ryder asked him. "Tell me, or I'll tell her it was an accident your arm got snapped in half."

Logan actually chuckled. "It's not a picture. It's a sketch."

"Of her naked?" Ryder wrenched his arm. "And you keep it in your nasty-ass underwear drawer?"

"What do you want me to say? That I didn't sketch her when we were together? Well, I did . . . all the fucking time. I have lots of sketches hidden away," he said, trying to piss Ryder off.

"I'll ask again, Grimm," Ryder said, squeezing his wrist, "do you have a sketch of my moon naked?"

Logan stiffened at Ryder's term of endearment for Janie and shook his head. No more taunts. Even if he knew he could hold his own against Ryder for a while, it would hurt a lot of people if he pushed his rival too far. So he said, "It's just the last sketch I did when we were together. She was wearing a nude cami and I was a horny kid. I used her hair to hide the straps. She only looks naked."

"Yeah right," Ryder said, but he released him and stood up. "Get rid of it."

Logan pushed himself up and allowed Gareth to guide him away.

"Do I have to knock you out before he does?" Gareth asked, laughing as Gawain sent them a glare for being stuck with Ryder. "And get rid of it," Gareth added. "You don't want anything falling into the wrong hands. Or for your girlfriend to find it. Then again, maybe she'll wise up and leave your ass."

Logan threw him a sour look. "It's just a sketch. I'll throw it out."

Gareth chuckled, leaning against a table as Logan snatched up a bottle of water. "So this new girl . . . is it real?"

"Yes," he said, sighing. "Well, I'm fucking up already so maybe not."

"Pretty dumb to expect her to get along with Janie, bro." Gareth picked up one of the paintball guns they had lying out and teasingly aimed it at his crotch. "What are you playing at with her?"

"They're using each other," Ryder said, a dark gleam in his eyes as he strolled over with Gawain. "Isn't that right, Grimm?"

"Fuck you," Logan said, placing his bottle down.

A taunting smirk stretched across Ryder's face. "My baby will be upset with that. She's possessive of my dick."

"Brothers are present . . ." Gawain looked ready to gag.

Ryder ignored him. "Tell me, Grimm, were you planning on using the blonde to make my girl jealous? Or was she using you for her twisted little desires to finally be the girl others envy?"

"I wasn't using Kylie for anything," he said, pissed. "She wasn't using me either. She needed my help. I just ended up liking her."

Ryder snickered, bumping Gareth's elbow before snatching the paintball gun from him. "Yet you had to wait for her to take my advice before you admitted it. Would you have really been like one of those silly romance stories Janie tries to tell me about and not tell the girl until the end of the book?" He laughed louder. "Not so big and bad next to a little blond girl, are you?"

"I was concerned about protecting her," he told them. "You know why I didn't tell her I liked her. And you're not going to say shit to her about it."

"Just like you won't say shit," Ryder fired back, standing straighter to show off his size and strength. "I mean it, Grimm. Not a damn word. If you fuck my girl over even more than you already have, you're dead."

Logan glanced at Janie's brothers, taking in their serious expressions. They were going to back Ryder—not him.

"There are limits to what we permit, Logan," Gawain said, disappointment lacing his words. "She's always the limit you do not cross."

None of Gareth's playfulness was present as he said, "Your girlfriend isn't one of us. And based on what the others said about her reaction to Janie, as well as yours to any threat you believe is against her, you need to be careful.

You're on thin fucking ice with every Knight, Godson, and Prince. Not to mention the others . . ."

"You could be looking at a renouncement," Gawain added.

"So I can't fucking have a girl if she isn't Janie?" He knew that wasn't what they were saying, but he didn't like being reminded of the little power he had around them—how much of a hold they had on his life.

"You know that's not what this is." Gawain stepped between the two of them. "You're a Grimm—you've read the stories. You put it all at risk for some family spat happening with a girl you don't even know."

"Family spat?" Logan shook his head. "She was being abused. She needed protection."

"You could've asked for help," Gareth said. "Properly."

Gawain's intense stare surprised Logan. "We won't protect you from *him*. Arthur's orders are for every Knight to stand down. Prince did the same."

"I can handle myself," Logan said, sliding his gaze toward Ryder.

"Sure you can," Ryder said mockingly. "You're such a successful hunter. Or is it reaper . . . hero. Or perhaps her wolf?"

It felt like the oxygen had been sucked out of his lungs, but he inhaled at the sound of Janie's voice carrying through the halls.

"Time to play up our bromance for my baby," Ryder said, staring him down. "I'll let you land half your hits so you can feel like a man in front of your new pussy."

"Ryder," Gawain said warningly.

Ryder fixed a fake smile on his face and aimed it at Logan. "I suggest you sell being my best friend because I might spill a little blood for the wolves to scent. You remember how they are, don't you? Or are you still pretending they're just fairy tales?"

"Babe," Janie shouted, darting her eyes between them. "I'll tell everyone you had to wound him before your spar if you play dirty."

"Get your gorgeous ass over here then." Ryder tossed the gun onto the table. "Let me play dirty with you."

"Jesus," Gawain muttered, walking away as Gareth laughed.

Logan tuned them out and locked eyes with Kylie. Everything they were warning him about was serious—things he needed to consider. But all he could think of was how Kylie needed help, yet she didn't want his.

Even an asshole like Ryder could heal what had been broken. But not him. All he'd do was fail . . . again.

Logan shook his head and turned away from both girls. The one from his past who he wanted to keep in his life forever, and the girl he wanted to protect.

Ryder, of course, saw his face. "You look pathetic."

He chuckled. "I hate you."

"I'd hate me too," Ryder admitted, glancing at the girls. "Get your shit together. I'm not watching my baby break down because she realizes she's the reason you and your blonde broke up."

Logan sighed, running a hand through his hair. "It wouldn't be her fault."

"Don't be dumb," Ryder said without menace. "To your blonde, Janie's the enemy. And you're asking them to play besties." He let that sink in. "Janie will do whatever you want her to, but your new piece . . . I don't think she will. She won't even play nice in public like we do with each other. So figure out how you're going to make shit work, or make up a convincing story for my girl so she doesn't hate herself for coming between you and the happiness she wants for you."

"How do you spout such wise shit?" Logan chuckled, but he was thinking over everything. Janie would blame herself, and Kylie, even if Janie could be a perfect support system, was proving she wanted help from no one, especially not Janie.

"I am wise, fucker." Ryder sent him a playful smile and reached out, snagging Janie by the waist. "Where you sneaking off to, beautiful?"

"I'm not saying," Janie said, ignoring Logan.

"Baby doll?" Logan called to her.

"Chicks before dicks," she said, trying to sneak away again.

Ryder laughed, lifting her up. "Sweetheart, you wound me. No one comes before me for you."

Logan ignored them. "Janie, what happened?"

She sent him a withering look. "Figure it out yourself. It's not rocket science, Logan. You know better than to walk away."

Ryder rolled his eyes and squeezed her ass so she'd calm down. "Babe, no getting angry at your little bestie." He smirked at Logan, no doubt for the 'little' comment, and continued. "He was just asking me for relationship advice. He's gonna sweep her off her feet."

The scowl on Logan's face didn't drop fast enough. Janie saw it, and her eyes narrowed. "Baby doll," he said, knowing she was pissed at him.

"I'm done talking to you," she said harshly.

"Just tell me what she told you," he begged. "Please."

She didn't answer. She simply turned toward Ryder and rested her head on his shoulder when her boyfriend lifted her up higher.

"Stop being a bitch, Grimm," Ryder told him, smirking while Janie couldn't see.

"I'm not," he said, halting at the truth. If Janie knew the shit Kylie had said about her, she'd either destroy Kylie, or Ryder would. He didn't want Kylie to be Janie's enemy, because even if Janie was mad at him, she was his only real friend. He couldn't abandon her. Not again.

Ryder sent him another teasing grin and squeezed Janie's ass before carrying her to the supply table.

Logan watched them as Kylie's stare burned a hole in his back. He could go and smooth everything over with her, but he didn't. Maybe the others were right; Kylie would wise up and leave. It was for the best, even if it sucked because she was fun when it was just the two of them. But his life wasn't as solitary as people thought it was.

He switched his attention between Janie and Ryder, and the Knight brothers. Kylie had no idea what being close to him really meant.

So he walked away again. He'd leave it up to her to decide.

She'd be safer that way, but if by chance she took a step toward finally helping herself, he'd stay. Even if it was wrong, a threat to all that mattered to him and the *families*, he'd see where they went.

Gareth gave him a teasing grin when he got close. "Ouch, Grimm. You should see her face."

"She has to want to get help," he said. "Forcing her to accept it isn't gonna work."

"True," Gareth admitted, laughing at his sister who was trying to escape Ryder's hold. "Just think about my sissy. You know she's all about heroes needing their Superwoman. But she's delicate right now."

He glanced at the girl who was once his whole heart and saw how big her smile was and how silly she was behaving. They all saw and knew what it really meant. But he also saw the Superman shirt she wore. "She's still trying."

Gareth nodded. "Don't fuck it up then. You know what's at stake."

"I know," he said, closing his eyes.

25

RED RIDING HOOD

Ryder's voice carried across the gym. "You're not using those."

Kylie looked up to see him glaring at Janie. It would probably cause most people to pee themselves, but not Janie. She acted like a fearless toddler with the notorious bad boy, and she was being scolded left and right because she apparently wanted to play with the training weapons that were left out.

It was hard to sit there and watch Janie have any bit of happiness while her heart was broken. Maybe it wasn't Janie's fault people wouldn't stop saying how much Logan wanted her, but she was still the source of tension when it came to her and Logan's relationship. It made it hard to really accept the kindness Janie had given her. It was almost maddening to feel comfortable with her—to laugh with her.

Because she could see it—what Logan did; Janie was sweet. She was delicate yet fierce. If she made an asshole like Ryder Godson smile, she must have a damn heart of gold.

Kylie pressed her lips together, thinking about how many guys, including Logan, Janie had. How did Ryder allow it?

"Maybe it's like a reversal," she mumbled. "I'm the Ryder, and I have to figure out how to get along with her."

Logan said something to Janie. It was soft, and his gaze was tender as he stared down at her.

Nope. No matter how sweet Janie could be, Kylie couldn't deal with it.

Girlfriends didn't get along with ex-girlfriends. Even divorced couples hated their ex-husband or ex-wife. They fought and only dealt with each other if they had kids together.

This thing with Janie was not how things were supposed to be. Logan was not supposed to be staring at his ex like she ruled his world.

Janie covered her ears like a little kid and turned her face away from Logan. All while Ryder gave him a taunting smile and hugged her.

A part of Kylie wanted to be calm and accept things were just different. She'd just had the mindset that she could make things work, but crap, it was hard to stay positive when Logan gave her the cold shoulder—all while Janie got attention from every guy in the building.

Sighing, Kylie tried to think over how she'd gotten to this point. Everything with Logan was totally not how things went in the books she'd read. He was the farthest thing from the other bad boy she'd thought about—Ryder. Ryder was a jerk, but he didn't look like the type to lie about his past.

Logan had lied to her face, and Ryder had warned her that Logan was a liar.

But she wanted him.

So the question was how did they move forward even though he wanted his ex around? Why did he want her around anyway? The girl had admitted to attempting suicide, and falling in love with another guy while they were in a relationship. Why did he want to hold onto that?

Then there was the apparent rape. Who blurted out that they were raped to someone they didn't know? The police hadn't believed her; they'd called her a liar. Was it possible Janie had lied? Was that why it was so easy to tell someone—she wanted attention? After all, Maura told lies all the time to get attention.

Was the rape the reason Logan felt chained to Janie? Yes, that had to be it. The others had said Logan felt guilty.

Still, why did Ryder let Logan stick around?

Kylie glanced at Logan. He didn't look at her, even though she knew he could tell she was watching him. He kept talking to Mark and Janie's brothers, who she had yet to meet.

Janie's battle cry pulled Kylie's attention away from her man-boy and the newcomers. The girl tried to make a run for it, but Ryder easily snatched her by the arm and pulled her to him. He kept her back to his front and effortlessly restrained her by wrapping one arm around her waist, pinning her arms to her sides. As Janie prepared to scream, Ryder, without looking at his girlfriend, used his other hand to cover her mouth and began speaking calmly to the others.

"How are you, love?"

Kylie jerked her head around, not realizing one of Janie's brothers had approached her. He looked to be in his late twenties, and had no resemblance to his sister. Well, she supposed that made sense if they were adopted. Still, he didn't seem to fit in at the gym. He was tall, tanned, and had short, brown hair, and he was dressed like he was attending a special-ops mission. "Oh, um. I'm good. Uh . . . How are you?"

He gave her a friendly smile. "Fantastic. I'm Gawain, Janie's brother. Mind if I join you?"

God, he has an English accent!

"I'm Kylie." She scooted a bit to give him room to sit. "And I don't mind you sitting here."

He chuckled, watching Janie flail in Ryder's hold. "So why is she trying to cheer you up?"

"Who?"

He nodded toward Janie, who had managed to turn around in Ryder's arms—and was attempting to bear-hug him to death? "Jane, my sissy. Normally, she only acts silly with us, but when she's trying to cheer someone up, she'll drag Ryder into her shenanigans."

"You call her Jane?" she asked.

A sort of wince marred his face, but his tone was neutral. "Most of us call her Jane or sissy. Her mum called her Jane."

"Oh," Kylie said, smiling a little at the sound of a grown man calling someone sissy. "I don't really know her. She's my boyfriend's ex. Well, if he's still my boyfriend."

"I'm sure Logan still considers himself your boyfriend." He grinned at her. "He wouldn't make a big deal out of just any girl."

Warmth flooded her body. He was so nice for not telling her how dumb she was, or how much Logan wanted Janie back.

"So what did Logan do?"

Kylie widened her eyes. "How do you know he did anything?"

He gestured to Logan. "He looked ready to kill something when he came out here. Janie asked him where you were, and he said you weren't feeling well. When she went to check on you, he tried to stop her, so she told Ryder to hold him. He pinned Logan down for a good ten minutes."

"He did?" Kylie checked Logan over to make sure he wasn't hurt. He looked fine. "Ryder hates me though. He wouldn't do anything to help me."

"Oh, I doubt he views it as helping you." He clasped his hands together as he leaned forward, watching Janie. "Don't let it get to you. Everything is for her. That's just what he is."

She frowned, finding it odd for someone to speak that way about Ryder. It was almost like he was saying Ryder wasn't human.

"He didn't hurt Logan," Gawain went on. "He only held him down and taunted him about you checking him out."

She choked on her spit. "What?"

He let out a light laugh. "Ryder and Logan have a unique way of dealing with each other. They hate each other but taunt each other about Janie behind her back—sort of a game, if you will. Ryder's not going to pass up the chance to turn it around. He reminded Logan that *everyone* looks at him—that you have too."

"I've never looked at him like that," she whispered.

He rolled his eyes. "Love, even straight men check him out. Then we have to go ravage a woman to remind ourselves we're not gay."

She laughed quietly, covering her mouth. "Okay, I don't feel so bad for looking then."

He winked at her. "Just try to boost Logan's ego when you're with him. It still stings quite a bit for him to see Ryder and Janie fit so well together."

Well, so much for someone not praising Janie and Ryder's relationship and pointing out how much it hurt Logan.

"Don't make that face." He chuckled, rubbing his hands together. "I meant to be purely informative. Logan's with you, but he's coping with a lot about their relationship, and seeking quite a bit of redemption with her."

"What does he have to redeem himself for? She broke his heart."

He smiled sadly. "I don't think he's been very honest about his past, especially regarding her."

"I kinda told him I don't want to hear about her, or be around her." She gave him a serious look. "No offense. I get she's your sister, and she's nice in her own way, but I can't really like her how he wants me to."

His eyes flashed with amusement. "She's not big on girl friends—I highly doubt she expects to be your friend. But even acquaintances can be friendly. Enough about her though. Tell me about you."

She startled as fight or flight instincts surged forward. "There's nothing to tell."

He frowned, his gaze falling down her figure but not in a creepy way. "Everyone has a story, love."

"Mine isn't one I want told. It's no one's business but mine." She crossed her arms, looking forward again. She refused to find Logan still giving her the cold shoulder, and she didn't want to look at any of the other shirtless guys, so she settled on Janie and Ryder again.

Janie still had her arms wrapped around Ryder's waist as he kept her from running off, but now she was puckering her lips and making '*Mmm*' sounds. Ryder was talking to the other Knight brother and Mark, but he'd pause to lean down and kiss her, then resume his conversation.

Kylie rubbed under her eyes to stop the stinging in them. She felt so damn emotional, and she hated it. All she wanted was for that to be her and Logan, and it would be if exes and bad boys hadn't come into the picture.

It would be better if Janie was actually mean too. But she wasn't.

"She's like a villain everyone loves," she whispered, only realizing she'd said it aloud when Gawain replied.

"I suppose she is the villain to some," Gawain said, his easy smile fading a bit. "I'm sure many will say she's a Mary Sue."

"A Mary Sue has to do with an author and their book."

He grinned as if he knew something she didn't. "Don't you know about our families? The fairy tales found in this town were written by the Godsons' ancestors. Blackwoods is home to the Godson Fairy Tales, Canada is home to the Knight Fairy Tales, Colorado is home to the Prince Fairy

Tales, and Texas is home to the Grimm's. The American Grimms, that is. They actually have no direct bloodline to the European Grimms."

Kylie gaped at him and had to force herself to speak. "Are you messing with me?"

"No." He chuckled, pointing at Ryder. "He has the largest collection—some aren't even permitted to be viewed by the public. There's a bit of a legend that the Godson collection was written by four gods. Three males and the moon, a woman. Actually, I think everyone in our family believes those three men and the moon created everything."

"Oh my goodness. *The Little Moon.*" She darted her eyes to Ryder. "No wonder he was so protective of the story in class the other day."

Gawain nodded. "They're more than stories. For our families, at least."

"Oh, wow. That kinda makes everyone seem—I don't know—important or something." She stared at Ryder, still not ready to look at Logan. "So the Knight, Godson, and Grimm families are acquainted in the past?"

"Yes."

"Wow. I actually hated learning about those fairy tales." Her cheeks heated. That probably wasn't the best thing to say to one of the Knights.

He shrugged. "They're not for everyone."

"So, since you guys are all adopted, you're not really related to those families?"

He smiled, but not in that charming way he had before. "If you believe only blood bonds make you family, then yes, we are not directly connected. We choose to be more open-minded and believe some souls are always meant to be tied together. Our father picked each of us, including Janie. We're destined to be together."

Wow, he's nuts. "Well, I don't believe in fairy tales," she told him.

He chuckled but gave her a pitying smile. "Few do, but the stories exist for a reason. They are dark and cruel lessons hidden in magic."

She grew tired of talking about fairy tales and searched for Logan. He had moved to the octagon with Mark, and just as she feared, he was still ignoring her.

When she and Janie had come out of the locker room, he'd barely glanced at her. All he had done was shake his head and turn away.

"It'll be okay," Janie had told her. "And you'll still show him he shouldn't have walked away. Girly balls, Kylie. Hold onto yours."

How could she *hold onto her balls?* Logan had left her. She'd experienced her first panic attack. It had been scary—dark and painful. Normally, darkness was comforting for her. Nothing touched her there; nothing could find her.

But as she'd listened to Janie's instructions, felt Janie's hand pressing against the pain as if to push away that darkness, the fight weakened. The claws she'd felt ripping her heart open seemed to come free, and it was her new enemy holding her hand when the darkness receded.

"Do you know why they're close?" she asked, her voice barely a whisper.

He sighed, lowering his gaze to the floor. "They're trying to heal and grow up. They want to see each other happy. They both want the other to see they're not a monster."

Did Logan see himself that way? It didn't seem like either one saw themselves so negatively. Logan was cocky and no one messed with him. Janie was flirty, and she had a boyfriend girls dreamed of having—and she had Logan. "But who heals with the person who hurt them? She broke his heart and is dating the guy she betrayed him with—why would he stick around?"

A tight smile graced his face. "I suggest you talk to Logan. There's quite a bit you need to learn about him."

Kylie didn't comment further. She knew when someone was done talking, and this man wasn't going to spill any beans on his sister.

"Well, it looks like they're going to fight, after all," Gawain said. "They were discussing strategies on a possible fight that Logan wants," he added, oblivious to her inner torment.

Kylie looked over to see Logan finally staring at her as Mark talked to him. She swallowed, trying not to cave under his dark eyes, and that was hard to do. Looking at him now was like looking at the sex god she first laid eyes on eight days ago. Beautifully dangerous. A *lie*.

"What do you mean a possible fight?" she asked, not breaking eye contact with Logan.

"There's an undefeated fighter from Canada who's been destroying everyone—the stuff of legends. He's a bit closer to Ryder's build, so that's why Mark is dying to get Ryder to come here again. The guy is huge, out of Logan's weight class. He'll have to bulk up and talk the fighter into dropping weight, but it would benefit Logan to get used to fighting someone bigger. Ryder could give Logan an advantage, because the rumor is this fighter's teammates are afraid to face him."

Kylie's stomach clenched at the thought of Logan fighting such a dangerous opponent. As much as she disliked Ryder, she wanted Logan to be prepared for whatever fight was coming his way.

She kept her eyes on her man-boy. His expression was difficult to bear. There was emptiness, but for a moment, guilt and anger all fought for dominance.

A sharp pain pierced her head, and she rubbed her temples. Logan's fierce look wavered, and he scanned her as Gawain patted her back.

"You okay, love?"

"It's just a headache." She kept watching Logan, waiting for him to come take care of her—to say he was sorry. But he didn't.

"Oh, I'm sure they have medication around here." He rubbed her back. "I'll go ask Evander. Sit tight. Or better yet, go wish Logan good luck. It's probably bruising his ego his girl hasn't even greeted him."

"He's the one who's ignoring me." She tried her best not to break the stare down Logan was having with her. No way was she apologizing when he walked away, then ignored her.

Gawain cracked a smile as he gestured for his brother to come over. "Boys aren't always brave enough to admit their faults. Some need a strong woman to show us she's still going to be there when we screw up. Go offer a truce before he gets the shit beat out of him because he can't stop thinking about you."

Ryder entered the octagon, and Logan turned away from her first. It felt like she'd won a small victory between them. That was probably all the balls she could muster right now—a crappy stare down.

The younger-looking Knight brother jogged over. He was about Logan's size and probably the same age as him too. "Hello." He grinned, holding out his hand. "You must be Kylie. I'm Gareth, Janie's most handsome brother."

Kylie shook his hand, smiling when Gawain shoved him and got up. "Keep her company while I search for Evander."

Gareth plopped down beside her as they watched Gawain head off. "So you're staying over?"

She grimaced but nodded. "Yes, thank you for letting me stay. It'll just be the one night."

He smiled. "He's a fool to push you two together. Try not to get too stressed—I promise you'll be in good hands. And she'll probably have Ryder around anyway."

Relief spread through her, and she sagged on the chair. "Thank you." She peeked at him. "For understanding."

"No problem." He sighed, pulling his phone from his pocket. Kylie noticed the contact before he declined the call: *L. Godson.* "Well, I've got something to take care of. I suppose I'll see you later, Kylie."

"Yes, I think so." She smiled, watching him rush off as a yell sounded from the octagon.

"Stop," Janie yelled, giggling as Ryder tossed her over his shoulder and carried her to the far side of the octagon.

Kylie jerked her gaze away when they started making out against the chain link. "Don't they have any decency?"

"Oh, for fuck's sake," came Gawain's voice as he marched toward the fence, "can you not wait until you're somewhere private?"

Ryder lifted his head, smirking over his shoulder. "Nope. Close your eyes. I'm getting unnecessary good luck kisses."

Logan shook his head at them and kept warming up with Mark.

"Here you are, Kylie."

She lifted her eyes and smiled at Evander as he held out two tablets. "Oh, thank you."

He nodded. "Of course. How are you feeling?"

"Good." She took the medication, smiling at him again. "I hardly feel anything."

"I'm glad to hear it," he said, subtly checking her over. "I'm here if you do require any help, okay?"

"Thank you," she said, happy that she finally didn't feel so smothered about Janie.

"I think he's waiting for you to go give him his good luck kiss." Evander chuckled and took a step toward the octagon before adding, "He'll need it against Ryder."

Her face warmed, and she nodded that she'd go see Logan. It hurt that he still hadn't come to her, but maybe these guys knew more about how boyfriends worked than she did.

So, standing and wincing when she felt sluggish, she made her way to the gate of the octagon.

"Logan," said Kylie, gaining his attention. "Can I talk to you before you start?"

He nodded and helped her climb into the ring. "Are you in pain?"

She almost smacked him right away but settled for giving him the attitude he deserved. "Is that all you have to say?"

He continued checking her over. "I'm sorry for yelling and walking out. I didn't want to say something worse than I already had. Did something happen with her?"

"Do you even care?" She couldn't believe he was ignoring the fact he'd left her thinking he'd broken up with her. Gawain had said Logan tried to stop Janie, and that's why Ryder held him down. It wasn't that they stopped him from going back to her.

He sighed, his eyes flickering over her shoulder. "I care. I care so much."

In an instant, her fury vanished, but she didn't want to let him off easily. "Listen," she said, trying to remember everything she'd absorbed since they fought. Her girly balls would have to settle for being brave enough to confront him. "I didn't mean to doubt you. Or to say such bad things about you and her."

Logan's gaze drifted over her face, but he stayed quiet.

"I'm sorry I let myself think the way I was," she went on. "But please understand, I'm not going to be okay with everything. You have no idea how hard it is not to compare myself to her when you're always praising her.

"She's not my friend just because she's yours; I'm probably never going to be her friend. She's your ex, you know? I can't deal with you comparing us or making it seem like you want me to be like her."

"I know," he said, his voice deep but soothing as he slid his hand into hers. "I didn't mean to make you think I wanted you to be like her. That's not what I was trying to do. She's just the best support I can offer you. Really, Hood. You have no idea how much she can help."

She nodded, so relieved to just hear him speak, especially since he was making it clear it was all for her. "I thought you broke up with me." Her heart raced because she hadn't meant to blurt out such a confession. She was supposed to be teaching him a lesson, but she couldn't help it. "You said you were done and walked out. If she hadn't told me you would've thrown me out if that was true, I would have left as soon as I could."

"I'm sorry, baby." He squeezed her hand as his other came up to pull her to him by her waist. "I feel like such a dick. I just didn't want to push you anymore. I'm not a good boyfriend, but I'm trying."

She sighed, melting when he kissed her forehead. It was so hard to hold him responsible for making her sad.

"Please give me another chance," he said softly.

"Yes," she said, then remembered they weren't alone. "Um, we can talk about all this later."

"That's probably wise." He smiled, scanning her attire. "You changed. Did you want to do some exercises after I'm done?"

"No." She scooted closer to him, wanting to melt into him. "I just wanted to show her I appreciate what she did."

He looked genuinely happy. "That's nice of you."

It felt like he was running over her heart every time he seemed happy about pleasing Janie. "Yeah. So are you ready to spar? Ryder seems calmer."

Logan smirked. "I have even more reason to beat his ass now that you're here."

"Don't try to butter me up. I'm still mad."

"I know you are." He cupped her cheeks. "You're hot when you're angry, though."

"You're such a pervert." She loved when he said stuff like that.

"You like my dirty talk." He chuckled, smoothing her hair back. "Are we good?"

"No."

"We'll talk after I'm done." He placed several kisses to her cheeks. "I really am sorry, Hood. I just want you to want me around. I want to support you."

"I do want you around and your support."

He grinned. "You're the most beautiful woman I'll ever see. I just wish you believed that."

She almost swooned. "Well, I don't know about being the most beautiful. Don't expect me to always feel confident. I am with you when we're alone, but that's 'cause—well, I don't know."

"You'll get there. I'll help you." He kissed her forehead. "You're doing so well, especially considering you've been forced to wear your hood up for years. I barely recognize you."

"Is that bad?" Her breathing became ragged. What was he saying? Was he saying what Ryder was—that she wasn't forced? Did he think she was lying?

"It's a good thing." He didn't seem to notice her distress. "I'm just saying you've made so much progress in such a short time. We only met a little over a week ago. It's really impressive that you can just come out, and you're talking to some of the most dangerous people you'll ever meet without any trouble."

"Yeah," she said, realizing how fast everything was happening, and that he was right. She was doing some things with ease.

"It seems like longer," he said, reaching up to hold the side of her face before sliding his hand into her hair. "I'm proud of you."

"Thanks."

He pulled her head to his chest. "You look exhausted."

"I am."

He hugged her, somewhat relieving the strain on her weak legs. "What happened? Is it your ribs or something?"

She shook her head, returning his hug as she decided not to bring up her panic attack. "I'll tell you about it after."

"You two didn't get into some secret catfight, did you?"

She laughed and smacked his back. "You would have liked that."

"Hell yeah, I would," he cheered. "Invite my ass next time."

"We didn't fight," she said, lifting her head to look up at him.

He gave her several small kisses to her lips and cheeks, letting their fight and her insecurities grow weaker and weaker.

He pulled back. "Why was she trying to take weapons to you?"

"You mean the things Ryder stopped her from getting?"

"Yeah." He waved his hand toward the wall. "She was going for the paintball guns. Were you planning on teaming up on me?"

"No." She couldn't believe that had been Janie's plan. "I'd never hurt you."

"Aw, honey." He kissed her forehead. "She's just playing. Those aren't even for training. They're to goof around with."

"Oh." She sighed, leaning against him. "I was about to say that she was crazy. She was talking weird and acting like a little kid."

His posture stiffened, but he held her close. "No, she's not crazy. She's just—" He let out a breath. "The sad ones are always the people who smile the brightest."

Kylie frowned. Was he talking about Janie's rape? It wasn't like he knew Janie blurted out her past, so she wasn't sure what Janie had to be sad about right now. Other than Ryder getting angry earlier, the girl should be fine.

"At least you've had a bit of time to bond with her. It won't be so awkward tonight." He grinned, but it was a nervous smile. "Right?"

She shrugged. "I guess."

"I realized you'd actually not spoken to her at all," he said. "You've kinda only talked to people around her." He frowned, caressing her hair. "I guess rumors about her and me are the worst ways to view her."

"I guess you're right," she said. "Well, I'll try to learn more about her, but don't expect us to be friends."

His body tensed, but he stayed quiet.

It worried her because she always said the wrong things to him. She was being honest, and it was making everything worse. She didn't want things to be bad between them.

So she pushed up on her tippy toes to distract him with a kiss him. With a smile, he lowered his mouth to hers. He pulled her closer before he pushed her mouth open so his tongue could meet hers.

She could kiss him all day. So powerful but gentle at the same time.

"You're going to give me a hard-on," he murmured.

She chuckled as he pressed a few smiling kisses to her lips. "You're so perverted. Can't we have one moment of you not telling me how turned on you are?"

"No." He kissed her before standing straight. "And I'm so fucking turned on with your little hood on. You look like Red Riding Hood."

"Is that a turn on for you?" She gasped. "Oh, gosh. Gawain told me about your families. I had no idea you were related to the fairy tales. You're all famous."

"Oh." He rubbed the back of his neck. "Yeah. It's no big deal. I wasn't raised to join the family legacies like the others."

"Legacies?" She must've missed something.

"Don't worry about it." He cupped her cheeks, kissing her again. This time, he kept it short and sweet. "I have to warm up."

"Oh—right. Um, kick his ass. Don't get hurt."

He chuckled, smoothing her hair back. "I'm imagining you playing sexy nurse with me afterward."

"Logan." She pushed his hands away. "Just concentrate on your fight."

"I think I can beat anyone knowing you're cheering me on."

She gave him a skeptical look, but she was melting. "Don't try to butter me up. I'm going to put you in one of those choke hold thingies."

He laughed. "I'll fight with one hand tied behind my back to even it up then. Sort of."

"Are you ready?" she asked, stopping him from embarrassing her.

He nodded, smiling and looking confident. "I think I'll let him hurt me just a little, though. Will you wear one of those sexy nurse costumes and take care of me?"

"Do you have one?"

His eyes went wide. "Are you serious? You'll dress up?"

She bit her lip, always surprised by what flew out of her mouth when he was around. "Do you want me to?"

He studied her. "Baby, I want to do everything with you. But only if it's something you want."

Oh, wow, that was the most perfect thing to say. "Then I'll dress up for you one day. Maybe I'll even be a real Little Red Riding Hood." She traced a Red Riding Hood tattoo on his forearm.

"I swear to God I'll lose my fucking mind if you dress up in a sexy Red Riding Hood costume."

"And would you dress up like the Big Bad Wolf?" Kylie watched him, confused when his smile vanished.

Logan shrugged, and that's when she remembered he seemed to have a strong dislike for the reference.

"I think I prefer Logan Grimm," she said softly, praying his smile would return.

"Who doesn't?"

He never missed a beat.

"You ready, Grimm?" Ryder asked.

"Yeah. Give me a sec." Logan looked back at her. "Good luck kiss?"

She didn't wait and pulled him down to her, instantly taken over by his kiss.

"God, I love," he whispered, pausing to kiss her harder before he pulled back, "these lips."

Her heart hammered away in her chest as he let his eyes drift over her face. He was staring into her eyes, and he looked happy.

"Stay with Janie," he said. "Don't talk to any guys walking around; they're not all good people."

"Okay."

He pecked her lips and grabbed her hand to pull her to the gate Ryder had just helped Janie out of. "And thank you, baby," he said, kissing her hand. "I'll make everything up to you."

"I'll try not to hurt him too bad, Blondie," Ryder told her before turning to glare at Janie when she smacked his butt. "Babe."

"Babe," Janie said, copying his annoyed tone. "You two play nice."

"I'm not nice," Ryder said, looking as if he really had no way of accommodating her request.

"See you in a bit," Logan whispered in Kylie's ear.

"Logan," Janie said, linking her arm with Kylie's, "don't hit my baby's face. I want him nice and pretty when I pop him in the nose for being a poop face."

Ryder scoffed. "He won't land a hit on my face unless I let him, baby girl. You don't have to act tough to protect me."

Janie rolled her eyes and tugged her away. "Never mind, Logan. Go ahead and hit him in the face."

"Babe," Ryder said, making Janie sigh and turn back to them, "don't go wandering around. Got it?"

Janie nodded as Logan seemed to give Kylie the same warning with his eyes.

Ryder winked at his girlfriend. "I'll behave."

Logan shook his head, smiling before resuming his warm-up.

Kylie watched Ryder scan the growing crowd before he went toward Logan.

"Not the way I envisioned you showing him your balls are bigger than his," Janie said as they walked to a set of chairs. "But you certainly stood up to him while proving you'll fight to keep him. Good job."

"Thanks." She smiled at Janie before nervously checking out the groups of rowdy fighters.

"Don't worry about them," Janie said, not looking at the crowd. "The boys get all protective—but no one will bother me . . . well, us."

Kylie returned her attention to the two man-boys as they bumped fists. "I guess a meanie like Ryder has his perks—no one messes with you."

Janie chuckled. "There are still monsters who don't fear the consequences—not even Ryder. Never forget that."

Kylie realized Janie, too, was incredibly wrapped up in the fairy tales her stepfather's ancestors had created. It had never been in her interest to listen to Janie when she spoke in class, but now that she thought about it, the girl spouted off philosophical stuff quite a bit.

It was dumb to get this way over stories, but they could've been drug dealers or killers. Instead, they were just some weirdos with rich families, and they liked to use their stories to make sense of things.

Well, she could pretend to go along with their nonsense. After all, Logan was a Grimm. So she grinned at Janie as best she could and said, "Yes, Master Anakin."

"Smartass." Janie beamed up at her. "But you are learning, my young Padawan. I knew the Force was strong with you. But smart off to me again, my young apprentice, and I might have to force choke you, bitch."

It was probably a real threat, but Kylie wasn't going to cower. Unfortunately, she didn't know any more *Star Wars* quotes. It didn't matter anyway, because Logan and Ryder's fight had started.

Pain tugged at her stomach when Ryder hit Logan with what seemed to be a testing punch to the face.

Janie grabbed her hand and squeezed. "It's okay—it's just a spar."

Ryder attacked with a more aggressive combo, hitting Logan in the cheek before Logan returned the favor.

Kylie's breath sped up as the crowd started cheering them on, her eyes on Logan as he showed no weakness, no fear against Ryder. He was a warrior fighting against a god. She couldn't stop her smile, remembering that Janie'd said Logan was a Batman fan, while Janie was all Superman.

Janie got really antsy, bouncing her leg before she yelled, "Superman ain't got nothing on you, babe!"

"Too bad Batman beats Superman," Kylie blurted.

Janie's eyes widened. "In your dreams." She turned, grinning at the octagon. "Kick his ass, babe!"

Ryder swung at Logan, hitting his stomach.

Kylie stood, hollering, "Come on, Logan!"

He locked Ryder up, landing a knee before Ryder somehow took Logan down to the mat. Logan blocked the next punch coming at him and locked Ryder in a hold of some kind, making the guys cheer even louder. And she cheered right along with them, out-screaming Janie.

26

KISS IT BETTER

"Ow."

Kylie smacked Logan's hand when he tried to reach up to his cheek. "Stop."

"Baby, it hurts." He stared up at her from where he lay on the sofa in his locker room.

She sighed and applied ointment to the cut on his eyebrow, softening her glare when he began playing with the hand she was resting on his chest. He'd showered after his draw with Ryder, so he was in a shirt now. Neither one wanted to yield during their fight, but it looked like they were both holding back. Eventually, they both nodded at each other, ending the sparring match.

"I know it hurts," she said, leaning back and smiling as he scooted over to give her more room on the sofa. "But you're supposed to put this stuff on. Evander told you to."

Logan rolled his eyes and pulled her down, shuffling so they could both fit on their sides, facing each other. "He's required to say that. That's his job." He tilted her face so he could kiss her, but she pressed her lips together. "Hood." He kept nipping her lips. "I'm wounded. You have to kiss me better."

She shook her head.

"Why? I know you'll make it better."

She stared at him, wondering if he had already forgotten how badly he'd hurt her.

He leaned away. "Am I still in trouble?"

She nodded, feeling her chest ache as he pressed sweet kisses to her cheek.

"I'm sorry," he said. "I should have calmed down and tried to understand how you were feeling. And I shouldn't have expected you to want to be around her, or compared either of you to each other—that wasn't what I really meant anyway. I just see how much Ryder does for her, and I wanted to be that for you. And then you basically accused me of wanting her over you, and of lying to you—it pissed me off."

"I shouldn't have said I hate you. I don't." She lightly trailed her fingers around his cut. "It was just a shock to look in the mirror and see myself. I usually avoid looking in mirrors. It's like I forget I'm not pretty when I'm with you."

"No, honey, you're beautiful." He held her cheek, kissing her as he took a deep breath. "I know what you mean, though. About forgetting, and that you feel upset when you see your wounds." He touched her side. "They do look better. Keep doing whatever you're doing. Everything's healing faster than I would've expected."

She frowned because nothing about her care had been different than any other time Maura had hit her.

"You're really doing great, Hood." He tugged her hair. "Nothing about you needs to change, except you need to stop hiding. You've done amazingly already."

"Sometimes I want to hide under my hood again." *In the dark.*

"That makes sense." He twirled her hair. "I want you to try to believe what I tell you about yourself. When I say you're strong, beautiful, brave—I mean it. So that's another thing I want you to try to get used to. The truth is you're a great girl. You've been through shit I can barely fathom, and you're alive. You're sweet and innocent." He chuckled, adding, "Well, when you're not my super freak."

"Logan." She rested her head against his chest, smiling when he ran his fingers through her hair. She'd always wanted this with a guy.

"Don't be upset. I dig the kinky shit." His laugh vibrated through his chest.

"Can I ask you something without you getting angry?"

"Yeah." He kissed the top of her head.

"Was I a bet?" She peeked up, seeing his eyes wide.

"No. Never." He held her cheek. "I swear."

"What about the bet I heard you placing when I was at your apartment the first time?"

Logan sighed, looking away. "I was talking to Chris. He was arranging a bet on a girl. I was putting my money in that I would fuck whoever he picked. It had to be someone I've never been with—which was always my preference."

She swallowed back her tears and continued in a low voice. "And those girls he had lined up for you, you were meant to pick one?"

He nodded, still not looking at her.

"But you brought me."

"I didn't care about the bet after meeting you, Hood. I'd actually forgotten until he walked up to us." He looked back at her, his gaze soft and begging. "I was fine with losing."

She felt her pain fade, but she wanted to clear up the doubts she had about him. She wanted to know him. "And Chris?"

He started rubbing her side as he talked. "It's more than me and him who bet on this. A lot of guys do it, a lot of people with money, but I'm usually a sure thing for anyone needing to score a win. He had money on me, so he was pissed you were with me. He knew I wouldn't bet you by the way I acted. Plus, you're a minor. We could have all gotten in trouble."

She frowned as it all came together. "So that's why he said I wasn't special. And it was Janie he was talking about."

"Yeah." He leaned forward to kiss her forehead. "I was eighteen when I started fighting, but I was still in school. I took her, of course, and everyone found out she was only fifteen. Chris didn't like it. He tried to say it was important to focus, and a young girlfriend would only ruin my future. It makes sense, but that wasn't really the problem. He just didn't want a girlfriend fucking up the way things worked with the team. And having an underage girl around, especially one with a family like hers, would be trouble for him. I guess he feared if she ever saw the shit going on, she'd tell the Knights, and they'd shut him down."

"What kind of stuff?"

He shook his head. "Shit I don't want you to think about. I swear I'm not doing anything like that anymore."

"But I'm underage."

"Only for a little while longer." He shrugged. "And I fired Chris."

"What happened after I left that night? Evander said some things . . ."

He leaned his head back, closing his eyes. "I was scared when I looked out in the crowd and saw you'd gone missing. He said you begged to leave, that you'd called for a ride. I was pissed. I thought he was telling the truth'."

"So you picked one."

"What? No!" He lifted his head, his eyes wide.

"I don't understand."

"I admit I got trashed." He gave her an apologetic look. "I was mad he let you go, but it was more because I thought you left on your own. I was worried about you. I know it was stupid of me to think you'd just accept me, but I'm not used to women turning me down. It infuriated me you would just keep letting yourself get hurt."

"I was scared, Logan."

"I know." He sighed, caressing her cheek. "I'm just a dick, and I don't always think shit through. But I didn't pick any of those women."

Kylie leaned forward to kiss him softly, to tell him that she believed him. His body relaxed and he hugged her to him, running his hand up and down her back. Smiling against his lips, she kissed him one last time before pulling back to see him pout. "I still want to talk," she told him as he sighed and nodded. "You did say we would."

"I know. What else do you want to know?"

She grinned as he began playing with her hair. "Why did you break Chris' arm?"

He darted his eyes away from the lock of hair he was twirling in his fingers to stare at her eyes. "Who told you that?"

"Trevor. At school today. And Evander told me about Chris winding up in the hospital—that it was about me."

His eyes moved all over her face. "It was about you. But not in the way you might think."

"I just want the secrets to stop. And you were a total jerk to leave me like that."

He smirked, making her smile like he always did. "Hood is getting feisty. I like it."

"Just talk." She laughed at his smile.

"Fine. But only because you got hot-angry. Don't be afraid to punish me later. And I want to know why you looked like you did after you both came out."

"Trust me, your punishment is coming."

"Can't wait." He chuckled and pecked her lips. "I like the way you evaded the last part there."

Sighing, she nodded. "I'll tell you, but I want some of this other stuff cleared up first."

"Fair enough. Okay, so I was mad?"

She nodded, understanding that he was talking about her leaving his fight.

"Well, there's normally celebrating and shit after I win. But I was pissed. I just wanted to search for you—but that would get me nowhere, so I got drunk instead. Chris kept trying to suggest one of the girls, but I kept blowing him off. Time was winding down on our 'clock', and I was getting angrier the more I drank. He said something about not believing I was acting like this over a naïve little girl. Then he had the nerve to say I need help if I only get hard for kids. I lost it and attacked him. Before I knew it, I'd broken his arm. Mark pulled me off, but the damage was done."

She grinned like an idiot, and she couldn't stop.

"That makes you happy?" He chuckled.

She nodded, giddy that he sort of defended her.

"Well, I don't regret it. I didn't know he'd told you what he did until the next morning. If I had known, I would have really beaten the shit out of him."

"I'm sure that had to do with Janie, though." It was petty of her, but she didn't care.

He shrugged. "It just added to my anger. He'd hurt two girls I care about. I'm glad to be done with him, and there are better agents out there anyway. Plus, Ryder hated his guts. As much as we piss each other off, we're good sparring partners. So it cuts out the extra drama none of us need."

"That's good, I guess."

"Yeah." He rotated his arm. "Fuck, he locked my arm up good."

Kylie leaned up, tracing the muscle. She couldn't tell what to look for, and he had tattoos and way too many muscles. "It was pretty cool to see you fight him. The fight lasted longer than the one you had before, and every fight I've seen Ryder in, he's easily wiped the floor with the guy."

Logan nodded. "He would kill if he went pro, but he won't. He has too much of their family business to deal with."

Kylie jerked her eyes up. "What's their family business?"

"I don't know, really." He avoided meeting her eyes.

"I thought your family worked with theirs."

"We do." He rubbed his face, sighing. "But I'm not like them. Wait until you see their homes. You're staying at the Knight house but I'm sure they'll take you to the Godson estate. It's insane."

She knew he was avoiding answering questions, but let him off this time. "Are they richer than Kevin?"

"Definitely." A faint curve of his lips hinted that he wasn't telling her everything. "Like I said before, our families don't need to have our names slapped on a town to know what's ours."

"Did you grow up rich?"

"Nah." He shook his head. "My dad got out of the game when they had me. I'm not in like the others because of my mom. She kept me from our traditions and the truth."

"Oh." She frowned, not sure what he meant by 'the truth.' "So it's like a cult?"

"No. I kinda can't say anything else." His gaze shifted away. "The Godson, Knight, and Prince legacies all have rules anyway."

"Prince?"

"Just drop it, baby."

She pouted. "But this is interesting. I just had homework on *The Little Moon* and *The End of Gods & Monsters*."

"Those are good." He grinned, pecking her lips. "Maybe just read them, and you'll figure stuff out. Anyway, I won't learn more unless I become a . . ."

"A what?"

He sighed, smoothing her hair back. "Nothing."

"Aw, come on."

"It's nothing." He chuckled, acting hurt when she gave him a little shake.

"Fine, can I ask a question about me?"

He smirked. "Is it about you naked?"

That reminded her of what Trevor had said, but she was sure asking him about it would only result in a fight. She'd just wait for the chance to check his drawer the next time she was at his place.

"I'm waiting, Hood."

"I want to know if you like me?"

He kissed her sweetly before looking all over her face, then said, "Hood, what have I been telling you from the first day we met?" When she didn't answer, he said, "I've said you're my girl. What do you think I mean by that?"

"I thought that was just you being you. You've never said more than you just want to take care of me—never that you actually liked me. You didn't want a girlfriend."

His brows furrowed adorably. "You think I don't like you?"

"I don't know what I think."

He kept staring at her like he was debating what to say. "Hood, I—"

Janie's voice rang out from the hall before he could start. "Can we come in?"

"Shit," he said before yelling, "Hang on!" Giving her an apologetic smile, he helped her up. "We'll talk later. I promise. You guys probably need to head home, though. I'm sorry I can't go with you over there, but I have to do some stuff with Mark. Anyway, you have school tomorrow."

"But—"

He pecked her quickly, kissing across her cheek so he could whisper in her ear. "I like you more than you know."

She smiled and received a few more kisses before he walked them to the door.

"But I promise we'll still talk later. That's not what I wanted to tell you."

"What do you want to tell me?"

He shook his head. "Later, Hood." Her pout only caused him to chuckle as he opened the door. "Hey," he said, greeting Janie, then looked at Ryder. "Are you done crying?"

Ryder scoffed and pulled Janie inside. "Bitch, I held back."

"So did I."

"Yeah right." Ryder plopped down on a chair before pulling Janie onto his lap. He looked a little sore, just like Logan, but neither looked like they had just beaten the crap out of each other.

Kylie watched Janie covering Ryder's jaw with kisses. He'd taken a hard hit there, and it was a little bruised.

Ryder smirked at Janie. "Baby, that's not where I need you to kiss to make me better."

"Hush, it's magic." She kissed his jaw again.

Was this the type of shit Logan was expecting? Kissing him better? She didn't want to be like Janie, or to remind Logan of her—and this had her thinking Janie had kissed plenty of Logan's wounds better.

Logan laughed as he gathered their things. "You think I didn't hold back?"

Ryder shook his head before turning his face to take the kiss Janie was aiming for his cheek.

Logan pressed a kiss to Kylie's temple, quieting those darker thoughts, as he slid his hand to rest on her hip. "You going to be okay staying with her?"

She nodded, smiling because Ryder was now frowning at his girlfriend's pampering. "Yeah. Maybe it will be fun—I haven't had a sleepover since I was maybe thirteen. Maybe this'll help me get to know her." Honestly, she didn't care to get to know Janie, but it would make him happy. And he'd already made it clear she couldn't stay with him. It really was better than going to the awkward situation she'd find at home.

"I hope you have fun then," he said. "And I know you'll like her. She's the best person I know."

Ugh.

"We have to get going, Logan," Ryder said, standing up. "I have to swing by my place so I can get some of her shit."

Logan smirked at Ryder as he took her hand. "You need me to buy you a teddy bear to cuddle?"

Ryder's eyes lit up in emerald flames. "Do you need my boot up your ass?"

Kylie's eyes went wide at the dark tone, but Logan just laughed and pulled her out of the room. Ryder didn't tug Janie ahead, like she expected, and she felt the tension rise between the man-boys.

"We're gonna have so much fun," Janie told her, grinning up at Ryder at the last second. "Babe, we can play hide 'n' seek."

"Doubt Blondie wants to play hide-and-seek," he told her, but he grinned over his shoulder at Logan, adding, "We fuck every time and get caught."

Surprisingly, Logan laughed. "I don't know why you're smiling at me. Makes me think you're swapping Janie's face out for mine."

Janie giggled as Ryder shook his head. "They have the best bromance, Kylie. You're going to laugh so hard with them together."

She doubted it, but she smiled at the girl anyway.

Ryder finally picked up the pace and dragged Janie ahead of them.

Logan lifted their hands and kissed her fingers. "He's gonna be moody about leaving her at her dad's."

"They really live together?" Kylie asked him.

"Yeah." He frowned. "Ryder's older brother's in town, and he's likely going to stick around. So it's best for her to be away from the Godson home. The Knights won't let him onto their property, so that's where it's safest for both of you."

"If he's is such a problem, why would you ask Ryder to call him? Is he the one you said would help if we needed?" She was fishing for information.

"Yeah." He smiled at her frown. "Don't worry about it. He's just a backup plan."

Her stomach was in knots about. "You're not going to have to deal with him, right?"

"Baby, just leave this to me," he said, harsher than she expected. "I know what I'm doing."

She bit her lip, not wanting to cause another fight or make him feel that she didn't believe in him.

"Just don't worry," he said softer. "I'm only using his help if we need it."

She nodded and stared at the couple ahead of them. They were back to being cute. She couldn't believe they lived together; she'd thought it was just for a few days when Janie brought it up before.

Logan squeezed her hand. "Do you need me to go get anything from your house?"

Like that would go over well. "No, I'll just wear this again."

"I'll find her something," Janie told them as Ryder opened the trunk of his car and loaded items. "And don't worry, I'll have her send you texts to show she's fine."

Logan smirked. "Good. But just record it if you two have a sexy pillow fight, and make sure you say dirty words to each other—maybe slip in a kiss or something."

Ryder's angry expression slipped, and he chuckled when Janie flipped Logan off.

"Stop being a pervert," Kylie when Janie tried to act like she wasn't paying attention.

"Stop being sexy and maybe I will," Logan said quietly. "Have fun, okay? And get your schoolwork done. If anything happens, I'll come get you, but I think you two will be fine. She really likes you. I promise."

"I'll be fine. Maybe I'll even get over some of my anxiety with her."

"You will." He smiled and pulled her closer. "I'll pick you up after school, okay?"

"Really?" She wanted that so badly. Just having her boyfriend show everyone she was special enough to change his day.

He nodded and chuckled at her big smile. "I'll be out front. We'll have to go back to the gym, but I'll work you out this time." He pecked her lips and pulled her tighter. "And I'll let you start my punishment."

"Grimm, will you shut the fuck up already?" Ryder had never sounded more annoyed as he guided Janie to the passenger side of the car. "Just kiss her goodbye. I have shit to do."

"Babe," Janie yelled.

"What?" he yelled right back.

"Let him tell her bye. Quit being a dick or you're cut off."

Ryder muttered curses and opened the door for his girlfriend, only to growl and start pulling things out to take to the trunk. "Woman, when the fuck did you put blankets in here?"

"It's a gift from Mark," Janie said. "Look at the moon!"

Ryder didn't look but Logan finally turned back to Kylie.

"Text me when you guys get to her house," he said.

She nodded but she sad about saying goodbye.

"I'll see you tomorrow." He caressed her hair before holding her chin.

"Okay. Um, have a good night." She darted her gaze, seeing a few men leave the gym as Janie caught her eye.

Logan chuckled and used both hands to cradle her face. "You're turning me into a pussy. I'll miss you."

She melted. This boy was never going to stay in trouble with her. All she could do was stand there, smiling as he lowered his lips to brush across hers. It was one of those kisses that wasn't quite a kiss, more like he was teasing her.

"You're supposed to say, I'll miss you, too, Logan."

She grinned against his lips. "I'll miss you a lot. Now hurry up and kiss me."

"I wish I could do so much more than that," he said softly, giving her the kiss that took her away from the world and to a place where it was just them.

"Any fucking day now," came Ryder's annoyed voice, yanking it all away.

Logan chuckled, guiding her to the car. "Take care of my girl."

Ryder popped the seat for Kylie to get in. "I only take care of mine."

Janie stood on the edge of the car, leaning over the top as she told Kylie, "He's happy to act guard dog for us."

"You," Ryder deadpanned. "It's all for you." But he flicked his gaze to Kylie. "Come on. You'll be fine with us."

A white Lexus pulled up on Janie's side, and before Kylie got in, she saw Logan and Ryder tense.

"Janie, get in the damn car," Ryder growled.

Kylie jumped at the dark tone as a man wearing an all-white business suit exited the car. He ran a hand through his gunmetal gray hair, then tugged his sleeves in place as his eyes locked on Janie.

"Get in the fucking car," Ryder repeated, taking a step toward Janie.

Logan pushed Kylie toward the door Ryder had opened. "Get in. Now."

"What's wrong?" Her gaze flew back to the man. His gaze was still on Janie and not on the furious bad boy nearing him.

"My queen," the man greeted . . . Janie.

"Get the fuck away from her," Ryder snarled, pushing the guy back.

"Babe, calm down," Janie said, wrapping her arms around his waist.

"Hood, get in," Logan said the moment the man looked right at her.

She froze under his cold stare, and damn near peed herself when his eyes gleamed with silver.

He actually looked a little familiar with his chiseled features and fierce gray eyes, but she was sure she'd never seen him before.

He shifted his gaze from her back to Janie, who had somehow managed to get between him and Ryder, and smirked.

Logan shoved Kylie harder, and she tripped but got into the car. She yelped as he tossed in her backpack and slammed the door in her face.

She couldn't hear what was being said, but Ryder was standing toe to toe with the man, holding Janie behind him.

Logan went over then, grabbing Janie by the arm as he opened the passenger door and pushed her in. "You're not helping. Stay here."

Janie glared at him, but Logan pinned her with a darker glare and shut the door in her face too.

"What's happening?" Kylie whispered as Logan turned to shake hands with the man in white and a second man who wore a black suit and a devilish smile.

"What happens every time his brother gets close to me," Janie said softly. "Ryder loses his mind and Logan ends up involved in something he doesn't need to be."

"That's Ryder's brother?"

Janie nodded. "Luc Godson."

Ryder turned his back on his brother and, flipping him off, rounded the car.

Kylie scrambled over to sit behind Janie since there was no room behind him, cringing when he slammed the door.

"Stupid motherfuckers," he said, starting the car.

"Babe, please relax," Janie cooed, reaching over to caress his clenched jaw.

He shot a frightening glare at Janie. "How can I fucking relax when he's after you?"

Kylie's eyes widened. That didn't sound good.

"He's not after me," Janie said, stretching over to kiss Ryder's shoulder. "I'm yours. You always scare him off anyway."

Ryder didn't reply. He just drove fast, shifting gears roughly as the street lights streamed past the window like falling stars.

As pretty as the sight was, the atmosphere in the car was suffocating, and she couldn't stand it. Maybe she'd try to be friendly . . . "Yeah, you're good at scaring people off," she said, earning a smile from Janie. "I mean, I didn't even know about those guys at our school who . . . hurt Janie."

"What?" His voice was so loud that she covered her ears. "Who fucking hurt you?" he asked Janie.

"I don't know," Janie said, frowning. "No one hurt me."

"Who the fuck are you talking about?" Ryder slammed on the breaks at a stoplight.

She braced herself so she wouldn't hit the back of Janie's seat, then searched for her seatbelt.

"Who?" Ryder yelled at her.

"The guys who raped her," she shouted before slapping her hands over her mouth.

Ryder went silent and grabbed Janie's hand. He lifted it to his lips and kissed sweetly before letting go so he could drive again.

Kylie lowered her hands while her heart pounded hard and fast. "Sorry. I didn't mean to blurt it out. I just meant that I had no idea those guys went to our school. They must be scared shitless."

"They don't go to our school," Janie said, settling back in her seat.

"Oh," Kylie said quietly. "That's good."

"Yep." Janie's head bobbed. "They're dead."

Continued in

LITTLE HOOD AND HER WOLF

CONTINUE

THE BIG BAD WOLF TRILOGY

LITTLE HOOD AND HER WOLF

-BOOK 2-

DECEMBER 2020

THE WOLVES ARE EVERYWHERE

-BOOK 3-

FEBRUARY 2021

CONNECTED SERIES

THE GODS & MONSTERS TRILOGY

AVAILABLE NOW

JANE'S TEAM

A High School Reverse Harem Romance

(A G&M ALTERNATE REALITY)

COMING SOON

THE SONS OF DEATH DUOLOGY
(A BIG BAD WOLF SPINOFF)

BEYOND FOREVER
(A GODS & MONSTERS TIME TRAVEL NOVELLA)

THE WOLF PRINCE
(A GODS & MONSTERS PREQUEL)

DEMETRIO

MATEO

JULIEN
(UNTITLED STREET GANG TRILOGY)

ACKNOWLEDGMENTS

Thank you to my family—to my husband Josiah, and my children, Tristan Nathan, Keira Natalie, and Evangeline Riley. I would not be able to write without your support, my loves. Thank you for sharing me. I love you.

Thank you to my alpha and beta teams who helped out with the original publication. I will never stop being grateful for your help and kindness.

Thank you to Micol Scalabrino for consulting with me on translations for Tercero's dreamy Italian exchanges with Janie.

To Monica, Tonia, and Shawn (Elise) thank you for allowing me to honor our friendship by immortalizing it in my story. I love you girls.

Thank you to Thander Lin for the beautiful cover art & design. I'm still stunned.

Emily Vaughan, you absolute legend. Thanks for pulling the rug out from under me and pushing me to make this happen. You're amazing.

Thank you to my mom and dad for encouraging me to write, to make something of myself.

To my Wattpad readers. We haven't had an easy time together. In fact, I think we both had moments we despised each other, but like any worthy relationship, the good outweighs the bad. Every message sent my way to encourage me to not give up stayed with me all these years and pushed me to give you my best. Thank you.

So long, I will see you again.

Janie Marie

JANIE MARIE

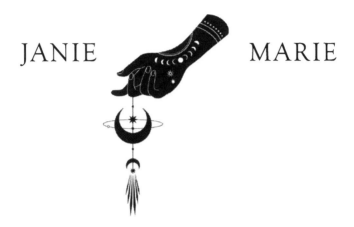

Janie Marie is an International Bestseller in Young Adult Contemporary Romance. She's a native Texan and resides in her hometown near Austin, Texas, where she devotes her time to family, pets, and her writing.

Much of her life experiences--good and a lot of bad--are where she has chosen to draw inspiration from to create her characters and stories. It's important to her to create the kind of characters she needs or needed at one point in time because she wanted to create something only the saddest souls would recognize as brave and strong.

Be ready for raw, emotional tales, as Janie never holds back. With her darkest thoughts she found light is still possible, that the sad girl can sometimes glow the brightest. Because she is beauty surrounded by darkness.

Facebook: www.Facebook.com/JanieMarie.author
Facebook group:
www.Facebook.com/groups/JanieMarieLand

You can also keep up with her on Instagram & Twitter
@janiemarie1617

www.janiemariebooks.com

Printed in Great Britain
by Amazon